Praise for Arlene James and her novels

"A unique plot with likeable characters creates an engaging combination."
—*RT Book Reviews* on *The Heart's Voice*

"*A Family to Share* is heartwarming and will cause readers to think about the true meaning of family."
—*RT Book Reviews*

"This is a terrifically lovely story."
—*RT Book Reviews* on *Anna Meets Her Match*

"Arlene James has an exquisite way with words and emotions in *To Heal a Heart*. The characters and intricate plot will resonate long after the last page is turned."
—*RT Book Reviews*

ARLENE JAMES
The Heart's Voice

A Family to Share

Steeple Hill®

Published by Steeple Hill Books™

STEEPLE HILL BOOKS

Steeple Hill®

Recycling programs for this product may not exist in your area.

ISBN-13: 978-0-373-65143-6

THE HEART'S VOICE AND A FAMILY TO SHARE

THE HEART'S VOICE
Copyright © 2004 by Deborah Rather

A FAMILY TO SHARE
Copyright © 2006 by Deborah Rather

CONTENTS

Books by Arlene James

Love Inspired

*The Perfect Wedding
*An Old-Fashioned Love
*A Wife Worth Waiting For
*With Baby in Mind
The Heart's Voice
To Heal a Heart
Deck the Halls
A Family to Share
Butterfly Summer
A Love So Strong
When Love Comes Home
A Mommy in Mind
**His Small-Town Girl
**Her Small-Town Hero
**Their Small-Town Love
†Anna Meets Her Match
†A Match Made in Texas
A Mother's Gift
 "Dreaming of a Family"
†Baby Makes a Match

*Everyday Miracles
**Eden, OK
†Chatam House

ARLENE JAMES

says, "Camp meetings, mission work and church attendance permeate my Oklahoma childhood memories. It was a golden time, which sustains me yet. However, only as a young widowed mother did I truly begin growing in my personal relationship with the Lord. Through adversity, He has blessed me in countless ways, one of which is a second marriage so loving and romantic it still feels like courtship!"

The author of more than seventy novels, Arlene James now resides outside Dallas, Texas, with her beloved husband. Her need to write is greater than ever, a fact that frankly amazes her, as she's been at it since the eighth grade. She loves to hear from readers, and can be reached via her website at www.arlenejames.com.

THE HEART'S VOICE

So that you incline your ear to wisdom,
and apply your heart to understanding.
—*Proverbs* 2:2

Chapter One

"Here's your chance."

Becca looked up from the shelf of canned goods she was stocking, glanced at her mother-in-law, Abby Kinder, and immediately turned her attention to the row of shopping carts parked along the front wall of the Kinder grocery store. Daniel Holden, tall and straight, tugged a cart free and aimed it toward the produce section. Becca felt a flutter of excitement inside her chest. With Easter just a week away, the time was right to begin repairs on her dilapidated ranch house. The weather was fine, she had managed to save a sum of money and it seemed that God had finally provided someone to do the work, at least according to the town scuttlebutt.

"You just don't expect the Marine Corps to turn out expert carpenters," she commented quietly. "I mean, soldiers, of course, and maybe mechanics, computer techs, even desk clerks, but 'carpenter' just doesn't seem to fit the mold."

Abby chuckled, swiping a feather duster over boxes

of pasta dinners. "You'd be amazed at the kind of training the military offers. Cody considered signing up, you know." She smiled wistfully, the pain of loss clouding her clear gray eyes even after these many months, but then she shook her silver head, the bun at the nape of her neck sliding from side to side, and her customary cheer reasserted itself. "His dad and I thought it was too dangerous, so then he goes out and takes up rodeo." She waved the feather duster, as if to say no one could predict what life would hold. Becca knew exactly what she meant. After years on the rodeo circuit, Cody had been killed in his own backyard by a high-strung stud horse.

Becca squeezed her mother-in-law's hand and went back to emptying the box on the tiered flatbed cart at her side, giving Dan Holden time to finish his shopping. Resolutely putting thoughts of her late husband out of her mind, she concentrated on the proposition she meant to make the tall ex-marine with the carpenter's skill.

Every day she drove past the Holden house on her way to and from work. Empty for longer than she'd lived in the sleepy little town of Rain Dance, Oklahoma, the elegant place had gradually taken on an air of abandonment and decay, but over the past three or four months that Dan had lived there, the old-fashioned two-story prairie cottage had seemed to come alive and take back its dignity. Now it stood fit and neat, as straight and tall as its owner and occupant, who just might be the answer to Becca's prayers.

When Dan turned his shopping cart toward the single checkout stand, Becca quickly wiped her hands on her apron and moved behind the counter. As Dan placed the first items on the rubber mat, Becca gave him a bright smile.

"How're you keeping, Mr. Holden?"

He nodded, but made no reply. She'd noticed that he was a quiet man, rarely speaking and often seeming shy, though with his looks she couldn't imagine why. He'd pretty much kept to himself since returning to Rain Dance after an absence of some ten or twelve years, but Becca figured he'd just been busy with the house. She rang up the first items and bagged them, talking as she worked.

"The word around town is that you're something of a carpenter."

He made no comment, didn't so much as look at her as he placed several cans on the counter. Becca licked her lips and took the plunge.

"Fact is, I'm looking for someone to help me fix up my old house, Mr. Holden, and I was wondering if you might be interested in taking on the project?"

It seemed a good idea. To her knowledge he didn't have a job, not that there were many to be had in this part of south central Oklahoma. Most folks depended on ranching, farming and intermittent oil field work to keep afloat, or else they were pensioners making the most of their retirement income. Living was cheap, if limited, in Rain Dance, which boasted a populati of some 500 residents within the narrow confines o limits and perhaps an equal number in the su area.

Without ever making eye contact, D

a carton of milk on the counter and reached back into his shopping cart for a box of cereal. She took his lack of reply as a good sign. At least he hadn't refused her outright.

"I've got a little money put aside," she told him, "and you've done such a fine job on your place, I was thinking we could maybe help each other out."

He plunked down a jar of pickles and a squirt bottle of mustard. She reached for the mustard, judging it a perfect fit for the space left in the shopping bag that she was packing. Their hands collided, and he looked up with a jerk, as if she'd burned him. She tried that smile again.

"So what do you think?"

He frowned as if puzzled, then muttered, "I think I have everything I need."

Becca felt her smile wilt. "I see." Tamping down her disappointment, she quickly rang up the rest of his purchase. "I guess that means you're not interested in the job?" He didn't dignify that with a reply, so she gulped and asked, "Might you be able to recommend someone from around here who could help me?" She'd been asking that question of everyone in town, and his name was the only one that ever seemed to come up.

Dan peered at the digital readout provided by the cash register and plucked bills from his wallet. She counted out his change, figuring that he was thinking over his answer, and left it on the counter. He picked it up, coin by coin, gathered his three bags of groceries and walked out.

Becca's jaw dropped, but she quickly snapped her

mouth shut again. The man hadn't answered her with so much as a shrug.

Abby had been hovering nearby with her feather duster, listening unabashedly to every word. She now looked at Becca with sad confusion on her face. "Well, he's sure changed. The Dan Holden I remember was a polite, outgoing young man. He wasn't much more than a boy, but still, that's not the same Dan Holden who left here for college. That's all I've got to say."

"I wonder what changed him," Becca mused, leaning a hip against the counter.

"God knows," Abby replied. "God always knows, and that's what matters, honey. If Dan can't or won't help you, God'll send someone else. You'll see."

Becca smiled and put aside her disappointment, knowing that her mother-in-law was right. She wouldn't have been so certain a few years ago, but she had learned, thanks to the Kinders. When she'd first arrived in Oklahoma as a nineteen-year-old bride of only days, she'd thought she'd made a terrible mistake. She'd met Cody at a rodeo and married the cute cowboy after knowing him for only two weeks. The rodeo life had seemed exciting to a country girl reared on an Iowa farm, but then she'd realize that she'd be spending most of her time in Rain Dance, which had seemed precisely the sort of place from which she'd thought she'd escaped, a dying town peopled with old folks and country yokels.

Then Abby and John Odem Kinder had opened their hearts and their lives to her. They'd shared their small house, their affection and, most important, their faith, and almost before she'd realized what was happening

Rain Dance had become home—and she had become a mother to a blond, blue-eyed baby girl. Cody had eventually scraped together enough winnings to buy them a place of their own on a quarter section three and half miles northeast of town.

The house had needed work even then, but the ranch had needed a good pair of breeding stock even more. They were hoping to start the horse herd that would provide the income that would keep Cody at home with his growing family, as Becca was pregnant again. Even without the much-needed repairs on the house, she wouldn't think of living anywhere else now, not even after finding herself a young widow with two children to support.

Rain Dance had its limitations, but she knew in her heart that this was where the good Lord meant her to be, so this was where she'd stay—even if she could see daylight through some walls of her little house.

Becca shepherded her daughter, Jemmy, into the pew near the front of the church where the Kinders sat, smiling as the four-year-old moppet preened in the simple blue-and-white-polka-dotted dress sewn for her by her grandmother. With her pale blond hair twisted into curls that most likely wouldn't last the service and a white straw hat tied with a blue ribbon under her chubby chin, she had sat for photos on the front steps of the narrow orange-brick church, giggling as John Odem had snapped away with his camera. Thirteen-month-old CJ had gone up onto his knees, trying to filch plastic eggs from his sister's Easter basket, his shirttail poking out of his navy blue shorts, matching bow tie seriously askew.

Finally Abby had brought the picture taking to a halt, warning that they would be late if they delayed any longer. Eager to show off her finery, Jemmy had insisted on accompanying her mother to the nursery, where CJ could play without disturbing the service, while her grandparents secured seats in the crowded sanctuary. By the time the middle-aged nursery attendant had finished gushing over how Jem's dress matched her blue eyes, the pianist had started to play the opening prelude.

As mother and daughter slipped into the pew, Becca smiled at the family in the seats behind them and patiently lifted her gaze toward the rear of the church while Jemmy climbed up onto the cushioned seat. Dan Holden stood in the doorway, a look of consternation on his face. Becca was struck by how handsome he was, standing there with his military bearing in well-pressed slacks, shirt and tie, his square jaw cleanly shaven, short, light brown hair neatly combed, sky-blue eyes searching the crowded pews for a seat.

She'd seen him here before, of course, but he usually slipped in a little late and took a seat on the aisle in the very last pew and then was gone again before she and her family had worked their way to the door. Today, however, even the back pews were packed. She saw him hesitate and then turn slightly as if to leave. Something in her couldn't let that happen. It was Easter Sunday, the day of all days when a Christian should be in church. Beckoning him with a slight crook of her hand, she quickly turned and slid into the pew, crowding close to her daughter in order to leave space for him on the aisle.

For several long seconds she didn't know whether or not he would take her up on her invitation, but then she felt his silent presence at her side and glanced up with a welcoming smile. Color stood in small, bright red patches high on his cheekbones, but he nodded thanks and folded his long frame onto the bench seat, elbows pulled tight to his sides. The pastor already stood in the pulpit, and he immediately lifted his voice to welcome all to God's house and comment on how nice it was to see so many in the congregation.

A few minutes later the music leader took over and got them all onto their feet for the first hymn of the morning. Becca joined in the singing. Jemmy climbed up into her grandfather's arms so she could see better, while Abby held a hymnal for him. His gravelly bass voice boomed so loudly that Jemmy covered her ears with her hands, which was exactly what John Odem had intended. It was a game they played, one of many. John liked to say that one of the most important lessons he'd learned in his nearly seventy years was to have as much fun as possible to help balance the difficulty that life often dealt. Having fun definitely included teasing his granddaughter. Smiling indulgently, Becca glanced at Dan Holden out of the corner of her eye. To her surprise Dan stared straight ahead, rigid and silent.

Realizing that he didn't have a hymnal, Becca briefly considered offering to share her own, but his stiffness made her uncertain. Compelled to seek another remedy, she looked down the pew, spying an extra hymnal in the pew pocket in front of her mother-in-law. Becca caught Abby's eye and pointed to the hymnal. Abby plucked it up and passed it to her. Becca immediately handed her own hymnal to Dan Holden, opened to the correct page.

He jerked, as if shocked by the gesture, and shook his head. His hand dipped with the weight of the heavy book before his gaze locked on her face, blue eyes piercing hers. Something there made Becca's breath catch, something intense and aching. His gaze moved from her face to the music on the page. The next instant he snapped the book shut, dropped it into the pew pocket in front of him and clasped his hands behind his back, a proud soldier at ease before a commanding officer.

Stung, Becca ducked her chin, brow beetled as she tried to figure out this guy. What was his problem, anyway? One moment he seemed charmingly shy and the next downright rude. It was almost as if he didn't know how to act around people. She now wanted to ignore him, but since he occupied the space right next to her, she couldn't help being uncomfortably aware of his every movement, or lack of it, to be more precise. During the sermon she noticed that he never took his eyes off the pastor's face. He appeared rapt, almost eerily so, and he seemed genuinely moved at several points. By the time the service progressed to the invitation, her puzzlement had deepened significantly. Dan Holden's actions and reactions just didn't seem to add up, and Becca's curiosity had definitely been piqued by the time the service ended.

As expected, the instant they were dismissed, he

turned into the aisle, but Becca impulsively reached out to trap him with a hand clamped firmly upon his forearm. He turned wary eyes of such intense attention on her that she once more caught her breath, but the next moment she heard herself babbling, "Oh, Mr. Holden, you remember me, don't you? I'm Becca Kinder."

"From the store," he mumbled in a voice so low that she had to lean close to hear him.

"That's right."

He glanced past her, his blue gaze sliding over Jemmy to John Odem. Becca released him, a little abashed by her forwardness now. He nodded at John and said, a little too loudly this time, "Mr. Kinder."

"Hello, Dan."

But Holden's gaze had slid right on past John Odem to Abby. "Ma'am," he said, and then he slipped away, edging and elbowing his way through the throng moving sluggishly toward the door. By the time Becca gathered her daughter to her side, he was gone.

"That man is downright peculiar," she said to no one in particular.

"Aw, I bet he's just having a little trouble settling into civilian life," John Odem said, tweaking Jemmy's ear.

Becca ducked her head. "I'm sure you're right."

"Maybe you ought to call on him, John," Abby suggested, crowding her family out into the aisle.

"Sure thing," John Odem agreed. "I'll go soon as that side of beef is delivered in the morning. Then you can do the butchering."

"Oh, no, you don't," Abby retorted.

"Why not?" John Odem asked innocently. "I figure it's time for some thumb soup."

"What's thumb soup?" Jemmy wanted to know.

"That's what we'll be having for supper once Grandma lops off her thumb with my butcher knife."

"Ewwww!" Jemmy exclaimed, wrinkling her nose.

"Stop that, John Odem Kinder," Abby scolded with mock severity. "We'll be having no disgusting soups, sugar," she assured her granddaughter, "because I'm not doing any butchering."

"You two are going to put this child off her feed for a month," Becca said reprovingly. "Honey, no one makes soup out of thumbs. Grandpa's just joshing you."

"Grandpa!" Jemmy scolded, sounding for all the world just like her grandmother.

John Odem laughed delightedly. When they drew even with the pastor, however, he did ask about Dan Holden.

"Anybody talk to that Holden boy since he came home, Pastor?"

The middle-aged preacher shook his head. "Not for lack of trying, John. He doesn't seem to have a phone. Shep Marcum and I have stopped by the house a few times, but no one ever came to the door. He seems to be keeping pretty busy."

"He seems to be keeping to himself," Abby commented, and the pastor nodded.

"That, too."

Becca bit her lip, mulling over this information. It seemed that Dan Holden didn't want to have anything do with anyone around Rain Dance, but if that were so, then why had he come back here?

The puzzle of Dan Holden just wouldn't leave Becca alone. She lay in her bed that night trying to decide what it was she'd seen in his eyes that disturbed her so, but try as she might, she couldn't come up with a solid explanation. Her first guess was loneliness, but why would a lonely man hold everyone at bay, avoiding conversation? Did his past hide something dark that he feared others would discover, something that shamed him? Maybe it was something that had forced him out of the Marine Corps, but what?

Maybe he was AWOL, absent from the military without leave.

No, that didn't make any sense. He would be plenty easy to find in a little town like Rain Dance, especially since he had family connections to the community. Besides, a Christian man with a guilty conscience would be compelled to make things right, and she felt in her heart of hearts that Dan was a true Christian. She'd seen the tears standing in his eyes when the pastor had described the suffering of Christ as He'd willingly paid the sin debt for all of humanity, witnessed the quiet intensity of his emotion as he'd listened to the dramatic reading of Scripture, watched his silent joy as the Resurrection was proclaimed. Yes, Dan believed. It was obvious. So why, then, did he bolt like a scalded hound whenever anyone tried to connect with him?

Maybe it was just her. Maybe she was the one he didn't want to have anything to do with, and he really

had been busy when the others had come to call. It was
a lowering thought, and one she felt compelled to put
to the test on Tuesday next.

She stayed late to close the store on Tuesdays and
Thursdays, so John Odem and Abby could have their
dinner together at a decent hour, and it had become the
family custom for the kids to eat with their grandparents
and on occasion stay overnight. This was just such an
occasion, so Becca found herself driving alone about
eight-thirty in the evening past the Holden place on her
way out of town. As she drew close to the house, she
naturally glanced toward it.

Dan Holden's profile appeared in an open living-room
window. He was sitting in a big, comfy chair watching
a large television screen. The way he sat there, so very
still, hands resting on the wide rolled arms of the chair,
had a lonely feel about it, and something inside Becca
said, "Stop."

She shivered, as if God Himself had tapped her on
the shoulder, and before she could even think to do it,
her foot had moved from the gas pedal to the brake.
She sat there for a moment, the engine of her battered
old car rumbling in competition with a cricket calling
for his mate. Then with a sigh she yielded to her initial
impulse and turned the vehicle into Dan Holden's drive.
She parked and got out, leaving the keys in the ignition
as usual. Reluctantly she let her tired feet take her along
the hedged walkway to the front steps and then up those
steps to the broad, sheltered porch. From this angle, the

light of the TV flickered against the windowpane, but now only that persistent cricket could be heard.

Becca knocked on the door. She thought its berry-red paint made a very pretty display with the pristine white of the siding, new grass-green roof and black shutters. She waited, but the contrary man couldn't be bothered to answer his door.

She tried again, her irritation growing. No response. Well, that took the proverbial cake. The man obviously didn't want or need a friend. It must have been a perverse imp who had compelled her to stop, but this time she was going to let Dan Holden know that his rudeness had been noted and marked. In a rare fit of pique she moved to stand directly in front of the window, which she pecked insistently with the tip of one forefinger before turning to stomp across the porch and down the steps on her way back to her car. Her feet had barely hit the paved walk when that red door finally opened.

"Who's there?"

For an instant she considered giving him a dose of his own medicine, just stomping off into the night without another word, but that was not Becca's way.

"It's me," she said, somewhat grudgingly. "Becca Kinder. I was just—"

The porch light suddenly blazed. "Mrs. Kinder," he said, surprise evident in his voice. "Is that you?"

Becca frowned. "I just told you so, didn't I?"

"Come up here into the light," he dictated, stepping out onto the porch, "and tell me what I can do for you." His voice had a stilted, uneven quality to it, as if he wasn't quite sure what tone to use.

Sorry that she'd come at all, Becca climbed the trio of steps again, realizing that she had no idea what she'd meant to say to him in the first place. An honest response was always the best one, so she licked her lips and said, "I was hoping you might be interested in working on my house now."

He cocked his head, as if he found something odd about that. "Sorry. Not possible."

"But you've done such fine work on this place," Becca heard herself arguing.

"Thank you," he said with a small smile. "Now I'm doing the garage apartment out back. Might rent it out."

Becca nodded, disappointed all over again. At least he had an excuse to offer this time. That was progress. Of a sort. "I see. Well, if that doesn't pan out and you find yourself needing work…"

He shook his head. "I'm keeping busy."

That was something with which she could certainly identify. "Just not enough hours in the day, are there?"

"Suppose not."

She searched for something else to say and finally gestured toward the western end of the south-facing house. "You ought to hang a swing over there."

He glanced at the end of the porch and back again. "Think so?"

"And paint it red," she added.

He rubbed his chin, smiling so brightly that she felt a kick in her chest. "Just might do that."

She felt positively warm all of a sudden, and the

thought occurred to her that he was a downright likable man when he wasn't being standoffish. "You know what else would be pretty?" she asked, basking in that male smile. He shook his head. "Two big white pots right here on either side of the steps, just spilling over with flowers, geraniums maybe, red to match the swing."

"My grandma used to keep flowerpots there."

"Well, there you go," Becca said.

He nodded. "I'll look into it sometime."

"Maybe when you're finished with that garage apartment."

"Maybe," he said, making it sound like two words instead of one.

Completely out of topics for discussion now, Becca glanced at the window looking into his living room. "You're missing your program," she finally offered lamely, "and morning comes early for me, so I'd best be going."

"Good night."

"Good night, Mr. Holden." She turned to go, but then a fresh thought hit her. "You know, there's a Bible study on Wednesday evenings that you might want—" She broke off. He'd already retreated and was closing the door. She brought her hands to her hips. There he went again! The man had practically locked up while she was still talking.

From the corner of her eye she caught sight of him moving back into the living room and reclaiming his seat in the chair. Must be some mighty interesting TV program he was watching. Curious, she stepped to one side and looked at the set. A commercial was playing, but she did note one interesting thing. The television seemed to be displaying closed captions, the words spelling out across the bottom of the screen. She was too far away to read them, and it could have been a disclaimer of some sort for the commercial, but she left wondering if she might not have discovered the clue to Dan Holden's odd behavior.

Chapter Two

Dan came into the store on Friday morning, a half day for Becca. He smiled and waved as he pulled his cart from the queue, then purchased milk and eggs and a piece of salt pork for "a mess of beans," as he said at the checkout.

"You must be missing military chow," she teased.

"Must be," he agreed shyly.

He turned his attention to a rack of television program guides mounted near the checkout, and Becca deliberately asked, "What sort are you having?"

He made no reply, just as she had expected, so she repeated the question once she had his attention again.

"Navy beans," he said with a grin. "Called them something else in the Corps."

"I prefer good old reds myself."

He chuckled. "Red seems to be a theme with you."

"I like red," she admitted. "That'll be 9.17."

"Bet it's a good color on you," he said, and then

ducked his head as that very shade bloomed on the ridges of his cheeks. He dug out a ten-dollar bill and plunked it on the table, mumbling, "You have a good day now."

"Oh, I will," she said, purposely not looking at him as she extracted his change from the cash drawer. "I'm expecting John Travolta to pick me up for lunch in his private jet." She peeked at him to see how he'd taken that, or if he'd even heard it, but he was already making for the door with his groceries. "Hey!" she called out. "Your change!" She wasn't the least surprised when he just kept on walking.

"What's the matter, honey?" Abby asked, appearing from the little office blocked off across the aisle from the checkout.

Becca dropped the coins into her apron pocket. "Dan Holden just forgot his change, that's all."

"How much?"

"Eighty-three cents."

"Oh, well, just give it to him next time he comes in."

"I'll take care of it," Becca said with a smile.

Abby nodded and turned back into the office, where she was tabulating invoices for payment. Becca patted the small bulge in her pocket and decided that she was going to pay another call on the handsome ex-marine, and this time they were going to have an honest talk.

Dan saw the flashing light on the panel mounted on the kitchen wall. Connected to a motion detector, it signaled him whenever someone approached his front door. He'd installed the panels in his bedroom, bath and here in the kitchen, and eventually he meant to have them in every room. Originally he'd thought he wouldn't need one in the living room, as it overlooked the porch, but little Becca Kinder's visit a few nights earlier had shown him that he wasn't as observant as he'd judged himself to be. He wondered how many other visitors he'd missed because he'd been too proud to admit that he might overlook what he couldn't hear.

Rising from the chair, he left his sandwich on the table and walked down the central hall past the staircase to the front door. Upon opening the door, he didn't know who was more surprised, Becca Kinder, who had apparently not yet knocked, or him at seeing pretty little Becca on his doorstep again, this time with a fat baby perched on one hip. It looked to be a boy.

"Hi."

"Hi, yourself," she said, holding out her right hand.

"What's this?" he asked, putting out his own palm.

"The change you forgot at the store this morning."

"Oh!"

He felt the burn of embarrassment again, and it galled him. What was it about this girl that kept him blushing like some awkward preteen? He slipped the coins into the front pocket of his jeans. Catching movement from the corner of his eye, he glanced left and spied her little girl skipping merrily across his porch, pale hair flopping. Becca was not a girl, but a woman and a mother, he reminded himself, and he'd do well to remember it. He still thought of Cody Kinder as the happy-go-lucky kid he'd once known, clomping around in a droopy cowboy hat and boots two sizes too large. Now here stood his family.

"Didn't have to bring this," he said, looking her in the eye. He always worried that he wouldn't get his volume right, but she neither winced nor leaned in closer.

She shrugged, and he dropped his gaze to her mouth. It was a pretty little mouth, a perfect pink bow. "No problem. It's on my way home. Besides, I wanted to ask you something."

He assumed that it had to do with her house and the repairs she seemed to think she needed. "All right."

"How'd you lose your hearing?"

He nearly dropped from shock. "How..." He stared into her wide, clear green eyes, sucked in a breath and accepted that the secret was out. "Explosion."

She nodded matter-of-factly, no trace of pity in her expression. She was a pretty thing, with her fine, straight, light golden-blond hair cropped bluntly just above her shoulders, the bangs wisping randomly across her forehead. Those soft olive-green eyes were big and round, but not too large for her wide oval face with its pointed chin and small, tip-tilted nose. Completely devoid of cosmetics, her golden skin literally glowed, and her dusty-pink mouth truly intrigued him. She was so easy to lip-read.

"I figured it was something like that," she said. "Mind if I ask how long ago it was?"

He shook his head, as much to clear it as in answer to her question. "About thirteen months."

She shifted the baby on her hip. "About the same time CJ was born, then."

What a coincidence, he thought, looking at the baby. She'd been gaining something precious while he was losing his hearing, along with life as he'd known it, his career, the future he'd envisioned for himself. Keeping his expression carefully bland, he switched his gaze back to her face.

"How did you know?"

"Little things. Abby says you were always friendly and outgoing before." He winced at the implication. "But you don't reply sometimes when you're spoken to." She grinned. "I thought you were rude."

He closed his eyes, appalled that he wasn't as smart as he'd assumed, then he opened them again to find that she was still speaking.

"…weren't singing and the way you watched the pastor so intently when he was preaching. Then there were the closed captions on the TV the other night."

He waved a hand, feeling ridiculous. Had he really believed that he could fool everyone? He'd thought that if he kept to himself and was careful he could lead something close to a normal life. Now he knew that wasn't true, and he felt sick in a way that he hadn't since he'd realized that he was never going to hear another sound. For some reason he felt compelled to try to explain it to her.

"It's not obvious at first."

"No, it's not. Took me a while to figure it out."

"I'm not comfortable announcing it." He hoped he hadn't stumbled over the word *comfortable*.

"I understand. And why should you if you don't

have to? How did you learn to read lips so well, by the way?"

"Training."

"Guess that's one good thing about the military, huh? They take care of their own."

"That's right. Helps that I wasn't born this way."

"I see. Is your deafness why you won't work on my house?" she asked.

He rubbed a hand over his face. "Yes."

She bit her lip. "Okay. Well, you don't have to worry that I'll say anything to anybody. I mean, if that's the way you want it."

He forced a smile. "Thank you."

"But since I already know about your problem, there's really no reason why you can't help me out, is there?"

He opened his mouth, then closed it again. She had a point. He sighed, then hoped she hadn't heard. It was hard to tell with her. "You better come in."

She shook her head, glancing at her daughter, who continued skipping. The child appeared to be singing to herself. Becca hefted the boy to a more comfortable position, and he noticed how small and childlike her hands were before quickly jerking his gaze back to her face. "That's okay. Jemmy likes playing on your porch."

He wasn't sure about the name. "Jenny?"

"No. J-e-m-m-y. Jemmy."

"Jemmy." He pointed at the boy. "CJ?"

"For Cody John, after his daddy and his grandpa."

Dan nodded his understanding. The child was huge, with fat cheeks and thighs, or his mother was very small, or both. Either way, she looked much too young to have two children.

"So will you help me fix up my house?"

She might be young, but she was persistent. Dan rubbed a hand over the nape of his neck. Was this God's will, that he work on her house? He was having a hard time figuring out what God had in store for him these days. He'd come home to Rain Dance simply because he had to go somewhere after the Marine Corps had medically retired him, and at thirty he didn't like feeling dependent on his parents, especially with his sister, Gayla, busily planning her fall wedding. By helping out Becca Kinder he'd at least be keeping busy.

"No promises," he finally said, "but I'll take a look."

She literally bounced, as excited as if she'd just won the lottery. "Oh, thank you, Mr. Holden!"

"Dan," he corrected automatically.

She smiled. "And I'm Becca."

"Becca," he repeated carefully. "Not Becky?"

"Not Becky," she confirmed, "but short for Rebecca."

"Okay, Becca. When and where?"

She started to answer him, but then she suddenly turned away. He followed her gaze and saw that Jemmy was about to slip off the end of the porch and down between the hedges. She stopped and cast a measuring glance at her mother, then resumed skipping again. Becca smiled at him and said, "As far as how to find us, just head east straight on out of town to the second section line. Then turn back north. We're on the left just over a mile down."

He smiled because she hadn't altered the speed or manner in which she normally spoke. "Two miles east. One north. On the left."

"Right. There's no section line road there, but you'll see the name on the mailbox."

"Kinder," he surmised.

"That's it." She flapped a hand happily. "Oh, you don't know how long I've waited for this! See you then." As she turned to go, he realized that he'd missed something important, and without even thinking, he reached out and snagged her wrist. A jolt of heat lanced up his arm. He instantly released her.

"Sorry. Uh, when?"

Her eyes grew even rounder, and apology was suddenly written all over her face. "I turned my head. Jemmy was about to crawl off into the bushes, and I didn't even think."

"It's all right." He brought his hands to his hips, just to be sure he didn't accidentally reach out for her again. "Tell me when."

"Monday's my day off, so anytime Monday would be great for me."

He nodded. "Monday."

She smiled, and he drew back, that smile doing strange things to his insides. He wondered if her husband was going to be there, and hoped that he was. It would be best to deal with Cody. Perhaps he should suggest it, but she was already turning away again, calling the girl to her side as she went. Dan backed up and closed the door. Then he suddenly remembered something he'd seen.

She wore her wedding ring on her right hand and no ring at all on her left. Thinking quickly, he weighed the significance of that, and then he remembered something else. One day down at the store he'd seen two women standing in front of the deli case, watching John Odem carve up a ham. One had leaned close to the other and apparently whispered something that had stuck with him. *What a shame about the boy.*

He knew now what it meant. Cody Kinder had died. That explained why Dan hadn't seen him around at all since his return, even why Becca had come to ask for his help. He thought of the boy he had known and felt a keen sense of loss tinged with shame. Cody had been younger than him, so they hadn't been buddies or anything, but Dan had always liked the kid as well as his parents, who had fairly doted on their only child. And to think that all this time he'd been too busy feeling his own loss to even realize what they had suffered.

He sighed and bowed his head.

Okay. I get it. Lots of folks have lost lots more than me. The least I can do is help Becca Kinder with whatever repairs she's needing. And I'll try to be less prideful from now on, Lord. Really I will.

For the first time in a long while a real sense of purpose filled him, and it felt good. Really good. He went back to his lunch, walking down the hall to the kitchen, completely ignorant of a loud squeak at a certain spot in the clean, highly polished hardwood floor.

Becca couldn't say why she looked for him to come into the store on Saturday, but she was disappointed when it didn't happen. Ever since he'd admitted his deafness to her, she'd felt that they shared a bond along with the secret. And yet she felt torn about the secret itself. Whatever his reasons for not publicly acknowledging his lack of hearing, it served only to keep him isolated. Most people would gladly accommodate his condition, allowing him to get back into the swing of things around the community. Perhaps with him working around her house—and she couldn't imagine that he wouldn't be—God would give her the words to say to convince him to let people know about his disadvantage.

She didn't see any reason to wait for Monday to speak to him, however, so on Sunday she kept an eye out, and sure enough he slipped in late and took up his customary spot on the back row. She didn't signal to him to come up front, though there was space in the pew, but she did rush out at the first possible moment, leaving Jemmy in the care of the Kinders. With barely a nod for the pastor, she hurried through the narrow foyer and down the front steps, catching up with him beneath a big beech tree that grew near the sidewalk and overhung the dusty parking area.

He stopped and turned when she tapped him on the shoulder. She suddenly found herself smiling like a goose.

"What's your hurry?"

He glanced down at the key in his hand and said softly, "Bean casserole."

She waited until he looked up at her again before she said, "Guess there's no point in inviting you to Sunday dinner, then, huh?" She'd meant to tease but realized belatedly that she was serious. At any rate, he missed the inflection.

"Nice of you." He shook his head apologetically. "Not a good idea."

"Because you'd be uncomfortable around John Odem and Abby," she surmised.

He seemed a little surprised by that, but then he didn't have any way of knowing that she routinely took Sunday dinner with the Kinders. "Yes," he said, and she had the distinct feeling that it wasn't exactly the truth—not all of it, anyway.

Suddenly struck by how forward she was being, she looked away. That's when Shep Marcum stopped by to shake Dan's hand and invite him to the men's Sunday-school class.

"Thank you for mentioning it, Mr. Marcum," Dan said slowly and politely, but just a tad too loud. Then again, Shep was nearly John Odem's age and hard of hearing. Maybe he wouldn't notice. "I'll think on it."

"You do that, son," Shep said, clapping Dan on the shoulder. "We'd sure be glad to have you." He glanced at Becca and winked. "Looking mighty pretty again today, Becca. That's a right attractive dress you're wearing."

Becca grinned. "Shep, it's the same dress I wear every other Sunday, and you know it."

"Well, it's still a nice one," he said jauntily, stepping off the sidewalk.

She laughed and slid a wry look at Dan. "He says that about the other one, too."

"The other one?"

"My other Sunday dress."

"Ah."

He looked down at his feet, missing the greeting called out by the Platters—not that he'd have caught it, anyway. Becca nudged his toe with hers, and when he looked up said softly, "Wave at Bill Platter and his wife. To your left."

Dan looked that way and lifted an arm in greeting before turning back to Becca. "Thanks. He coming over?"

"Nope. Heading for the car. They always go to her mother's in Waurika on Sunday."

Dan nodded, keeping his gaze glued to her face. "Graduated high school with Bill."

She lifted her eyebrows. "He looks older than you."

"He is. Held back, dropped out for a while."

"Is that so? Then you'll be surprised to hear that he's a big man around here now. Pretty well-heeled. Owns an insurance agency in Duncan."

His mouth quirked at the word *hear*, but she didn't apologize, sensing that would compound the mistake. "Surprised he's living in Rain Dance, then."

"How come? You're living in Rain Dance now."

He looked away, mumbling, "Inherited my house."

She stood silently until he glanced her way again. "Is that the only reason you came home, because you inherited your grandmother's house?"

He turned away as if he hadn't understood her, but then he turned back again and looked her in the eye. "Not sure. It is home."

She smiled. "Yeah. I feel the same way. I couldn't think of living anywhere else after Cody died."

He asked gently, "Not long ago?"

"Twenty-one months," she told him. "Just after I found out I was pregnant with CJ."

His eyes widened. "Must've been tough."

She nodded. "But we're managing. I'm even finally going to get my house fixed up."

He chuckled and tossed his keys lightly, signaling his intention to take his leave. "We'll see. Tomorrow."

"Tomorrow," she echoed, adding, "Look left again and acknowledge Effie Bishop."

Dan turned his head and smiled at the elderly woman, calling out in that same careful, measured way, "Good to see you again, Miss Effie." He looked back at Becca as he moved into the parking area and mouthed the words "Thanks. Again."

She smiled, waved and went in search of her family, marveling at how he handled himself. No one who didn't know him well would realize his predicament, at least not with her acting as his ears. She found a strange satisfaction in that, one she didn't much want to ponder.

Dan brought his white pickup truck to a halt behind Becca's old car and studied the sight before him. He shook his head and killed the engine, automatically pulling the keys. The truck was spanking new, with fewer than two hundred miles on it. He'd ordered it specially equipped as soon as he'd made the decision to move back to Rain Dance, but it had never seemed so plush or shiny as it did now, sitting in front of Becca Kinder's shabby little house.

The house didn't need repairs, he realized with dismay—it needed demolishing. The roof line was uneven, the shingles a patchwork of colors and type. Over the low porch it sagged dangerously, and he saw that one of the support poles had sunk through the rotted wood and past the untreated joist to the ground. The house itself was built atop a foundation of cement blocks placed about two feet apart, so the floor probably rolled like an ocean inside. Besides that, every inch of wood siding needed scraping and painting. Windowsills were buckled. The damage was such that he could tell she'd been living like this for a long time, and that knowledge pricked him, though he supposed that he should've expected it.

Despite running the only grocery store in town, the Kinders had always been poor as church mice. None of them, Cody included, had ever seemed to mind. Dan remembered his grandfather saying that John Odem was a good man who had no head for business, that he gave credit to everyone who asked and probably collected only a fraction of what was owed him. That apparently still held true, and while Dan admired the generosity and pleasantness of the Kinders, he couldn't help feeling a little irritated on behalf of Becca and the kids. No wonder she'd pressed him for help.

He got out of the truck and walked across the dirt yard to the porch, noting as he stepped up onto it that the floorboards were warped and broken. The whole thing would have to be replaced. The patched screen door opened and Becca stepped out, looking freshly scrubbed and smiling a happy welcome.

"It's nearly ten. I was getting worried you wouldn't show till after lunch."

"Your morning off," he pointed out. "Thought you might sleep in."

She waved that away. "I'm a morning person, always up with the dawn." She hugged herself. "I love it when the world's still and quiet, like I'm the only person awake anywhere."

He smiled, not because he identified—for him the world was always still and quiet, and he missed the bustle and racket of it keenly—but because she never bothered to police her speech with him. Becca was just Becca. Period. He liked that, admired it. In a funny way he was even grateful for it. She made him feel…normal. Whole. He reminded himself that he was neither.

"Come on in," she said before leading the way inside.

He followed with some trepidation and found himself standing in a living room that couldn't have been more than ten feet square. Poorly furnished with an old sofa, a small bookcase, a battered coffee table, a cheap floor lamp and a small television set on a wire stand so rickety that it leaned to one side, the place was shabby but spotless and cheerful.

Becca had obviously made a valiant effort. A colorful quilt covered the ratty sofa. Bright yellow ruffled curtains fluttered in the morning breeze. An oval, braided rag rug covered a significant portion of the torn linoleum floor, and sparkling beads had been glued around the edge of the yellowed lamp shade. The bookcase bulged with neatly stacked rows of paperback novels, children's storybooks and Bible study materials. Best of all were the framed photos hung artistically on the wall, so many that they almost obscured the faded, old-fashioned wallpaper, along with a homemade shadow box of dried flowers and a variety of inexpert coloring-book pages pinned up at Jemmy-height. Jemmy sat on the floor industriously working on another while watching cartoons.

Becca waved him into another room. He glimpsed a sunny bedroom as he walked past an open doorway, then came to stand in the disaster that was her kitchen.

It looked like something straight out of the thirties, with a tired old propane stove, a tiny ancient refrigerator, peeling wallpaper that exposed its rough backing, a shallow tin sink and virtually no cabinets. The only work surface was an old table that obviously functioned as eating space and stood over the slanted entry of an old root cellar. A pair of unfinished shelves comprised the only storage, and a single naked lightbulb provided the only illumination, since the window and possibly a door had been boarded over. To top it all off, the baby sat in a rusty high chair in the very middle of the floor, naked except for a diaper, his hair, face and chest smeared and sticky. With one hand he clutched the remains of a banana while rhythmically banging a spoon on the metal tray with the other. When Dan caught his eye, the filthy little cherub offered him the piece of mushy banana. Dan pretended not to notice and quickly diverted his attention.

Becca reached out and removed the spoon from the baby's hand with a patient shake of her head. "Sorry about the racket." Realizing what she'd said, she put a hand to her head and, eyes twinkling, said, "Sorry for apologizing."

He found himself smiling. Although the place was an appalling wreck and he was just beginning to realize what a job he'd let himself in for, he couldn't do anything but smile. She was one of a kind, Becca Kinder, as natural and uncomplicated as a woman could get. Widowed much too young, she worked long hours at the store owned by her in-laws, obviously didn't have a penny to spare, lived in appalling conditions and still managed to be happy and make a warm if humble home for her two children.

He'd do what he could, of course. He wouldn't be able to live with himself if he didn't, though he realized in that moment that he would be getting something important out of it, too. Because just by being herself and by treating him as if he wasn't handicapped, as if he was someone to depend upon, as if he had something of genuine value to offer, she made him understand that it was so. Plus, he could make a real contribution. He *could* help her. To what extent he wasn't yet certain, but her life and the lives of her children would definitely be better once he was through here. She couldn't know what a gift that was, and even if he'd had the words to tell her, he doubted that he could express it sufficiently, so he just looked her in the face and asked, "Where were you wanting to start?"

She gave him a bright, brilliant, happy smile that lightened his heart. Then he felt something brush his hip and looked down to find his jeans decorated with mashed banana.

Chapter Three

"Oh! I'm so sorry! CJ, stop that!"

Becca grabbed a dishcloth from the edge of the sink and rushed to scrub at the banana smeared on Dan's jeans. He jumped back. She followed and scrubbed at him anyway, and he could tell that she was speaking but not what she was saying, as she was bent over, concentrating on the stain. He tapped her on the shoulder, and she suddenly looked up.

"Work clothes," he said with a shrug. "No big deal."

She frowned, but it turned into a smile as she turned to scrub her son. Dan thought it a wonder the little tyke's skin didn't come right off. She looked at him over her shoulder. Apparently she had enough experience at this sort of thing that she didn't need to see what she was doing in order to do it.

"This is all my fault," she said. "He didn't really want that banana, but I was trying to keep him occupied. He tends to hang all over me when I'm not working."

You should stay home, he thought, and then realized from the look on her face that he'd spoken aloud. He hastily added, "If—if you could."

She nodded. "But I can't. They stay with the woman who lives next door to John and Abby, so they're close to the store, and by juggling our schedules we make sure they aren't there more than a few hours a day. That's why the butcher counter isn't open all the time anymore."

Dan had actually wondered about it, and had decided that John Odem wasn't getting any younger and had probably cut back his hours for that reason. Now he knew that John wasn't taking it easy somewhere while his wife and daughter-in-law ran the store. These Kinders were a wonder, with all their good-spirited hard work and caring.

"When CJ's older," Becca went on, "I'll take them both into the store with me. John Odem's going to set up a playroom, and Jemmy can help watch her brother."

Dan smiled lamely. "Good plan."

"CJ's still clingy, though," she said. "He's at that stage, you know."

Dan didn't know. He didn't have the slightest notion about kids. He'd always imagined that one day he'd find some girl and settle down to parenthood, but soldiering had kept him too busy to do anything about it, and then one day it had taken the possibility away from him.

He knew that he couldn't be a fit parent. His own childhood experience told him that. When he thought about all the times he'd been awakened in the dark of night by some bad dream or frightening noise and how his mom and dad had rushed to his side at his call, he understood his own inadequacy. Thinking about the times he'd tried some silly stunt and injured himself had forced him to admit that his inadequacy could put a child at real risk.

No, he didn't know about kids, and he probably never would know more than the basics, even though his baby sister was planning a fall wedding and would, presumably, one day make him an uncle. He had to believe that God had a reason for the way things had turned out, and maybe Becca was showing him what that reason was. The skills he'd learned at his grandfather's and father's knees seemed to be playing an important role in it. Carpentry had always been an enjoyable pastime for Dan. Working with his hands gave him a certain satisfaction. Maybe it was meant to be more.

A small, delicate touch fell on his shoulder, and he realized with a jolt that Becca was speaking to him, but he hadn't been paying attention.

"I thought we'd start in here with some plasterboard. If you could just get it on the walls for me, I think I could get it plastered and painted. I've been reading up on how to do it."

He blinked and looked around the room. She'd been reading up on tape and bedding. "I can take care of it," he said, bringing his gaze back to her face. "All."

Her relief was palpable. "Oh, good. New plasterboard would patch up some of the holes."

He made a mental note to check the insulation before he nailed up any drywall. He'd bet his bottom dollar that this place didn't have a lick of insulation.

"Of course, I'll be wanting cabinets," she was saying. "Nothing fancy, you understand. They don't even have to have doors."

He'd never build her cabinets without doors, but he just nodded.

"And I would love it if we could replace that nailed-over back door," she went on. "I don't like not having more than one exit, you know?"

"For safety," he said, and she smiled.

"Now, this is the most important part," she said, reaching over to place her hand flat against the rough boards covering the outside wall. "There's a window under here, too, and I've always figured it would be the perfect place for an air conditioner. Some summer nights it's just so hot out here that my babies can't sleep."

His mind was racing. How in heaven's name had they survived an Oklahoma summer without air-conditioning? It meant 220 wiring, though. No doubt the whole place would have to be rewired. He wondered if this old house even had a fuse box. He tried to pay attention to what she was saying even as his brain whirred with what was needed: insulation, wiring, window, door, light fixtures, probably plumbing. Plasterboard and cabinets were way down the line. He made himself concentrate on the movement of her mouth and was stunned to read what it formed next.

"Two thousand dollars isn't a lot, I know, but I can get together more as we go along. It ought to make us a good start, don't you think?"

Sensing her hope and her eagerness, he couldn't make himself say what was on the tip of his tongue. He told himself ruefully that before he'd lost his hearing and become unsure of his own speech, he'd probably have blurted out that a measly two thousand wouldn't get this one room into really livable shape. Now he just covered his dismay with a nod and asked to see the rest of the house, explaining carefully that he needed to see what was behind certain walls.

She led him on a full house tour, which didn't take long, even with the baby attached to her hip. He wondered if she was going to survive this child's infancy with a straight spine, since she seemed able to walk only at an awkward angle while lugging the great brick.

Her bedroom was in the same pitiful shape as the rest of the place, but the tiny bath and second bedroom had been added to the house sometime in the past few years and were structurally sound, at least. Unlike the papered walls in her room, he couldn't see daylight through cracks. No wonder she wanted drywall in the rest of the house.

When they reached the second bedroom she put the baby down for a nap in a wobbly old crib squeezed into the corner next to the low, cotlike thing apparently used by the little girl, judging by the ruffly pink spread. The baby wailed, his chubby face screwing up and turning dark red, but Becca just bent low and kissed him, patting his belly until he calmed and rolled onto his side. The child was still awake when she led Dan from the room, but if he kicked up additional fuss, Dan couldn't tell and she didn't let on.

Back in the living room, he sat down to talk over what was going to happen next. Dan felt a distinct catch in his chest as he began to marshal his thoughts. She had so little. If he told her what this place really needed, she'd no doubt be upset, but would still want to do what little could be done with the funds she possessed. He decided that, though he couldn't lie to her, she didn't have to be overwhelmed with all of it at once. Besides, he could save her some real money by simply using what he had on hand, like the base cabinets he'd pulled out of the garage apartment. He'd thought them too old-fashioned to use, but they were solid and about the right size. Originally he'd intended to recycle the wood, but, stripped and refinished, the cabinets would make a welcome addition to her kitchen, especially if he dressed them up with doors that he could build in his shop out back of the house. She need not know that they were used—or free. And he certainly didn't have to tell her that he would take no profit on this job. That was his business, after all.

Jemmy crawled up into Becca's lap as she waited patiently for him to speak, and he figured it was polite to at least smile at the child. She brightened noticeably when he did so.

"You're right," he told Becca, switching his gaze to her face. "Start in the kitchen."

She closed her eyes with obvious relief. "Then you'll do it? You'll take the job?"

He nodded, waiting until she opened her eyes again to speak, realizing a heartbeat later that he need not do so. She could hear, for pity's sake. "I will make a plan for you to approve."

"Oh, you don't have to do that," she said, still smiling. "Just do what you think best."

"Best to have a plan," he said, and she shrugged.

He rose. "Get my tape. Make some measurements."

She hugged the little girl and bowed her head to say something to her. Jemmy looked up, delight and wonder in her eyes, and clapped her hands. Then suddenly she came off her mother's lap, zipped across the small space that separated him from them and was suddenly standing on his feet, her arms wrapped around his legs in a childish hug. He could feel her breath on his jeaned thigh, the movement of her lips but he was too stunned to comprehend even that she was speaking until she glanced back at her mother and then turned her face up.

He caught the words *nice man* and *Mr. Dan*. He looked helplessly at her mom, but Becca just sat there smiling. With a lump the size of his fist in his throat he couldn't have spoken even if he'd known what to say, so after a moment he gently dislodged the child and went straight out the door. Only as he was looking through the toolbox fixed to the bed of his truck did he once again regain his composure.

He took the plan to the store for Becca to see. It was a scaled-back, highly simplified version of the one he'd worked on almost nonstop for the past thirty hours. Hand drawn on simple white notebook paper, it was really nothing more than a floor plan of her kitchen with the cabinets, door and window set in place. He'd listed the work to be done, but it was only a brief overview and included such uninformative items as Basic Wall Preparation, Electrical Upgrade and Plumbing Adjustment, along with Door Installation and Cabinet Installation.

As he'd expected, she cared only about the final result, asking, "What color will the cabinets be?"

"Your choice. Paint or stain?"

She had to think about it, but then she shook her head. "Whichever is cheapest."

He shrugged.

"Which is simplest, then?"

"Paint."

She grinned. "I like yellow."

He chuckled. "Exact color later."

"When can you start?" was her only other question.

He checked his watch. If he could get to the building supply outlet in Lawton today, he could start work in the morning. "Tomorrow."

She clasped her hands together in front of her chest, and tears filled her eyes. Alarm shot through him.

"It'll take a while," he warned, but she shook her head happily.

"I don't care. It'll be started. You know what they say. Once begun, sooner finished."

She turned to the cash register and opened the drawer. Extracting an envelope, she turned back to him, then carefully placed it in his hands. He knew what it was even before he thumbed back the flap. She'd just handed him her life's savings in cash. Humbled, he quickly decided against trying to return it. Instead, he'd earn the trust she had just placed in him.

He left her a copy of the plan and drove straight to Lawton, some seventy-five miles distant. Surprisingly, he found a number of good sales, so the two thousand dollars bought him just about everything he'd need to get her kitchen into decent shape. It seemed that he wasn't the only one with a plan. He decided to let God worry about everything else.

It took him three days to get the kitchen wiring done, the new door and window framed in, the glass installed, the walls stuffed with pink fiberglass insulation and the longed-for plasterboard on the walls. Since the electricity had to be off, Becca and the kids stayed in town with her in-laws for a couple of nights, but by the time he got the door hung on the third evening she was there with both little ones and a bag of groceries in tow. She sent the girl back into the living room and gave the kitchen a careful look.

"I can't believe how much you've gotten done," she said, placing the bag on the table that he'd pulled across the floor and out of his way. "It's ready for the tape and plaster."

He nodded, feeling a spurt of pride. "Tomorrow."

She adjusted the baby on her hip and smiled, looking around the room. "I could help," she said, facing him.

He shook his head. "My job."

She sighed, but he saw the smile in her eyes. "Okay, if that's the way you want it."

"Yes."

"Hungry?" she asked, pulling a paper napkin from

the bag and preparing to dust the tabletop. "I brought plenty. The least I can do is make sure you eat."

He'd brought a sandwich for lunch, but the aroma of roast beef was making his stomach rumble now. Deciding that it would be impolite to refuse her offer, he looked at his dusty hands and checked his wrist for the time. Sixteen minutes after seven! No wonder he was hungry.

"Better wash up," he said.

She nodded, and he moved toward the newly installed back door, picking his way around tools and scraps of building material. He felt something very light bounce off his back and stopped, turning. She pulled another napkin from the top of the bag. He looked at the wadded one on the floor, then back to her.

"Where you going?" she asked before starting to wipe off the tabletop.

"Spigot out back."

She lifted her eyebrows. "Why not use the bathroom?"

The bath was the most feminine room in the house, pink and flowery and as clean as a surgical suite. Cody had obviously added the room and the kids' bedroom onto the house himself and managed a fair job of it. No doubt he'd have had the whole place whipped into shape by now, had he lived. Instead, Dan was doing the work. It didn't seem right, and Dan was never more keenly aware of that than when he was standing in her little bathroom looking at her pink fixtures. He couldn't help wondering if Cody had installed them to please her. He certainly would have.

Shaking his head, he slapped at the legs of his jeans and said, "Too dusty." Then he escaped out the back door to bend over the rusty old faucet at the corner of the house. By the time he returned, Becca had unpacked a number of disposable containers from the bag, and the girl had dragged the high chair in from the living room, where he'd moved it.

Becca was talking, but he didn't try to follow her, his interest taken by the food as she opened the containers. He saw sliced brisket, baked beans, potato salad, coleslaw and a thick, rich barbecue sauce. She held up a bundle of butcher's paper and unwrapped it, displaying three large pickle wedges and small banana peppers. He reached for one of the pickles, mouth watering.

She inclined her head toward the root cellar. "There's bread in a box on the steps."

He bit off a hunk of the tart pickle as he moved to open the flimsy cellar door. Inside, about four steps down a steep flight of rickety stairs, sat a cardboard box full of foodstuffs that Becca had removed from the kitchen shelves the night before he'd started work. A plastic bag of sliced white bread lay on top. He stooped and picked it up by the wrapper. By the time he carried the bread back to her, Becca had set the table with paper plates and plastic forks.

Jemmy hopped up on one of the pair of available chairs, but Becca spoke to her, and she started getting down again.

"Stay there," Dan said, reaching for a short stepladder. It made a tall but adequate stool when he sat on top of it. Becca put the baby in his chair and sat down.

Four people seated around a rectangular table in the littered kitchen made for a very crowded room, but Becca's smile and his own satisfaction in a job progressing well overrode any awkwardness as Becca began filling plates. She piled his high, and he let her, suddenly ravenous. From pure habit he began to bow his head, then he felt a jolt as Becca took one of his hands in hers. Jemmy's little hand slid into the other. His gaze flew to Becca. She had bent her head but lifted it again, eyes closed, as she spoke a simple grace.

"Thank You, Lord, for all Your many blessings, family, home, this delicious food and especially for Dan and all the good things he's brought to us. We have need, Lord, and You've sent this fine man to help. Bless him for his willingness to share his talent."

Dan felt a kick inside his chest. A fine man. He inclined his head and silently asked God to make him worthy of that description. When he looked up again he saw that Becca and Jemmy watched patiently. He looked at Becca and followed the seemingly natural impulse to squeeze her hand. She smiled. It was like warm sunshine bathing the cluttered, half-finished room. She pulled her hand back and began eating. Jemmy did the same, so he dug into his own food.

"Good," he said after swallowing.

She nodded and dabbed at her mouth with a napkin before saying, "John Odem cooks a couple times a week for the deli case. Monday it was a huge ham and macaroni and cheese."

Dan nodded. "I bought some. Real sweet."

"Yeah, he likes that brown-sugar-cured ham."

They concentrated on the meal for some time, then Dan noticed that Jemmy reached for one of the small yellow peppers on the butcher paper with the pickles. He shot a quick glance at Becca, who smiled and said, "She eats them all the time. John Odem again."

Dan chuckled and watched with interest as the little girl gingerly nibbled the succulent yellow flesh. "Hot?" he asked when she met his eyes.

She shook her pale head. "Nah, na if yont ea te sees."

"Not if you don't eat the seeds," he repeated carefully, realizing that she was eating around the ball of seeds inside the pepper. She nodded and kept nibbling. He felt an odd glow of pleasure. Children were often difficult to understand because they didn't always get words right, but he'd followed Jemmy. She was smart for her age, or maybe her diminutive size made her seem younger than she was. "How old are you?" he asked.

She grinned and held up four fingers, spouting rapid-fire words, few of which he caught this time. Lost, he looked to Becca, who ducked her head to hide a smile before lifting it again to say, "Jem's telling you that she had a party on her birthday, which is February tenth, and that you're invited next year. It's going to be here in our 'newed' house, by the way."

"Newed?" he repeated uncertainly.

Laughter danced in her soft green eyes. "Abby told her the place was going to be 'like new.' So in her mind when you're done it'll be 'newed.'"

He glanced at Jemmy and smiled. She beamed at him with something akin to hero worship. Just then something flew right past the end of his nose. He looked down to find a corner crust of bread on the table next to his plate. When he glanced in the direction it had come from, he noticed that both Jemmy and Becca were laughing. Even CJ, who had obviously launched the missile, judging by the white stuff oozing from his fist, was grinning broadly, showing off the few teeth he possessed.

"I'm sorry," Becca said. "He saw me throw the napkin to get your attention earlier."

Dan looked at the boy, and something in that little face seemed to be saying that he craved the same attention that Dan had been showing his big sister. Without even thinking about it, Dan picked up the scrap of bread and tossed it back at the boy. It was just long enough and just curved enough, incredibly, to hang on the boy's bit of a nose. For an instant Dan couldn't quite believe what had happened, and neither, apparently, could anyone else, but then the little imp grinned, put back his head and laughed so hard that his round little body jiggled all over. His whole being seemed to light up, even as he collapsed into the corner of the chair, laughing. The kid was so purely tickled, that crust of bread now clasped in his plump hand, that everyone was laughing, Dan included. He laughed so hard that his chest shook and tears gathered in his eyes. It almost hurt. He hadn't laughed like this, felt this good since…so long.

He wiped his eyes and looked at the smiling faces

around him. It was time to be happy again, time to stop licking his wounds and concentrate on the good in life, on the good that he himself could do.

Chapter Four

"You don't have to keep feeding me," he said slowly.

Becca had noticed that when he spoke carefully and precisely, his tone often lacked inflection, but when he blurted out or tossed off words, his speech was almost normal. This sounded like something he had rehearsed, at least in his mind, and she wasn't at all surprised. They'd enjoyed several meals together in her quickly evolving kitchen, and though he often seemed pleased and relaxed, she had identified a growing unease, a certain tension developing between them.

"You have to eat," she said, making sure he could see her face as she laid out the food. "Besides, it's the least I can do. You're working long hours, and you can't be making much money on this job."

When she thought about the material he'd used so far, she wondered if he could be making any profit, especially considering those cabinets. Even without the doors, which he said he was still building, they improved the room a thousand percent. And then there was the cookstove, which he'd said was used. She had no reason to doubt him, except that he'd pretended not to see when she'd asked where he'd gotten it. She kept wondering if his garage apartment had an empty space where the cookstove used to be, and the idea made her cringe inside. She wasn't above a certain amount of charity, frankly, but even she had her pride.

"Don't need money," he said matter-of-factly, filching a potato chip from the open bag on the table. They were still eating deli food. She looked forward to the day when she could cook him a real meal.

"Everybody needs money," she replied.

He held up four fingers, counting off the reasons he didn't. "Medical disability. Military retirement. Inheritance. Good investments."

"And the rent on that garage apartment?" she asked.

"Soon," he said nonchalantly, averting his eyes.

She didn't let him get away with that. Reaching across the side chair that stood between them, she placed a hand flat against the center of his chest. He looked down at it, then slowly lifted his gaze to her face. "You can rent an apartment without a cookstove, then?" she asked pointedly.

He blinked and chewed. She lifted an eyebrow insistently. Finally he grinned. "Got a stove same place I got yours. Used. Dealer in Duncan."

She narrowed her eyes, thinking that he'd worded his reply rather oddly. "It's not the same one, then?" He shook his head. "You swear?"

His mouth quirked. "Never swear. Much. When I hit

my thumb with a hammer, maybe." She laughed, and he grinned. "Not the same," he promised. "Honest."

She couldn't help noticing that his eyes crinkled in a most attractive way at the outside corners when he smiled, and for the first time she was truly glad that he couldn't hear the husky tone her voice had acquired. "I just don't want to take advantage of you, Dan—no more than I can help, anyway."

"I understand."

"I know you do. You're just such a blessing to us, and I can't tell you how grateful I am."

He shook his head. "I am blessed. You work hard." He poked a thumb at his chest. "I get checks in the mail."

"You deserve those checks," she told him, looking up into his chiseled face. He was a handsome man, with those blue eyes, and a good one, too. That much had become very obvious.

CJ banged on the metal high-chair tray, but she ignored his bid for Dan's attention, keeping it all for herself.

"Maybe I do work a lot," she said, "but it's because I have to, and it's nothing compared to what you do out of the kindness of your heart." She thought of the clean white kitchen walls, the glass light fixture snugged against the stain-free ceiling, the door and the window where the compact air unit would soon be installed, the butter-yellow cabinets and mottled-gold countertop set with a white enamel double sink. After hanging the cabinet doors and connecting the stove to the propane, he was going to add shelves around the refrigerator and build a new cellar entrance set flat into the floor, since she needed the cellar space for additional storage and the floor space for the dining table. He intended to install new cellar steps, too, as well as strip, seal and paint the kitchen floorboards. After that he'd rip off the porch and build her a new one that she and the kids could actually enjoy. It was almost too much, and she felt tears gather in her eyes.

"Thank you," she whispered, going up on tiptoe to kiss his cheek. He needed a shave, and the delicate rasp of sandy whiskers lightly abraded her lips. She'd almost forgotten what it felt like to kiss a man's rough cheek.

Suddenly he whirled away and moved to the back door, but then he paused and looked over his shoulder. She couldn't read what crowded into those blue eyes. "Welcome," he mumbled, and slipped outside.

A moment later she heard the water running from the spigot in back of the house and looked ruefully at her new kitchen sink with its shiny faucet. Her fingers wandered up to touch her lips, and for a moment she wondered what it would be like to kiss Dan Holden on the lips, to be kissed by him.

A vague guilt pricked her. Was she being disloyal to Cody and the Kinders by thinking of Dan as more than an answer to prayer? Maybe she was more selfish and needy than she realized. She marveled at how much God loved people. For no reason she could understand He loved her enough to let her stumble across Cody, to bring her here to Rain Dance and the Kinders, to give her two healthy children and meet every one of her true needs. He'd even shown her joy and peace in the midst of heartbreak and loss. Was it asking too much, wanting too much to wonder if the pleasure that she found in Dan's quiet company might be more than fleeting?

Could God mean Dan Holden for her?

She was almost afraid to think it. But somehow she was more afraid not to.

Becca said a quick prayer as she twisted in her seat. She'd kept an eagle eye out for Dan Holden all morning, and through the tall, narrow church window she'd just glimpsed his lean form striding up the path toward the building. Her heart sped up, and she told herself sternly not to be a fool. She'd seen the man almost every day for the better part of two weeks now, ever since he'd started work on her house, and today would be no different. Except somehow it was.

They were great friends now, maybe even more. Or maybe they could be. She wasn't sure, frankly, though she'd prayed and prayed about it. Lately she'd wanted very much to talk to Abby about her feelings for Dan, but she hadn't dared. For one thing, Abby was her mother-in-law. For another, she didn't feel free to discuss a certain issue with Abby or anyone else. Dan's deafness was his business, after all.

Dan appeared in the doorway from the vestibule, and Becca bounced up to her feet, motioning for him to come forward and join her. He glanced around uncertainly, but then he started down the aisle, right past the place where he usually sat. She plopped down again and briefly closed her eyes with a mixture of relief and excitement before turning up a smile for him as he slipped into place beside her. Abby and John Odem leaned forward to offer their own smiles, which Dan returned with nods. Jemmy, however, fairly shouted, "Hello, Mr. Dan!" just as the organ started playing. Dan didn't see.

Becca nudged his knee with hers, mouthed Jemmy's name and gave her hand a little wave. Dan instantly looked at Jemmy, smiled and waved as the congregation rose to its feet. Becca opened the hymnal to the correct page. Then, mindful of his desire not to broadcast his disability, she moved it sideways so it would look as if they were sharing. His gaze dropped on her before shying away, even as his hand rose to help support the heavy book.

Standing shoulder to shoulder with him—well, shoulder to forearm—Becca quickly found her place, using the tip of her forefinger to locate the word with which she picked up the lyrics. Quite without thinking, she followed the words with her fingertip for several seconds as she sang, before two realizations hit her simultaneously. One, Dan was tapping his toe in time to the music. Perhaps he couldn't actually hear the sound of it, but he could feel the beat. And two, he was following the words to the song as she sang them by following the progress of her fingertip.

A feeling of deep satisfaction crept over her. It wasn't much of a service, really, nothing at all on the scale of what he was doing for her. Dan could read the words to any song for himself at any time, while she could never in a dozen years do what he had done to her house. But by helping him to follow along in time to the music, she felt that she was helping him join in somehow—not with the singing, but maybe with the praising. And wasn't that the most important part? Or was she searching for something that didn't truly exist, assigning more significance to a simple courtesy than was warranted?

They went through the remainder of the service much as they had at Easter. Dan took his cues from those around him and paid particular attention to every word the pastor said, but this time Becca realized that he couldn't really catch each and every word, for often the pastor turned his head or looked down at his text or distorted words for emphasis. Becca began to realize how confined Dan's world had become, and she tried to think of ways in which she might help him. She could record the sermon and then repeat back every word to Dan in some private place, or she could write it all out for him to read at his leisure. That seemed to limit his participation in the experience, but those were the best ideas she had at the moment. She decided to discuss the possibilities with him.

After the service, Becca kept pace with Dan until they were out of the foyer. Then she grabbed his arm and tugged him down a hallway, explaining, "I have to get CJ."

He blinked at her, a question in his eyes. It was the long way around to the nursery.

"I want to ask you something."

He nodded and kept his gaze on her face as they hurried along the narrow corridor. She glanced around to make sure she wouldn't be overheard and said, "You're missing words during the sermon. Pastor doesn't know to keep his head up when he's speaking."

"Like you do," Dan said with a smile.

"I could help you fill in the blanks," she said, coming to a stop. Quickly she told him her idea for recording the sermon and speaking it back to him or writing it all out. He bowed his head, and she just hated it because she couldn't tell what he was thinking, but then he looked up again, and his smile and the blue of his eyes felt very soft.

"Becca," he said slowly, "I get enough of the sermon to fill in the blanks for myself."

"Oh."

"You don't have to find ways to pay me back."

"I'm not." She bit her lip. "Okay, maybe I am, but I just want to help."

He smiled. "You have. I needed to know *I* could still help someone."

She gaped at him. "Are you kidding? Why, if I had one tenth of the skills you do, I—"

"Wouldn't need me," he said, cradling her cheek with his palm. "I wouldn't have a friend." He grinned. "Not one who'd share her songbook."

Even as a warm glow suffused her, she whispered, "You'd have more friends if you'd just let everyone know—" He dropped his hand and looked away, effectively cutting her off. She realized only after he did that they were no longer alone. Two women were walking toward them, Amanda Cox and Jane Robertson, both Sunday-school teachers with classrooms on this hall.

Becca tossed them a wave and headed for the nursery, Dan at her side.

When the nursery worker handed CJ over the half door, he surprised everyone by making a grab for Dan, who grappled awkwardly with him until CJ got an arm around his neck. Becca felt warmth flush into her cheeks.

"Come here, you," she said, reaching for her son. "Dan doesn't want to lug you around."

But CJ drew back from his mother. Dan hefted him in his arms as if getting a feel for his weight, and said, "I'll carry him."

"He's heavy," Becca warned needlessly.

"Like lead," Dan agreed, looking at the boy, who grinned at him around the finger in his mouth.

Embarrassed by her son's grab for Dan's attention, Becca took the diaper bag and hurried through the church to the front lawn, where Abby and John Odem waited with Jemmy. The friends with whom they'd been chatting broke off and moved away as Becca and Dan approached with the baby.

"Sorry to keep you waiting," Becca said. She slung the straps of the diaper bag over one shoulder and reached for CJ. "I'll take him now."

But Dan moved toward John Odem, saying to Becca, "He's too heavy for you."

John took the boy and parked him on a hip, quipping, "You're a little mountain, aren't you, boy?"

Abby was laughing. "You won't believe it, but Cody was the same way. His age caught up with his size at about six."

Dan nodded and said, "Yes, ma'am," meaning he hadn't really caught what she'd been saying. "You folks have a nice day," he added just a little too loud as he prepared to take his leave of them.

"Wait a minute, Dan," Abby said just as he turned away, and Becca quickly reached out to snag him by the arm. He glanced at her, then turned back to Abby as she said, "Why don't you join us for dinner today? I've got a pot roast in the oven. It ought to be ready about the time I get the bread made."

"Yeah, and nanner pudding," John Odem added, using Jemmy's word for banana. Dan was staring at Abby and didn't even know John had spoken.

Jemmy saw an opportunity to draw even with her brother on the attention scale and started hopping up and down pleading, "Please. Please. Please."

Dan looked at her and then at Becca, who was holding her breath. Suddenly he nodded.

"Thanks."

Becca's smile broke free, even as she worried how he was going to pull this off. She wouldn't have him embarrassed or shamed for the world. Abby busily started directing everybody.

"John, get these kids in their car seats. Becca, you show Dan the way over. Jemmy, don't you step foot in the parking lot without holding your grandpa's hand." As she herded John and the kids toward their car, she said over her shoulder, "Dan, we could use some ice. That freezer in front of the store isn't locked."

"Come on," Becca said quietly, making certain he

could see her face even as she moved to his side. "We have to stop by the store for a bag of ice."

He nodded and dug out his keys with one hand. The other just sort of naturally cupped Becca's elbow. She waved at a few folks as he handed her up into the passenger side of the truck, then took a look at the inside of the vehicle as he walked around to the driver's door. She noticed at once that the radio had been replaced by a flat black screen with tiny domed lights placed at intervals around its perimeter.

He settled behind the wheel, inserted the key into the ignition switch and began buckling his seat belt. Becca tapped his forearm, pointed to the black screen and asked, "What's this?"

"Global satellite positioning system," he said, starting up the engine so the thing would come on.

"That's like a moving map, isn't it?" she said, buckling her own belt.

He nodded and ran a finger around the lights, saying, "These let me know when there's a loud noise and where it's coming from."

"Like a siren or car horn."

"Like that," he confirmed.

"Cool."

He put the transmission in gear, looked over his shoulder and backed the truck out of the space. Within seconds Becca saw that conversation would be difficult. He was a very attentive driver, which meant that he had to keep looking around him all the time, alert for what he couldn't hear and the alarm wouldn't recognize as important.

When he pulled up in front of the store, she unbuckled her belt and hopped out of the truck to hurry over to the freezer positioned next to the store entrance. She extracted an eight-pound bag of ice, carried it back to the truck and placed it on the floorboard before climbing in herself. As she was buckling her safety belt again, Dan asked, "Is that always open?"

"Sure."

"Anybody could take ice," he pointed out.

Becca shrugged. "Most folks will tell you next time they're in the store."

"Not all."

She shrugged again. He shook his head and drove the truck across the small parking lot to the street. "Turn left," she instructed. Realizing he couldn't have seen her, she reached across the wide bench seat, tapped his shoulder and pointed left.

He turned left. At the stop sign she pointed left again. He chuckled. "I know the way. Lived on this street."

"Oh."

Abby must have known that. So why had she told Becca to show him the way to the house? Her interest in Dan must be more obvious than she'd realized. Becca sat back and thought about Abby. It must hurt her mother-in-law to know that Becca was forming an interest in another man. Yet she'd invited Dan to Sunday dinner. Becca wondered what she'd ever done to deserve the Kinders and all the good things they'd brought into her life.

When Dan pulled the truck to the side of the street in

front of the small, modest Kinder house, Becca started to get out, but he stopped her.

"You didn't tell them," he said, and she knew that he was referring to his deafness.

"Of course not." She picked up the bag of ice from between her feet. "But don't worry, I'll help you stay on top of the conversation. You'll have to stay close to me, though."

He looked at her, smiled and took the ice from her, saying, "Thanks."

Feeling some trepidation at the task ahead, she got out of the truck and joined him on the buckled sidewalk. Together they moved across the grass to the concrete steps that led up to the stoop and the door. With one last smile of encouragement, Becca opened the door and ushered him inside. The small, crowded living room was dark and cool. Becca quickly snapped on a lamp.

Abby appeared in the doorway to the kitchen, wearing an apron over her Sunday dress. "Come on in," she said, disappearing again. "John's changing the kids' clothes." Becca knew that she ought to help John get the children out of their Sunday clothes, but she dared not leave Dan on his own. He followed her into the kitchen, carrying the bag of ice.

"Where do you want this?" he asked.

Standing in front of the small, high table where she did most of her kitchen work, Abby stirred buttermilk into the depression she'd made in a bowl of flour and other dry ingredients as she answered him. "Just put it in the sink there, hon."

Becca pointed to the sink, but Dan didn't even look at

her, let alone budge. Instead he just stood there holding the bag of ice by the end with one hand. Then he said, a little too loud, "You'll have to look at me when you speak to me, ma'am."

Abby did look at him then, obviously surprised, but no more so than Becca when he calmly announced, "I can't understand you if I can't see your mouth move. I'm deaf, Mrs. Kinder."

Becca clapped a hand over her heart, which had just given a decided lurch. Abby dropped the spoon into the bowl with a clatter.

"Oh, my soul!"

Dan looked down, then carried the ice to the counter and laid it gently in the sink, demonstrating that he had gotten Becca's message after all. Tears gathered in her eyes. He had obviously already made the decision to go public with his problem when he'd accepted Abby's invitation. Becca wanted to let him know how proud she was of him, and the only way she could think to do it without making a complete idiot of herself was with a touch. Slipping her hand into his, she briefly squeezed and retreated, but not before getting a quick squeeze back.

He leaned a hip against the old-fashioned, chrome-edged counter and folded his arms, facing Abby. "Should've told everyone sooner," he admitted. "Hard thing for a soldier who isn't one anymore."

Abby came around the worktable and enveloped him in a hug. "I'm sure glad you came home," she said.

Dan could obviously tell that she was speaking but couldn't know what she was saying, so he looked to Becca. She told him out loud what Abby had said so that Abby would know she hadn't made herself understood.

"She's glad you came home."

Dan smiled and hugged Abby back. "Me, too."

Just then Jemmy bolted into the room in her bare feet, wearing shorts and a T-shirt. "Mr. Dan, Mr. Dan! I gots a turtle in a box in the yard. Come see." As she spoke, she ran out onto the closed-in porch that served as a second bedroom. Becca called her back into the room, while Abby dabbed at her eyes with the hem of her apron.

"Honey, what have I told you about speaking to Mr. Dan?"

Jemmy looked up at Dan and asked politely, "Want to see my turtle? Please."

Dan smiled. "Sure."

"But not until you get some shoes on," Abby instructed.

Jemmy bolted for the porch again, crying, "They're under the bed. Mr. Dan can help me."

Becca caught her by the shoulders and turned her back to face Dan. "I'll help you with your shoes, but you have to remember to look Mr. Dan in the face when you speak around him."

"How come?" Jemmy wanted to know, not for the first time. Becca had always told her that it was the polite thing to do, but this time Dan went down on his haunches next to Jemmy and told her the truth.

"I have to read the words on your lips because I can't hear."

She checked briefly to be sure his ears were where they should be and repeated her question. "How come?"

"A big boom damaged the nerves in my ears. It was so loud it knocked me out of the room, which was underground, and put me to sleep for a long time."

"How long?"

"Two days."

Jemmy's eyebrows went up. "How come you were under the ground in a room? Was it a storm? Sometimes we might go to the cellar if a bad storm comes."

"I was looking for bombs." He glanced up at Becca and added dryly, "Found some."

She bit her lip to keep from laughing, because it really wasn't funny.

"Why were you doing *that?*" Jemmy wanted to know.

"It was my job," he said simply. "I was in the military."

"What's miltry?"

"A soldier," Becca explained.

Eyes rounding, Jemmy blurted to Dan, "You're a soldier?"

"I was," Dan answered. Then he looked up at Becca and said, "Now I'm a carpenter."

"Like Jesus!" Jemmy announced importantly.

Knowing he'd missed that, Becca waved his attention back to her daughter.

"What?"

Jemmy said, "Jesus was a carpenter. He made chairs and crosses and stuff."

Dan smiled. "That's right."

Abby suddenly shoved a paper towel full of pieces of cabbage at Becca, saying thickly, "Ya'll go on and tend that turtle while I get my bread in."

Knowing that she was anxious to have a good cry in private on Dan's behalf, Becca nodded and turned Jemmy toward the porch. Dan rose and followed.

Like the rest of the house, the porch-become-bedroom was cramped and faded, much as it had been when Cody had slept here on the full bed as a boy. Dan took that all in before turning to pay indulgent attention to Jemmy who babbled about her turtle while Becca wrestled shoes onto her feet.

Those shoes would have to be replaced soon, as Jemmy was outgrowing them, but Becca couldn't worry about that now. It was a beautiful spring Sunday in Oklahoma, and the world felt bright and glorious, especially as Jemmy blossomed and preened for Dan.

It struck Becca then how much her little girl missed her father. John Odem did his best to fill in, but it wasn't the same as having a daddy to poke twigs at your turtle and smile as you tried to impress him with what a responsible pet owner you were. Becca had been too busy to notice how hungry her children were for male attention, but as always, God had seen the need. And sent Dan Holden.

Chapter Five

Crouched over a patch of sand with Jemmy, Dan enjoyed the sunshine as he watched the little girl feed bits of cabbage to her turtle. He felt lighter somehow, breathed easier, as if a weight had been lifted from his chest.

Apparently a previous owner had written the turtle's name, Buddy, on its back with a black marker, and Jemmy had suffered through weeks of worrying that the writer would return to claim the animal. During that time the Kinders had posted a sign in their store window, much as people often did for stray cats and dogs. Dan had smiled when he'd seen it.

Found—Turtle
Doesn't answer to the name Buddy.

Jemmy petted the hard shell, watching with satisfaction as her silent companion munched at the pale green hunks of cabbage. Turtles had always struck Dan as stoic creatures, but every time Jemmy brushed her fingertips over the turtle's back little Buddy closed his eyes, looking for all the world like a turtle that had found a piece of turtle heaven. Maybe he himself had been a little bit the way he'd imagined turtles to be: slow, unemotional, silently enduring a lonely existence. Now, for some reason, he felt a kinship with this little fellow.

Dan wondered where the turtle's original owner might be. Surely anyone in the area would have seen Jemmy's sign. There wasn't another grocery store for miles around, and a turtle couldn't have traveled far on its own. Could it? Maybe he and Buddy were more alike than he even knew.

Have you been around the world, Buddy? Dan wondered. Did you travel far away and somehow find your way home again, like me?

He felt a tap on his shoulder and looked up at Becca.

"Dinner's ready."

He nodded and stood to watch as Jemmy carefully transferred Buddy to his cardboard box house with holes cut in the sides. She placed the box, with a bed of yellow grass and a large bowl of water inside, beneath the shade of an oak tree.

Becca waved Jemmy forward, then followed her into the house. She said something to the child, who nodded and rushed on into the kitchen. "You'll want to wash up, too," Becca said, turning to him. "You can use the kitchen sink as soon as Jemmy's done." She followed the child, presumably to be sure that she washed her hands sufficiently.

The instant he stepped up into the house, a mélange of rich, complex aromas tickled his nostrils and made his stomach rumble in anticipation. While he waited for his turn at the sink, he looked around the back porch. It had been sealed off with heavy plastic sheeting and plywood to make a bedroom, with a metal rod hung across one end for a closet. Atop that rod and the odds and ends of clothing that hung from it lay a battered old tan felt cowboy hat that Dan recognized as belonging to Cody, a memento of the boy he had been. That hat said to Dan that the Kinders were irrefutable proof that happiness wasn't about things or money—not that he'd ever really believed that. Still, he'd always had nice things and plenty of money to buy more if he needed or wanted. He had good parents and wouldn't wish for any others, but he couldn't help feeling a little envious of Cody at the moment. How simple and fulfilling his life must have been.

Simple, fulfilling and short, Dan reminded himself as Becca beckoned him. While he washed up, she helped Abby carry food to the table. With his hands clean and dry, he moved out into the space that served as the dining area. It was nothing more really than an awkward corner at the end of the living room where doors from all the other rooms in the house—bedroom, bath and kitchen—could swing open without colliding, but Abby had managed to tuck a round, claw-foot table and a number of mismatched chairs into it. Obviously no doors could be opened when the table was occupied, so the kitchen door had been removed from its hinges. John Odem was already sitting at the table when Dan arrived, with CJ propped up by pillows and tied with a dish towel to a chair beside him. A space equal to the boy's reach had been cleared on the tabletop. Deprived of more interesting utensils, he smacked the table repeatedly with his hands.

John Odem said something and pointed to a chair across the table from him, but Dan was uncertain if it was meant for him or someone else until all the females moved to other chairs. He waited until Abby, Becca and Jemmy were seated before pulling out the chair and sitting down. He positioned himself and scooted up to the table. The cushion felt a little lumpy and uncertain, but he didn't let that bother him—until he looked up and saw that everyone was staring at him.

Suddenly Abby glared at John Odem. Obviously scolding him, she shook her finger, speaking furiously. Unsure what was going on, Dan looked at Becca.

"John Odem's a great prankster," she explained with a wry smile, "and this time he meant to pull a trick on you, but the joke's on him." She moved her gaze to John and told him what Abby apparently had not.

"Didn't hear?" John said. "How could he not hear that?"

Abby apparently spelled it out for him. John's mouth gaped open so wide that Dan began to fear his upper denture would fall out. Then John smacked his knee and began to laugh. The old man howled until tears ran in rivulets down his craggy face.

It certainly wasn't the sort of reaction Dan had

expected, but it all began to make sense when Becca said, "There's a whoopee cushion under the seat pad of your chair."

A whoopee cushion. Dan rolled onto one thigh and thrust a hand beneath the pad tied to the chair, extracting a small, collapsed bladder with a nozzle on one end. John Odem went off again, and this time Dan joined him.

Abby rose from her seat and snatched the thing from Dan's hand, her face red with embarrassment. She took the carving knife to it, sawed right through the rubber, and as she worked she lambasted poor old John Odem. Dan could see her jaw working but not what she was saying. Whatever it was, John took it all in stride, laughing at himself as easily as he'd laugh at anyone else.

The situation was pretty darn funny, and laughter, it turned out, seasoned a meal to perfection.

Dan shook his head regretfully, looking down at the easy chair John had invited him to take after turning on a basketball game on the TV. "Put me right to sleep," he explained. Catching the wave of Abby's hand from the corner of his eye, he turned to her.

"We don't mind if you take a little nap, Dan."

He smiled. "You ought not, after all that good food." He patted his middle.

"Well, then, stay and take a snooze," Abby insisted.

"Have to go, but thank you." He walked across the room and kissed her cheek, explaining, "I talk to Mom on Sunday. She'll worry if I'm late."

Abby nodded and patted his shoulder. "You go on then, son, but you come back again real soon."

"Yes, ma'am."

She turned and spoke to Becca, who ducked her head and moved to open the front door for him. He wasn't certain what had been said until they stepped out onto the stoop and she pulled the door shut.

"I was told to show you out." He smiled his understanding. She tilted her head to one side. "Can I ask you something?" He nodded. "How do you 'talk' to your mom?"

"E-mail. Chat online."

"Oh. Of course. So you don't have a phone, but you do have a phone line."

"For the computer and security system. For emergencies."

"That's good."

He wrinkled his nose and admitted, "My parents worry."

She smiled. "I understand."

"I know." He swept his gaze over her face and said simply, "Thank you."

Her eyes held his for a long time before they slid away. "It wasn't as hard to tell Abby and John as you thought it would be, was it?"

"No." Now that it was out in the open, he found that he was glad.

She wrapped her arms around herself as if suddenly chilled, and he felt the impulse to put his own arm around her, pull her close to his side. He looked away to gather himself, but her clean scent lingered.

When he looked back, Becca asked, "Will I see you tomorrow?"

He hadn't worked the past Monday, figuring she needed some peace and quiet on her day off. Besides— and it was the oddest thing—as comfortable as her company often was, she made him uneasy, too.

"Summer's coming," she pointed out when he hesitated. She didn't have to say that the heat would make her and the kids miserable and the outside work unbearable for him.

He didn't hesitate any longer. "I'll be there."

She brightened. "Good."

He saluted her with a little wave and went down the steps, pausing at the bottom to remove his keys from his pocket. It had been a lovely afternoon—relaxed, funny, companionable. He'd felt a part of something again, more at home than with his own family, who tried to hide their pain at his loss with well-meaning smiles.

Feeling a tug on his pant leg, he looked down to find Jemmy at his knee. She'd gone outside to tend her turtle the instant she'd been excused from the dinner table, but had apparently made her way around the house in time to catch him before he left. She crooked her tiny finger at him, and he dutifully bent low to read her words, but to his surprise, she just wrapped her thin little arms around his neck and hugged him tight.

For a moment he couldn't breathe, but it had nothing to do with the stranglehold Jemmy had on him. For an instant he knew what it would be like to have a child of his own, a fragile little person who loved without reserve. He felt a sharp pang of regret, and then she pulled free and ran back to her beloved turtle. Dan blinked, put properly in his place—one rung below Buddy. Then he stood and caught the look in Becca's soft green eyes.

Suddenly he knew that his feelings for Becca were becoming complicated, even more so because they seemed to be reciprocated. Surely she wasn't looking at him as a new daddy for her children. That wouldn't do. He could never do the things that real fathers did, or even fit husbands, for that matter.

Troubled, he turned and went on his way.

Dan woke before the sun and fought back the impulse to dash straight out to Becca's. He dressed in lightly starched jeans and a soft, drab green, military-issue T-shirt, the tail neatly tucked in, and tugged on his comfortable lace-up work boots, no longer shined to a spit-polish gleam. After taking his time shaving, he scrambled some eggs and made a pot of coffee for breakfast. Even after that, it was still too early to go out to Becca's, so he thumbed through the local, county-wide newspaper.

Increasingly restless, he prowled the house after he finished the paper, but the emptiness and silence seemed unusually oppressive. He'd almost forgotten what a lonely world it was without sound to fill it: the tick of a clock, the hum of a ceiling fan lazily circling overhead, the ring of a telephone or doorbell… Funny he should think of those things now after all these months.

Desperate to keep busy, he turned on the TV set,

but morning television couldn't hold his interest, and he couldn't seem to settle down to serious reading. He decided to go through the toolbox in the bed of his truck, reorganize things a bit. That was good for a long while, at the conclusion of which Dan figured he had the neatest toolbox for miles around. He glanced at his wristwatch. Eight o'clock. Still too early to show up for work on Becca's day off.

He opened the hood of the truck and checked all the fluids, then he checked the air pressure in all the tires and even swept out the floorboard and shook the mats. Finally he stacked the carefully painted cabinet doors in the bed of the truck, making sure to cushion them with an old quilt, and climbed behind the wheel.

It was just after nine when he pulled up in front of Becca's house. Barely had his feet touched the ground when the screen door flew open and Jemmy tore out of the house wearing a flowered cotton nightgown with a ruffle around the hem. She barreled straight into him, threw her arms around his legs in an exuberant hug and began jumping up and down, talking all the while. She caught his hand and pulled him toward the house. Surprised, he could only wonder if something had happened to Becca or CJ. Scooping Jemmy up into his arms, he literally ran toward the house, only to see Becca calmly step out onto the porch in cutoff jeans and a faded yellow blouse with the tail tied at her waist.

"What's going on?" he asked, hoping his panic didn't show.

She sipped from the glass of orange juice in her hand,

smiled and told him, "You've been invited to breakfast with Jemmy and her dolls. She was worried you wouldn't get here in time."

He smiled with relief, though he had reservations. Jemmy had adopted him into the family, but she didn't understand what problems came with him. Framing his face in her small hands, she turned it so he could see her speak.

"It's a breakfast party in my bedroom and we got strawberries with cereal and juice."

He thought of his father sitting at a child-sized table, pretending to drink tea from toy cups while his sister babbled imaginary conversations with her dolls, and his heart squeezed. Setting Jemmy on her feet, he said, "Had breakfast," and quickly turned back to the truck.

How Jemmy took that or what Becca might have said to her once his back was turned, he couldn't know and wouldn't think about. Some distance was needed here, and yet he hadn't been able to think about anything else this morning except seeing Becca and the kids again. Just looking at Becca, all clean and fresh, made regret clench in his gut. He shouldn't have come today, but it was too late to make excuses and go.

Grimly determined to be strong in this, Dan hauled his tools into the house and set to work. He had cabinet doors to install, a floor to scrape and a full box of inexpensive self-stick vinyl tile to lay down before he could say that the kitchen was finished and get at that porch. He got busy, as near blind to the goings-on around him as he could make himself and still get the work done.

It was easy to tune out, really, with no sound to distract him and the precise placement of hinges and handles to absorb him. He worked steadily but swiftly, step by logical step, measuring, marking, drilling, placing, setting, tightening until every screw in every hinge on every door was in its proper place.

The cabinets looked fine, 1,000 percent improvement if he did say so himself, but the work was nowhere near being finished. He went down on his knees and began scraping the ancient linoleum away from the floorboards with a spackling trowel, which he'd sharpened for the job. When he felt something touch the sole of his boot he warily moved into a crouch, pulling one foot up beneath him, and looked over his shoulder.

Becca was standing barefoot among a scattering of screws from a box he'd left on the seat of a chair he'd pulled away from the table to serve as a kind of workbench. In her arms she held baby CJ, red faced and wailing as she pried screws out of his fists. Realizing at once that the one-inch screws were small enough to be swallowed, Dan shot to his feet.

"He okay? Any in his mouth?"

Becca jostled the crying baby while using her thumb to force his chin down and get a look inside his mouth. She turned a calm face to Dan. "No, I don't think he'd gotten that far with them."

But he could have. The hair rose on the back of Dan's neck. That baby could have swallowed a whole box of screws. And Dan would've had to stumble over him to even know. Incredibly, he watched *her* apologize.

"He shouldn't have been in here. Jem spilled her cereal and I was distracted with..."

Dan turned away. He knew it was rude, but he just couldn't bear to let her apologize for his failings. Another man would have heard the child there. This only reinforced his resolve to keep his distance.

Disappointment hit him, as profound and deep as on the day he'd finally understood that he was never going to hear again. On that day he'd sat through an awkward consultation with his doctor conducted almost entirely in writing, then he'd gone quietly into his hospital room and sobbed, only to look up and find that a nurse had entered without his knowledge. That had seemed the crowning humiliation and a harbinger of what his life was going to be like from that point on. Turning his back on that embarrassed nurse had been his only option that day. Getting away from Becca was all he could think to do now.

"Done for the day," he announced, and started gathering up his gear. He dumped what he could into his portable toolbox, slapped the drill case under his arm, grabbed the flat metal squaring tool and headed for the door. Becca caught him by the arm as he passed her. Her small hand fit perfectly into the bend of his elbow and sent heat radiating up and into his chest. He forced himself to look at her face, seeing distress—and understanding. He felt bare, naked, raw. Whatever he expected her to say, it wasn't what he read on her lips.

"The cabinets look wonderful."

He nodded and pulled away before she could say

more, moving quickly through the house and out to his truck. He didn't stop moving until he was once more safely behind the door of his own home. Just him. And the silence.

Chapter Six

Becca settled the baby more comfortably on her hip and sighed as she stared through the screen door at the level new floor of her porch and the empty road beyond. It had been days since she'd laid eyes on Dan. He was invariably gone when she got home in the evenings. Obviously he was avoiding her, and she didn't know why. She suspected that it had to do with the kids, even though that didn't make much sense to her.

Right up until Monday he'd been patient to the point of indulgence with them, but she was beginning to wonder if it didn't have more to do with his natural politeness and his circumstances than with Jemmy and CJ themselves. When Dan gave you his attention, it was necessarily intense. The lack of hearing and his dependence upon lipreading required him to lock his gaze on you, and the piercing blue of his eyes made the contact almost tangible. Unfortunately, a child wouldn't understand that such focus might not be personal. From

Jemmy's and CJ's ends, the connection went right down to the core of their own need.

She hadn't realized how much they wanted a daddy. Even now Jemmy's memories of her father were pale, like a movie on a fuzzy TV. CJ had no memories of him at all. He was born into a world without daddies, at least as far as he knew. Yet he worked as hard for Dan's attention as Jemmy did, driven by some innate craving for a father figure.

Though while they both naturally gravitated to Dan, he continued to hold some part of himself aloof. From everyone. Oh, at times she'd sensed the possibility of more between Dan and herself, a deeper knowing, a magnificent sort of emotional connection, but circumstance had made him an artist at pulling back into himself, and he had definitely pulled back from her and the kids.

Maybe she'd read him all wrong. Maybe he just didn't like kids and was too polite to say so. And maybe it had more to do with the shock and self-condemnation she'd seen in his eyes when he'd realized that CJ had gotten into that box of screws.

She sighed again and turned away from the door. The half-finished porch depressed her.

Oh, it was lovely how he'd squared it up with the front of the house. For the first time the floorboards were neat and level. The corner posts rested not on the ground itself but on a foundation of cement blocks, which had in turn been set on footings of gravel laid into a trench hardened with lime. He'd even built a skirt around the lower edge of the floor so critters couldn't set up housekeeping underneath. Once a skunk had gotten in there and made the house unlivable for nearly a month. She wouldn't have to worry about that happening again. But without the shelter of the roof, the incomplete porch made the house feel abandoned and hopeless in a way that the old, rickety one never had. It made *her* feel abandoned and hopeless.

Foolish notions, she told herself. No child of God was ever hopeless. She was proof of that, and Dan Holden was part of it. He'd come just when she'd needed him most, just when her faith in her ability to provide a stable, comfortable home for her children had begun to waver. She couldn't shake the notion that the timing had been as right for him as for them. Hadn't he said that he'd needed to be needed, to know that his life had purpose and value?

He had more purpose and value than he knew, because the fact was that she missed him. She missed his steady, pleasant manner, even his terse conversation and that air of wounded pride, for if Dan Holden had anything in abundance it was pride. Considering that fact, she wondered how he managed to cope with his handicap at all and suspected that it was only by the grace of God and his own deep faith.

Perhaps that faith was why she felt a serenity with Dan that she'd never known with Cody, whose exuberant personality had brought fun and adventure into her life, but little peace. Cody's own belief had been sincere and absolute, but his happy-go-lucky nature had not lent itself to serious contemplation, and she had the feeling that Dan had done a whole lot of that, at least since he'd lost his hearing.

They did have one thing in common, Cody and Dan. They were both strong, masculine men who somehow made her keenly aware of her femininity without making her feel weak or foolish, as her father and brothers often had. She hadn't realized how important that was until she'd lost it. Now she could have a chance for that again, with Dan, if only he felt the way that she did. She just didn't know. She didn't even know how to find out. Abby always said that the only thing to do when a body didn't know which way to go was to get down on your knees, so that's just what Becca did.

By Sunday she was certain that God didn't mean her to give up on Dan Holden yet.

Once more she watched and waited for him, and when he finally appeared in church she summoned her nerve and signaled for him to join her, but Dan pretended not to see and reverted to his old pattern, taking a seat in the back pew and slipping out before anyone could engage him. She realized that she was going to have to force a confrontation, but it wasn't until after dinner that Becca decided to visit him at his house again.

She looked at Abby, who'd just mentioned that she was going out back to sit in the shade with Jem, and simply said, "I'm going to Dan's."

Abby's smile communicated understanding. "I was wondering how long you'd let it go."

"I don't want to push, but I have to do something.

He just suddenly pulled back, and I don't even know why."

Abby nodded and patted her cheek. "You're good for him. That much is plain."

"Not to him, apparently."

"Well, maybe somebody needs to set him straight."

"I'm not sure anyone can."

"God can, if He wills."

"But I'm the one who has to talk to him," Becca pointed out.

"I'll say a prayer for you," Abby promised.

Becca smiled, hugged her mother-in-law and went out.

Not until she was halfway across the front yard did she decide to walk. It was only about a half mile to the Holden place, and she needed the time to gather her thoughts. She'd reasoned out a calm, careful approach that went right out of her head the instant she realized that a strange car was parked in front of Dan's house. She almost turned around, but it was too late for that. Dan was on the porch with two visitors, and she'd already been seen. Dithering for a moment, she didn't know what to do, whether to wait until the couple left or interject herself into the situation. Then one of the visitors, a woman, turned and smiled at her. A moment later Dan lifted a hand and waved her forward.

Becca felt embarrassed and horribly conspicuous as she moved up the walkway and climbed the porch steps, but then she noticed that Dan was speaking to the strangers in sign language. Intrigued, Becca moved closer. Dan rested his hands on his hips for a moment and gave her a look that said he didn't quite know what to do with her before quickly beginning to sign again. This time, he also spoke.

"Linda, Max, meet Becca." He spelled out her name, his fingers flashing the symbols at lightning speed.

The woman, a tall, thin brunette, looked at Becca with palpable interest. "Hello," she said warmly, her hands casually interpreting her words into sign language. "It's nice to meet you."

"I'm sorry to intrude," Becca apologized. "I didn't realize Dan had company."

"Oh, we're on our way out," Linda said, continuing to sign. "Max and Dan became friends in therapy last year, and we just wanted to stop by on our way home to Oklahoma City and see how he's doing."

Becca looked at Max. "That's nice."

Linda signed for Max and said to Becca, "My husband doesn't read lips very well. He doesn't have the knack, and since he cannot speak, we communicate by sign language."

"I see."

Max spoke to his wife with his hands, and Linda turned to Dan. "We really have to be going," she said, leaning in to kiss his cheek.

"Good to see you," Dan told her.

Then he signed something and shook Max's hand as Max smiled and nodded and Linda said to Becca, "I hope we'll see you again sometime."

"That would be nice."

Just before they started down the steps, Linda

looked back over her shoulder. "I'm glad Dan's doing so well."

"Very well, I think," Becca said, glancing at Dan.

He lifted a hand in farewell to his friends, then took Becca by the elbow and steered her unceremoniously into the house. The instant they were out of sight and earshot, he backed up about three steps and folded his arms.

"What?"

Becca bit her lip. Now that the moment had arrived, she wasn't sure how to begin, so once more she dithered. "I—I didn't realize that you had company."

"Even *I* have friends," he said, managing to sound sarcastic.

"Well, of course you do," she snapped. Bowing her head, she tamped down her impatience before looking up again. "They seemed very interesting people. I take it you were in therapy with Max?"

"Took therapy *from* Max."

"The sign language."

"Yes. Not everyone can lip-read. Max was born deaf."

"I see."

"He doesn't miss sound," Dan went on. "Never knew it."

"So he doesn't feel sorry for himself," Becca reasoned, realizing belatedly what she'd implied. "I didn't mean that you do."

Dan parked his hands at his waist and changed the subject. "Something wrong?"

"You tell me."

He made a face, as mute as his friend Max.

Becca licked her suddenly dry lips and looked around the neat foyer, taking in the large, lovely house even as she tried to find the right words to begin what promised to be a difficult conversation. Her house, in comparison to this, was a tumbledown shack, and the Kinders' wasn't much better. Dismayed by that knowledge, Becca searched for some way to reconnect with this man who had somehow lodged himself inside her heart.

"Would you teach me sign language?"

Dan stared at her for a full fifteen seconds before saying flatly, "No."

"Why not?" At last the words tumbled out. "What's gone wrong between us, Dan?"

He blinked and frowned. "Nothing."

"You know that's not true."

He shrugged as if to say that he didn't know what she wanted from him.

"You're avoiding me," she accused, "and I don't even know why."

Bowing his head, he brought his hands to his hips and said slowly, "Becca, it's best."

Flexing her fingers, she fought to keep her hands relaxed at her sides and waited until he looked at her. "I don't believe that."

Suddenly he threw up his hands. It was the first time she'd heard him shout, and she covered her ears, knowing that he couldn't realize how loud he was. "I'm not fit for you!"

She stomped forward, making him look at her. "That's not true."

"It is!"

Wincing, she automatically covered her ears again, then dropped her hands almost at once, but not before a look of sheer agony came over him.

"I can't even hear myself! People stare when I'm too loud. Don't fit in. A freak." He closed his eyes. "Easier alone."

Her hands at his shoulders, she shook him until his eyes popped open. "You're not a freak."

"Not a whole man."

"That's crazy."

"Not the man for you."

"How could you possibly know that? You haven't even given us a chance to find out!"

He leveled his gaze and enunciated each word carefully. "You're a mother. I can never be a father."

So that was it. She felt an odd sense of relief. It wasn't her, then. It was his fear of inadequacy. "You think you can't be a father because you can't hear. That's baloney."

He shook his head, an agonized look on his face. It was the same expression he'd worn the day that CJ had gotten into that box of screws. "Kids get hurt, cry for help. If my child were in danger, I wouldn't know!"

"That was my fault with the screws," she told him, "and I can hear just fine. There must be ways to minimize the risks."

"Can't think of any. I've tried!"

Stepping closer, she looked up into his face. "Things

have a way of working themselves out if you just give them a chance."

He swallowed and said, "I have to accept my limitations."

"And sometimes you have to at least try to move beyond them," she countered.

He shook his head stubbornly. "Not fair to the kids, you."

"Your deafness is not a problem for us. So you can't hear, so what?"

"So what? CJ almost swallowed screws. I didn't know!"

"You couldn't be expected to."

"My fault," he insisted stubbornly.

"Next time you won't leave them in reach."

Dan shoved a hand over the top of his head and said desperately, "I don't get half what Jemmy says."

Becca reached up and placed her hand in the hollow of his shoulder just above his collarbone. "Dan," she told him, "what you hear with your ears isn't nearly as important as what you say with your heart. Think on that, will you? And while you're at it, think on this." Going up on tiptoe, she angled her head and brought her mouth to his.

For an instant she thought he would pull away, but then his arms came around her, and for a brief, sweet moment she knew the joy of being held again, of being wanted again. Suddenly she remembered that she had instigated this, that he was too polite to do anything but kiss her back, and chagrin at her own forwardness made her break away. Appalled at what she'd done, she turned tail and left without even a word of farewell.

Dan was loading his tools into the back of the truck when Becca drove up to the house with the kids. She parked the car, got out and looked at him frankly, letting him know that she was surprised to find him still there. He was surprised himself, but he couldn't deny that he'd wanted to see her again. He'd missed her, much more than was wise, since she'd come to his house four days ago, since she'd kissed him. He stopped what he was doing and watched as Becca moved to the back door of the car and reached inside to free the children from their safety restraints.

Jemmy piled out first, pushing past her mom to reach the ground. She stood leaning against the car fender, watching Dan warily, her bottom lip stuck out. He felt like the biggest heel in the universe, but he didn't know yet what to do about it. He was so afraid of doing the wrong thing, the selfish thing.

Closing the toolbox, he waited for Becca to speak. She approached with CJ on her hip, moving in that twisted, leaning gait that she somehow made look graceful and natural. She studied the completed porch before switching her gaze to his face.

"Looks great."

He nodded and let the feeling of a job well done flow over him. "It'll look better painted."

"Is that next?"

He nodded. "Then walls and air conditioning."

"So the cool air doesn't go right out the cracks," she surmised correctly.

He grinned. "Cheaper that way."

She looked down. He wanted to put his arms around her, but he didn't dare. That kiss was never far from the surface of his thoughts. He still didn't know how his arms had come to be around her or how he had lost himself so completely in the simple meeting of their mouths, but it was just one more danger in what felt like a whole minefield of possibilities that surrounded this woman.

She looked up again after a moment and suggested, "You could stay for supper."

He frowned and said, "Crock-Pot's on." It was the absolute truth. He'd put in a frozen chicken that morning. Only now did he realize that he'd done it to protect himself from staying to supper.

"All right, then," she said before looking over her shoulder at Jemmy.

"She okay?" he asked, concerned by the manner in which the child hung back.

"She's upset because I wouldn't let her have ice cream before we headed home. She'll be done pouting soon."

He tried to look at Jemmy without being too obvious about it. Was she crying over there? He couldn't tell in the waning light, and he didn't think it wise to get into the middle of a mother-daughter spat, so he stayed where he was, although it felt wrong somehow.

"Better go," he said, moving to the driver's door of the truck.

When he looked back at her, she said, "I wish you'd stay."

He sent his gaze skittering off, trying to pretend that he hadn't understood. His heart was pounding so hard that it hurt. He wanted to stay, but he knew that it wasn't wise. Nothing had changed, after all, just because she'd kissed him. He opened the door, but then he turned back to her.

"Can't make peace with it, Becca."

"I can see that."

"I'm sorry."

She shook her head. "I can't fault you for honesty, Dan. You obviously just don't feel the same as I, we, do."

He wanted to tell her that it wasn't so, but something had risen into his throat, and he couldn't have spoken even if it had been right to do so. Instead, he just stared at her, hoping that his emotions didn't show on his face. God knew that he wanted her, but she and her kids needed a whole man. They deserved that.

Finally he forced himself to get into the truck. Reaching up, he adjusted his mirror, more to break the connection that he felt with Becca than because it needed alteration. An image of Jemmy materialized. She was leaning across the fender of her mother's car with her arms flung out and her cheek pressed to the metal, as pathetic a picture as he'd ever seen—and quite calculated. He fixed the view and checked the side mirror. Becca was at the window, so he rolled it down, grinning at the child's dramatics and his own susceptibility to it.

"Give her ice cream," he pleaded, wrinkling his brow in supplication.

Becca smiled. "I will. After dinner. If she behaves herself."

He nodded and started the engine. Becca called to Jemmy, who dragged herself listlessly from the car and trudged toward her mother as if going to the guillotine. Becca traded a knowing look with Dan and held out a welcoming arm. He chuckled and rolled up the window. As soon as Jemmy was held safely to her mother's side, he backed the truck around her car and turned it down the road. When he glanced up into his rearview mirror again, it was to the image of Becca and those two kids standing there in the dusty yard of their little house.

It seemed all wrong somehow, but he couldn't quite figure out why. Whatever it was, it surely had nothing to do with him.

Chapter Seven

Dan made himself a tasty supper of chicken and dumplings by following a recipe e-mailed to him by his mother. It was way too much food to eat at one sitting, but that just meant that he wouldn't have to cook again for a while—and that he couldn't risk staying late at Becca's for at least a couple of days. Funny how his life had narrowed to whether or not he could safely spend time with her and the children.

Sitting at the table over his plate, he wondered if Jemmy had gotten her ice cream and knew that she most likely had. Unless she showed up her little self, her mama would have no reason not to keep her word. He hoped the imp was properly grateful. Even tonight with her put-upon face and mistreated-miss act, she'd made him want to smile.

CJ would get ice cream, too, of course, and gobble it down with all the finesse of a baby bird. By spoon or hand, it didn't make any difference to that boy. Yet even as he was cramming it in or opening his mouth in automatic demand for more, he was watching everything and everyone around him. More often that not, Dan had to admit, the boy was watching him. Who was he kidding? The light of hero worship in that child's eyes made him feel ten feet tall. But what would he see in those green eyes, so like Becca's, when he failed to respond to his cries?

Dan felt as if he had one foot nailed to the floor and couldn't go anywhere except around and around in circles. One moment he wondered if he could really belong with Becca and the kids, and the next he had to face the fact that he could not be all that they needed. He thought of Becca: her pretty, peaceful face, those wide, soft eyes, that Cupid's-bow mouth, the perfume of her—all Becca without any hint of anything artificial, just clean and feminine—her endless patience, forthrightness, her happy faith…. Why did feel as if he'd lost her when he'd never even had her? He felt so confused. For days he'd been praying about it.

Don't let my desires keep me from doing the right thing, Lord. Show me what's best and help me do it. I want to do what's best for Becca and the kids.

Only by talking to God could he find a measure of peace that allowed him to go about his business.

Rising from the table, he cleaned up after his meal and wandered into the living room to catch the late news. The weatherman predicted a chance of rain tomorrow. Good thing he'd gotten the roof on Becca's porch. With that thought, he took himself upstairs to bed, as weary as ever he had been in his entire life.

* * *

Dan awoke with a jerk. It was dark inside his room and as still as the grave, despite the opened window beside his bed. Still tired, he first rolled onto his side and looked at the clock on the bedside table. Three in the morning. The tingle of his nerves told him that he would sleep no more this night, and he resignedly rose to a sitting position.

His natural circadian rhythm had been disturbed for a time after his concussion. He'd essentially slept for days after the explosion, only to awaken for the first time in the middle of the night to an eerie silence, feeling his own heartbeat and breath in a way he never quite had before. For a time he'd been frightened and disoriented by the tilt and sway of his world. Then he'd realized that he was aboard a hospital ship. Some hours had passed before he'd fully understood that he could not hear a blessed thing, not even the rotor staccato of the helicopter that ferried him to an air base for transport home to the States.

After that he'd slept only fitfully for months, a combination, the doctors had said, of stress, jet lag, disorientation, worry and idleness. He'd soon discovered that no easy remedy existed, for the simple reason that he could no longer rely upon an alarm clock to tell him when to get up. An orderly had awakened him on the ship, but gradually he'd had to learn to pace himself, develop a routine, read his own body and organize his life around an uncertain beginning to his mornings.

It was his habit to lay out his clothing for the next day. He got to his feet, and without bothering with the light pulled on the jeans that he'd left folded over the foot of the bed, shrugged into the T-shirt waiting atop the dresser and picked up his boots, into which he'd poked a clean pair of socks. He carried the heavy, familiar footgear out onto the landing and down the stairs, where he went into the kitchen for a glass of milk.

He poured the milk by the light of the refrigerator and drank it all, standing, then poured another glass and fished around in the cookie jar for a couple of stale macaroons, which he carried in his teeth as he walked through the dark house to the study. Might as well catch up on his correspondence while he had a chance. E-mail had been piling up in his box. Sitting down in the comfortable leather desk chair, he laid the cookies on the blotter right next to the tall glass of milk and pulled on his socks and boots before settling down to his little feast. One cookie into it, however, he lost his enthusiasm for the second.

What was wrong with him? Even during his time in the hospital he hadn't felt like this. Fear as real as the chair beneath him gripped his heart, and he began to pray with a fervency that bordered on panic. In the midst of it he found himself remembering the last verse of the forty-second Psalm.

"Why are you downcast, O my soul? Why so disturbed within me? Put your hope in God for I will yet praise Him, my Savior and my God."

He lifted his head. Something was wrong. The hair rose on his forearms and the back of his neck. His skin prickled and tightened. He felt the crack of thunder in time to turn his head to see the flash outside the window.

In that blink of light he saw the branches of the trees swaying wildly. A moment ago it had been as still as death without a breeze of any sort, but in the time it had taken him to dress and come downstairs for a glass of milk and some cookies, a storm had arisen. Storm. The word whirled through his mind, followed instantly by another, much more ominous.

Tornado.

Jumping to his feet, he hurried out onto the front porch, right to the edge of the steps, where he paused, steadying himself with one hand on a sturdy square column. The smell of rain filled his head and lungs, but even as the wind died away to a chilling breeze, lights began to come on around town. He watched them, one by one, then caught sight of a police vehicle at least two blocks down, speeding toward him with flashing colored lights.

The warning siren must have sounded, which meant that a twister had actually been sighted! And as deaf as he was to the alarm, Becca and the kids would be, too. The horn was mounted atop a pole on the edge of the school grounds and could not possibly wake them from a sound sleep so far from the center of town. Rain began to pour down in sheets, as suddenly as if someone had turned on a tap. It was foolhardy to drive in such a tempest, but he couldn't take the risk that the storm would miss Becca's place.

Galvanized, he ran back into the house, taking the stairs two and three at a time as he made for his bedroom. Grabbing keys, wallet and a flashlight from the nightstand, he pelted back down the stairs and out of the house to the truck parked in the carport. He gunned the engine in Reverse all the way out into the street, then forward as fast as he could go, the rear end slewing from side to side on the rain-slicked street.

The trip out to Becca's house had never seemed longer, even as the rain began to let up. When he turned off the county road onto her sandy drive, he wondered why in the world anyone would build a house so far off the road. As he bumped over the last little rise, the truck rocked crazily, and it was then that he saw the gray funnel cloud begin to dip down out of the churning black mass overhead, and he laid on the horn. The flashing red light on his warning panel let him know that it was indeed blowing. He could only pray that they had time to get to safety.

Bailing out of the truck before the engine had even died, he crammed the flashlight into his back pocket and ran for the house. Becca met him on the porch in her nightgown and robe. The air had grown ominously still again.

"Get to the cellar!"

Eyes wide, she turned back into the house without a word, and he followed, right on her heels, straight to the kids' room. Becca went to the crib, and as Jemmy roused, Dan swept her up into his arms.

"Hang on to my neck."

He realized that Becca was grabbing clothing, and he took it from her, bundling it into his arms with Jemmy even as he pushed Becca back into her own bedroom. He gave her two seconds to snatch up what she could for herself, then seized her by the arm and propelled her into the living room and across it to the kitchen. Shoving aside the table with one hand, he threw open the cellar door, beyond thankful that he'd installed a new one along with a sturdy set of stairs. All but tossing Becca and CJ down those steps, he dropped down behind them and let the counterweight on the door slam it shut.

For a moment he stood there at the bottom of the steps in the pitch-black darkness, pumping damp air in and out of his lungs, heart racing as he waited for the light. Then he realized that if he wanted light, he was going to have to provide it for himself. Still clutching Jemmy, who had a stranglehold on his neck, he let the clothing fall and reached into his back pocket for the flashlight, then flicked it on.

Becca stood a few feet away, jostling a screaming CJ. A trickle of sand drifted down from overhead, and Dan's skull felt as if it was being compressed slightly.

"We're okay," he said, as if to reassure himself. "We're okay."

But he sensed the maelstrom whirling overhead, and the skin prickled on his arms and legs. Jemmy was trembling, and Becca's face was ashen with fear. She looked up at the ceiling, jiggling the baby, and Dan wondered what she was hearing.

"Can you hear me?" he asked, and she lowered her gaze to his face, then gave him a nod. "Too loud?" She shook her head. Willing his heart to slow, he sucked in a deep breath through his mouth. It tasted of dirt, dampness and panic. Perhaps it was his inability to hear the storm that allowed him to calm himself. Now he had to calm the others. "Settle in. Get comfortable."

He carried Jemmy over to a wooden box about as old as he was and carefully set her atop it. Shivering, she pushed hair out of her face and looked up at him with wide, solemn eyes, trusting him to keep her safe. He took stock. Becca had stored a jumble of things down here, including some of Abby's canned peaches and pickled okra. He spied an old kerosene lantern and went to check it for fuel, slipping past Becca and the baby in the narrow confines. Calmer now but still sniffling, the boy reached for him. Dan smiled, but took care of the lantern first. Luckily, it felt heavy with sloshing liquid.

"Matches?" he asked Becca, and she reached into a corner of a dusty shelf, coming up with a small box. While he lit the lantern, she pulled out two cheap, folding lawn chairs, the type with woven plastic seats, and placed them within the circle of light. To save the batteries, Dan switched off the flashlight and placed it, lens down, on one of the shelves that lined the narrow, dusty, underground room. When he turned to Becca, she handed him CJ, then followed the boy right into Dan's arms, all soft and warm and woman. A moment later he felt Jemmy wrap herself around their legs.

"It's okay," he said against the top of Becca's head. "Safe." Had any woman ever smelled better than this one? he wondered, closing his eyes for a moment.

Thank You, God. Thank You. I know You woke me just in time.

CJ grabbed hold of his ear, but Dan wasn't ready to

give up that sweet, soapy perfume just yet. Presently Becca pulled away a little, and when she wiped the tears from her cheeks he realized that she'd been crying. She turned her face up and asked, "How did you get to us in time?"

He gave her a lopsided grin. "Went fast."

She punched him lightly in the midsection. "You took a big chance driving out here in this kind of storm."

"You can't hear tornado siren."

"Neither can you."

He chuckled, feeling the tension in his chest begin to loosen. Oddly, it made him feel a little weak in the knees. "Better sit."

He pulled around one of the chairs and gingerly lowered himself into it, shifting the baby onto his knees. Jemmy had glued herself to her mother. Becca pulled the second chair close and sat down facing Dan, Jemmy on her lap. As she kept casting worried glances upward, Dan figured the storm must sound pretty fierce.

"What time is it?" she asked.

He shrugged, not having thought to grab his watch. "Half past three? Not sure."

She tilted her head. "How did you know?"

He understood perfectly well what she was asking. Leaning forward slightly, one hand steadying the boy, he told her. "Just woke up. Felt wrong. Knew it was coming here."

"Thank God," she said fervently.

"Yes. Thank God."

Jemmy suddenly jerked and cried out, clutching her mother.

"What?" he asked. Becca answered, but she was looking up, so he didn't understand. "Becca!" he said sharply, and she abruptly dropped her gaze, blinked and answered him.

"Something hit the door."

No telling what that was, but it meant something had been flying around inside the house. "Raining?"

"I think so. It's quieter now."

"Good." At least, he hoped it was good. Frankly, he wasn't too sure just how watertight this old root cellar was, but he saw no point in dwelling on that at the moment.

"I was in a typhoon once," he said—anything to distract them.

"What's a typhoon?" Jemmy wanted to know, turning her face up to him. It looked as if she'd pronounced it *tied-foon*.

"Big storm at sea," he told her.

"Were you on a ship?" Becca asked, and he nodded, answering Jem's question before she could ask it.

"Big, big boat, lots bigger than a house." Jemmy's eyes went wide. For the first time he realized that her eyes were almost the same color as his, as blue as a cloudless sky. "Wind blew hard. Ship went up and down." He rolled his arm and hand in the air, demonstrating what the troughs were like during a typhoon in the open sea. "Like a roller coaster."

"Nuh-uh!" Jemmy said skeptically. Then, "What's a roller coaster?"

Her mother explained that. Then he told them, as best he could, how they'd lashed themselves into their bunks while dishes and various gear had tumbled and crashed, rain and seawater deluging everything topside. "Scary," he said finally, realizing that he'd talked more in those minutes than he had in many months.

CJ slapped a wet hand against Dan's cheek just then, and Dan realized that his hand wasn't all that was wet. "Any diapers?" he asked.

Becca bit her lip and said, "I'll check." Shifting Jemmy off her lap, she went to the foot of the steps and gathered up the things they'd dropped earlier. "Might as well get dressed," she said, carrying them into the light. She placed the lot on the chair and plucked out several items, including a disposable diaper, which she held out to Dan. "Think you can manage CJ while I take care of me and Jemmy?"

"Try," he said uncertainly, looking at the bits of clothing as he took them into his hand. He looked up a moment later to find her waiting.

"Well, turn around," she said, making a twirling motion with her finger.

"Oh." He got up and turned the chair so that it faced the wall, CJ and his clothing tucked under one arm. He sat down again and started trying to figure out what went where.

The diaper was first, of course. Fortunately CJ lay placidly with his head upon Dan's knees while he managed it. He'd dismantled sophisticated weapons less confusing than all those folds and gathers and tabs, and it wasn't until he had the thing on that he realized it was backward.

"Again," he said with a sigh, but CJ had been patient

as long as he was going to be. It became a real wrestling match, and for once Dan was glad he couldn't hear, for he was sure there was much laughing going on behind him. Nevertheless, he finally got the squirmy critter corralled and saddled. Then came the actual clothing, which turned out to be a one-piece shorts-and-shirt thing with a bewildering number of snaps. He fastened the crotch together twice before he got it right, and by then CJ was completely out of patience. Hitting a moving target at a hundred yards was nothing, Dan concluded, compared to getting a tiny sock on a busy foot. In the end, Becca came to rescue them both.

Dressed simply in faded jeans, gray T-shirt and running shoes, she wasn't wearing any socks, either. "Let's just forget about these," she said, tucking those tiny stockings into a pocket. "Anybody hungry?"

Jemmy jumped up and down, the ruffled hem of her favorite flowered nightgown belling out to reveal the cuffs of the shorts she wore underneath. Apparently Becca hadn't managed to grab her a top. At least she had snagged a pair of tennis shoes for her. As Becca reached for two jars of sliced peaches and a small box of plastic forks, Jemmy knocked into the empty chair. She stilled at once. Becca obviously chose not to scold the child in these trying circumstances, a decision Dan found wise.

"We'll have to eat out of the jar," she said, handing one to Dan. "Try not to get syrup all over yourselves. We may be wearing these clothes for a while."

She smiled, but Dan saw the worry in her gaze and nodded mutely. Becca calmly set her chair upright and parked herself in it, Jemmy coming to lean against her knee. Dan held the plastic fork in his teeth while he twisted open the jar, feeling the *pop* that told him the seal was good and the fruit safe to eat, but he hesitated before he put the fork into the jar, looking up at Becca. She seemed to know exactly what he was thinking and reached out her hand for his. He clasped her fingers and bowed his head.

"Dear Lord, thank You." It was all he could get out, but it was enough. Becca squeezed his hand and let go. When he looked up, she was forking a peach slice into Jemmy's mouth.

The best that Dan could manage with CJ was to lean the child way out over his legs and quickly slide a whole peach slice into his gaping maw. The boy could swallow almost without chewing, and half the quart jar was gone before Dan got his first bite. He ate the rest with CJ sitting quietly against his chest, drank the syrup, dropped the fork into the empty jar—which he placed out of the way on a nearby shelf—and wiped his sticky mouth with the palm of his hand. When he looked down at CJ, he saw that the boy slept. Jemmy was drinking the syrup out of the jar she'd shared with her mother.

"What do you hear?" he asked Becca.

"Nothing for some time now." The look on her face said that, much as she dreaded it, they could probably safely look outside.

"Wait for daylight," he suggested, and she nodded agreement. Neither had to say that the dark could hide unknown dangers if the storm had done much damage.

Dan didn't know how long they sat there, her cradling Jemmy, him holding a sleeping CJ, but the air had gotten close and stale and his joints felt stiff and uncomfortable when he finally rose.

Jemmy, too, came to her feet, so he slid CJ into his mother's arms and reached for the flashlight. "Let me look first."

Becca nodded, and he slid his palm against her cheek before he went to the stairs. Dread filled him, but it was easy enough to set aside. They were all alive and well. And together. He'd not ask for more than that.

He climbed the steep steps, put his shoulder to the door and shoved upward, but it barely budged. Not a good sign. He pocketed the flashlight and tried again, feeling something heavy slide around on the top of the door. He looked back down into the cellar, saying, "Becca, help me."

Becca rose and placed CJ in the seat of the chair, instructing Jemmy to stand in front of him and keep him trapped in his seat. Jemmy seemed to relish the job. Becca squeezed up the steps beside Dan and placed her hands flat on the underside of the door. He pulled her up higher.

"Use your back."

She maneuvered until she got her shoulders pressed up against the door. Dan craned his head out of the way to accommodate her. He patted her legs to let her know that she should push with those rather than just her back.

"On three." She nodded, and he counted. "One, two, three."

For a moment he didn't think they'd make it, but then whatever it was blocking the door slid free and the door literally flew open. Gray light flooded the stairwell. Dan caught Becca as she lost her balance, steadying her with his hands.

"Wait," he said, promising her with his eyes that no matter what they found, all would be well. She shrank back, and he climbed up out of the hole of the cellar into…chaos. And open air. The refrigerator had been blocking the door, but that was about the only recognizable shape he saw. Becca's house lay in jumbled piles of debris, bits of newly installed insulation fluttering like pink dandelions in the breeze. Even the floor had buckled and tilted crazily. It wasn't light enough to see much more, but what he could see was catastrophe.

He turned back to the cellar and looked down to find Becca waiting with wide, uncertain eyes, CJ on her hip, Jemmy's hand clasped in hers. He reached down and drew her gently upward, saying, "Sorry, honey."

Tears filled her eyes, but for a long moment she looked only at him. Then she took that last step up and out. Wandering slowly forward, she clasped her son to her and took it all in. Dan let her go, let her deal with it, but when she reached the spot where her new porch had stood, now swept clean of even the sand that had once covered the hard ground, she fell forward onto her knees. Yanking Jemmy along with him, he rushed to her side and went down onto the dirt with her, pulling her into his arms, pulling Jemmy in with them, CJ wedged between their chests.

She sobbed, but the children, oddly, remained dry-eyed. With Jemmy it was shock, with CJ confusion. Dan held them all as close as he could get them and waited it out. Presently Becca began to pray. He couldn't hear what she was saying, but it didn't matter. As he held her with her face tucked into the curve of his neck, he could feel the words against his skin, and though he couldn't identify a one, he knew the essence of them, for they were the same words that his own heart prayed.

Why?

Help.

What now? How do we fix this?

We survived.

Thank You.

Chapter Eight

They sat on the ground for a long time as daylight gradually brought the devastation into full relief. Becca didn't want to look. She didn't want to leave the shelter of Dan's arms. If ever she had doubted that Dan Holden was the answer to her prayers, she would not do so again. He had saved them. God had used Dan to save her and her children.

"What do we do now?" she asked his shoulder.

His only reply to that was to bracket her face with his hands and tilt her head back because, of course, he couldn't have heard her. She smiled wryly and saw in his bright eyes a tender concern that brought fresh tears to her own. The children began to stir.

Jemmy sat flat on the ground, leaning against both Becca and Dan, and now she rubbed her eyes as if awakening. CJ had slipped down to Dan's lap when he had shifted off his knees to sit with his legs folded back beneath him and slightly to one side. Her poor baby was holding the hem of Becca's T-shirt and the sleeve of Dan's as if he needed to be doubly sure that he was anchored to this world. He tugged uncertainly at her, and she straightened away from Dan to smile blearily at CJ and take him into the fold of one arm, wrapping the other around Jemmy.

"I don't know what to do next," she said to Dan, feeling stupid.

He got to his feet, dusting off his jeans with busy whacks of his hands as he glanced around the immediate vicinity. "Head for town."

Jemmy stood, keeping close. Dan reached down and pulled Becca to her feet by one arm, CJ sliding into position on her hip. He held her gaze for a time, as if willing her to be strong. Becca steeled herself, full of dread, then turned and caught her breath.

It was even worse than she'd first thought.

Broken, soggy bits of debris were snagged in the bushes that had grown up around the fencerow. Much of it was tangled in twists and curls of barbed wire. A cast-iron skillet and a single fork, the plastic dish drainer, the broken handle of a broom and the sides of a rattan clothes hamper were strewn about the yard. Her car lay on its side, missing its hood and most of its glass. A fence post had been embedded in one wheel well and stuck out at a crazy angle. She saw a wooden block and a tiny die-cast car in a clump of grass. What was left of her television set had been buried by one corner in the dirt next to it. The old hickory tree that stood about fifteen yards to the east of the house was now bald and split. Worse, Dan's truck was wrapped around it.

"Oh, Dan," she said, turning to him.

He shrugged. "Insured."

"Well, thank heaven for that," she said, not even wanting to think about her own situation.

Bringing his hands to his hips, he said. "Guess we walk. Or I do."

She glanced around once more. "There's no point in hanging around here. We'll all go."

"You sure?"

She wasn't really, but she couldn't think of anything more depressing than sitting here alone with the kids. "If you don't mind. We'll have to take our time."

He reached for CJ and her hand. "Plenty of that."

She took Jemmy's hand with her free one, and they started off at a sedate pace, Dan matching his gait to Jemmy's. They hadn't gone very far, just a few yards down the road toward town, when Becca felt her spirits begin to lift. The air tasted clean, crisp. The bright sun felt gentle. The sky had never seemed so blue. She began to realize that the post oaks lining the bar ditches that flanked the dirt road were alive with fluttering movement. She squeezed Dan's hand, and he turned his head to look at her.

"Birds are singing."

He nodded and looked up, pointing with his chin. A pair of small brown wrens dipped and darted, cavorting like happy children. Becca burbled laughter, glad to be alive, and Dan's strong right arm came around her shoulders, squeezing and momentarily throwing her off stride. Then he pointed to one side.

"Rabbit."

They stopped and stayed still until Jemmy spotted the

small gray hare with white tufted ears. It hopped off as soon as she began to speak to it, but she smiled, wonder in her eyes. Becca shook her head at that. Jemmy had seen rabbits before, even held and petted tame ones, but the whole world had become a gift with their survival of the storm.

A little farther on, Jemmy herself caught sight of a tortoise sticking its head up from a depression in the ground. It retreated into its shell as she ran toward it, but presently poked its head out again, beady eyes rolling. Becca stopped her from reaching for it, and Jemmy immediately put up a fuss to take it home as a friend for Buddy.

"This is a wild thing, Jem, not a pet."

Jemmy's lower lip began to tremble. Just then Dan crouched at the edge of the depression, CJ on his knee and a twig in hand. He dropped the end of the twig in front of the tortoise's head, and the critter snapped with shocking speed, yanking the twig from Dan's hand as it again retreated. Jemmy jumped back with a yelp.

"Bad turtle!" she cried.

Dan wrapped his arm around her and brought her close to his side, saying, "Reckon he's had a tough time, too. Better leave him be. Okay?"

Jemmy dashed a tear from one eye with a dusty hand. "'Kay."

He nodded and patted her arm before rising to his feet once more. They started walking again, but Jemmy's mood had soured, and she complained of being tired and bored. Becca began to hum a familiar song, and soon Jem was singing along and skipping ahead. Becca was beginning to feel fatigued herself. None of them had gotten much sleep, and the adrenaline surge of terror had abated. She wondered how long they could keep up the pace.

Sure enough, they hadn't gone quite a mile when Jemmy began to flag. Dan paused long enough to hand CJ to Becca and swing Jemmy up onto his back. A spurt of guilt shot through Becca, and she mentally castigated herself. She should've stayed at the house with the kids and waited for him to return with help—except the house no longer existed. The devastation boggled her mind. She didn't dare think about it yet. Better to concentrate on the here and now.

"You can't carry her the whole way," Becca told Dan, feeling hot and drained.

"Won't need to," he said, striding ahead, his hands behind him to support Jemmy, who had wrapped both arms and legs around him.

Dirt gave way to pavement, which made the walking easier but hotter. They trudged on, not speaking or pausing except to shift a child into a more supportable position. At the end of the second mile they stopped to rest. Becca's tongue was sticking to the roof of her mouth. Her feet felt sweaty, and CJ had started to fuss. She swept a place free of stones in the dirt at the edge of the road and sat down cross-legged, CJ in her lap. Dan and Jem did the same. Becca's forearms had started to sunburn. She wasn't as brown as Dan or even Jemmy. She shielded CJ with her body as best she could and sighed, pushing damp, scraggly hair away from her face.

She must look a sight, but what could she do about it now?

She caught Dan's eye and said, "Wish someone would come along."

Dan nodded, squinting into the distance, his forearms balanced on his knees. "Me, too."

"I wish I had some chocolate milk," Jemmy announced.

"When we get to town," Becca promised. Providing it's still there, she added silently, biting her lip. Just how hard had the town been hit? she wondered. Were Abby and John Odem safe? She wished she had some way to let them know that she and the kids were okay. Dan seemed to be reading her thoughts.

"Don't worry," he said. "Be okay."

She nodded and put on a brighter face, though a real smile seemed to elude her.

They sat there until the ground got too hard for comfort. When Jemmy rose, so did Dan. He reached down for CJ, who went readily into his arms, and once more hauled up Becca, who let him, even as it occurred to her that she had come to depend on him even for small things like this. She pushed away a sense of desperation and fixed her mind on just getting to town.

Dan looked down at Jemmy. "Walk a bit?"

She nodded and moved between him and Becca. He lifted CJ onto his shoulders, clasping his hands behind the baby's back. CJ grabbed an ear and a fistful of hair. Becca took Jemmy's hand and squared her shoulders. Off they went.

That last mile seemed to stretch on and on forever.

Heat radiated in silver waves off the pavement. The sun had grown harsh, mocking. Becca held tears at bay with a willing numbness. Dan had shifted CJ to his chest and instructed Jemmy to walk in the shadows that he and Becca cast as they trudged along.

They didn't pass another soul all the way into town, but as they drew closer they could see signs of damage. Trees and highline poles were down. Shingles and leaves and bits of other matter littered the ground. Becca's concern for Abby and John Odem grew.

"Didn't set down," Dan pointed out. He didn't say, and she didn't have to be told, that a tornado didn't have to touch the ground to do a great deal of damage.

Jemmy began to complain and then to cry, and they were blocks yet from Dan's house. He looked to Becca, the first real signs of worry puckering his brow. "Can you take CJ?"

She wasn't really sure that she could, but she nodded and held out her arms. Once he was on her hip, the baby felt part of her again. Dan scooped up Jemmy and held her against his shoulder, stiff and sniffling, but before they could move forward, a black-and-white patrol car turned from behind an empty building onto the street and came toward them. Dan waved it to a stop, and Clay Parks got out, one of only two deputy police officers employed by the city. He was a compact man with a boyish face and easygoing manner.

"You folks all right?"

"Just tired," Dan said, sounding it. "Mrs. Kinder's house was destroyed. We had to walk in." He didn't offer any explanation for him being with them.

"Say, I'm sorry to hear that," Clay told her.

"Can you tell me if Abby and John Odem are okay?" Becca asked urgently.

Clay nodded, the brim of his brown felt cowboy hat rocking to and fro. "Saw Abby not two hours ago. They had some damage at the house. Otherwise they rode it out just fine. She was worried on account of not being able to reach you, with the phones being down. Power's off, too, but the chief called it in on his cell. Oughta be back on in a few hours."

"Could you take me and the kids over there?" Becca pleaded. "We're about done in."

"Drop us at my house," Dan countered.

Becca bit her lip uncertainly. "I don't know. Maybe we should go straight to Abby's."

Dan shook his head. "My house is closer."

"That might be best," Clay said. "The Holden place seems untouched. Besides, the Kinders are at the store, doing what they can there. I'll let Abby know where you are."

Becca nodded. She hadn't even thought about the store. What would they do if their only source of income had been destroyed? She couldn't make herself think of it just yet, and since Dan was already handing Jemmy down into the back seat of the police car, she let him propel the situation along, as she had been doing. He reached for CJ next and stepped back to let Becca slide in beside Jem before dropping down on the outside, CJ on his lap. As Clay turned the car around, Becca laid her head back and felt an ache spread from her feet up.

After a bit Dan asked a little loudly, "Anybody hurt?"

"Haven't heard of any fatalities or serious injuries," Clay answered. "Got some damage, all right. Lots of roofs tore off and chimneys down, few busted windows. Mostly straight-line winds and lightning, I figure."

Dan looked to Becca. She lifted her head and repeated what Clay had said. "No fatalities or serious injuries so far as they know. Lots of damaged roofs, chimneys and windows. He figures it was mostly from straight-line winds and lightning, so I guess you were right about the twister not setting down here."

Dan nodded and turned his gaze out the window. "That's good."

Clay looked into his rearview mirror, tilting his head back so he could see Becca. "You sure he's all right? Something wrong with his ears?"

Becca leaned forward. "Dan's been deaf since he was hurt in an explosion in the military."

"Is that so? I never knew. Heard he was working out at your place, though."

"He came out to warn us," she told Clay, wanting to set the record straight. "Good thing, too, because we took a direct hit. If we hadn't got to the cellar quick, we wouldn't be here now."

"Boy, that was some lucky!" Clay exclaimed.

"More than lucky, if you ask me," Becca said. "We had to walk in because Dan's truck got wrapped around a tree."

The deputy whistled as he pulled over in front of Dan's house. "He got insurance?"

"He says so."

Dan opened the door and got out.

"What about you?" the deputy asked.

Becca grimaced. "Little bit."

"It's a complete loss, is it?"

"Except for the land."

"Can't take the land, can they?"

Might as well, Becca thought. With a sigh she started to slide across the seat, then paused, blinking back tears. Her voice shook when she asked, "Could you ask Abby to bring over diapers and clean clothes? We're always leaving stuff at her place."

Clay Parks looked over his shoulder, sympathy in his eyes. "I sure will, ma'am."

"Thanks."

She grabbed the hand Dan extended to her and stepped out of the car. Broken tree limbs littered the yard, and the shrubs were looking kind of bare. A window screen lay on the front lawn, and the gutter was down on one side. Otherwise, the place looked the same as before.

"I hafta go," Jemmy whined, climbing out of the car. Becca nodded as she took CJ from Dan, who bent at the waist and waved to Clay.

"Thanks."

"No problem."

Dan straightened and looked at Becca as the police car pulled back onto the street. "This is best," he said. "Room for Abby and John, too, if need be."

She figured they'd have to wait and see before deciding who was going to stay where, but she was just too tired to say so. "Right now what we need is a bathroom," she told him.

"Got two of those," he said. They walked slowly up the path and onto the porch, straight to the front door, which was standing slightly ajar. "Guess I didn't shut it good," he said, pushing it wide. He pointed to the stairs. "Up there."

Becca started Jemmy up the steps. Dan caught up and took CJ from her. She nodded a weary thanks and kept Jemmy climbing, though the stairs seemed to get steeper as they went. Finally they reached the landing, which opened onto a glaringly bare central hall with a window seat at the far end overlooking the backyard.

"Center door on the left," Dan said. "My bedroom and second bath next. Two bedrooms on the right. Plus, garage apartment out back."

Becca knew he was really saying that he had more than enough space for her and the kids and the Kinders, too, but that was a temporary solution beyond which she could not begin to think. She concentrated on taking care of Jemmy.

The bathroom was long and narrow, with a claw-foot tub at one end beneath a small curtainless window. A gas heater stood between the tub and the toilet, with the sink placed closest to the door. Everything was white except the hardwood floor, faucets and the oval mirror above the sink—even the trash can.

"Get some towels," Dan said, walking across the hall to the linen closet positioned between the two extra bedrooms. As he carried the towels back to her, she saw that CJ was asleep on his shoulder.

"We'll just be a minute," she promised.

"Take your time."

She helped Jemmy, then sent her out and took a turn herself. After she washed her hands and face and slurped some water as Jem had done, she felt better, and when she opened the door Dan was standing there alone.

"Abby's here," he explained.

Becca hurried down the stairs, Dan on her heels. Abby appeared in the wide living-room entrance, and Becca fell into her arms. Abby steered her back into the big comfortable room, where CJ slept in one corner of the sofa and Jem slumped in the other.

"Thank God you're all right," she was saying. "I was so worried about you! We didn't know a thing until we woke up this morning and half the roof was off the house. We've been at the store packing ice into the freezers ever since. John reckoned it had missed you, and people were waiting when we got there, wanting batteries and nonperishables." She stopped and took Becca by the shoulders. "Dan says you got hit hard."

Becca nodded, and the tears started to come. "It took everything, Abby, even Dan's truck. If he hadn't come to warn us…" She trailed off and shook her head.

Abby turned to Dan. "How on earth did you know? We slept right through it."

"How *did* you know?" Becca asked, stepping forward and wiping at her tears with both hands.

Dan slid his hands into his pockets and shrugged. "Just woke up. Storm came, and I knew I had to get to you."

Abby clapped a hand to her chest. "Divine intervention, that's what it is."

Dan nodded and looked at his feet. Becca covered her mouth with her hand and sat down in the nearest chair. She'd always suspected that God had a specific reason for bringing Dan Holden into her life, but it wasn't at all what she'd thought! Suddenly the future seemed even more of a puzzle to her than ever.

Okay, Lord, she prayed silently, *now what?*

"So long as everybody's alive and well, we can work everything out," Abby was saying. "Logically, I guess the first thing is getting you settled."

Dan said, "Here. I'll move out to the garage apartment."

"Oh, no, Dan," Becca protested, looking up sharply. "We can't put you out of your own house."

"Dan's right, honey," Abby said. "We've got no place for you now. The back porch is flooded, and everything in it is ruined. Plus, a corner of the kitchen is open, and we've got to fix that first or lose it, too."

"The kids and I will rent your apartment," Becca suggested to Dan, but he shook his head.

"Too small. Not finished. Just a bedroom, really."

"Now you listen to Dan," Abby put in. "We'll figure out something else later."

"Room here for you and John," Dan said to her.

"No, no," Abby said. "We're fine where we are."

He nodded. "I'll help make repairs."

"Thank you, Dan." Abby accepted with heartfelt gratitude. "Gracious, we already owe you so much."

"Settle for a ride to Duncan," he said with a self-deprecating smile.

"You can take our car," Abby offered instantly, but he shook his head.

"It's better if someone else drives."

"Becca can. I'll stay here with the kids."

"Becca's tired," he pointed out.

Abby looked at Becca and said, "I'll take you, then." Realizing that Dan couldn't have caught that, she faced him and repeated it.

He nodded and walked over to Becca. Going down on his haunches, he laid a hand on her knee. She realized that she was letting him decide everything for her, but her brain felt dull and blank, and she could feel his certainty like a comforting blanket. Rejecting that required more strength than she could muster at the moment.

"Get comfortable," Dan said deliberately. "Abby brought diapers. Help yourself to anything you need. Kids will be hungry."

Jemmy perked up at that and struggled up onto one elbow. "Chocolate milk," she pleaded, "and cookies."

Dan rose, chuckling, and ruffled her hair. "Be back soon as I can," he said to Becca. "Rest. Eat. Use anything you want."

Becca felt close to tears again. She didn't want him to go. It suddenly felt as if she couldn't possibly cope on her own, but she knew that was just weariness and shock. She'd been on her own for nearly two years and much of the time before that. She looked up at him.

"Take care of what you need to," she said, "and don't worry about us."

He smiled and walked out into the foyer, his heavy boots clumping over the floor. Abby kissed her cheek and followed.

Becca sighed and bowed her head, leaning forward until her forehead touched her knees. *You'll take care of us,* she thought to God. *I know that. But still I worry. Help me not to, and keep me from doing anything foolish.*

When she sat up again, Jemmy was standing at her elbow expectantly. Becca looked to C.J., who was sleeping soundly in the corner of the couch. She didn't have anywhere safer for him at the moment. She'd just have to trust that he wouldn't wake in the next few minutes.

She'd just have to trust, period, she mused, and went to raid Dan's kitchen.

Chapter Nine

John Odem wanted them to bring back as much bagged ice as they could carry. His stores were severely depleted due to the power shortage as people, like him, tried to save the contents of their refrigerators and freezers. As she aimed her ten-year-old sedan northward, Abby worried aloud about what was to become of Becca and the children, the cost of repairing their house and saving their merchandise and the plight of others hit hard by the storm. Dan didn't mind. He only caught a word or two here and there, and his thoughts were preoccupied with a swirl of plans of his own. By the time they completed the forty-some-mile trip he'd decided on a definite course of action.

He had Abby take him by the insurance office first, where he filed a report on the truck and pretended not to notice Abby telling the agent how he'd "saved" Becca and the kids. He was promised a visit by an adjuster within twenty-four hours and a check soon after. After leaving the insurance office, he and Abby drove straight to the bank, where he withdrew a sizable amount of cash. The next stop was the automobile dealership.

It didn't take long to explain what he needed and why, choose a red, midsized, double-cab, short-bed pickup truck, tell the man what he intended to pay for it—cash on delivery—order the warning system, leave a significant down payment and insist that it be ready within three days. When the sales manager pointed out that he'd have to send a man to Oklahoma City to find the necessary equipment, Dan forked over another hundred bucks as an incentive and walked out while the man was still talking. He hadn't thrown his weight around in quite a while, but he hadn't forgotten how to do it, and in some ways being deaf actually made it easier. The whole transaction took less than ninety minutes, and he had little doubt that the truck would be ready when he returned for it, and if not, he'd know why. He didn't have time to be patient or politic.

The final stop was the local discount department store. With Abby's help he picked out whole new wardrobes for Becca and the kids, about a week's worth of apparel, including dress clothes for Sunday. He bought nightgowns, shoes and a supply of baby goods, as well as a crib, high chair, car seat, diaper bag and a clever little monitor set with lights that flashed when it picked up sound. In fact, he bought two of those.

The most personal stuff he left to Abby, who put together a selection of shampoo, conditioner, brushes, combs, clips, deodorants, creams, underclothes and such. While she was doing that, he wandered the toy section, entertaining himself with the amazing array of gadgets designed to teach and enthrall a kid. He had no idea that toys had changed so much, but the old favorites were still around, too, and he made sure to buy a combination of both new and familiar items, as well as half a dozen books.

His two final purchases were an inexpensive but feminine wristwatch and a Bible, a modern, fully annotated study version with a supple leather cover dyed rose-pink. He'd have liked to have her name embossed on the front, but they didn't do that there, so he settled for a flowered bookmark with "Rebecca" printed on it in flowing script.

Abby fussed about the amount of money he was spending, but he pretty much ignored her. When he added 150 pounds of bagged ice to the total, she flat threw a fit, and he wound up letting her cover that part herself, then doled out cash for the rest with a sense of real satisfaction. Abby shook her head and informed him that his generosity was apt to get a different reception than he imagined.

"Our Becca's a real independent little mite, you know. Comes from being the third of seven children growing up poor on an Iowa farm."

He hadn't known that about her, and it occurred to him that he hadn't really bothered to find out. What Abby said about her objecting to him outfitting her and the kids was no doubt true, but he was willing to risk her disapproval in this case. It simply had to be done, and so far as he could see, he was the only one around who had the money to do it. She could kick up all the fuss she wanted, but in the end she'd accept his charity, for lack of a better word, because she really had no other immediate choice. Besides, he'd had more fun shopping for her and those kids than he'd had at anything in a very long time. She'd just have to swallow some of that pride. It wouldn't kill her. That much he knew from personal experience.

By the time the old car was loaded down with everything they'd purchased, it was riding pretty low, and Abby had a time holding the thing on the road, but Dan was too tired to care. He kicked back and snoozed the whole trip home, coming awake again only when they pulled to a stop in front of Kinder's Grocery. The lights inside the store meant, thankfully, that the electricity was on, and John Odem was as busy as "a June bug in August," as he put it, which according to Abby meant two months behind and fading fast. Dan helped Abby move the ice with the assistance of a wheelbarrow, then he climbed back into the car and let her drive him to his house, where they began the process of off-loading the remainder of their purchases.

The box containing the unassembled baby bed was tied to the roof of the car with nylon twine, the knots of which had tightened to the point where they would have to be cut. Dan carried in as many bright blue shopping bags as he could manage, left the lot in the foyer and went to grab a utility knife from the small box of tools that he kept in a cabinet over the washer and dryer just off the kitchen. When he returned to the foyer, Becca was there, her hands on her hips, outrage clouding her drawn face. She was wearing one of his T-shirts, which was many sizes too large for her, and a pair of his drawstring gym shorts.

As he brushed past her and hurried back outside to finish the unloading, he noticed that she was barefoot and smelled of soap and water. Obviously she had bathed. He met Abby on her way in with a clutch of bags and told her that he'd take care of the rest. Wisely choosing to leave the remainder of the sacks on the front porch, he went back to cut free the boxed crib. Becca met him on the front steps, primed for bear.

"What do you mean, Dan Holden, by taking this on yourself? You might have asked me what I—"

He put his head down and moved right past her, hauling the cumbersome box with him and trying not to notice how fetching she looked in his clothes. As he shoved his way through the small mountain of discount-store shopping bags on the floor of his foyer, he mused that not being able to hear did have some benefits, after all. No doubt she was giving vent to some choice words right now, but he didn't have to acknowledge them as he manhandled the boxed baby bed upstairs and into the front room on the right.

This room had belonged to his uncle, his father's older brother. Ted was a pipe fitter who'd spent the majority of his career working in the Middle East, socking back money for a retirement he was clearly unwilling to consider, despite being well past the age when most men hung up their welder's masks. Never having married, he seemed intent on leaving Dan and his sister a minor fortune. Dan didn't figure he'd mind having a needy little boy take up residence in his old childhood room.

Besides, it was time the room was cleared of its decades-old memorabilia and decoration. He'd hunt up some boxes tomorrow and clean out this room and the one next to it, which he intended for Jemmy. Every little girl should have her own room, he mused, or at least not have to share with her brother. In the meantime, he could make space for the crib by simply shoving aside some of the furniture. Becca could decide later what would stay and what would go. After opening the box and extracting the instructions, he figured out what tools he would need, then gathered up his patience and went back downstairs.

Becca was sitting in the living-room chair, her head in her hands. CJ was playing quietly on the floor, dressed simply in a diaper. Dan asked cautiously, "Where's Jem?"

Becca lifted her head to glare at him. "Out back playing."

"Abby?"

"She had to get back to the store."

He nodded. Time to pay the piper, then. "Want to go out front so you can yell at me?"

She cut her eyes to the side and folded her arms. Finally she shook her head. He dropped down to sit on the floor in front of her, one knee drawn up with his arm wrapped around it.

"Had to be done, Becca."

"Doesn't mean I have to like it," she said, keeping her gaze averted.

He moved his toe back and forth, trying to think what to say to that. "Could be worse."

She pushed her hands through her hair and glowered at him, saying, "Yeah, we could be charity cases with nothing more to our names than the clothes on our backs, a useless piece of land and a stock of canned peaches and pickled okra."

He dropped his gaze and said, "I can help." When he sneaked a peek at her, she was sitting forward with her forearms on her knees, mouth flattened, gaze level. She opened her mouth, but then her eyes filled, and she put her head back to keep the tears from falling. He gave her a moment, then got up so he could look down into her face.

"It's been a long, hard day," she said, mouth trembling.

He nodded. He was feeling it himself—the weakness that came with being emotionally drained. "It'll get better," he promised.

She sat up straight again, looked him in the eye and said, "Thank you."

He shrugged. "You're welcome."

She sighed. "You must feel like God's dumped us on you."

He chuckled. He actually felt as if he was finally understanding why it had all happened, why God had brought him back here, what his real purpose was. He finally understood that being deaf was next to no hardship when all things were considered, that he'd traded his hearing and a career for a *life* and that he was no less a man than before. Maybe just the opposite.

Now was not the time to say these things, though. It wasn't about him. She had been through a serious trauma. She needed time to adjust, to accept, to under-stand, and he needed time to work out some details and get everybody settled. The details, actually, were a good distraction.

He pulled the folded instructions from his back pocket and waved them at her, saying, "Now *I* could use some help."

She took the paper from him, glanced at CJ and said, "Okay, but what about that mess in the front hall?"

He waved a hand. "Dig out what's needed later. Leave the rest for tomorrow."

Sniffling, she nodded. "Fine."

Backing up, he said, "I'll get the tools."

"I'd better check on Jemmy," she replied, starting to rise, but he pushed her back down.

"I'll do it." He was happy to do it. Just plain happy, in fact, which didn't make a lot of sense because he really did hurt for Becca and all that she had lost. Furthermore, he knew perfectly well that more difficult days lay ahead before they could really say that they had weathered this storm, yet life suddenly felt right to him.

He found Jemmy in one of his old sport shirts, but-toned up to the neck and stuffed haphazardly into her shorts, sweeping the floor of her imaginary playhouse with a fallen tree branch. She looked up and smiled as he approached. He smiled back and instructed, "Stay inside the fence. Okay?"

She nodded and continued her play, talking and shak-ing a finger at some imaginary troublemaker.

Yes, he thought, giving a few more moments to her little drama, this was what life was really about, and he might never have known if left to his own devices. Like Uncle Ted, he might have awakened one day in a place far from home with the realization that his only heirs were nieces and nephews of whom he'd seen too little over the years. He understood now that he didn't want to be like Ted, and a profound sense of gratitude washed over him. With it came the whisper of an almost forgotten Bible verse.

"In everything give thanks; for this is God's will for you in Christ Jesus."

In everything give thanks. Everything.

Even deafness, as incredible as that seemed.

Becca quickly realized that putting together a crib was a daunting process that in this case could have been a disaster. For one thing, reading instructions aloud to Dan proved less than efficient, especially when those instructions appeared to have been written by an individual with only a vague understanding of the English language. He simply couldn't watch what he was doing with his hands and the movements of her lips, too. This necessitated much study of intricate diagrams and a good deal of trial and error.

If that wasn't bad enough, CJ greatly complicated the procedure. He desperately wanted to get in on the act. Two adults down on the floor with an interesting array of wood and metal parts spread out between them looked like great fun to him. A situation tailor-made for bedlam. They spent at least half their time removing things from his reach or taking them away once he had gotten his hands on them. This naturally produced a series of infantile protests, complete with back arching and squeals of outrage.

Through it all Dan remained cheerful, patient and—somehow—productive. Just when her own frustration or CJ's reached fever pitch, Dan did or said something to lighten the atmosphere. Once he even pretended to skewer himself with a long, thin piece of metal, reeling about the room on his knees and finally collapsing on his back with arms and legs lifted toward the ceiling and jiggling like some insane cartoon character. CJ threw himself onto Dan's belly with a shriek of delight, although a moment before he'd been screaming in demand of the dangerously long, thin metal piece, which Dan quickly passed to Becca before pitching the child into the air and catching him for a prolonged ticklefest. By the time he let the little urchin up for air, she had the rail guide firmly attached to the side of the bed and the conflict was forgotten.

As the parts disappeared into the whole, CJ began to lose interest in the process and realize that the result of the game was all about him, too. He knew a crib when he saw one, and he was ready to climb in well before it was safe to do so. Dan worked at a feverish pace then, having mastered the intricacies of the design, while Becca herself paced the floor with CJ in her arms, babbling a running dialogue on the delights of this new wonder. Once the mattress was installed, the casters locked and the side raised into place, she deposited her rambunctious son in the crib. CJ grasped the slender wooden rails and shook them with all his tiny might, as if to exert his mastery over his new abode. It was then that Dan realized he hadn't purchased the appropriate bed linens—as if she'd ever had any.

"A regular sheet will do just fine," she told him, and then had to let him placate CJ while she folded and tucked the thing into place.

CJ went back into the crib and refused to get out until they both pretended to leave the room. Grinning at each other in the hall, they let him howl for a moment before swooping in to scoop him out of the bed once more and carry him off downstairs to the kitchen, where Jem was discovered helping herself to another glass of milk, her second since lunch. Her skill at this endeavor was clearly demonstrated by puddles of milk on the counter, table and the floor in front of the refrigerator. She had not, however, broken any glasses or turned over any chairs in the process. Becca coaxed her into entertaining her brother with a set of plastic measuring cups and other extraneous utensils while dinner was being prepared.

Dan kept a well-stocked larder, and the freezer tucked into a corner of the utility room proved to contain enough meat to feed them for months to come. The chest-type freezer seemed to have held its seal well and adequately preserved its contents, so it was just a matter of determining what could be prepared most quickly. They decided on hamburgers, though the package in Dan's pantry contained only three buns and he declared himself hungry enough to eat a whole cow. In the end he ate one burger with bun and all the fixings, another with white bread and a third patty all on its lonesome, not to mention canned pork and beans and fruit cocktail.

Afterward they loaded the dirty dishes into the

automatic washer—such luxury!—and adjourned to the living room for a little television, very little, as it turned out. Jem was asleep before she fully stretched out on the rug in front of the set, and Becca herself was fading fast. Even CJ, who had napped much of the day away, seemed worn out. When Dan shut off the set and stooped to gather up Jem, Becca was only too glad to let him carry the child up the stairs.

What followed was unique in Becca's experience. Whenever Cody had been home, it had been his habit to take a few moments for himself while Becca prepared Jem and got her into bed. Later, often after Jemmy was already asleep, he would slip into the room and kiss her good-night. He even stood sometimes and watched her slumbering peacefully, a smile of fatherly pride on his face, but it had never occurred to him, apparently, to actually get her ready and tuck her in, and in all honesty it hadn't occurred to Becca to let him, perhaps because Jem was a girl and because her own father had never taken a hand with his children except in discipline. John Odem provided fine help with the children as a general rule, but even when they were around at bedtime, he was usually the first one to bed. Whatever the reason, she didn't expect Dan to help out with bedtime chores, even though they would be sleeping in his house.

It came as a shock when, after producing pj's and other necessary items from the mound of shopping bags in the foyer, he wrestled CJ into a dry diaper and shirt while she changed Jemmy. Then while she got the baby down, a more time-consuming task than normal, he calmly toted Jemmy into the bathroom and held her up to the sink so she could brush her teeth, which involved much more giggling and spitting than it should have. When Becca was finally able to slip away from CJ, she found Dan sitting on the side of a twin-size maple bed reading a book to Jemmy in such a soft voice that it was almost a whisper. Jem looked up and lifted a finger to her lips, as if to say that it would be rude to ask him to speak louder. Feeling a pang at her heart, Becca stood in the doorway, arms folded, back against the casing, and waited until he was finished. As she tucked Jemmy beneath the covers, she noticed a small, roughly triangular pink plastic box standing on the shelf above the bed. It was the only feminine thing in the room.

Out in the hallway Dan handed her a corresponding piece that he'd clipped to the back of his belt. "Monitor," he explained. "In case she gets scared." He shrugged. "First time sleeping alone, strange place."

Becca stared at the gizmo in her hand, watching a tiny light flash green as Jemmy coughed in the other room. He'd thought of everything. In the old house she'd heard through the wall every time one of her babies had so much as rolled over in the night, but this place was different—not just larger but more solid. She nodded, a lump in her throat, but when she looked up to thank him, he produced a second receiver, a blue one.

"CJ," he said succinctly.

She stared at him for a long moment and saw the weariness and concern around his eyes. He needed a shave, but the shadows on his jaws and chin just made the blue of his eyes look brighter and more vivid. She ached to feel his arms around her once more, but too much had happened for that now. She was too dependent on him suddenly, too much of a burden. She had dared to dream of finding love with him, of an equal and mutually beneficial relationship. For a while she had imagined that she could be his ears, his bridge to the hearing world, but this long, traumatic day had shown her he didn't really need a thing that she could provide. Just the opposite, in fact. He surely didn't need the trouble she'd brought to his doorstep.

If God had any purpose at all in bringing her into his life, it was to show him how little assistance he really needed. No, she rather feared that the need was all on her end. That, it seemed, was the story of her life, and she was purely tired of it, tired to the bone. In more ways than one. It must have shown.

"Better grab some gear," he said suddenly, moving toward his bedroom. "Shift stuff around tomorrow."

"No need for that," she told him, but his back was to her, so he couldn't know. She stood in the doorway of his room, head bowed as he packed up.

Large and spacious, the room was simply furnished with a ridiculously large bed, a single side table and a dresser and chest of drawers that matched each other but nothing else. He pulled things from both and tossed them into a small black kit bag, working quickly, then moved into the well-appointed bath to pick up his personal toiletries. She hated putting him out of his room, but it was only temporary. Tomorrow, she decided wearily, she would figure out what to do. He moved toward her, zipping the bag as he crossed the room.

"I'm sorry about this," she said, catching his eye, "but it won't be for long."

He smiled, stopping in front of her. "It's okay," he said, and then he reached around her, the bag swinging lightly against her back as he hugged her briefly. "Sleep well."

He was at the top of the stairs before she even thought to return his polite good-night, and then he was gone. She stood in the silent house, pink and blue monitors in her hands, and felt the weight of broken dreams around her.

Chapter Ten

Dan spent Saturday morning salvaging as many of his tools as he could from the wreck of his pickup truck. The toolbox had flown open at some point, but a number of the larger items were still inside. His levels were broken, the blade of a circular saw had been bent beyond redemption, but he had the tools necessary to help John Odem get a tarp over his back porch where the roof had been blown away. Clouds were building in the west when John dropped him back at the house, and he'd barely started on the late lunch Becca had prepared for him when the insurance adjuster arrived, having driven over from Lawton. Becca showed the fellow in, introduced him as Alan Hampton and insisted on fixing him a sandwich, which he accepted with a happy smile and words that Dan didn't quite catch.

"Can't very well eat in front of you," she said, sitting down across the table from Dan.

Hampton was a youngish fellow, affable and self-assured but nondescript physically. After making short work of the sandwich, he took out a long form and an ink pen and began asking questions about the storm, which either Becca or Dan answered. It went fairly smoothly. She was so good at helping him understand all that was being said that Dan doubted the young man even realized he was talking to a deaf person. Hampton would be writing and speaking at the same time, so Dan would totally miss what he was saying. Then Becca would ask something like, "Can you remember your Social Security number off the top of your head?" or "The mailing address here would be the same as the physical address, wouldn't it?"

Dan would concur or make some relevant correction, and they'd move on to the next question. One time she looked at him and said very deliberately, "You never did tell me the exact date you bought that truck or who you bought it from, either."

Dan had to grin at that one. "Don't suppose I did." He recited the date and place in Oklahoma City where he'd purchased the now wrecked truck, and the insurance adjuster wrote it all down.

When Hampton asked why Dan happened to be out that night, Becca supplied the answer. "It was a mission of mercy, pure and simple."

Grateful that she hadn't made more of it than that, Dan added simply, "Sirens can't be heard out there."

Hampton nodded his understanding and asked, "Anyone hurt?"

"No," Becca told him, looking at Dan. "Everyone's just fine."

"Can't mind a wrecked truck too much, then, can

we?" he said, and Becca and Dan both agreed that they could not.

The form was filled out pretty quickly after that. Hampton thanked them both and left to go check out the damage, promising to return later with a settlement check. Dan offered to show him the way, but he felt confident that he could find the site on his own, so Dan let it be. He didn't really care whether or not the fellow knew that he was deaf, but he was coming to the conclusion that he and Becca worked well together. In fact, they seemed to fit pretty much like glove and hand.

"That went fine," he said to her as soon as they were alone.

"Should've," she answered, getting up to clear the table. "Though why they have to ask some of that stuff is beyond me."

He nodded in agreement, then softly said, "You didn't have to run interference for me."

He knew he'd gotten it wrong or that she'd taken it wrong when she stiffened. "Oh, I'm sorry."

"No, no," he protested, but she kept going.

"I didn't even think. I mean, it was sort of automatic."

"It's okay," he said quickly.

"No, really, you manage just fine on your own."

"You don't understand," he tried to say, but Jemmy skipped into the room then, announcing that CJ was awake from his nap.

"The monitor?" Dan asked, glancing around the room.

"I forgot it," Becca admitted with a grimace before going to rescue CJ from his crib.

Dan tamped down his impatience. Not only had he gotten the tone all wrong, his timing obviously left much to be desired. Pushing out a long breath, he looked to Jemmy and swirled a finger at the littered table. "Want to help?"

"I'll get it," she said, whirling away. Puzzled, he rose and brought his hands to his hips, his gaze skittering around the room. A red light was flashing on the alarm panel. Someone was at the front door. He stepped out into the hall just in time to see Jemmy swerve almost into the wall as she ran toward the foyer. Following, he came upon her talking to two women, one elderly, the other a mere teenager with dark, short hair caught up in all manner of clips and barrettes.

"They come to see you," Jem announced, looking up into his face. He looked at the two women.

"Are you Mr. Holden?" the girl asked. He nodded, and she went on. "Gram needs your help. The roof's plumb off the bathroom, and there's a leak coming out from under the house. John Odem down to Kinder's said you was the one to call on account of she hasn't got insurance, only he said we wasn't to telephone, you being deaf and all."

Dan blinked, increasingly aware of the old woman's hands as she wrung them. Worry emanated from her squat, stooped form.

"It's gonna rain again," she said, and something in her face told him who she was.

"Mrs. Schumacher?"

She nodded dumbly. He looked to the girl. "Are you Evelyn's daughter?"

"Yeah. I'm Jessica." He knew that Evelyn and her husband had died in a car crash when he was a junior in high school. Mr. Schumacher had been gone many years even then, dead of heart failure, it was said. These two were alone in the world. Dan sighed inwardly. He couldn't refuse to help.

"Got a car?"

"Yeah, out front."

"Room for my tools?"

"Yeah, I guess."

"Anything to cover the roof?"

"John Odem gave us a tarp."

He jerked a thumb over his shoulder. "Go get my toolbox and some rope." First he took Jemmy by the shoulder, looking down into her face. "Tell your mom where I've gone, okay?" Jem nodded. He went to get what tools he could carry.

It was wet, dirty work. He got the tarp in place just minutes after the rain began to pour, so the Schumacher women could use their bathroom, but the interior walls would have to be replaced, and the old house sagged alarmingly at one corner, where water seeped out of a broken pipe. Already drenched to the skin, he found an opening in the crawl space and slithered under the house on his belly. The break was all the way on the other side of the house, naturally, so it took some time to reach it, and about half the way was through mud. The water leak had apparently driven out some sort of critter, an opossum or skunk judging by the "nest" that Dan came across. Unfortunately the same could not be said for the spiders, but he knocked the webs out of his way and kept going.

He found the leak in a joint of pipe. That would be easy enough to fix. The bigger problem was the section of broken foundation beam that had caused the pipe to stress. The creosote-coated twelve-inch-square beam had broken off above ground level, leaving a jagged chunk of wood poking up and two others on the ground beside it. The beam had probably already been rotted, so the force of the storm had made the house sway enough to splinter it. If he could get that corner of the house up, the leak would stop pretty much of its own accord.

After crawling back the way he'd come, he had to hose himself off in the yard, even with rain falling, before he could go to the house and discuss the situation with Mrs. Schumacher. She told him that she had an upright piano sitting in that corner, so Dan took off his boots, dried himself with a towel as much as possible and crept through the crowded, untidy house to shift the furniture and move that piano. Once that Herculean job was accomplished, he borrowed the jack from the trunk of their car, found a few pieces of lumber sturdy enough to serve his purpose and set about temporarily leveling the house. In order to do so, he had to remove some of the siding around the foundation and make himself a special lever with which to work the jack. Even then it took all his body weight to coax the jack into lifting that corner of the house.

The good news was that he didn't have to crawl the

full length of the house to check the leaky pipe again. All he had to do was lie in the mud under the newly exposed corner of the house and convince the flashlight to work in the rain. After drying the joint with some rags supplied by Mrs. Schumacher, he smeared it with plumber's putty and wrapped the area in duct tape. Weary and filthy, he once more knocked on the Schumacher door and told Jessica that he was ready to be taken home. This being without transportation was getting old fast. He promised to return as soon as the weather cleared to fix the roof, replace the broken foundation beam and put back the siding.

Mrs. Schumacher wept and tried to offer him money, but he put her off, saying the job wasn't finished yet, and that he'd have to check the price of certain supplies. Upon seeing the blood drain from her face, he assured her that the job probably wouldn't cost more than a couple hundred dollars to complete and that she could pay it out a little at a time. He would not, of course, charge her for more than the supplies, and perhaps not even all of those if the cost seemed too much for her, but she didn't have to know that.

By the time he slogged up the steps to his own front door, he was craving a hot shower and a cold drink. He removed his boots on the porch, then stood dripping in the front foyer for a few moments, wondering how best to keep from creating a huge mess. Finally he decided to ask Becca for a towel. He peeked into the living room and saw that it was empty. So far as he could tell, no light was on in the kitchen. Everyone must be upstairs. He'd have to call out to her. At least he didn't have to worry about waking the baby. Oddly, he had to think how to go about shouting. It felt so strange, sucking in his breath, putting back his head and forcing the word up out of his throat.

"Bec-ca!"

For a moment he could only wonder if he'd made himself heard, but then she was there at the top of the stairs. She said something, but he couldn't quite make it out at that distance and figured he could let it go for a minute.

"Towel, please."

She turned and disappeared into the upstairs hall. Just seconds later she was on her way down to him, a pair of folded towels stacked on her arms. "You look like a drowned rat," she said, handing over the first one.

"Feel like one, too," he admitted. Smiling sheepishly, he mopped his face and moved to his chest.

She gave him an arch look, then draped a towel over his head and began rubbing briskly at his hair. Laughing, he let her tend to him. It felt good—unfamiliar but good. Finally she whipped off the towel and stood with it tossed over one arm, her hands at her waist.

"So what were you doing? Jem said two women came for you."

He nodded. "Mrs. Schumacher and her granddaughter." He briefly explained while toweling his pants legs. When he straightened again, he found Becca shaking her head.

"You can't help playing the hero, can you?"

"Huh? Just a temporary fix."

Becca folded her arms. "Who's going to do the real work?"

"Me. Can't afford to hire anyone."

Becca flapped her arms, and the towel with it. "There. You see. Abby told me you were going to do their work, too."

He shrugged. "So?"

"So you can't fix the whole world, Dan. Much as you might like to, you just can't fix the whole world." With that she dropped the towel, whirled and stomped quickly up the stairs.

Dan stood there, his mouth agape, as swamped now by confusion as he had been by mud and rain earlier. He couldn't imagine what was going on with Becca. She was a Christian woman, as generous as she could be. Surely she didn't expect less from him. It must be the stress of her situation. She hadn't wanted to go to work today and leave the children, but it seemed to Dan that they were handling their new circumstances better than she was in some ways. He'd just have to be patient with her, he supposed.

With that in mind, he draped the towel he was using around his neck, then moved forward and picked up the other one from the floor before beginning to climb the stairs. He went straight to his bedroom and across it to the bath, but the instant he stepped through the open bathroom door, he realized that Becca was already in the room. Quickly he ducked his head.

"Oops. Sorry." Before he could even back out the door, however, she had hold of him, her fingers curled around his forearm. He looked up uncertainly.

"It's for you, silly."

Frowning, he glanced around the room and saw the water running in the shower. "Oh. Thanks."

"By the time you gather up some clean clothes, it ought to be hot."

"Right. Great."

She shooed at him impatiently. "Go on. Get your things. When you're done, I'll wash what you're wearing."

Backing out into the bedroom, he said, "I can." He didn't want to put her to any trouble.

She rolled her eyes, following him. "Fine."

He turned toward the dresser, and when he turned back again, she was gone, having pulled the bedroom door closed behind her. She was in a strange mood. Dan scratched an ear, realized that he was itching all over and headed for the shower.

Becca stood at the kitchen sink, her back to the door, and gulped down tears. A maudlin feeling of helplessness enveloped her. She brushed impatiently at her damp cheeks and told herself that she was being an idiot. Of course Dan would go to help the Schumachers, just as he'd help Abby and John Odem and anyone else who needed it. Even her. She knew that she must not make the mistake of thinking that made her special. Dan was a talented, generous, caring man. Why that should make her cry, she didn't know.

She had plenty to cry about, of course. The storm had taken her home, the one place she could call her own, and she just didn't know what she was going to do.

She didn't even have as much insurance on her house as Dan had on his truck. She'd never be able to rebuild with what she had coming, at least according to what her agent had told Abby, who'd notified the company of Becca's claim, since Dan didn't have a telephone. She wouldn't know for certain until the adjuster came, and she didn't know when that might be. Maybe God would work a miracle in the meantime. For now, everyone was okay.

As comfortable as Dan's house was, though, and as happy as the children seemed here, this was not their home, and she couldn't think of it as such. But she couldn't think what else to do, either. Somehow she had to find a way to provide her family with a home of their own, but she didn't have a clue how to do it. She'd just have to put her faith in God, rack her brain and be patient until He showed her the way.

Her insides still felt shaky, which was why she hadn't gone to work today. She just didn't trust herself to handle the stress right now, and Abby insisted that she and John had everything under control. Thankfully, tomorrow was a day of rest and worship. She'd feel more centered if she could just get to church, focus on something greater than her problems. Monday was soon enough to begin searching for solutions to her problems.

Meanwhile, thanks to Dan Holden she and her babies were safe. They had a roof over their heads, food to eat and clothing to wear. She was going to put these worries, these fears, behind her and simply gather her strength. God would continue to provide, and she would continue to be properly grateful, instead of wishing and hoping and making more of this situation than either Dan or God intended.

She knew how to do this, after all. She'd suffered loss and disappointment before, and she had always survived by trusting God. Feeling calmer, she squared her shoulders and went to tend her children.

When Dan emerged from the bedroom, clean, dry and freshly garbed, he was glad to find that Becca's strange mood seemed to have lifted. She smiled warmly at him as he walked into the living room, and asked what he had in mind for supper. Truth was, he hadn't had time to think of it, so he just shrugged. That was when she looked to the foyer and announced, "There's someone at the door."

Dan looked through the window, spotted an unfamiliar vehicle parked out front and turned back into the entry area. He opened the door to find the insurance adjuster on his porch, looking damp but satisfied.

"Come in," Dan invited, but Alan Hampton shook his head.

"I'll just leave this and go." He offered Dan a sheet of paper, saying, "It's a total loss. Soon as the weather dries up a little, we'll send someone out to haul off the wreckage."

Dan looked down at the form. A check was attached to the bottom. The amount was just about what he'd expected. "Thanks," he said. "Stay to supper?"

"That's kind, but no. I need to get back, and it's a long drive."

Dan nodded, folded the paper and offered his hand. "Appreciate your promptness."

"What I'm paid for," Hampton said, shaking Dan's hand. "Give my best to your wife."

Dan opened his mouth to correct that assumption, but the fellow was already turning away, and he didn't see any point in calling him back on account of a harmless error. He supposed it was a natural mistake. Thinking back, he realized that he had never properly introduced her because she had been the one to answer the door. Now that he considered it, they hadn't even actually said that it was her and the kids he'd gone out in the storm to warn. Shaking his head, he turned back into the house—and found Becca standing at the foot of the stairs. Obviously she had heard. He could think of no other reason for the ashen look of her face.

"Should've set him straight," Dan said.

Her gaze slid away. "Don't suppose it matters."

He nodded. She said something, but he didn't catch it, since she was turning toward the kitchen. He wondered for a moment if he should go after her, tell her that he hadn't bothered to correct Alan Hampton's supposition because he liked the idea of her being his wife, but he knew that it wouldn't be wise just then. She needed time to come to terms with her situation first. Jemmy appeared to ask if she could watch TV, and he went to turn on the set, reminding himself to be patient.

Chapter Eleven

D an put a pork loin in the slow cooker early the next morning and insisted that the Kinders would take Sunday dinner at his house, since parts of Abby's kitchen were still drying out from the storm. Abby agreed on the condition that she be allowed to prepare the rest of the meal. Becca bit her lip to keep from saying that she'd been looking forward to some "normal time" at the home of her in-laws and went along with the plan, but she couldn't help feeling peevish as Dan handed her down into the back seat of Abby and John Odem's old car for the ride to church.

"He's mighty fond of that slow cooker," she grumbled.

"You say something?" Dan asked, cramming in next to her. The kids' car seats took up almost all of the space, so he lifted his arm across her shoulders in order to make more room.

She shook her head, telling herself that his being deaf did have some advantages. Then she felt contrition.

Losing his hearing was obviously the worst thing that had ever happened to Dan, and she wouldn't take one full moment's pleasure in it. Of course, if he hadn't suffered that loss, he wouldn't have come back here to Rain Dance to live. He'd be off making the world a safer place with the marines, and she'd never have met him, leaving her world a much more dangerous situation than she might have imagined. Funny how God worked things sometimes. She wished she knew what He was working out for her and the kids just now.

"Oh, ye of little faith," she whispered, scolding herself.

Dan lifted his hand to cup her chin and angle her face toward his. "What?" His voice was a little too loud, given their proximity and the intimate tone of it. She was sitting on one thigh, practically in his lap, and their lips were very near to touching. She dropped her eyelids, shuttering her gaze.

"Talking to myself."

He took his hand away, saying teasingly, "Better watch that."

She knew that he was telling her that he could read her lips even when her words were inaudible, and she felt a fresh stab of guilt. How could she think or speak unkindly of him when he had been so good to her? Suddenly overwhelmed by the confusion of her own emotions, she felt the prick of tears. Silently, as if attuned to her every thought and feeling, Dan brought his arm down around her and folded her close. She turned her face into the hollow of his shoulder and thought desperately, *Oh, God, please don't let me fall in love with him now.*

It hit her then that she had finally come to the root of her problem. The house was gone and, yes, that was cause for immediate concern, but what she feared most just now was that during this trying time her heart would run away with her better judgment. After all, she'd practically thrown herself at the man not long ago, and he'd made it plain that he didn't think he could or should be a father and husband. That hadn't stopped him from being a generous, caring friend, a sanctuary from the aftermath of the storm. *Hero* was not too strong a word for Dan Holden. On the other hand, *pathetic* pretty well described her at the moment.

Becca blinked away the tears, lifted her head and put as much space between them as she could manage within the cramped confines. By the time they reached the church, she felt bruised but more in control. During the service she managed to ignore Dan and concentrate on worship. It was balm to her troubled soul, and when her name was read, along with others in need after the storm, and special prayers were offered, outward calm finally began to transform into inner peace.

God had not forgotten her. Security rested always in Him, not in buildings or money or even other people. Solutions could be found for every problem. Patience and acceptance were possible; surely contentment could not be too far behind them.

After church, people stopped her to ask how they might help, but she asked only for prayer, and then was amazed to find that one petition that she hadn't even thought to offer up had already been answered. Flozelle Reed was a tall, thin widow nearing sixty who resembled a schoolmarm out of some old Western more than the banker she was, but she had been second vice president of the State Agricultural Bank for nearly twenty years. She was not a formal member of the church, but she often showed up for one reason or another. This morning her purpose seemed to be nothing less than lightening Becca's load of worries, though Becca couldn't know that at first.

"I understand your house was destroyed, Mrs. Kinder," Flozelle said, standing in the aisle in front of Becca with a patent leather handbag dangling from one thin arm.

"Yes, I'm afraid so," Becca admitted, aware of Dan at her elbow taking in every word.

"Your insurance won't cover the loss."

"I'm aware of that."

"We didn't require more coverage because the mortgage is small compared to the value of the land."

"I believe you explained that to me after my husband passed, Mrs. Reed."

Flozelle nodded with apparent satisfaction. "It is, however, more than enough to pay off your mortgage, and State Agricultural is prepared to suspend interest and payments until you receive settlement."

Becca hadn't even thought about her mortgage payments. Somehow, with the house gone, they hadn't seemed relevant any longer, but the mortgage more properly pertained to the land than the house. Now Flozelle was telling her that she wouldn't have to worry about making payments for a while. Then again, the balance due would take more than half of the expected settlement. Still, it was a generous gesture.

"Thank you, Mrs. Reed."

"You'll be receiving formal notification," the woman told her, "so do remember to have your mail forwarded."

Another matter that Becca hadn't even considered. "I'll do that, ma'am. Thank you again." She would have everything sent to Abby's.

Flozelle tilted her head, wreathed in iron-gray braids, and asked kindly, "Have you thought what you'll do now? The bank might be willing to loan you an increased amount of principal if you should choose to use your insurance settlement as a down payment on a new domicile, but it wouldn't be much more than you're carrying now, say forty thousand. That could buy a nice mobile home, though given your recent experience you might not want to go that route."

Mobile homes, while economical, were notorious magnets for tornadoes. Ironically, Becca and Cody had actually considered one before Jemmy was born, but had decided against it for that very reason. It might be the best course for her now, though.

"I'll have to think and pray on it, ma'am, but I do appreciate you bringing it up."

To her surprise, Flozelle reached out and patted her hand. "I'm a woman alone in the world, Mrs. Kinder. I try to be sensitive to those in my own boat." She swept a politely speculative gaze over Dan and turned away.

Becca breathed her first real sigh of relief since Dan

had closed that cellar door on the raging storm. Never had she been so glad to have attended a church service. All the niggling doubts and worries of the past two days seemed to dwindle away, and she could only marvel.

"Good news?" he asked, steering her toward the exit.

Very good news, she mused, nodding. Her faith had not been misplaced. God was already giving her direction, options. Thought and prayer would surely reveal the best course in due time. In the meanwhile, she had only to remember that God, not Dan Holden, would ultimately work out everything.

They joined the Kinders and the children on the sidewalk out front and headed for the car. Jemmy begged to go by her grandparents' house to check on her turtle. Since John Odem wanted to change his clothes anyway, it was decided that he would drop off everyone else at Dan's and take Jem with him to the Kinder house. He would return as quickly as possible with a pair of more comfortable shoes for Abby and her favorite apron.

At the house, Dan escorted Abby to the kitchen and turned her loose with orders to make herself at home, then he went out back to the apartment over the garage to change into casual clothes, having moved most of his things the previous evening. Becca changed, too, and stripped CJ to his diaper and shirt. Before hurrying back downstairs, she laid out play clothes for Jem. Abby was already at a loss when Becca walked into the kitchen with CJ on her hip.

"Doesn't that boy have a good cast-iron skillet? I can't fry up a proper mess of squash in that flimsy thing."

She pointed to the offending aluminum equivalent on the counter.

"We haven't been frying much," Becca said, meaning *any*. Her mother-in-law was old school when it came to cooking technique, but Becca herself preferred a healthier mode of general food preparation. "Do you want to just boil the squash, or should I go ask?"

"Do you mind running out back to ask him? John's been talking about fried squash all week, and there's plenty in the refrigerator here."

Becca handed CJ to his grandmother, figuring she could move faster without his added weight to haul around. "I'll be right back." She moved quickly through the utility/mud room and out to the garage and then up the steep staircase that led to the apartment. She knocked on the door, realized how foolish that was and tried the knob. The door parted from the frame, and she stuck her head inside to look around.

The living area was small but adequate, with a window that looked out over the backyard. A bar had been built between the kitchen and the living room, giving the place an open feel. As of yet it didn't have a top on it, and there were no cabinets at all. She stood there pondering the significance of that until Dan came out of a short hallway that obviously led to the single bedroom and bath. He was pulling a T-shirt over his head, and as he tugged the tail down, he stopped in his tracks.

"Becca."

She pointed at the kitchen. "Where are the cabinets?"

"In the shop downstairs," he said, sucking in his

already flat belly in order to tuck in his shirt. "Haven't finished them yet."

"You didn't put them in my house?"

He froze, but then he shook his head, and his hands finished their work. Face oddly impassive, he said, "The old ones. They were in my way."

She nodded, even more aware than ever how pitiful she must seem to him. Even his uninhabited garage apartment would have nicer cabinets than her house would've had. Maybe that was for the best, all things considered. "They're kindling now."

"Candles?" he asked, face screwed up.

"Kindling," she enunciated crisply.

"They are. You're not," he pointed out.

"True."

He smiled and changed the subject. "Need something?"

"Oh. A cast-iron skillet. Abby wants to fry up some squash."

"Cabinet over the fridge. Hard to reach. I'll get it."

"You must not use it much," she observed, careful to keep her face in view as they turned to leave together.

"Not much."

"Healthier ways of cooking," she said as they went down the stairs side by side.

He nodded and added, "Good corn bread pan."

Once they reached the kitchen, he pulled down the skillet, then Abby sent him on his way, insisting that she would cook. When John Odem and Jemmy returned, they had the turtle with them, Jemmy insisting that the poor thing was lonely and scared since its "house" had been destroyed by the storm, too. To her way of thinking, it was only right that it come to live with them at Dan's now. Dan just smiled and said he'd build it a proper pen. Becca couldn't let her daughter think that this arrangement was permanent, however.

"Sweetie, you understand that we're only staying in Dan's house temporarily, don't you?"

Jem screwed up her face much as Dan had done earlier. "What's temohairly?"

"It means only for a little while," Becca explained. Jemmy's mouth took on a mulish set, so Becca made it clear. "We will not be staying here for long."

"But we don't got a house no more," Jem pointed out.

"We'll get another one," Becca assured her.

"With my own room?" Jemmy asked doubtfully, her preference for staying put obvious.

All Becca could say to that was, "We'll see," but she realized that the likelihood of providing more than she had before was slim. Still, her family would be best served by removing themselves from Dan's house as quickly as possible. Newly resolved, she promised herself that her time of grief and shock was at an end. It was time to move forward.

"Your truck's ready," Becca told Dan, hanging up the telephone in the tiny office of Kinder's Grocery. "Let's go get it."

Dan smiled. Having his own transportation again would undoubtedly make things easier for him. He'd certainly been anxious about it, popping in and out of the store all day—between giving estimates and making critical repairs for folks hit hard by the storm—to see if the dealer had called.

His "to do" list was getting longer and longer, much of it on hold until he had the proper transportation. Becca had to bite her tongue to keep from telling him to slow down. She'd had her say on that subject Saturday, even though it really wasn't any of her business. Besides, it was undoubtedly better if they both stayed too busy to get in each other's way. She couldn't help getting a chill when she thought about him crawling around on rooftops and under old houses by himself, though. What if he should fall or become trapped? He couldn't hear if a beam was about to give way and go crashing down. She shook off the concern.

"I'll ask Abby if I can borrow her car," she told him, swinging out of the office to go in search of her mother-in-law. She returned minutes later with the keys and both kids. Abby couldn't be expected to watch the children and the store at the same time, and since Monday was a regular day off for Becca, the normal baby-sitter wasn't available.

They loaded up and set out. Dan was so anxious that he kept rubbing his hands together in anticipation. It was difficult to drive and converse, so she contented herself with an understanding smile. She hated being without wheels, too. That was something else for which she'd have to find a solution, since she'd carried only liability on her old junker.

CJ dropped off to sleep fairly quickly, it being his nap

time. Jemmy amused herself with a book for a time, but then she began to whine about being bored and thirsty. Since she was in the back seat, Dan didn't realize that any problem existed, and Becca kept it that way, turning her head toward the window whenever she reasoned with or scolded her daughter.

By the time they reached the dealership, Jem was in a real sulk. Dan got out of the car, glanced into the back and bent at the waist to speak to Becca through the open door. He jerked his head toward Jemmy.

"What's wrong?"

"Nothing a soda pop won't cure," Becca assured him, and Jemmy instantly brightened.

"Sounds good," he said. "Better yet, how 'bout dinner out?"

Becca turned in her seat and looked pointedly at CJ. "We'll have two cranky kids on our hands if we wake him early."

Dan squatted in front of the open door and said, "Take Jem for soda, meet me later."

Becca glanced once more at the back seat, sorely tempted. She couldn't remember the last time she'd eaten in a real sit-down restaurant, but then she found her backbone and shook her head. "You go on. I don't want to inflict them on any unsuspecting diners. We'll just pick up something on our way home and see you back there later."

Dan bowed his head for a moment, but then he rose. Draping an arm across the top of the car, he bent to look inside. "Need money?"

"No! Abby cashed a check for me this morning."

She could hear his fingers drumming against the roof of the car. Finally he straightened and closed the door. Becca knew a moment of regret, but she was determined to set aside all negative emotions and face the future with calm assurance—on her own, since that seemed to be what God intended. Certainly she could not allow herself to become any more dependent on Dan Holden. The poor man was already trapped by his own generosity and good intentions. She could not, in good conscience, add to or prolong the load he was shouldering. As soon as possible she would find a way to move her family out of his house. At a safe distance again, she felt sure that they could be friends. Until then, she was determined to be as little burden to him as circumstances would allow.

Dan looked at Becca with something akin to shock and hoped that it didn't show. Weariness pulled his exasperation close to the surface, and he struggled to subdue it before speaking.

"You want me to build two rooms onto the Kinders' house?"

Becca nodded eagerly and smoothed a sheet of paper against the top of the kitchen table with both hands. "We've figured it all out. With their settlement and mine—or what's left of it after I pay off my mortgage— we could add two rooms to Abby and John's house. That way the kids and I would have a place to live until I sell the ranch."

"Already do."

"I mean a permanent place. Well, semipermanent."

"Why move again?"

"Why not? It isn't like we've got tons of stuff to cart around anymore. Besides, we've put you out of your own home long enough."

"No, you have not."

"Oh, you're very sweet, but this isn't a workable situation for us. Everybody wins my way. Abby and John get a bigger house without borrowing money. I can take my time selling the ranch and ought to make a nice profit eventually. Might even get a new car out of it, since I won't have to make mortgage payments. This really is best."

Maybe she was right, Dan thought. The past few days had been so busy that he hadn't had time to talk to her about the future. He'd been consumed with purchasing and hauling in supplies, making repairs and promising to make repairs. Maybe it was all for the best. Maybe he was fooling himself with the idea that he could be a proper husband and father. Becca certainly seemed no more comfortable here than she had at the beginning—less so in some ways. He had the distinct impression that she went out of her way to avoid him. Maybe she had come to understand what he didn't want to face. He felt duty bound to point out one flaw in her plan, however.

"Jem won't get her own bedroom."

"She will eventually. The wait won't kill her."

He didn't say that it was an unnecessary wait, that they could all just stay put right where they were from now on as far as he was concerned. Instead he nodded weary concession and finally said, "Can't get to it for a while."

"I know you're busy," she said, but she pecked at the paper with a fingertip. "When do you think?"

He shrugged, avoiding her gaze. "Hard to say."

Becca bit her lip. "Would you rather I tried to find someone else?"

He felt a sharp pain right in the center of his chest. "No."

"I've got money now, and I've heard there have been some builders coming around since word got out about the storm."

"They overcharge."

"One of them has to be honest."

He just looked at her, torn between hurt and anger. *Now* she would turn to somebody else? He had to find his voice and pummel it into some semblance of normalcy. "Your call, Becca," he said and left the house, straight out the back to the bare, lonely garage apartment where he'd camped for days now.

It seemed pretty clear that Becca had changed her mind about him. Either that or the old saying about familiarity breeding contempt had proven true.

He wanted to hit something. Instead he went to sit on the too-small bed with his head in his hands, finally rising to bathe and change. He couldn't sit across the table from Becca and the kids, pretending that they were going to be a real family soon. Telling himself that he owed her nothing, he got back into the truck and went in search of a lonely dinner. A drive-through was out of the question, of course, so he went into a fast-food restaurant in Waurika and picked up a chicken sandwich and fries, which he ate parked on the shore of the lake northwest of town, trying not to think of the dreams he'd been spinning since the storm.

The house was dark when he returned. He climbed the stairs to the garage apartment, pulled off his boots and fell into bed otherwise fully clothed, sick at heart. The next morning, Friday, he left without looking in on Becca and the kids. Nor did he stop in the house that evening or the next. Instead he worked, daylight to dark, ate elsewhere and generally kept himself busy and apart. It was the loneliest time of his life. The silence had never been so empty.

Chapter Twelve

Dan backed the long truck out of the garage and down the driveway to the street, where he parked it and got out again. He'd been debating with himself all morning whether or not he should offer Becca and the kids a ride to church. John Odem might well be on his way over here to pick them up, or she might be planning to walk. It was only a few blocks, after all, but the weather had warmed up considerably, and without a stroller, Becca would have to carry CJ. Having had some experience at that, Dan didn't think it a wise choice. So he found himself climbing the steps to his own porch and knocking on his own door like some stranger.

Jem opened the door, wearing the same dress she'd worn the previous Sunday, but this time her mother had caught up her fine, pale hair into a neat ponytail and tied it with a scarf in a big floppy bow. He recognized the scarf as one that Abby often wore. To his gratification, Jem's face lit up. She hurled herself at him, throwing both arms around his legs. He could feel her talking and felt a pang because she'd forgotten already that he couldn't hear. He gave her a rub between her shoulders, something more than a pat, less than a hug, and then gently set her back, turning her little face up in one hand. Mercy, she looked so like Becca.

"Where's your mama?"

She turned and pointed up the stairs, speaking again, and then she ran up them as fast as her little legs would carry her. Dan stayed where he was, no longer feeling comfortable in his own house. After a few minutes Jem appeared again, this time with the diaper bag in tow. A second later Becca stepped into view, CJ on her hip. About halfway down the stairs she looked up, one hand on the railing, and said, "I didn't think to tell Abby to come for us."

Jemmy jumped the last few steps and landed at his feet in a flurry of skirts and thumping diaper bag. He reached down for the bag, and Jem came right up into his hands herself. Swinging her up into his arms seemed the only reasonable thing to do. How slight she felt, settling against him.

Becca stepped down into the foyer and looked up at him. "Haven't seen much of you lately. I was afraid we'd have to walk."

He cleared his throat and tried to modulate his tone. He hadn't spoken much in the past few days. "Been busy."

Her brow furrowed. "I see."

He stepped aside and let Becca open the door. As he followed her across the porch and down the steps,

Jem laid her little cheek against his and wound her arm tightly about his neck and throat. He felt his heart cracking open.

"What's Dan doing back there?" Abby whispered, and Becca turned her head to find him parked in his old place on the back pew.

She wanted to cry. He had pulled so far back from them that at times he seemed like little more than a memory. She really hadn't even expected him to offer them a ride to church this morning, but he was too thoughtful not to. He'd drawn some pretty firm boundaries lately, nonetheless. It seemed that he was taking back his life from the Kinder clan, and she certainly couldn't blame him for that. God knew that he'd gone more than the extra mile for them already.

He'd helped Jem down out of the big, four-door truck, but as they'd walked toward the church building he had fallen behind, once more separating himself from them. Jem didn't understand. That had become obvious over the past few days, and Becca couldn't find a way to explain it to her except to say that Dan was used to being by himself most of the time. Becca did understand, but it still made her want to cry.

She looked at Abby and said, "Maybe he's more comfortable in the back."

"I want to sit in back," Jemmy complained.

"You're a Kinder," Becca said softly but firmly. "This is where the Kinders sit. Now, hush up. Service is starting."

Jemmy folded her arms mutinously, but she kept quiet until after the service. "Dan's leaving," she pointed out stridently as they crowded into the aisle. "I wanna go with Dan." Thankfully his back was turned and he couldn't hear, or rather, see her.

"Dan's busy," Becca told her. "He has things to do today. We're going to Grandma and Grandpa's and stay out of his hair."

Jem started a whine, but Becca didn't scold her. She knew just how Jem felt.

They drove home with Abby and John Odem. The Kinder house had never seemed so small and cramped to Becca before, especially in the kitchen when Abby asked if something had "gone wrong" between her and Dan.

"Of course not," she answered briskly. "Dan's a good, good friend, and he has a right to his space. He's used to being alone, you know, and this has been a really busy time for him."

Abby nodded her understanding at that, but Becca saw a flicker of disappointment in her eyes. She would not let Abby see her own.

Dan knew something was wrong when he saw that Abby was still in her bathrobe. The sedan pulling up in front of the house on a Tuesday morning was not an unusual sight, really, but seeing Abby get out from behind the wheel in a bathrobe and fuzzy slippers was a definite tip-off that this was not a routine visit. Dan braked the truck to a halt short of the street and put the transmission in Park. He drummed his fingers on the steering wheel for a moment, debating the wisdom of getting involved. In the end he closed his eyes and asked God what he should do. Then he killed the engine, got out of the truck and walked up to the front door.

This time he didn't knock; he just opened up and strode into the foyer. Becca sat on the stairs, her head in her hands. Abby stood at the bottom, one arm folded across her middle, the other hand cupping her chin.

"What's wrong?"

Becca looked up, and Abby turned. She spread both hands in a gesture of helplessness. "Stella's son came by the house early this morning to let us know that she had a stroke last night."

Dan couldn't be sure of the name. Names were always difficult. "Stella?"

Abby nodded, and her gaze traveled to Becca, whom he belatedly realized was speaking. He caught the last words.

"Around the corner from Abby, and she's my baby-sitter."

He digested that. "Stella lives around the corner from Abby." Becca nodded. "She's your baby-sitter." Another nod. He looked at Abby. "How is she?"

Abby pressed her hands together. "They think she'll be okay, but it's going to take time, and she's past seventy, so even if she eventually comes home again, she probably won't be able to see to the kids."

Becca rose. "I'll just have to take them to the store with me. We were planning on it eventually, anyway."

Abby said something to her, remembered that she was excluding him and turned to repeat herself. "We don't have anything ready. How are we going to corral them? John always intended to put together a play space for them, but there hasn't been time." She looked to Becca, saying, "You'll just have to stay home, sugar, today at least." Becca nodded miserably, and Abby added, "Now, don't you worry. We'll manage without you, and your salary will be the same."

"I can't let you do that," Becca protested. "You can't pay me for work I don't do."

"You need the salary," Abby argued.

Dan missed the first part of Becca's reply. "Until I find someone else to watch over the kids," she went on. "I'm more worried about you and John carrying the full load without me."

"I can do it." Dan didn't even realize that he'd spoken aloud until they both looked at him with something akin to shock on their faces. For an instant he desperately wished that he could take the words back, but then he realized that it was the only sensible solution. He could take care of the kids; he knew he could. "The monitors," he said, as if that explained everything, and to his mind it did. He could clip one to each of their shirts and carry the others himself. That way he'd know if Jem was calling out to him or if the baby had awakened from a nap. He could manage, surely.

"Don't you have a job going somewhere?" Abby asked.

He shrugged. "Put it off a day or two." Becca seemed to be mulling it over. "I can, Becca," he insisted in what he hoped was a soft, sincere tone.

She flipped a hand dismissively. "Oh, I know that."

Her brow wrinkled. "I just hate to take advantage of you, Dan—I mean, more than I already have." She tossed up her hands in a gesture of helplessness. "Seems like no matter how hard I try to stand on my own, I just wind up leaning on you."

"I don't mind," he said, feeling something warm spread inside his chest. Becca dropped her gaze, but she was smiling wanly. He realized Abby was speaking.

"A temporary solution, anyhow."

"Will you call Claude Benton?" he asked her. He looked at Becca and added, "Roof's in the dry so it won't leak. It'll wait." Becca nodded her understanding. He jerked his chin toward the door, saying, "Put away the truck." He'd started to turn for the door when something else occurred to him. "Jessie Schumacher," he said. Jessie would be a good baby-sitter for the summer, part-time, anyway. He'd been around her enough to know that she was responsible and caring. "Good girl," he told Becca, "despite…" He swirled a finger around his head. Becca chuckled.

"They all wear their hair like that now."

He shrugged, smiling just because she'd laughed.

"I'll give her a call, see if we can work something out."

"Here," he said, pointing at the floor. "Not there."

"That would be best," Abby agreed. "Old lady Schumacher still has everything she's ever owned. I mean, every cereal box, and it's all right there in her little house."

"Pretty much," he agreed, smiling. The old gal was eccentric, but she was a dear. Still, he wouldn't want to think about Jem and CJ careening around her tiny, crammed place. Here they'd have room to play. Becca was looking concerned, so he said, "Jess can't do it, we'll find someone else."

She nodded at that and he went out, feeling better than he had in a while, though it probably wasn't acceptable for him to find pleasure in her difficulty. Still, it was nice to be needed. It was especially nice to be needed by Becca and her kids.

Jem slipped off the edge of her chair to her feet, abandoning the peanut butter and jelly sandwich that he'd just trimmed for the second time. He brought his hands to his hips, about to ask what she thought she was doing now, but before he could form the first word she was out the door and off down the central hall. Exasperated, he started after her.

It had been an eventful morning, with Jem spilling her cereal on her feet and him repeatedly waking the baby, first by accidentally bumping into the wall that CJ's room shared with Jem's while he was helping her change her soggy shoes and socks, and then by closing the door too loudly after putting the little character down for a nap. In the interim CJ had been fussy and demanding, so much so that Jemmy had once stood in front of Dan with her hands over her ears as he'd cradled the howling baby and announced, "You're lucky you can't hear!"

He watched now as she swerved toward the wall, brushing it with her sleeve, and headed on toward the door. Must have company, he mused, recalling that he'd seen her perform that particular veering maneuver before and always right about the same place. Curious. He hurried down the hall to the foyer, getting there just as Jem pulled open the door. She did a little hop, and John Odem swung her up into his arms as he stepped over the threshold.

"What's this here?" he asked, flicking a finger at the pink monitor clipped to the front of her shirt. It was a little heavy, but Dan was going to look into getting her a belt.

Whatever she said in reply to John Odem's question made John smile, but then most things did. He winked at Dan.

"Belled the cat, eh?"

"Sort of."

John nodded and said, "Thought I'd better check on y'all. Need anything?"

Dan glanced at the blue receiver clipped to his waistband, relieved to see the tiny light on top blinking green, and shook his head. "Learning secrets of pb and j."

"Ah." John Odem poked a finger into Jemmy's ribs knowingly. "Gotta trim every speck of brown crust off and slice it diagonally so it makes two equal triangles."

"She measures," Dan confirmed, lifting an eyebrow at Jemmy, who giggled and spoke to John Odem. He glanced at Dan in surprise.

"Buddy the turtle has a rabbit?"

Dan grinned. "Found it in his pen this morning."

"Eating clovers," Jem confirmed.

"Set it loose," Dan said significantly, and Jemmy nodded importantly.

"You can't get pet rabbits from wild. You got to *buy* them, so we're gonna get one from Duncan, aren't we, Dan?"

"If Mama says okay."

John Odem sent him a doubtful look about that, but Dan just shrugged. He'd had to do some fast talking at the time. Besides, he didn't figure Becca had *all* the say. He could keep a pet if he wanted to, which he'd have to do if she absolutely put her foot down about it. In the meantime, Jem would be happy with a furry little bunny to nuzzle. He could see it now, soft and white, with a tiny pink nose. He was counting heavily on the cute factor to win Becca over.

John Odem looked at Jem. "Say, aren't you supposed to be eating a peanut butter and jelly sandwich?"

Dan realized then that John Odem hadn't stopped by just to check on them. He obviously had something on his mind, something he didn't want to say in front of his granddaughter. Dan felt a moment's unease, but he said nothing as John set Jemmy on her feet and she ran back down the hallway toward the kitchen. When she came to that spot, she swerved again.

"What's that?" he asked John Odem. "A kid thing, some game?"

"Naw, she's just avoiding the squeak."

"Squeak?"

"In the floor."

Dan brought his hands to his hips again. "There's a squeak in my floor?"

John chuckled. "Loud one."

"Where?"

They walked forward, Dan going first, until they came to the place where Jem always veered close to the wall. He stepped aside, and John Odem moved past him to demonstrate. He set one foot dead center of the hardwood floor and rocked forward, putting his weight on it. Dan motioned him aside and placed his own foot right where John's had been. As he shifted his weight onto it, he felt a pronounced give in the planking.

"Better get under there," he said, figuring that a foundation support had given way.

John Odem shivered. "Better you than me. I don't like close spaces." He grinned when he said it, but that was John Odem Kinder's natural expression, so Dan figured he meant what he'd said.

"Want to sit?"

"Good idea. Let's try the living room."

Dan followed this time, and as John Odem made himself comfortable on the couch, he took a seat across from him in the recliner. "What's on your mind?"

John smiled. "To the point. Okay. Well, then, Becca and Abby've been talking up this building-on thing, and I'm wondering how you feel about that."

Dan looked down, flicking his fingertip against an imaginary speck of lint on his jeaned thigh. "Be a while before I could get started."

When he looked up again, John Odem was sitting forward, his forearms resting on his knees. "That's not what I mean, Dan. Fact is, I figure you're wanting to keep her."

"I want to marry her," Dan corrected, not much liking the way John had phrased that.

Only when John reared back did Dan remember that old saw about letting cats out of bags. Now, what had possessed him to blurt that out?

For a moment John just stared at him, and Dan imagined all that could be going through his head. He wasn't a "whole" man. He would never be a model father—the way he kept waking the baby and other things proved that. Just that morning he'd handed over a bowl of milk and cereal to a four-year-old without so much as a warning to be careful. No wonder she'd spilled it all over her feet. He couldn't even find a squeak in his own floor without help! No, he would never be anyone's idea of the perfect family man, not even that of an easygoing jokester like John Odem. Dan figured he was in for some straight talk—not that John could say anything to him that he hadn't already said to himself at one time or another. Still, he owed the older man the courtesy of hearing him out. He girded himself for an unpleasant dose of reality, but the last thing he expected, though perhaps he should have, was for John Odem to slap his thigh and go off into gales of laughter just before hopping to his feet and breaking into a jig.

"Hoo, boy!" John said, stabbing a finger at him. "I knew it! I knew it!" He lunged forward, grabbed Dan's hand and began pumping it enthusiastically. "I told Abby. I told her, but she said Becca said you wasn't interested." He flapped his lips at that, making Dan blink.

Wasn't interested? He shifted forward in his seat. "She is the one not interested," he enunciated carefully.

John seemed surprised, then genuinely skeptical. "Naw, that can't be right." He stroked his chin thoughtfully for a moment, then he shook his head. "No, it ain't that." He sat back down and shook a finger at Dan, saying, "That gal, she's had her eye on you since the day you showed up around here again, not that she was on the lookout, mind, 'cause she's not that sort."

Dan disciplined a smile. "I know."

"She's interested," John assured him with a nod. "What makes you think she's not?"

Dan shrugged and rubbed his palms down his thighs. He glanced casually at the monitors affixed to his waistband, very aware that his heart was racing. "She doesn't like leaning on me."

"She don't like leaning on me, neither, but I tell her that's what family's for."

"Not family."

"But you want to be."

Dan looked down again, uneasy revealing so much of himself. Finally he just nodded, but then he had to face John. "Thought once…" He shrugged. "Yes."

"You haven't said anything to her, have you?" John Odem surmised.

"No."

"Don't you think you oughta?"

Dan looked him in the eye. "Do you?"

"Sure do."

Dan noticed he was breathing a little more deeply. "You approve?"

"Of course I approve." His eyes clouded, and his customary cheer bled from his face. "I'm not saying it's an easy thing, my boy being gone, but there's the fact. It's about Becca and the kids now, and that little gal shouldn't be alone."

"Not alone," Dan said softly, wanting John to understand that he knew and appreciated how much a part of her life he and Abby were.

John Odem flapped a hand dismissively. "Abby and me, we're not gonna live forever, son, not in this world. We always knew God would have someone else for her, and we been praying for you even before we knew it was you, just as we prayed for Becca from the time Cody was a little lump till the day he brought her home to us."

Dan smiled, truly moved. "Thank you, John."

"Thank you," John said, getting to his feet again. Dan did likewise as John Odem glanced around him. "This is a good situation for her, for all of you. She'll see that, too. Soon as you ask her, it'll all come clear."

Dan gulped. "Just ask, then?"

John shrugged, chuckling. "Course, boy—no other way I know of."

Dan shifted his feet. "Shouldn't I ask her father first, maybe?"

John shook his head. "Naw, I wouldn't think so. Becca's the third of seven kids, you know, and the Stoddards seem to figure she's not much concern of theirs no more. Oh, I'm not saying they aren't good people. You can just look at Becca and see they've done some things right, but there didn't never seem to be no question of her moving back into the family fold after Cody passed. 'Sides, I doubt Becca herself would cotton to it, her being a grown woman and a mother and all. I'd just get the question past my teeth if I was you, and leave the rest to Him that knows best." He pointed at the ceiling as he said that, and Dan nodded.

Getting the question past his teeth, as John Odem put it, seemed a daunting endeavor just then, but he was glad to know that John approved of the match.

"Glad you came," he said to John, shaking the older man's hand.

"Me, too," John replied, waggling his eyebrows. "Got out of cleaning the fryer."

Dan laughed, and John took his leave, calling a farewell to Jem, who shouted something in reply, according to the flashing red light on the monitor. An instant later CJ's flashed red, too. Dan sighed, shook his head and called out for her to stay put while he went after the baby. He'd grab a diaper and change the caterwauler downstairs, then he'd open a jar of something to feed the little chunk and try not to doubt the wisdom of John Odem's advice—or think too much about what Becca might say.

Chapter Thirteen

Jemmy pinched her finger in the pantry door, causing a large blood blister to rise on the pad of it. She ran into the living room, slinging it wildly and bawling. Dan calmed her, looked it over and walked her back into the kitchen for a piece of ice, which was the only way he could think of to ease the sting. He'd barely applied the ice when she gasped, jerked toward the door and pointed toward the living room.

"What's that noise?"

He looked down at the monitor. The little light was rapidly flaring red. Dropping the ice in the sink, he rushed back to the living room. CJ was sitting inside the fireplace with the folding brass screen on its side in front of him, howling like a banshee. Horrified, Dan rushed forward and snatched him up, examining him for injuries, beginning with his head. Thankfully, he didn't find so much as a red mark on the boy, but when he glanced at his own hand he found that it was black with soot. Groaning, he looked for something to wipe his hand on, found nothing and decided to check CJ's back, which was black from his thighs to the crown of his head.

Dan closed his eyes, wondering what else could go wrong, which was exactly when CJ threw up all over his chest. Dan jumped back, holding the baby at arm's length, and stared down at himself, stunned. For a moment he couldn't think, let alone move, then he realized that a lot of bathing was going to be involved with this, and for a moment he thought he might cry. He looked at Jem, holding aloft her bloodied finger, and wondered if he was cut out for fatherhood, after all.

She scratched the back of her leg with the front of the opposite foot and calmly said, "He does that sometimes when he cries a lot."

Dan lifted his eyebrows. "Cried a lot today."

She nodded solemnly in agreement.

Dan sighed. "Got to clean up. You be all right?"

She shrugged. "Sure."

"Just sit here, watch cartoons," he instructed.

"Okay," she said, "but I'm hungry and I want a snack."

He made a face, painfully aware that he reeked. "Almost dinnertime." How could she even think about food right now?

She made a huge show of sighing, plopping down on the floor and slumping forward dejectedly.

"Don't open the door for anyone you don't know," he warned firmly.

She nodded and pressed a hand to her belly as if suffering hunger pangs. Dan rolled his eyes as he headed

for the door, CJ dangling from his hands. He was sucking his fist contentedly as if throwing up had solved
everything. Dan climbed the stairs and headed straight
for the master bath, where he deposited the child in the
deep claw-foot tub and quickly stripped off his shirt,
turning it wrong side out. It was black everywhere he'd
touched it. Very gingerly he removed the monitor receiv-
ers from his waistband and laid them on a shelf. Then
he knelt and stripped CJ.

Quickly, one hand on the baby at all times, he ran
water until it heated, then plugged the tub and let a few
inches gather. Using plain old hand soap, which was the
only thing he could reach, he scrubbed the kid head to
toe, being extremely careful not to get any in the baby's
eyes. Then he simply laid him back in the water to rinse
away the suds. In the process, he cleaned his hands. He
scrubbed his chest with a soapy washcloth, then rinsed
it the same way and snagged a towel off the bar behind
him to dry off. CJ was trying to sit up by then, but succeeded only in flopping over onto his belly and sliding
around, which he found extremely funny.

He was slippery as an eel, but Dan finally managed
to get him wrapped in the towel and into his arms. He
tossed his shirt and CJ's into the tub, then carried the
boy into his bedroom to diaper and dress him. Leaving
CJ in his crib, he went back to rinse out their clothing,
retrieve the monitors and dig a fresh shirt out of his
dresser. When he returned for CJ, the boy was standing in the crib shaking the side rail like a monkey in a
cage. Dan laughed, and CJ beamed at him, reaching up

with both arms. Maybe he was right the first time and he could do this, after all.

Clean and dry, he carried the boy down the stairs, wondering if he shouldn't rustle up something for Jemmy to eat. It really was getting close to dinnertime, but she was a growing girl, after all. He walked into the living room, musing that he needed to get a fixed screen for that fireplace if he could find one at this time of year, and opened his mouth to ask Jem how she felt about an apple. His blood ran cold when he saw a strange man sitting on his couch.

"Jem!"

She popped up from the chair, snagging his attention. "Danny," she began. At least, he thought she was calling him Danny; at the moment he was both too relieved and too angry to care.

"I told you, don't open the door!"

She blinked and shrank back. "But I know Mr. Dixon."

Dan shifted CJ to his hip, aware that his heart was still beating at double time. It was true that he'd told her not to open the door *for anyone she didn't know,* but he'd meant her mother or grandparents. Seeing her stricken face now, he swallowed and turned to the stranger.

"Dixon?"

The man rose to his full height. He was a large, bluff, handsome man somewhere in his fifties, a rancher by the look of him and the pale straw cowboy hat resting on its crown on the sofa cushion. He put out his hand, pale gray eyes twinkling. "Call me Frank," he said.

"Dan Holden." They shook hands briefly. To Dan's surprise, CJ reached for the other man.

Frank Dixon patted the boy on the head, winked at Jemmy and said, "We're old friends. I'm Becca's neighbor. Own the section to the north of her place."

Dan frowned, still not sure what to make of a fellow who would just waltz into another man's house and make himself to home. "Uh-huh."

Frank Dixon hooked his thumbs in his belt and said, "I'm sure sorry about the storm. Broke my heart when I stopped by there and saw nothing but the foundation of the house still standing. Sure wiped her out."

Dan nodded. "Yes."

"Thank God she and the children made it through unscathed." He shook his head. "It's a pity what that little gal's been through. Anything I can do for her? Anything at all? I saw the car was mangled. I could loan her one of my trucks. Wouldn't be any bother."

"Nice of you."

"I'd sure do that and more for sweet Becca."

Dan frowned. The use of another vehicle would be convenient, and he had no right to turn down the offer on Becca's behalf, but he couldn't quite stomach the idea of Dixon stepping in at the eleventh hour, so to speak.

"We're getting by just fine for now."

"Good. That's good." Dixon rocked back on his heels, lips pursed. "I was told that she might be interested in selling her acreage. Thought I might sound you out about it."

Dan felt his heart thump in his chest. Seemed as if Dixon thought Dan might have more claim on Becca than he really did, and here was his chance to foster that idea, but he couldn't take it that far. "Becca's land," he finally said. "Speak to her."

"I see." He looked down at his toes, and Dan missed what he said next. He tapped the big man on the shoulder. When he looked up, Dan motioned with his hand that he would have to speak face-to-face. Before he could say that, however, Jemmy stepped close to his side, wrapped her arm around his leg and spoke. Dan knew by the expression on Dixon's face that she was telling him about his deafness. Dixon looked up quickly. "Sorry. I didn't know."

"It's all right. I read lips."

"Very well, apparently."

"Well enough."

Frank Dixon smiled. "You wouldn't remember me, but I knew your daddy when he was principal out at Jefferson Elementary."

"Not surprised."

The big cowboy rocked back on his heels. "I suppose Becca's down at the store?"

Dan glanced at the clock on the mantel. "Might be."

Dixon pursed his lips. "Would you tell her I came by? I hate to see her sell up after all she's done to hang on, but I'd give her a fair price."

Dan made a quick decision. Frank Dixon struck him as a friendly, well-meaning—if a little too familiar—fellow, and Becca was wanting to sell. He tried not to weigh his own personal interests against that. "Sit, wait a spell. Could be on her way home now."

The big man smiled. "Don't mind if I do." He lowered himself onto the couch once more.

Dan took the chair that Jem had vacated, aware that he owed her an apology. He hadn't meant to shout at her, and the whole thing was his own fault, but she had to know that it wasn't safe to open the door without him or another adult present, not even in Rain Dance. They could have that talk later. He might as well start mending his fences in the meantime, he figured, so he looked at Jem and patted his knee. She happily scrambled up to his lap next to CJ, and he gave her an affectionate squeeze. They traded a smile before he turned back to their company.

"So, Frank," he said, "you a rancher?"

Dixon nodded and launched into a recitation of the stock he was raising. He was still talking about Angus crossbreeds when Jem alerted Dan to Becca's presence. She came into the room carrying grocery sacks and saying, "I brought home supper." But then she stopped in her tracks. "Frank."

The sacks were quickly deposited on the end table, and in short order she and Frank Dixon were hugging each other. Dan felt his heart drop like a stone. Apparently Dixon was plenty familiar. Even when Becca broke away, she was still smiling at and talking to Dixon.

All Dan caught was, "So good to see you." Then she turned to the children.

Jemmy jumped off his lap and threw herself into her mother's arms. After hugging her, Becca swept up CJ and kissed him, still talking to Dixon. She never even spoke to Dan. In fact, she turned her back on him in order to continue speaking to Frank Dixon.

Face and throat burning, he got up and made himself scarce, gathering in the grocery bags and carrying them into the kitchen. So much for getting that certain question past his teeth. At the moment his teeth were clamped so tightly that he couldn't have gotten a whisper through them.

It was a double-edged sword, Becca thought. On one hand, it cut through all her problems. With the money Frank was willing to pay her for her quarter section of land, she could replace her car and get about making a home for herself and her children. On the other hand, it meant the end of dreams—first that which she and Cody had struggled so hard to fulfill and also the one she had been so tempted to believe in since she'd first asked Dan Holden for his help. Perhaps that was as it should be. A dream without God's will in it was as insubstantial as a puff of smoke and about as worthwhile. Still, she wouldn't be human if she didn't feel some trepidation and disappointment. She had some suspicions about Frank's sincerity.

She put that aside as best she could, reasoning that this was proof of God's intention. Why, only that morning John Odem had warned her that it could take months, years even, to find a buyer for her property. Yet that very afternoon Frank had walked in with a generous offer. She really should have called the Dixons right after the storm. Instead she'd sat around feeling sorry for herself and making Dan feel responsible for rescuing her.

Poor Dan.

CJ on her hip, she walked into the kitchen. While she'd talked with Frank, Dan had put away the groceries, set out the carry-in and gotten down plates.

"Sounds like you've had a hard day," she said. Then she shook her head and waited patiently for him to look up and notice her.

"Your friend gone?"

Dan's voice was strangely stilted and without inflection sometimes, but at others it sounded raw with emotion. She figured the emotion that she was hearing now had to do with the day he'd had rather than with Frank, but she was happy enough to discuss the latter.

"I should have thought to call Frank and Iola."

"What?"

She said it again slowly. His face puckered up.

"I-o-la?"

"Iola Dixon, Frank's wife."

Dan's face went oddly blank. "Married, is he?"

"Well, sure. Their son and Cody were best friends. I think Frank is the one who put cowboying into Cody's head."

"That a fact?"

"Um-hm. The Dixons have always been good to us. He bought all my stock after Cody's death, and he doesn't even raise horses. He's always sworn he sold them at profit, though."

"Now he's offering to buy your land."

She nodded. "I can't help wondering if he really needs the land or if he's just being nice." She shifted

CJ on her hip. "He says he's thinking about building a feedlot."

For a long moment Dan said nothing, then, "Could bring in jobs."

"Hadn't thought of that." She bit her lip. If Frank was serious, she wouldn't be the only one to profit from his generosity.

"So?" Dan asked.

"Am I going to take his offer? Most likely. Unless..." She shrugged.

"Don't like being rescued," he concluded.

"It's not that," she told him honestly. "I just don't want to take advantage."

He smiled and shook his head, advising, "No rush. Pray on it."

"Yes, I'll do that."

He nodded at the containers in the center of the table. "Smells good."

"Barbecue," she told him, "and we better get to eating it."

She turned to call Jemmy, and he pulled the tray off the high chair for CJ. In half a minute they were seated around the table and filling their plates. They talked over the meal about the day he'd had. She couldn't help smiling sympathetically when he told her about CJ. She'd already had the story from Jem.

"The first time he did that to me," she told Dan, "I thought sure he had a terrible disease. That reflux thing or some such. Turns out Cody used to do it, too. Sorry you had to get nailed. I should've warned you."

Dan smiled ruefully. "Know better next time." He

nodded at Jem, saying, "Caught her finger." He made it sound like a confession.

"I heard about that," Becca said, glancing at her daughter knowingly. "What I haven't heard yet is what she was doing that she wasn't supposed to be when it happened."

Jemmy tucked in her chin. "Just getting something to eat."

Becca looked at Dan, eyes laughing. "Always eating lately. Must be gearing up to grow." She looked at Jemmy. "Next time you ask first."

"I asked," she insisted, skewing her gaze sideways.

Becca laid down her fork. "But did you ask so Dan could see you?"

"No-o-o."

"I didn't think so, and see what's come of it?"

Jemmy bowed her head. "I'm sorry." Becca lifted her chin with her hand and instructed her with a look to repeat herself to Dan. "I'm sorry, Daddy."

Becca gasped and dropped her hand as if she'd been burned. She shot a look at Dan.

He looked positively stricken. "If I could hear," he said softly, "wouldn't have happened."

If he could hear, Becca thought to herself, she'd be digging a hole to disappear into right now. It wasn't the first time Dan had failed to pick up on something, and she couldn't say she was sorry. She glared at Jemmy, kept her head turned and whispered fiercely, "Don't you say that again, young lady."

Jemmy folded her arms mutinously. Quickly Becca

turned to Dan, engaging him more to keep his attention diverted from Jem than anything else.

"This isn't about you," she said crisply. "It's about her strange notions."

At that Jemmy leaned sideways and hissed, "I don't want a dead daddy no more."

Becca sat frozen for a full five seconds. Time itself seemed to stand still. Finally she turned slightly and took her daughter's face in her hands. "It's not fair, Jem," she said softly. "You can't just pick a daddy and claim him." Jem wrenched her eyes around to look at Dan out of their corners, such longing there that Becca could have wept. "He's been good to us. We'd be bad friends to press him for more, honey."

Jem gulped and nodded. Becca released her, and both subsided into their chairs. After a deep breath, Becca faced Dan once more. His brow was wrinkled with confusion. She cleared her throat and said, "It's got nothing to do with your lack of hearing. She'd have found some way around the rules, wouldn't you, Jem?"

Jemmy looked at Dan with big hangdog eyes and softly confessed, "I'd of asked real soft 'stead of a-hind your back."

Dan grinned. "That's honest. Apology accepted. Sorry about your finger."

"That's okay," she piped up, staring at her fingertip. "I like it." She held it up for all to see and announced, "I'm polka-dotted!"

Everyone laughed, and the atmosphere lightened a bit. Becca changed the subject to Jessica Schumacher. Jessie could give them only mornings because she'd taken a part-time job helping the school librarian move and reorganize the high school library in order to make room for an array of computers.

"We can manage with that," Dan said.

"Are you sure? I really don't—"

"Want to take advantage," he finished for her. He looked at the kids and smiled. "We'll be fine."

"I'm going to ask around for permanent help," she promised. "Somebody will turn up. They always do."

"Somebody has," he told her quietly, and bent his head over his meal, effectively putting an end to the discussion.

Chapter Fourteen

John Odem showed up just after lunch the next day. Dan was clearing up the dishes, and he turned around to find John in the doorway. He almost started, but he'd turned around so many times lately to find Jem shadowing him that he was beginning to get used to finding himself with company.

"Got anything cold to drink?" John asked, grinning ear to ear.

Dan nodded toward the refrigerator and reached up to pull down a tumbler from a cabinet. "Ice tea."

John took the glass and helped himself. After taking a long swallow, he topped off the glass and turned back to Dan. "Real sweet, just like I like it."

"Jem, too."

"Where do you think she got it from?"

Dan chuckled. "What's up?"

"Nothing. It's my break. Every day but Tuesday and Thursday I work a split shift—four or five hours after opening, four or five hours in the evening to close. I usually go pick up the kids and take them home with me till Becca comes, then I go back to the store. Figured I'd just hang out with you today instead."

Dan blinked at that, but John didn't notice; he'd turned toward the hallway. Bemused, Dan followed him toward the living room. When John reached the center of the hall he winced and looked back over his shoulder. "When you gonna fix that screech?"

"Screen?"

"Scree-*ch*."

"Oh. The squeak."

John pointed at the floor. "That's no piddly squeak, son. That's a banshee in your floor."

"Soon," he said, figuring he'd better get to it quickly before something significant gave way.

John nodded and continued into the living room. He switched on the television before taking the armchair, making himself right to home. Dan figuratively shook his head. Looked as if he had company.

Life had sure changed. Not so long ago, his was the only face he saw in an average day, and only then for as long as it took him to clean up. He'd forgotten what it was like to have people in his life on a routine basis, friends dropping by, others to consider before he started some project or took himself off to bed. It was more complicated this way, but it was also richer.

"Where's the kids?" John asked when Dan looked back to him.

Dan glanced at the monitors clipped to his belt. "CJ's sleeping. Jemmy's out back. Checking on her now." With that he left the room, retracing his steps. When he reached the center of the hall he stopped to feel the give in the floor. Better get under there as soon as possible. If John was going to be around for a while, and it appeared he was, maybe he could slip under there today to take a look.

He went out to find Jem playing with her turtle. He had a hard time figuring out how she could get such enjoyment from a creature with so little personality. Maybe it had something to do with the fact that it paid her no mind and couldn't speed off, since she seemed to jabber nonstop to it as she constantly changed the direction in which it plodded. She was looking forward to the rabbit he'd promised, and they'd built a hutch this morning, but he'd had no opportunity to go shopping. Thankfully, she seemed content with the possibility of getting one for now, and he figured it was a possibility so long as her mama didn't catch wind of their scheme too soon.

"Jem," he called, and she looked up with a smile that squeezed his heart. "Your grandpa's here." He watched her get up off the grass and run to put the turtle back in its pen.

"Do we have to go, Danny?" she asked as she ran up to him.

There it was again. Her pet name for him. He smiled and smoothed a hand down the back of her pale head. "Naw, thought you'd like to know he came for a visit."

"Oh, goody," she said, slipping her hand into his.

They turned and walked back to the house, where she crawled up into her grandfather's lap and settled down to watch a game show. This was how it should be, Dan thought. Becca had to see that eventually. God had shown him; He would show her.

"John," he asked, clearing his throat, "do you mind watching the kids awhile? Want to check under the house about that squeak."

"Sure, son, you go ahead," John said, tilting back his head. "Better you than me."

Dan handed over CJ's monitor and went to change, being careful not to wake the napping boy. Looking in briefly, he found the babe sleeping on his stomach, two fingers in his mouth and his rump sticking in the air. Things had gone easier for them all today, thankfully. He went quietly down the stairs, along the hall and through the kitchen, snatching a flashlight from the utility room as he headed out the back door.

The foundation skirt opened in the back right next to the water spigot. Dan removed the portable section and set it aside before going down on all fours. He could understand why this sort of thing unnerved some people, but he'd done his share of tunneling and working in close quarters during his time in the Corps. This was nothing compared to some of the work he'd done setting up demolitions and ferreting out explosives. Oddly, that experience served him well now that he'd turned his efforts to building. Funny how life turned out sometimes.

When he'd been whole, he'd taken some extreme chances, often volunteering for the most dangerous jobs. Many times he'd remarked that it was the element of danger that made what he did exciting. Now he was thrilled to stand and watch a little girl talking to a turtle.

He took pride in making a lunch she'd eat on the first try and keeping her baby brother happy. Just this morning he'd coaxed CJ up into an independent standing position. Soon the little fellow would take his first steps, and Dan wanted to be there to see it, right alongside his mother.

That was something else he figured he'd better take care of soon, though when he thought of it, his heart pounded as it never had when he'd put his life on the line. Flopping down on his belly and crawling into the dark unknown seemed like a piece of cake in comparison.

Becca looked at Jessica with pure horror. "How long?"

"Five hours," Jessica told her. "When I got here this morning, he had him a kind of little sled thing with tools and a bag of cement on it all ready to go. Said something about a squeak in the floor."

Becca knew all about that squeak in the floor. Dan had explained at dinner last evening that a wood support pier had dried out and shrunk, leaving the floor joist to sag. It hadn't cracked yet, but soon would if he didn't get it shored up. When he'd tried to wedge a block of wood in there, however, the beam had started to crumble, so he would have to dig and pour a cement footing for something called a jack pier. She couldn't see how anyone could dig a hole and pour cement under a house without tearing up the floor first, but he'd just shrugged and said there were ways. He'd spoken briefly then about a time when he and his team had actually tunneled beneath a building with their hands under cover of darkness and in dead silence. He hadn't said what for, and she wasn't sure she even wanted to know, but she'd pointed out then that he hadn't been working alone.

"And he knew you had to leave before noon?" she asked Jessica.

"He said if I'd fix the kids' lunch, he'd come in at eleven forty-five and feed it to them."

"But he didn't come in." Becca bit her lip worriedly.

"And I've just got to go," Jessie said, handing over CJ. "I'm sorry to bring the kids to the store like this. I was supposed to be at the school by one, and I did try to get his attention with a flashlight first. Didn't do any good to holler for him."

"Dear heaven," Becca said, wondering if he was hurt and trapped under there.

Jessie gave Becca a mildly censorial look and said, "You really ought to get a phone in your house." She made a face and added, "Everybody but me has a cell phone."

"I don't," Becca muttered, spreading her feet to balance CJ's weight on her hip. She was much too worried about Dan at the moment to really think of anything else, let alone correct Jessie's assumption that Dan's house was any part hers or that she and the kids would be there long enough to warrant putting in a phone. "Thank you, Jessie, and I'm sorry about this."

As the girl hurried away, Becca turned and called for Abby. Jem had already run back to the deli counter to filch a taste of something from her grandpa. Abby appeared, an anxious look on her face at the sound of Becca's voice.

"Could you watch CJ for a minute? I need to go check on Dan."

"What on earth?" Abby began, taking her grandson into her arms.

"He's been under the house for hours, and he knew that Jessica had to leave by noon."

"You don't think he's been hurt or passed out under there?"

"I just don't know. It's awful hot out. What if he's got heat stroke?"

"Take the car," Abby said. "And maybe you ought to take John, too, just in case."

Becca shook her head, already hurrying away. John would be next to useless in this kind of situation, and Abby couldn't handle the store and the kids on her own. She'd find out what had happened, and if necessary go next door and phone for emergency assistance.

After parking the sedan behind his truck, she rushed around back to find the gaping hole in the foundation skirt. A water hose ran from the spigot outside under the house, its tautness telling her that it had been employed for some purpose. Going down on her hands and knees, she called out to him, even knowing that he couldn't hear her. Peering into the dark, she saw nothing. Could he have gone into the house?

Quickly she shimmied backward and pushed up to her feet. Then she ran across the covered patio and into the house, through the laundry room and the kitchen. The hall was empty, too. For the sake of thoroughness she continued across the hallway into the formal dining room, which was seldom used though the pocket doors between it and the living room were routinely left open. No Dan. She ran for the entry, stuck her head into the study and then climbed the stairs as fast as she could go. She swung into the master bedroom and right on into the bath through the open door. No one.

Back out into the hall she went and through the remaining bedrooms and the second bath. Where could he be? The apartment.

Dashing down the stairs and out the back of the house, she ran for the garage, praying aloud, "Oh, God, oh, God, please let him be okay. Oh, please. Oh, please."

Her leg muscles burned with the effort of racing up those steep steps, but she didn't slow until she came to the door. Wrenching the knob, she thrust the door open and literally leaped into the living area. A glance showed her nothing to alleviate her fears. The bedroom and bath proved similarly unhelpful. She was almost sobbing as she ran out again, leaving the door open behind her. She pounded down the stairs, across the drive and through the yard, hitting the ground on knees and palms in front of the foundation opening.

It occurred to her that she should've located the flashlight that Jessie had used, but she wasn't going to waste any more time looking for it. Instead, she dropped to her belly and dug her elbows into the soft dirt just inside the opening, pulling her body forward and into the dark. Blinded by the sudden shift from bright sunlight to inky darkness, she couldn't see a thing.

Craning her neck, she butted her head against a floor joist, driving her teeth together with jaw-cracking force. She ducked down and crawled on, gradually becoming aware that it was cooler here than outside in the sunshine. She heard a rustle of movement, and the word *snake* instantly popped into her head.

Galvanized, she picked up the pace, heedless of her now raw and aching elbows. She didn't bother calling out, knowing that it was wiser to save her energy for what might await ahead. A flashlight suddenly blinked on.

"Becca?"

The light swung around. No longer blinded, she recognized shapes in the gloom: a board on runners stacked with tools, a small shovel and round plastic tub, a large, thick paper bag empty of its contents, levels, rubber mallet, hammer, long, heavy rubber gloves. She saw, too, a scattering of chat or gravel and a number of miscellaneous bits of lumber. In the midst of it sprawled Dan's long, muscular body, one arm flung out, chest gently rising and falling. At least he was alive. Thank God.

"Where are you hurt?"

"What?"

"Where. Are. You. Hurt?"

He flopped over onto his belly and skewed around. "I'm not. Just resting. What's going on?"

Relief flooded her. *Thank You, God.* She touched his face with her hand, somehow needing that physical connection to finally put her fears to rest. Sweet heaven, what would she do if anything ever happened to him? She thought of Cody and what it had meant to lose him, and the horror of also losing Dan brought hot tears to her eyes. Anger quickly followed. "What do you mean, you're not? You've scared the life out of me!"

"Scared?"

"You were supposed to relieve Jessica at eleven forty-five!"

He shoved his wrist into the light beam, checking the time on his watch. "Oh, man."

They stared at each other for a long moment, the flashlight between them. He'd been working and lost track of time. That's all it was. She was ashamed to say that she'd panicked and assumed the worst, but all she'd been able to think at the time was that she might have lost him, too. How she could lose something that wasn't even hers she didn't know.

Finally he said, "Let's get out of here. Go on."

She turned, with some difficulty, and began crawling for the opening. Her muscles felt weak and depleted. Dan pulled ahead, taking the flashlight with him, and got through the opening first. When she finally pushed her upper body out into the sunlight, he reached down and hauled her to her feet. She came to rest against his chest and he held her there, his strong, capable hands clamped around her arms just above the elbows.

"Sorry, honey. Time stands still in dark and silence."

She dropped her gaze. "We thought you'd gotten hurt under there."

"Just busy. Lost track of time."

"You're telling me! It's going on two." Okay, it was almost half past one. In *principle* it was nearly two, which didn't begin to explain why the sap was grinning at her.

"You came to rescue me," he said, linking his hands in the small of her back.

Suddenly she realized how close they were standing, their bodies actually touching, and her heart thumped pronouncedly. She attempted to step back, grumbling, "I came to read you the riot act."

He just grinned and pulled her against him again. Lifting his hands to her face, he slipped his fingers into her hair.

"You came to rescue me."

He bent his head, and somehow she was on her tiptoes, so that their mouths met and melded into sweetness. Cupping her head, he tilted it. Love poured out of her, an endless supply, too long pent up and yearning for expression. Finally he pressed his forehead to hers.

"Don't close up tonight, do you?"

"No."

He lifted his head and let his hands fall away. "Home about six?"

"Yes."

"Where are the kids?"

"At the store."

"Send them back with John."

"All right." She backed away, feeling slightly dazed and disoriented.

"Better change," he said meaningfully, and she looked down at herself.

"Mercy!" Well, what had she expected after dragging herself through the dirt? "Just look at me!"

He lifted his gaze to hers and said loudly, "You're beautiful."

She couldn't help laughing, even as her heart flopped over inside her chest. "I am?"

He just smiled.

It spread through her then—a rare, wonderful knowledge. Everything had changed. The world had fixed itself somehow, as if God had smiled and pronounced creation perfect. All of her worries, all of her fears—some of them unnamed and so unacknowledged until just now—all of her confusion was swept aside in the space between one breath and the next. She didn't know how or why yet. In fact, she had no answers at all at the moment. Yet everything was right, just fine, exactly as it should be.

"I'll get cleaned up," Dan said, moving toward the apartment.

She stood there like a complete idiot, caught in some heavenly snare, until he disappeared across the drive. Turning suddenly, she hurried into the house to do the same.

"So'd you get finished?"

Dan shook his head at John Odem and explained. "Concrete has to cure. Then put in a pier jack."

John shuddered. "Don't know how you do it. Don't even want to know."

Dan shrugged. "Used to it."

"When you gonna finish Claude Benton's roof?"

"Tomorrow, hopefully."

"I told him you'd get to it soon as you could when he

came into the store today. He said not to worry. Want me to let him know you'll be there in the morning?"

"Yes, thanks." He shifted his weight from one foot to the other. "About the kids…"

"What about 'em?"

Dan lifted a hand to the back of his neck. "Could you stay with them till I get back?"

John nodded. "Sure. Where you going?"

"Duncan. Important. Be quick as I can."

John Odem dangled his hands at the ends of his arms, as if shaking the feeling back into them, and said, "I reckon we can manage something."

Dan took a deep breath. "Thing is, don't really want 'em here when Becca gets home."

John's eyebrows went straight up. "Care to tell me why?"

Dan looked him in the eye. "Question to ask. In private."

John's eyebrows climbed higher. "About time, I'd say. Dixon's at the store now, talking to Becca. He wants to bring a fellow out to look at the property, says he's going to build a feedlot."

"That so?" John nodded sagely, and Dan asked, "How do you feel about it?"

"Her selling the place?" John shrugged, his gaze skittering away from Dan's. "That's her business."

"Cody's land," Dan pointed out gently.

John Odem sighed. "Keeping it won't change anything. She could use the money for college funds for the kids. I reckon Cody would want Frank to have it." But it was the end of Cody's dream, and they both knew it.

John clapped a hand on Dan's shoulder. "It's as it should be. I wouldn't change it if I could, and that's the truth. No father could take heaven from his son, and I can't say God hasn't provided what we've been missing."

Dan had to look down to hide the sudden sheen in his eyes. "Thanks, John."

John pounded his shoulder. "Welcome to the family, Dan."

"Not yet," Dan pointed out, smiling.

"You will be," John assured him. "I knew soon as she started stopping by Mrs. Buckner's."

"Buckner? The one who taught fifth grade?"

"Same," John acknowledged with a nod of his head.

Dan cocked his, puzzled. "Must be a hundred years old." Why would Becca be seeing old Mrs. Buckner? he wondered.

"She's only eighty," John replied, "and still sharp as a tack." Then he waved a hand and asked, "Got any of that sweet tea?"

Dan chuckled. "Help yourself."

"Think I will," John said, moving toward the cabinet. He took down a glass, then turned to grin at Dan and said, "Flowers wouldn't go amiss."

Dan smiled his thanks for the advice, wishing that his stomach hadn't just turned to cold jelly. "See what I can do."

Chapter Fifteen

Fearing he would be short for time, Dan dug out his darkest jeans and pressed them to a military crispness, along with a blue short-sleeved sport shirt that his mother swore was the very color of his eyes. Then he shaved and dressed, buffing his best tooled leather cowboy boots to a shine. He threaded the matching belt through the loops of his jeans, put on his good watch and faced himself in the mirror.

You're deaf, he told himself mentally, as he had so many times before. It had started as a necessary reminder of how his life had changed and gradually had become a test of sorts. Today it felt more like a simple statement of fact, and for the first time it was not followed by a pang of regret but by a brand-new reality check. *You're in love.*

He would not even think about whether or not the sentiment was mutual. He'd find out soon enough. It was possible, he discovered, to feel elation and terror all at once.

Quickly he descended the stairs, kissed the kids, told

them he'd see them later, dropped a grateful hand on John Odem's shoulder and went out to the truck. He fought the urge to speed all the way to Duncan.

Becca slipped through the front door and stopped. The house felt utterly empty. Wherever John Odem had gone with the kids, it wasn't here. She shook her head, feeling hot and irritated. This had been the weirdest day. First Jessica had shown up at the store with the kids, igniting in her an unreasoning terror that had resulted in a belly crawl through the dirt under the house and a toe-curling kiss that she could not even think about for fear of making more of it than was truly there. Then John Odem had shown up at the store with the kids and disappeared again just as she was ready to get off work. She had no idea where they'd gone or what mysterious errand had been important enough for Dan to alter their plans for the day—or where he was now, for that matter.

Painfully aware that she had already overreacted once that day, she was determined not to let her imagination carry her away, but she couldn't help feeling a niggling concern that bordered on annoyance. Surely Abby knew where John had taken the kids, though she'd feigned ignorance, shrugging and telling Becca to head on home.

"We'll get them back to you before bedtime," she'd said, and Becca wondered why even then she'd felt suspicious about that. Jemmy and CJ were undoubtedly safe with their grandfather. Telling herself that she just wasn't used to having any time on her own, she resolutely closed the door, left her small handbag at the foot of the stairs and wandered into the kitchen for something cold to drink.

She pondered whether or not to start dinner and decided to wait, though her stomach rumbled in protest, until she had some idea how many she'd be feeding. Peevishly she wondered if everyone else would eat without thought of her and leave her sitting here alone, starving, all evening. She grabbed a carrot and munched it while she poured a glass of tea, which she carried into the living room.

Stepping out of her shoes, she curled up in the armchair and used the remote to turn on the television, flipping through the channels. Dan had satellite here, so something was always on, but she'd never really developed the TV habit and had no idea what might hold her interest. She settled on a familiar syndicated program from her childhood, but before she could really get into it, she heard Dan's footsteps in the kitchen, accompanied by the faint rustle of paper and plastic. Sliding to the edge of her seat, she prepared to rise, but Dan appeared in the dining room just then, rubbing his hands together.

"Hi. Getting some quiet time?"

She twisted on the seat so that he could see her face. "Yeah. Do you know where John and the kids are?"

"Not a clue. Hungry?"

"Starving." She started to get up again, but he waved her back down.

"Stay there. I brought in Italian. That okay?"

She tilted her head in curiosity. "Where did you get Italian food?"

"Duncan. Watch your program. Won't be a minute."

With that, he stepped back and pulled the pocket doors shut.

Becca stared at those closed doors for a moment, decided that he felt he had to make up for scaring her that morning and gingerly sat back. That niggling feeling that all was not as it seemed deepened, however. She endured two more minutes of recorded laugh track before deciding that enough was enough. Aiming the remote control, she shut down the system and rose determinedly to her feet. Striding across the room, she reached for the twin doors, then paused long enough to listen for a moment before sliding them apart.

The table had been set with summer-green place mats and napkins. A small wire basket at one end of the dark, ornate table contained soft, steaming bread sticks. Dan carried two glass goblets into the room and placed them on the table before pulling out a chair for her.

"Sit."

"What's going on?" she asked suspiciously, slowly moving to position herself.

"Thought we'd eat like adults for once," he answered, moving away.

He quickly returned again bearing two of his grandmother's gold-rimmed floral china plates, which Becca had often admired in their mirrored cabinet against the far wall. Reaching across her shoulder, he set one laden plate before her. The aromas of spicy tomato sauce and tangy salad dressing set her stomach to rumbling in anticipation. He laid down the other plate and disappeared again while she was saying how good the food smelled. Seconds later he walked into the room and skirted the table to his own place. Becca's eyes widened at the sight of the vase of hybrid roses in his hands, creamy yellow buds, the color graduating to vibrant pink at the tips of the curling petals.

"These remind me of two favorite women." He pulled out his chair and sat down, saying, "Grandma loved yellow roses. Mom's favorites are hot pink. Makes these special."

"They're beautiful," Becca said. Then she looked him in the eye. "Are we celebrating?"

He shrugged. "Why not?" He reached across the table for her hand. "Mind if I pray?"

"Of course not."

He bowed his head, speaking slowly and deliberately. "Father, thank You for the reminder that this world contains as much beauty as difficulty. Troubles bring us wisdom, so thank You for them, too. My ears don't hear sound, but my heart does. Thank You for this food and this woman. Amen."

He let go of her hand and picked up his fork. Truly moved, Becca stared at him until he glanced up and smiled. He lifted a piece of rotini to his mouth and hummed approval. Once again that feeling that all was utterly right with her world washed over her. What difference did it make what John Odem was up to? Her children were safe with their doting grandpa. Dan had brought her a lovely dinner. Roses adorned the table, and she was now convinced that Frank Dixon truly wanted her property in order to build a feedlot, which would in turn bring a few much-needed jobs to the area and take care of her financial worries. She looked to her plate and picked up her own fork.

They ate in comfortable silence interrupted only

by her own voice saying, "This is very good. Thank you."

He just nodded, smiled and went on eating. Finishing way ahead of her, he lounged in his chair, one arm draped over the back, until she finally pushed away her plate.

"I am stuffed," she exclaimed, confessing, "I always eat too much when I'm really hungry."

He swept his gaze over her. "Doesn't show. In fact, you ought to have dessert."

She shook her head. "Thanks, but I really shouldn't."

"Doesn't take up much room," he insisted, rising to his feet. "Italian ice." She rose, too, and began clearing the table, but he took the plates from her hands. "No, no. My shindig."

"Dan," she said, "you don't have to do this. I'm the one who overreacted this morning. It wasn't your fault. You were working hard, and the time just got away from you."

"True. Now sit." He used his elbow on the top of her shoulder to urge her back down into her seat. "Be right back."

She slowly lowered herself onto the chair seat. Something was up, but she couldn't imagine what. Looking at those beautiful roses in that elegant vase, she felt a spark of hope kindle inside her, but she quickly squelched it, afraid to let her imagination run amok. Dan swept back into the room then with a single-footed ice cream bowl of heavy cut glass. He set it in front of her with a flourish, then instead of returning to his place, he dropped down onto the seat of the chair at the end of the table. Were they to share? Becca wondered, looking at the small, ornate bowl. She tilted her head, confused by the yellow-and-pink petals in her bowl.

"These are rose petals."

"Ice underneath."

She fought the impulse to lift a hand to his brow to test it for fever. "What're you doing?"

"Trust me," he said, handing her a spoon. "Go on."

Her heart began to race as she carefully, delicately brushed back the velvety petals with the tip of the spoon until the light caught something in the bottom of the bowl—not ice but gold.

"Oh, no."

The spoon clattered to the table, and with trembling fingers she divided the petals and pushed them apart. Two rows of tiny gold beads formed the band, widening in the middle to create a setting for a large, square-cut stone. Simple, elegant, unique. Definitely an engagement ring—with a very large diamond. She clapped her hands to her cheeks.

"Oh, no!"

She immediately turned to Dan, aware that he was frowning but not quite registering that fact. She was too busy dealing with a host of others. One, from sheer habit and long practice, naturally rose to the fore.

"Please tell me that's not a real diamond!"

"Think I'd give you a fake?" he asked incredulously.

She clapped her hands to her cheeks again. "Oh, no!"

"You don't like it."

"It's beautiful! But you can't—"

Suddenly he sat forward, circled her wrists with his

long, strong fingers and tugged her hands away from her face. "Becca, I can be a good husband and father."

"I know that. That's not the point."

"What is?"

"It's too big!"

"What?"

"It costs too much money!" she shouted.

He shook his head as if he hadn't understood a word, and released her. "What does?"

She poked a finger at the crystal bowl, on the verge of tears. "A diamond like that!"

His mouth fell open, and he rolled his eyes. "You won't marry me because the diamond's too big?"

"No! Yes! I mean…" Oh, what was wrong with her? She shook her head. This was not the important part. The important part was "Why?"

"Why?" he echoed uncertainly. "Why do I want to marry you?"

A tear sneaked out of the corner of her eye. She reached up a hand to deal with it, saying very clearly, "You're a natural-born hero, Daniel Holden, but you can't rescue the whole world."

"Not trying to." He caught her hands again and pressed them together, palm to palm, with his own. "Becca," he said earnestly, "God took my hearing to get me here to you."

Her chin began to wobble. "To rescue us from the storm, you mean?"

"To rescue *me*." He clasped his hands around hers. "I was so busy I couldn't hear God saying I wasn't doing what He wanted. He had to make me *really* listen. Understand?"

She had to ponder it a moment, but then she nodded. "I think so." Pulling her hands away, she wiped both cheeks. "But that doesn't mean you're supposed to marry me."

"Becca," he said, "I can't imagine my life without you and the kids. I don't want to."

The sobs caught her by surprise, and she wasn't sure what they came from—relief, joy, stubborn fear. Maybe all of it. Her heart felt so full suddenly that it seemed about to burst. The look of dismay on Dan's face just made her cry all the harder.

"Don't. Please, Becca, be happy. Forget everything else. I just want you to be happy. You deserve it. Sweetest, dearest, most beautiful woman on earth."

She laughed and sobbed and found herself horribly mute when she most wanted, needed to tell him what she was feeling. Suddenly she knew just how to do it. Her hands stumbled through the gestures. Once, twice. The third time he slipped off his chair onto his knees and wrapped his arms around her.

"I know," he said. "I love you, too. Love you so much."

She laughed and sniffed and laughed until he pulled back, smoothing her hair away from her face with his big, warm, protective hands. "Where did you learn?"

She tried to tell him, but her voice broke. She spelled it out with her fingers. B-u-c-k-n-e-r.

He smiled. "So that's what that was about."

She nodded and gasped and held on to him by his shirt, her hands grasping the fabric at his sides. He sat back on his heels and quickly signed something. All she got was "you" and "me."

"I'm not very good yet," she told him. "You have to say it."

He went more slowly this time, speaking as he signed. "Will you marry me?"

She covered her trembling mouth with one hand and nodded decisively. Beaming, he reached into the bowl and scooped out the ring, which he then slid onto her finger, saying, "Don't like it, we'll exchange it."

"I love it, but can we afford it?" she asked anxiously.

Dan chuckled and got to his feet, pulling her up and clasping his hands in the small of her back. "Not rich, but well fixed. I can give us a good life, Becca."

She bit her lip and looked at the ring, her hand resting lightly against his chest. "Come to think of it, I'm going to have some money, too. Frank's serious about the feedlot, you know."

"There you go. All that worry, you don't even need rescuing."

She blinked at him in shock. "That's right!" Why hadn't she realized it before? God had taken care of everything, as always, even her own stupid fears. "I've been an awful fool," she managed to say, glad he couldn't hear the screeching whine of her voice.

"No. No, no. Crisis confuses everything. I was confused, too, for long time." He smiled wryly. "Then this morning *you* came to rescue *me*, and I finally heard."

Her pulse quickened. "What did you hear?"

He cupped her face in his hands and smiled down into her eyes. "Your heart speaking to mine."

She slid her arms around his neck and laid her head on his shoulder, feeling the warmth and strength and rightness of his embrace. "I'll marry you, Dan Holden," she whispered, "and thank God every day for you." She knew that he heard, just not with his ears.

"A real wedding," Dan insisted later, sitting on the sofa next to her, his arms looped about her shoulders. He couldn't stop grinning, couldn't stop marveling, couldn't stop touching her, loving her. He smiled as she considered, watching the cogs turning in her mind. Sweet Becca, she just couldn't seem to stop counting pennies, but then she did.

"I'd like that, too. I didn't have it with Cody, didn't think it was important, and even if I had, my folks couldn't have provided cupcakes, let alone wedding cake. Besides, he had to be in Calgary in two days. I'd like a church wedding this time, the last time."

The last time. Dan liked that.

"Nothing fancy," he said, "but with my folks and yours, if they'll come." He felt strong, certain. Whole. Funny how that had nothing at all to do with physical perfection.

"I'm not sure they will," Becca was saying, "but we'll invite them."

"Okay. When?"

She shrugged. "As soon as we can work it out. I want to talk to Abby and John. And Jemmy."

He nodded. "Better see how the kids take to it first, huh?"

Becca cut him a look. "Oh, they'll 'take to it,' all right. Trust me on that."

"CJ's little," Dan mused. "Don't figure he'll mind. Jem might be little confused, but she'll be okay eventually."

"Eventually," Becca echoed. It almost seemed like a

question. She shifted around on the couch to face him more fully, drawing up one leg. "You don't read lips as well as you think you do, hotshot."

He frowned, targeting his concentration. "How's that?"

Her lips twitched. "Jemmy decided some time ago that you are her father."

"What?" He couldn't have gotten that right.

"You think she's been calling you Danny, don't you?"

His brows drew together. She *had* been calling him Danny. Unless… His eyes widened. "Daddy?"

"Yep." His jaw dropped, and Becca just grinned. "We've been around and around about it, but she's one stubborn little girl."

"Daddy," Dan whispered. He'd thought he'd never be anyone's daddy, and then he was without even realizing it. He had to duck his head, the tears catching him unawares. Becca slipped her hand into his, and he heard it again.

"I love you. Just as you are."

He got to his feet, pulling her up with him. "Let's go."

He wanted to hear Jem call him "Daddy" and John Odem call him "son" and Becca tell them all that she loved him and trusted him enough to be his bride. He wanted to hear Abby's delight and CJ's sweet confusion and silly bids for attention. He could already hear Cody whispering that he should take care of them, make them his own.

The sound of a heart speaking was a beautiful thing.

* * * * *

Dear Reader,

Hearing impairment is a serious issue in my family. In 1996 my beautiful niece Hillary gave birth under very trying circumstances that even involved airlifting her newborn daughter a hundred miles away to a special hospital. After fearing that our Madison wouldn't survive or could do so only with extreme medical problems, we thanked God to find that her sole impairment was loss of hearing. What a blessing she's been to us!

Her parents have always treated Madi as the perfectly normal child she is, so our darling not only speaks normally, reads on grade level, enjoys television and, yes, even music, she's also made significant accomplishments in her young life that few hearing children have achieved. Last year, her parents allowed her to enroll in competitive cheerleading, and her team went on to win two national championships in the mini-tot division. Madison herself won the American's Elite National Championship for Individual Dance at the age of six in Kansas City, Kansas. A world champion at six! How's that for inspiration?

As Madi could tell you, love, strong support, hard work and prayer can overcome any personal challenge, which is Dan Holden's message for us in this book. Like Dan, Madi knows she's "challenged," and that's sometimes daunting, but—also like Dan—our little rosebud has bloomed huge under the bright light of personal accomplishment. I hope you enjoy their story. And look out, world, here comes Madison Bowles! (Go get 'em, baby.)

God Bless,

Arlene James

A FAMILY TO SHARE

For we do not have a high priest who cannot
sympathize with our weaknesses, but one
who has been tempted in all things as we are,
yet without sin. Let us therefore draw near
with confidence to the throne of grace,
that we may receive mercy and may
find grace to help in time of need.
—*Hebrews* 4.15–16

For the Stines, with much affection.

Chapter One

"Lovely," Sharon pronounced, backing away from the trail of ivory satin ribbon that she left curling around a tendril of ivy on the floor, the finishing touch to a canopy of cascading ribbons and greenery.

"It is beautiful," Connie said, gently tugging on her left earlobe as she pictured her older sister, Jolie, standing beneath the canopy beside Sharon's brother, Vince.

Jolie met tall, good-looking Vince Cutler after she'd moved into his old apartment. He'd forgotten to have his personal mail forwarded, and the two had met after he'd dropped by to pick up what the post office had sent to his old address. One thing had led to another and now the two were about to be married.

Connie couldn't have been happier for her sister. God knew that Jolie needed someone like Vince, especially at that point in her life. The whole thing was terribly romantic. Every wedding was romantic, Connie supposed, but especially on Valentine's Day when the couple were as much in love as Jolie and Vince. The wedding was still hours away, but there were already tears in Connie's eyes.

Helen, one of the youngest of Vince's four sisters, folded her arms and nodded decisively.

"I think it's the prettiest wedding we've ever done."

"Ought to be," Donna, the youngest, cracked, "considering how much practice we've had."

"And you know that if we'd left it up to Vince," Olivia, the second-oldest sister, drawled, "he'd have hauled in a couple of hay bales, stuck a daisy in one and called it done."

Everyone laughed, but it was good-natured teasing. All of the sisters were married and seemed delighted that their adored only brother had found his life mate, even if Jolie *had* decorated his house in Western style, or something between Texana and cowboy chic, as she put it. For the Cutler women, chintz and kitsch seemed to be the height of home fashion, but Connie certainly couldn't fault their wedding decor.

In fact, Connie couldn't have been happier with Jolie's soon-to-be in-laws. They had even helped mend the rift that had existed between Connie and Jolie, a break that had resulted from a custody battle over Connie's young son, Russell. Vince had pushed Jolie to reconcile with her family, and for that, Connie would be forever grateful. According to Marcus, Connie's and Jolie's brother, that just went to prove that God does indeed move in mysterious ways.

Marcus, who was the pastor of this endearing old church where the wedding would take place, had been accorded the happy privilege of performing the ceremony, and Connie knew that he treasured the very idea of it. No one had regretted the break with Jolie more than Marcus had, but since the family had been mended, he'd have the joy of officiating at his sister's wedding ceremony. Wanting to look his very best on this momentous occasion, he had gone to the barber shop that morning for a professional shave and cut.

"Just think," he'd said as he kissed Connie's cheek before walking out the door of the house they shared, "one day I'll be doing this for you, too."

Connie doubted that very much. Marcus, bless him, was so good that he couldn't understand that most men would hold her past against her, at least the sort of man that she would even remotely consider as a father for her son. Jolie, on the other hand, deserved a kind, caring, upright man like Vince. Connie had cheated herself of that privilege, but she couldn't be too maudlin about her situation; if she hadn't made certain mistakes, she wouldn't have Russell.

Thoughts of her eighteen-month-old son woke a quiet yearning for the sight of his sweet little face, and Connie glanced at her wrist to check the time. If she hurried, she ought to be able to give Russell his dinner in the kitchen at the parsonage before she had to start getting ready for the wedding.

As if she could read her thoughts, Sharon announced, "I think we're finished here."

"Better be," Olivia said, gathering up her decorating supplies. "Mom's hair appointment is in thirty minutes."

"Oh, that's right!" Helen gasped. "We'd better swing by the fellowship hall and pry her out of there ASAP."

"I don't know what she's been doing over there all this time anyway," Donna said. "All she had left to do was arrange a few relish trays."

Sharon rolled her eyes. "That's like saying all Genghis Khan had to do after he conquered Asia was ride a horse across it. She'll have rearranged the serving tables and had the baker redecorate the cake by now."

"She'd better not," Olivia declared, heading for the door.

Olivia had spent hours that morning arranging those serving tables just the way she wanted them, but Connie wasn't fooled into thinking that anything but the most best-natured arguments would ensue. The Cutler clan loved and treasured one another. They teased mercilessly, but since Jolie and Vince had gotten engaged at Christmas, Connie had not witnessed a negative expression stronger than a grimace from any member of the Cutler family. Nevertheless, Olivia made a hasty retreat in the direction of the church's fellowship hall.

The other sisters followed her in rapid succession, waving at Connie and saying that they'd see her in a little while. Connie smiled, genuinely admiring the Cutler sisters, each in her own way. As the last one hurried off, Connie took a final measure of the chapel.

The white of the antiqued walls had aged to a soft butter-yellow, which complemented the gold carpet and pale, natural woods in the room. Tall, narrow stained-glass windows glowed vibrantly in the afternoon sunlight, while brass gleamed overhead.

The altar had been draped in an ivory satin cloth and topped with a basket of bloodred roses and a gold cross. The canopy of ivory ribbon and greenery elegantly draped the brass kneeler before it.

A tall, heavy glass pedestal decorated with twining ivy stood to one side, holding an ornately carved unity candle. The Cutler sisters had crafted unique bouquets of greenery with lengths of red satin cloth gathered into soft, billowy clumps, which now adorned the ends of the pews. Connie found them especially appropriate for Jolie, who, though very pretty, was not, as Olivia put it, the "girly" type.

The final touch was an artful scattering of almost two hundred tiny votive candles in simple, clear glass containers, which Vince's older nephews would light at the beginning of the ceremony.

The attendants' dresses were a shade of pale yellow trimmed with green ribbon, which, oddly enough, brought the whole scheme together perfectly. When Jolie had first chosen that particular shade, all of the sisters had protested, but it hadn't taken long for everyone to realize that Jolie had not only her own distinctive style but also a gift for putting colors together.

It truly was going to be a beautiful wedding.

Smiling, Connie went to pick up her son at the church's day care, situated on the back corner of the grounds.

Rather than erect a shiny new building, the congregation had opted to purchase houses surrounding the historic old church, link them with covered walkways and renovate them for administration, education, fellowship hall and day care spaces. In doing so, they had created a quaint campus reminiscent of a gingerbread village with the chapel at its center. The result felt more like a community than a church, and Connie would be forever grateful for the haven she'd found here.

Snagging her tan wool coat from a peg in the foyer, Connie shrugged it on over her straight-legged, brown knit slacks and matching turtleneck sweater. She felt that the monochrome color scheme made her look taller that her mere five-foot-three frame and balanced her top-heavy figure.

In actuality, her neat, curvy shape was well proportioned to her height, giving her ultrafeminine appeal that her taller, leggier older sister had often envied. Connie, however, remained unaware of this fact, just as she remained unaware that her wispy, golden-blond, chin-length hairstyle often garnered more appreciative glances than her sister's long fall of straight, thick, golden-brown hair.

The one trait that the two sisters shared, other than their jade-green eyes, was a simplicity of style. In Connie, that translated into an almost-elfin elegance that made her seem vulnerable and quintessentially female, as opposed to Jolie's earthy, Amazonian womanhood.

Unfortunately, like many women, Connie tended to concentrate on her shortcomings. When she gazed into the mirror, she saw not a pert nose but a childish one, not a classically oval face but a too-sharp chin and wide cheeks, not a full, luscious mouth but a mundane one, not arresting, gold-fringed eyes like jade glass but odd-color eyes and lashes that were too pale.

As she tugged open the door and stepped onto the covered walkway, a cold gust hit her with the force of an icy slap. The wind had a wet, chilly feel to it, but the sky remained blue and clear overhead.

February usually yielded an ice storm that would paralyze north central Texas for at least a day or two, but so far so good. *It could ice up tomorrow,* she thought, *right after Jolie and Vince head off to a beach in Mexico for a honeymoon.*

She was thinking how lovely that beach was going to be as she walked up the ramp to the day care center and pulled open the door.

A late-model, domestic luxury car was parked beneath the drive-through cover, but Connie thought nothing of it. Parents came and went all day long, and from the sound of wails in the distance, some little one had either fallen ill or gotten injured. Of course, if it had been serious, an ambulance would have beaten the parent here.

Connie smiled at Millie, a spare, quiet, attentive woman whom everyone referred to as "The Gatekeeper," and jotted her name down on the pickup sheet beneath that of Kendal Oakes.

Ah, that explained a great deal, she thought.

Mr. Oakes was a new member of the church, having just recently moved to the community, although he did not reside in Pantego itself. Sandwiched between Arlington and Fort Worth, Pantego, along with Dalworthington Gardens, was regarded as a small bedroom community. Landlocked by its larger neighbors, it had little opportunity for growth. As a consequence, many of the church's members came from outside the community.

Unfortunately, Kendal Oakes's young daughter had already earned a reputation as a problem child, and it was no wonder considering what she'd been through, poor thing. Connie felt deep compassion for the troubled toddler and her father. Marcus told her that Mrs. Oakes had died suddenly months earlier and that the child, Larissa, had suffered great trauma as a result.

Connie knew Mr. Oakes only in passing, but she'd had dealings with Larissa that past Sunday when she'd stopped by the church's day care to check on Russell and found herself calming the shrieking child. The day care attendants—most of them older ladies—were beside themselves when she happened along, and their relief was painfully obvious when Larissa unexpectedly launched herself at Connie and held on for dear life. It took several minutes for the sobbing child to exhaust herself, but she was sleeping peacefully against Connie's shoulder when her father arrived to gently lift her away.

Recognizing a deep sadness in him, Connie supposed that, like his daughter, he must still grieve his late wife dearly. He had whispered his thanks, and in truth Connie hadn't minded in the least, but she'd come away from the experience more grateful than ever for her son's placid—if somewhat determined—nature. It was a trait, or so Marcus insisted, inherited from Connie. It certainly hadn't come from his biological father.

She pushed thoughts of Jessup Kennard to the farthest recesses of her mind as she walked along a hallway toward the toddler area. No good ever came of dwelling on anything to do with Jessup. She prayed for the man regularly, but she couldn't help but feel relieved that he would very likely spend every day of the rest of his life locked behind bars. And yet, she'd have done much to spare her son the shame of carrying the name of such a father.

Wails of protest had turned to angry screeches by the time Connie turned the corner and came on the scene. Kendal Oakes was doing his best to subdue his child above the closed half door of the room, but while he attempted to capture her flailing arms and twisting little body, Larissa was alternately bucking and clutching at her teacher, Miss Susan.

For some reason, all of the day care workers went by the title of "Miss." Only twenty and still a college student, the young woman looked as if she was near to tears herself, while Miss Dabney, the day care director, hovered anxiously at her shoulder.

Tall and whipcord-lean, Kendal Oakes looked not only agonized but also out of place in his pin-striped suit and red silk tie tossed back haphazardly over one shoulder. One thick lock of his rich nut-brown hair had fallen forward to curl against his brow, and the shadow of his beard darkened his long jawline and flat cheeks. He was speaking to his daughter in a somewhat exasperated voice.

"Larissa, please listen. Listen a minute. Daddy is taking you to play with Dr. Stenhope. You like Dr. Stenhope. Larissa, Dr. Stenhope is waiting for us. Come on now."

"Is she ill?" Connie wondered aloud, and for one heartbeat, everything froze.

All heads turned in her direction and Larissa stopped screaming long enough to see that someone new had arrived. The next instant, the child propelled herself out of her caregiver's arms and straight into Connie's, clapping her hands around Connie's neck and grasping handfuls of Connie's hair and coat.

Grappling with the sudden weight of a flying body, slight as it was, Connie staggered slightly. Larissa lay her head on Connie's shoulder and sobbed inconsolably. The sound of it tore at Connie's heart, and by the look in his cinnamon-brown eyes, it ripped Kendal Oakes to shreds.

For a moment, Connie saw such despair in those eyes that she mentally recoiled. She knew despair too well to wish further acquaintance with it.

The next instant, compassion rushed in. The poor man.

"I'm so sorry," he said, but she shook her head and instinctively stepped back as he reached for his daughter.

Connie noticed that he had quite large hands, with wide palms and long, tapered fingers.

"It's all right," she told him softly, hefting the child more securely against her.

Larissa felt warm, her tiny chest heaving, but whether it was with exertion or fever, Connie couldn't tell.

"Has anyone been able to take her temperature?"

Kendal shook his head grimly. "It's not a physical ailment. Dr. Stenhope is a pediatric psychiatrist."

Poor baby, Connie thought, rocking from side to side in a gentle swinging motion. Connie knew that the child had to be under two; otherwise, she would have been in a different class than Russell. So young and already under the care of a psychiatrist. It was heartbreaking.

Larissa's weeping subsided to huffs and gasps. Connie reached up and instinctively patted the child's back. Kendal stared at her hand as if he was studying just how she did it. He betrayed a patent desire to learn how to handle his daughter, and once more Connie's heart went out to him.

After a moment, he glanced reluctantly at the thin gold watch encircling his wrist and grimaced.

"We really have to go."

Cautiously, almost apologetically, he reached for his daughter, but as those big hands settled at her heaving sides, Larissa shrieked and arched her back, clutching on tighter to Connie. The one clearly in pain, though, was Kendal. Leaning closer, he pitched his voice low and spoke to the bucking child.

"Larissa, we have to go. Dr. Stenhope is waiting for us. Don't you want to see Dr. Stenhope?"

What Larissa wanted was to hang around Connie's neck like a necklace, and she fought for several moments, shrugging and twisting and clutching. Her father patted and cajoled and stroked, but Larissa screamed and flailed in sheer anger. Finally Kendal grasped her firmly by the sides and pulled her away from Connie.

"I am so sorry. She misses her mother still. She…" He gave up trying to speak over Larissa's shrieks, turned her chest to his and gulped. "I'm sorry," he said again before striding down the hallway, Larissa's head clasped to his shoulder to keep her from hurting herself as she bucked.

"You don't suppose…" Miss Susan murmured, breaking off before completing the thought.

Connie glanced at her, sensing what she was thinking, what they were both thinking, Miss Susan and Miss Dabney.

"No," she said firmly. "I don't believe he would harm that child."

It seemed a logical conclusion, Connie had to admit, but she'd seen child abusers up close and personal during her many years as a foster child. She'd seen the children come in, battered in body and spirit, and watched as the state tried to retrain the parent and reunite the family. If the abuse had been mild enough in nature and the parent willing to work at it, the outcome had sometimes been good. Too often, it had not. More than once, a child of her acquaintance had died after reunification.

Everything she knew told her that the worst that could be said about Kendal Oakes was that he might not be a very skilled parent, but he was obviously trying to get help. It occurred to her that she might have handled this situation better herself.

"Miss Susan, would you get Russell ready to leave, please? I won't be a moment," she said crisply, turning to follow Kendal down the hall.

He was moving quickly and she had to run to catch up, but she was with him when they reached his car. He fumbled in his pocket for his keys. Larissa wailed, but she no longer struggled. When he had the keys in hand, he pressed the tiny button on the remote that unlocked the doors.

"Here, let me get that," Connie offered, reaching for the door handle.

She pulled it open and stepped aside as Kendal bent down, clutching Larissa firmly. He deposited the child in her car seat, but when he attempted to pull the straps of the safety harness up over her shoulders, she crossed her arms and kicked him. He jerked back but said nothing, caught both of her feet in one hand and held them down as he reached for the harness straps with the other. Obviously, he wasn't going to get it done with one hand.

"Can I help?" Connie asked.

"Would you mind?"

She heard the cringing in his voice, the shame at what he perceived to be his personal failure.

"Not at all," Connie said brightly, squeezing into the open space beside him.

Larissa stopped crying the instant Connie drew near and allowed her to gently uncross her arms so her father could slide the harness straps in place and bring them together over her chest. Connie smiled and attempted to keep the child engaged while he fit together the two sections of the restraint system and pushed them into the lock.

"There now. That's right," Connie crooned. Larissa watched her avidly, as if she was memorizing her face. "What a pretty girl you are when you aren't crying." She stroked her hand over the child's pale-blond hair and heard the lock click at last. "All ready to go see the doctor?"

Larissa blinked and jabbed two fingers into her mouth. Her nose was running, so Connie dug into her coat pocket for a tissue. She had second thoughts before she touched the tissue to that tiny nose, but Larissa turned up her chin and closed her eyes while Connie gently cleaned her nose. But then Connie pocketed the tissue once more and backed away. Larissa's eyes popped open and she howled like a banshee, drumming her heels and reaching toward Connie.

Dismayed, Connie could only watch as Kendal closed the door on his daughter's howls of protest.

"Oh, dear."

"It's all right," he said, two bright red splotches staining the flesh drawn tight over his cheekbones. "When she gets like this…" He clutched his keys. "She'll calm down in a few minutes. She likes Dr. Stenhope, I think."

Connie couldn't control her grimace and then had to explain it.

"I don't have anything against psychiatrists. It's just that your daughter is so young for that sort of care. I know the two of you must have been through a lot."

The look that he turned on her said it all. The man was confused, harassed, deeply worried.

"I don't know how else to help her," he admitted bluntly. Then he cleared his throat and smiled. "I appreciate your assistance."

"Anytime."

He would have turned away, but Connie impulsively reached out a hand, setting it lightly on his forearm.

"I'll pray for you," she told him softly.

A muscle in the hollow of one cheek quivered as he lay his much larger hand over hers.

The next instant, he abruptly jerked away and stepped back, saying, "Please do."

Quickly, he opened the front door of the car and dropped down behind the steering wheel. In the backseat, Larissa still reached for Connie, her cries both angry and desperate.

As the sedan drove away, Connie pictured the child inside.

She really was a beautiful little thing with her pale-blond hair and plump cheeks. She had her father's cinnamon-brown eyes, but hers were rounder and wider, and something about the way Larissa looked at a person felt vaguely troubling. It was as if she constantly searched for something, someone.

Connie sensed the child's fear, anger and frustration, emotions with which she could strongly identify. She had never known her own father and had few pleasant memories of her mother, but she remembered all too well being separated from her brother and then later her sister. Alone and confused, she had desperately sought comfort from those in whose care she had been placed, only to find herself also suddenly separated from them. That pattern had repeated itself over the years.

At times, the anger and neediness had overwhelmed her, but unlike her older sister, Jolie, Connie could not express herself in cold contempt or outright displays of temper. Instead, she tended to hide away and weep endlessly for hours, then blindly latch on to the first friendly person she could find. All too often, they hadn't really been her friends at all. It seemed to be an unwritten law that the users of this world could recognize the neediest of their companions at a glance. Thank God that He had led her out of that.

Chilled, Connie folded her arms and turned back into the building. She smiled at Millie and walked down the hallway to her son's room.

Russell was ready and waiting for her, his coat on, a sheet of paper to which cotton balls had been glued clutched in one hand. Miss Susan held him in her arms behind the half door, rubbing his nose against hers. He giggled, throwing back his bright-red head, and spied Connie.

"Mama!" he called gaily, his big, blue eyes shining.

He leaned toward her and she caught him up against her, hugging him close.

"Hello, my angel. Were you a good boy today?"

"Sweet as pie," Miss Susan said.

Connie smiled in response. "Say bye-bye to Miss Susan."

Russell raised a hand and folded his fingers forward. "Bye-bye."

"Bye-bye, cutie. See you soon."

"Thank you, Miss Susan."

"Anytime. We're always glad to see him."

"Well, if I start school—or when, rather—he's apt to become a regular."

"That'd be fine," Miss Susan told her. "He's such a happy, little thing."

Connie knew whom she had to thank for that.

Oh, it was true that Russell possessed a sweet, placid nature, but even the best-natured child would fret and act out in the grip of insecurity, and Russell could easily have been such a child. Being born in a prison was not the best way to start out in life, but Jolie, bless her, had seen to it that he had a loving, structured home until Connie, with the help of their brother, could see to it herself.

She and her son didn't have much money or even a two-parent home, but they were blessed nevertheless.

Connie thought of Larissa Oakes and the turmoil that seemed to spill out all around her and she hugged her son a little closer.

Truly, they were blessed. They had Marcus and Jolie and now even Vince and the other Cutlers. Whatever terrors and shame her past held, whatever uncertainties and limitations clouded her future, her little boy would always know love and the security of family and faith to keep him strong and whole.

She couldn't ask for anything more.

Chapter Two

No wedding could have been lovelier, Connie thought, walking slowly down the aisle while clutching a half-dozen red roses nestled in ivory tulle.

Vince was grinning from ear to ear and had been since he'd walked out of the side door of the chapel with Marcus and a trio of groomsmen. Both her brother and her soon-to-be brother-in-law were more handsome than any man had the right to be. One dark, one golden, they made an interesting contrast—Vince with his black hair, dressed in a simply tailored, black tuxedo, Marcus in the sumptuous ecclesiastical robe that he chose to wear on such occasions.

Marcus nodded subtly as Connie turned to take her place in front of the other attendants: Vince's two younger sisters, Helen and Donna. Sharon and Olivia sat to one side, having taken other roles in the ceremony, while their husbands ably corralled the numerous Cutler children.

Connie took her position and gracefully turned,

Get **2** Books **FREE!**

Steeple Hill® Books,
publisher of inspirational fiction,
presents

Love Inspired

A series of contemporary love stories that will lift your spirits and reinforce important lessons about life, faith and love!

FREE BOOKS! Use the reply card inside to get two free books by outstanding inspirational authors!

FREE GIFTS! You'll also get two exciting surprise gifts, absolutely free!

GET 2 BOOKS

IF YOU ENJOY A ROMANTIC STORY that reflects solid, traditional values, then you'll like *Love Inspired®* novels. These are heartwarming inspirational romances that explore timeless themes of forgiveness and redemption, sacrifice and spiritual fulfillment.

We'd like to send you two *Love Inspired* novels absolutely free. Accepting them puts you under no obligation to purchase any more books.

HOW TO GET YOUR
2 FREE BOOKS AND 2 FREE GIFTS

1. Return the reply card today, and we'll send you two *Love Inspired* novels, absolutely free! We'll even pay the postage!

2. Accepting free books places you under no obligation to buy anything, ever. The two books have combined cover prices of at least $11.00 in the U.S. and at least $13.00 in Canada, but they're yours to keep, free!

3. We hope that after receiving your free books you'll want to remain a subscriber, but the choice is yours—to continue or cancel, any time at all!

EXTRA BONUS

You'll also get two free mystery gifts!
(worth about $10)

FREE!

allowing the short train of the flared skirt on the long-sleeved, high-waisted dress to settle into an elegant swirl about her feet. A moment later, the flower girls stepped into view: Vince's nieces, Brenda and Bets.

Brenda was a few inches taller than her cousin, but they were dressed identically in pale-yellow dresses with long-sleeved velvet bodices and short, full, chiffon skirts, white anklets edged in lace, and black Mary Janes. Their hair had been caught up into sausage curls on opposite sides of their heads and each carried a small basket filled with rose petals, which they sprinkled judiciously along the white satin runner on which they walked. One of Vince's nephews had unrolled the runner along the aisle earlier before two of his cousins had entered to light the many candles now glowing and flickering about the room, their light refracting against the stained-glass windows.

The double doors at the end of the aisle closed behind the girls. Once they reached their assigned spots, the organist switched from Debussy to the wedding march and the crowd rose to its collective feet.

The doors swung open again, revealing Jolie on the arm of the man who would shortly become her father-in-law. Larry Cutler couldn't have looked prouder walking his own daughters down the aisle, and none of them could have looked any more beautiful than Jolie did.

She wore her mother-in-law's circa-1960s dress, and the simplicity of the Empire style, with its delicate lace hem, suited her well. A short, close-fitting jacket of ivory velvet was added to make the sleeveless bodice suitable for a winter wedding. Along with the lengthy but fragile veil that rested atop Jolie's head beneath a simple coronet and trailed along behind her, it lent an elegant air to what would have otherwise been a sadly outdated gown.

The bridal bouquet was made up of pale-yellow roses, their stems tied together with velvet ribbon. To please Vince, Jolie had left her long, golden-brown hair down, the coronet sitting just far enough back on her head to keep her bangs out of her eyes.

This was perhaps the first time Connie had ever seen her sister wearing makeup. Nothing heavy—a touch of blush, mascara and a glossy, pink lipstick that called attention to her pretty mouth. The effect was astonishing, though.

Vince looked absolutely stunned, entranced by the vision that glided toward him, and he didn't snap out of it until Marcus announced in a clear, ringing voice, "I give this woman in marriage." At which point, Larry kissed her hand and placed it in Vince's.

Larry then did something that would stay with Connie for a very long time.

He leaned forward and hugged his son tightly.

It was unexpected, at least to Connie. She wasn't used to seeing two grown men, father and son, masculine and strong, display a deep, easy affection for a special moment.

Connie couldn't help but think that Russell would never have that.

Because of her—because of the mistakes she had made—her son would never know the love of a father so complete that embarrassment simply did not exist in the same sphere with it.

Tears immediately gathered in her eyes and she had to look away.

She wasn't the only one crying at that point. Vince's mother and oldest sister were already dabbing at their eyes. Sharon, in fact, had a difficult time getting through the Old Testament reading that she had chosen. Olivia delivered the New Testament portion more easily, but she was in tears, too, by the end of the music.

Marcus, bless him, elevated the ceremony from tear-filled to joyous simply by his demeanor as he delivered a short homily on the blessings and responsibilities of marriage and read the vows, which the happy couple spoke loudly and clearly.

In a small departure from the norm, it had been decided that it was best if the ring bearer—the youngest of Olivia's three sons—made as short an appearance as possible in his formal role. This arrangement also gave him a real moment in the spotlight as he now came forward, carrying the actual rings attached to a small pillow by ribbons. Connie and the best man, Boyd, a friend and employee of Vince's, met him at the head of the aisle and took the rings from him, then moved into position once more while shepherding the young boy into his spot among the groomsmen, who were his uncles.

The rings were exchanged.

Marcus lit two taper candles and passed them to the bride and groom, who together lit the unity candle while the organ played. Then they knelt at the altar and received their blessing.

Finally, the moment came when Marcus pronounced them man and wife, followed by "You may kiss your bride."

To her shock, Connie found that she couldn't watch.

It was ludicrous. She had seen the two kiss before, and she'd always felt such delight for her sister's sake. She knew that Jolie deserved the kind of love that Vince showered upon her. Yet, in that moment when they publicly sealed their lifelong commitment to each other, Connie could not bear to witness it.

Somehow and very unexpectedly, it was as if a knife had been driven into her heart, as if she were witnessing the death of all her romantic notions, silly as they had been. Even as the newly married couple turned to be presented to the assembly as Mr. and Mrs. Vince Cutler, Connie could not look at them. She applauded along with everyone else and she truly was happy for them, but she suddenly felt as if a sob was about to break free from her chest.

She knew what it was, of course. She had felt envy before but never like this—never with this searing sense of pure loss—for surely this moment was as close as she would ever come to a wedding of her own.

Not even time could diminish the mistakes that she had made. Only in Heaven would she be able to say that it no longer mattered. As Marcus often said, God removes the consequences of sin in the hereafter, but in the here and now, our choices often yield terrible fruit.

The sad result of her choices was that no decent Christian man would ever want her for his wife, and that was as it should be. She thought that she'd faced and accepted that harsh truth, but suddenly she realized that deep down she harbored a very foolish hope, which now surely had been properly dashed.

It was all for the best, she told herself. She was not like Jolie. Unfortunately, she was much more like their mother, and this just served to prove it. No matter how much she had tried to deny it in the past, the emotional neediness of Velma Wheeler was very much her legacy to her youngest daughter.

Disgusted with herself, Connie fixed her smile and followed her sister and her new husband down the aisle. The best man—a perfectly nice, married gentleman— escorted her, but it was all she could do to hold his arm until they had cleared the room.

At once, she was swept into a joint hug by the newly married couple, and then it was fairly chaotic for several moments as the remainder of the wedding party joined them. Telling herself that she would be thankful for this reality check later, Connie allowed herself to be hurried into a side room while the photographer snapped candid shots and Marcus told the guests how to find the hall where the reception would be held.

After the guests had headed toward the reception site, the wedding party hurried back into the sanctuary for a few group photos. Then the attendants trooped over to the reception en masse while Jolie and Vince struck a few poses as husband and wife.

It was a happy, talking, laughing mob in the reception hall. Connie couldn't have counted the number of hugs that enveloped her, and yet shortly after the new Mr. and Mrs. Cutler arrived, Connie found herself standing alone in a corner watching the festivities. She felt apart, solitary, sealed away behind an invisible wall of past mistakes.

Some prisons, she had learned, were not made of bars.

Squaring her shoulders, she scolded herself for letting regret stain this of all days. After sending a quick prayer upward, she fixed her smile and forced one foot in front of the other until she was in the midst of the throng once more.

Marcus sauntered forward, free of his clerical robes, a cup of punch in one hand and a relaxed smile on his face. He glanced across the room to the table where Jolie and Vince were seated. Russell lolled on his aunt's lap, playing with the edge of her veil, which she'd looped over one arm before taking her seat.

"I never expected this," Marcus said, surprised when his sister jumped slightly. He shouldn't have been. She held herself apart too much. It sometimes seemed to him that Connie had not yet left prison behind her.

"What?" she asked uncertainly.

He waved a hand. "This. Somehow, I never thought about it. There always seemed to be so much else to worry about, and now suddenly here we are, a real family doing just what real families do."

"It's the Cutlers," Connie said. "They're just so normal that they make you feel normal by association."

"I don't know," he mused, his green eyes narrowing. "I think we might be more normal than we realize."

"You, maybe," she countered softly, then immediately amended that. "And Jolie. Definitely Jolie."

He cocked his head. "Not you?"

"Not me," she answered softly.

He looped an arm around her shoulders in brotherly support.

"You may be the most normal of us all, Connie."

She shook her head and Marcus sighed inwardly. Sensitive and caring, Connie had suffered the most after their mother had abandoned them. As a result, she could not seem to stop punishing herself for past sins. She carried such needless guilt, such overwhelming shame. It was one of the reasons Marcus had convinced her to regain custody of her son. Going against Jolie had hurt him, but he had known Jolie would survive. He hadn't been so sure about Connie, and yet here she was, as lovely and sweet as ever.

He followed her adoring gaze to her son. No longer entertained by the delicate edging of Jolie's veil, Russell suddenly flopped over and tried to pull himself upright on Jolie's lap by tugging at the bodice of her wedding gown. Vince immediately reached over and plucked him off Jolie, settling him in his own lap, but Connie was a very conscientious mother. She had a gift for it, frankly, if Marcus did say so himself.

She immediately started toward her rambunctious son, saying, "Uh-oh. Someone is restless."

Marcus followed in her wake, watching the way that Russell so readily came up into her arms.

"He looks so adorable in that little suit," Jolie said, her eyes shining.

Her smile looked permanent, Marcus was thankful to note.

"Marcus insisted that he had to have one," Connie said, sliding a look at Marcus. "He spends too much on us, doesn't he, munchkin?"

"Don't be silly," Marcus scoffed. "If you'd let me pay you for keeping house—"

"You do pay me," Connie interrupted tartly. "You're putting a roof over our heads."

"It's more than a fair exchange," Marcus argued.

"Somehow, I don't think he minds," Vince told Connie, smiling at Marcus and clasping Jolie's hand in his.

Marcus saluted him with his punch glass.

"I'm sure he doesn't," Connie replied, "but I do. That's why I'm intending to go to school and learn a trade of some sort."

Marcus studiously kept a grimace off his face, even as Jolie sat forward, exclaiming, "That's great!"

"You have to know that we'll help in any way that we can," Vince assured Connie.

"Thanks, but that's the point, isn't it? I have to be able to help myself. Still, since you're not working at the cleaners now, Jo, maybe you could watch Russell a couple of days a week? They won't charge me to keep him here at the day care, but I know he'd rather spend some time with you. It would give him a nice change, at least."

Jolie literally beamed. "That would be wonderful!"

Marcus smiled to himself, so very proud of both of his sisters.

While Connie had been in prison, Jolie had cared for Russell as if he were her own child, and in many ways he was. It was entirely understandable that Jolie hadn't wanted to give him up, but once Connie had been released, Marcus had known that—for her sake as well as Russell's—she had to take over guardianship of her son. She hadn't believed herself worthy of mothering a child, but no one who knew her could say that now. Marcus's one regret was that Jolie had gotten hurt in the process, and he had feared that the resulting break in the family would be permanent.

Thank God that had not been the case.

Vince had helped Jolie find a way to forgive and reconnect with her family. Considering that they'd fought a custody battle over the boy, Connie showed great compassion and wisdom in asking Jolie to help care for Russell. Thankfully, Connie understood that Jolie would always share a special bond with Russell and that he needed Jolie to be his aunt. Now, she could be.

Marcus only wished that Connie could forgive herself for her past mistakes as readily as she forgave others. He hated to think about Connie not spending her days with her son, but he understood why she felt that she had to go to school. Somehow, though, something told him that it wasn't the right thing to do, not at this time. Still, he kept his opinion to himself.

One thing he had learned was that God always had a plan for His children, and Marcus had no doubts that, when the time was right, God would reveal His plan for Connie.

Connie tacked her smile into place and took her son to find his sippy cup and something appropriate with which to fill it. She loved her sister, and she had no doubt that it was wise to have Jolie watch Russell whenever she could, but she felt stretched thin at the moment. She had not expected this day to be so hard for her. That it was seemed irrefutable proof that she was not the person she should be.

Father, forgive me, she prayed silently. *I want to be better. I really do.* It was a familiar but heartfelt refrain, and she determinedly set out to enjoy her sister's wedding reception.

Russell was yawning by the time the bride and groom cut the cake. It finally seemed acceptable for Connie to make her escape. The Cutler sisters, however, would hear nothing of it. The bridal bouquet was yet to be tossed, they declared, and Connie was one of only four unmarried ladies present over the age of twelve. She couldn't very well refuse to line up with the others. It was her only sister's wedding, after all.

She wanted the floor to open up and swallow her whole when she actually caught the thing, though *caught* was too fine a word for what happened.

As was usually the case, the florist had made a replica of the bridal bouquet for the traditional toss. That way, the bride could keep her real bouquet and the lucky, next-to-be-married recipient could keep the silk copy. The silk flowers were quite lightweight and sailed merely a few feet over Jolie's shoulder before bouncing off Connie's chest.

The bouquet plopped to the floor, as Connie had made no real attempt to catch it, but Russell, who was at her feet, promptly snatched it up and presented it to her, proud as a peacock. Everyone laughed and Connie felt her cheeks flush with embarrassment because surely too many knew how ridiculous the idea was that she would be the next to marry.

A great deal of effort went into her smile for the photos, and when she left the room a few minutes later, a sleepy Russell snuggled against her chest, she felt like the worst sort of ingrate. God had blessed her, despite her mistakes, and she told herself firmly that she would not allow envy and regret to rob her of gratitude. Nevertheless, she was glad to finally get away.

Draping her coat over her shoulders, she pulled the edges together around her son and carried him swiftly across the compound. By the time she reached the neat little house that they shared with her brother, her feet were killing her and her arms felt like lead weights. It was a great pleasure to kick off her satin pumps, deposit the silk bouquet on a handy shelf and gently lower Russell onto the changing table.

Russell was sleeping already, but he roused as she changed him. Softly singing a lullaby, she kept her movements slow and easy as she removed his wedding finery and slipped him into footed pajamas. She dropped down into the bedside rocker with him. Moments later, he was deeply asleep again without a care in the world, his face sublime.

Then it came, the sense of awe, the vast relief.

How could she feel envy when she was here in this warm, cozy house instead of a cold, impersonal cell? She had her son with her—not only an empty ache in her heart—and she had just come from her dear sister's wedding. Moreover, her kind, generous big brother would be home shortly, still beaming, no doubt.

"Thank you, God," she whispered, blinking back tears as she lay her son in his crib.

Perhaps she would never have what Jolie did, but she had more than she deserved. It was enough.

Kendal gently closed the door to his daughter's room and leaned against it, sighing with relief. Bedtime had not been the ordeal that he had feared it would be this evening, which was not to say that the day hadn't been difficult enough. The session with Dr. Stenhope had not gone well.

Usually, Larissa tolerated the grandmotherly psychiatrist with cool indifference. Today, however, she had wailed and struggled until Dr. Stenhope had yielded the direction of her exercises to a younger assistant. Kendal didn't need a psychiatrist to tell him that his child was fixated on younger women, women who apparently reminded her of her mother on some level, women such as Connie Wheeler.

He turned off thoughts of the petite, compassionate

woman, allowing himself instead to indulge a remnant of the rage that he'd felt since the death of his wife. Intellectually, he knew that he was as much to blame for this situation as Laura was and the great guilt that he carried quickly eclipsed the anger. True, she'd shut him out after Larissa was born, but he'd allowed it to happen. It was as if Laura hadn't known how to be both a wife and a mother at the same time, and he hadn't known how to overcome his own hurt and disappointment to help her.

He now realized how selfish and convenient that had been. Oh, he'd told himself that, as Larissa grew older, Laura would relax and allow him to take a hand in raising their daughter, but Larissa had needed him then as much as she did now. He could not escape the fact that he had been as unfair to his daughter as Laura had been to him.

It had been horribly easy to take a backseat. His mortgage brokerage had burgeoned with the lowering of interest rates and he'd been focused on turning it into a real player in the field. That, too, had been a convenient excuse.

The ugly truth was that his marriage had never been what he'd hoped it would be. Even before Larissa was born, the relationship had shriveled into cold politeness. He should have fought harder to breach Laura's defenses of silence and impersonal interaction. He should have been the husband and father that God had meant him to be, even if Laura hadn't been capable of being the wife and mother he'd envisioned.

Now, it was too late to be a husband to Laura.

Who could've imagined that she would die so abruptly, especially from something as seemingly innocuous as a few ant bites? It was Larissa who needed him now.

To think that Larissa had been there, alone, with Laura at the time of her death was bad enough, but for the child to have spent the next day and a half wailing in her crib, waiting for her mommy to come and get her...

He shuddered at the memory. As long as he lived, he'd never forget how Larissa had fought and struggled, reaching for her mother as the ambulance crew wheeled the body from the room.

He hadn't even handled that part of it well.

Yes, he'd been in shock himself, but a real father would have *instinctively* protected his child from such a sight. Nearly nine months later, he was no closer to being an adequate father. His little girl merely tolerated him, preferring even a strange woman to him, and all Dr. Stenhope could say was that he shouldn't take it personally!

At times, he wondered if making the move from Tulsa to Fort Worth had been wise. He was willing to do anything—*anything*—to help Larissa. All the doctors and literature said that Dr. Stenhope was the foremost authority on detachment disorders in the entire southwestern part of the country, but Stenhope's treatment didn't appear to be making any headway with Larissa. She certainly hadn't offered him the level of counseling and advice on parenting that he'd expected. Yet, he'd had other reasons for making the move—specifically, Laura's parents.

He was too tired to even think about the Conklins right now. Sometimes he thought he was too tired to breathe. Nevertheless, he still had papers to look over and dinner to clean up after, if hot dogs and canned corn nuked in the microwave could be called *dinner*.

Off to the kitchen, he scraped ketchup from the plates and stacked them in the dishwasher before wiping down the table, floor and wall. Larissa's table manners left much to be desired, but he dared not do more than sit stoically while she slung food around the immediate vicinity. He could imagine what she'd do if he actually reprimanded her.

After the domestic chore was accomplished, Kendal moved to the home office that he'd set up next to his bedroom and opened his briefcase. Rubbing his eyes, he settled down behind the mahogany desk to peruse the documents that had been handed to him that day. The new office was up and running, but they weren't yet fully staffed, so these days he wore several hats as far as the business was concerned.

Any other time, he'd have been thrilled that things were going so well, but now he had more pressing matters on his mind, so much so that the numbers just didn't want to compute tonight. After a couple of hours, he gave up and went to check on Larissa.

She didn't even look peaceful in her sleep. Her eyes twitched beneath her closed lids, and her mouth was constantly pursed. As if she were aware of his disappointment, she sighed and flopped from her side onto her back. Her little hands flexed and then she sighed again and seemed to relax. Kendal bowed his head.

God help her, he thought. *Please help her.*

He meant to say more, but the words wouldn't come out. They felt too trite and repetitive to make it beyond the ceiling, let alone to God's ear. That, too, was his fault. His mom used to say that if he felt far from God, he was the one who had moved.

He missed his mom.

Ironically, that was something that he and his daughter had in common, if only she could know it. His own mother died when he was twelve, having contracted a viral infection that had attacked her heart, and the sadness had never really left him. He understood Larissa's pain more than she could possibly realize, but that seemed of little value at the moment.

Slipping out of her room, he wandered around the dark, silent house. In the few months that they'd been here, he'd come to like this place, situated as it was in a safe, gated community on the eastern edge of Fort Worth. The residents could bike or run around the common green or even ride horses and picnic beside the small lake or creek. There were tennis courts and a weight room, too, but no community pool, as most of the homes, including this one, had their own.

When he'd purchased the property, he'd envisioned Larissa having pool parties and class picnics in a few years. It made a nice contrast to imagining his daughter institutionalized, which was what he really feared would happen.

Too exhausted to keep those fears at bay, he shut

himself into his bedroom, where he collapsed onto his pillow. The house felt cold and empty, even though he could hear the central heater running and knew that Larissa slept just across the hall. Or was it that the coldness and emptiness were inside him?

He didn't know how this had happened. He'd never meant to move so far from the God of his youth, never expected to be so unhappy in his marriage, so inadequate a father. Only God knew how desperately he wanted to fix it, but he simply didn't know how. He tried again to pray, but he'd said the words so often that they no longer seemed worthwhile.

Gradually, he began to slide toward sleep. As he felt his body relax, his rebellious thoughts turned to a subject he had hoped to avoid: Connie Wheeler.

The minister's wife was a kind, considerate woman. She was also lovely—all soft, dainty femininity. He sensed a gentle, willing spirit in her. Larissa was certainly taken with her, and she seemed to have a way with the child. Was it possible that she could somehow help them? Maybe, he mused, as awareness drifted away, that was why God had led him here, to this place and to that church.

He slept on that hope, more comfortable than any pillow, and by morning it had become a notion with a life of its own, a growing part of his consciousness. He tried not to give the idea more credence than it deserved, but throughout the difficult morning, he found himself returning to it, clinging to it, comforting himself with it, even praying that it might be so.

Larissa didn't want to eat and didn't want to take

her bath or have her hair brushed. She didn't want to be changed, and she certainly didn't want to be dressed. Forcing her into her clothes, he prepared her for the day as best he could. In his desperation, he wasn't above bribing her.

"Don't you want to go to nursery school? Don't you want to see Miss Susan? How about Miss Connie?"

He had no idea whether the minister's wife would be around today or not, but he'd have promised the child Santa Claus if it would have stopped her from fighting him. But it didn't help. Larissa remained distraught.

She quieted as soon as they pulled into the parking lot of the day care center, though, and his relief fought with his resentment. His daughter would rather spend the whole day at nursery school, where she wasn't even particularly happy, than two hours with him. The worst of it was, he'd rather be apart from her, too. As he dropped her off, he was aware of a shameful eagerness on his part. He couldn't wait to get to the office, where people actually smiled at him and at least pretended to be glad to have him around. He knew what he was doing there, what was expected of him, and he didn't have to feel that he was inflicting himself on anyone.

How pathetic was he to let a toddler hurt his feelings so much that he wanted to turn away? It was one thing to feel that way about one's spouse, but one's *child?*

Father, forgive me, he prayed, driving away. *I know I disappoint You as much as I disappoint her. And forgive me for that, too.*

The words seemed to bounce off the windshield and sink heavily into his chest, weighing down a heart already heavy with woe.

Chapter Three

Connie opened the door to the church's administrative building and smiled at her brother's secretary, Carlita.

"*Hola,* Miss Connie."

"Hello, Carlita. How are you?"

"*Muy bien.* Do you wish to see the pastor?"

"Yes, I do, actually."

"Go on back. He's been in conference with Miss Dabney for some time now. Surely, they are just about finished."

Connie slipped past Carlita's desk and moved toward the hallway off of which several offices opened, saying, "If they're still talking, I'll wait outside the door."

"If you like, I'll bring you a chair," Carlita offered.

Connie shook her head. "Not necessary. Thanks."

"*De nada.*"

Carlita went back to her typing, her long, black braid swinging between her plump shoulder blades as she turned her head toward the computer screen.

When Marcus had hired the single mother of four,

she had spoken little English, but her need had been great and corresponded precisely with her efforts. Little more than a year later, Carlita was a model of cheerful, dependable efficiency and another of Marcus's success stories.

Stepping into the hallway, Connie saw that the door to her brother's office was only partially closed. She paused a moment, bending her head in an effort to discern whether or not the meeting was coming to an end. She hoped that it was. She had made a decision this morning, and she wanted to speak to Marcus about it before she lost her resolve. Just then, a familiar voice spoke with unexpected sharpness.

"But the child is simply unmanageable."

"When she's frustrated," Marcus replied calmly. "That's what you said a moment ago—that she's unmanageable when she's frustrated and that she dislikes men. I'm not sure that's cause for dismissal."

"It wouldn't be if she wasn't frustrated so much of the time!" Miss Dabney argued.

"All children get easily frustrated. You've told me so often."

"But they don't all throw thirty-minute temper tantrums on a routine basis!"

"Is she a danger or an impediment to the other children?" Marcus asked, the very model of patience.

Miss Dabney's answer sounded grudging. "I suppose not, but she demands a lot of time and attention from the staff."

"I know it's difficult," Marcus said soothingly, "but I'm sorry, Miss Dabney I'm not comfortable dismissing Larissa Oakes. Please, can't you be patient a little longer? Her father is trying to help her."

"If you ask me, he's half the problem," the day care director retorted.

"I'm sure he's doing the best he can under the circumstances."

"She ought to be sent home for the day at the very least," Miss Dabney grumbled, sounding fairly frustrated herself. "She's simply out of control, and I'm afraid she's going to make herself sick if she keeps on the way she is right now. In fact, we have her in the nurse's room."

Marcus sighed. "All right." From the sound of it, he picked up the telephone. A moment later, he dialed a number and only seconds later began speaking.

Connie bowed her head while the call was being made. She'd heard a commotion coming from the infirmary when she'd dropped off Russell a few minutes earlier, but she'd assumed that a child had scraped a knee or something equally innocuous. Probably distance and a closed door had muffled the sounds.

Remembering how distraught little Larissa had been the previous times that she'd dealt with the girl, Connie felt an immediate, almost visceral, impulse to go to her, but it was not her place to do so.

What, she wondered, *would Kendal Oakes do if the church didn't provide day care for his daughter?*

Poor child.

Poor father.

Suddenly, the door swung wide open and Marcus halted in mid-step, jerking his head up.

"Sis! Oh, hi. Did you want to speak to me?"

"It can wait," she told him, backing up.

He held up a finger, almost in supplication.

"One moment."

Stepping into the hallway, he addressed the secretary. "Carlita, would you call down to the nurse's station on the intercom and have Larissa Oakes brought up here, please?"

"Sure thing, boss. Pronto."

"Thank you." He turned back to Connie. "What's wrong?"

"Nothing's wrong. Why would you think something was wrong?"

"Well, you usually wait to talk to me at home, that's all." He smiled and patted her shoulder. "Let me rephrase that. What's so important that it couldn't wait?"

She shook her head, now oddly reluctant to broach the subject of returning to school.

"Uh, nothing actually. We can discuss it later."

"But—"

"Excuse me if I was eavesdropping just now," she hurried on, "but is there a problem with Larissa Oakes?"

Before Marcus could answer, Miss Dabney appeared in the doorway, arms folded.

"You've seen how she reacts," the day care director said.

"Yes," Connie replied, "it's very sad."

"Sadder than either of you even know," Marcus added.

"I know she's experienced trauma in the past," Miss Dabney stated, "and I'm not unsympathetic to the child's situation, but it's very tiring dealing with these scenes day after day."

Connie felt sure that causing those scenes was equally exhausting for Larissa, but she didn't say so out of respect for the director. The whole thing was very puzzling. Connie didn't know if Larissa was hypersensitive, frightened or just spoiled. Perhaps all three.

"Do you know what set her off this time?" she asked Miss Dabney pensively.

"Davy Brocha's dad came at naptime and Larissa had picked up this stuffed tiger of Davy's that he had dropped. Well, Mr. Brocha was in a hurry and maybe he was a little abrupt, but he wanted to take the tiger with him, so he let himself into the classroom, went over and plucked it out of her grasp." Miss Dabney lifted both hands in puzzlement. "She screamed and fell over backward. You'd have thought he'd shot her. Of course, he wasn't even supposed to be in there, but with any other child it wouldn't have mattered. With Larissa, it means at least half an hour of uncontrollable screaming. He tried to comfort her and that just made it worse."

Concern furrowed Connie's brow. So Larissa really was averse to men in general, she mused, not just her father.

"I see."

She didn't really. What could cause such a reaction in a child so young? Whatever it was, Miss Dabney was right about one thing: Larissa clearly was out of control. Connie could hear her shrieks long before the staff nurse carried her into the office.

"Oh, my," Marcus murmured, and he hurried forward

to comfort the child. "Why are you crying, sweetie? Don't you know that no one here will hurt you?"

He reached out a hand to pat her back, but Connie stopped him.

"Marcus, don't."

He never touched the child, but she twisted out of reach anyway, nearly throwing herself out of the nurse's arms.

For a moment, it was pandemonium as everyone rushed to contain the thrashing child before she could hurt herself. Then suddenly, a sharp clap brought everyone to a freezing halt.

"Stop that!" Carlita ordered, her hand still on the book she'd slapped down on the desktop.

The sudden silence felt deafening in its intensity. For an instant, they all stood locked in that silence. Then Larissa's mouth opened up into a howl.

The next instant, the howl became a pathetic burble as the girl spied Connie. She threw out her little arms beseechingly, crying something inarticulate.

Connie did the only thing she could: She hurried to take the shuddering child into her arms.

Larissa wrapped all four of her limbs around Connie and dropped her head onto Connie's shoulder, sniffling and gasping with her tears.

Marcus raised both eyebrows.

The nurse—a young, normally cheerful woman with an infant of her own—looked from Carlita to Connie and drawled, "One of y'all is a genius."

The remaining three looked at Carlita, who shrugged

and said matter-of-factly, "With my kids, first you got to get their attention."

"Words of wisdom," Miss Dabney muttered to Connie, who was rocking Larissa from side to side.

The atmosphere had lightened considerably. Larissa took a deep, shuddering breath, but she was quiet.

"Why don't we take her into my office?" Marcus suggested softly, lifting a hand.

Keeping her movements slow and gentle, Connie preceded Marcus past Miss Dabney and through the hallway into his private office, where she took a seat in the corner. The day care director followed while Marcus instructed Carlita to expect Kendal Oakes and send him right in. Finally, he joined the two women and the child in his office, skirting around behind the desk between Miss Dabney's chair and the bookcase.

The room was small but well arranged, and Marcus enjoyed the view of the chapel in the compound square a great deal. The world seemed a fine place from his office window. Marcus often took comfort in the view during difficult moments. He gave himself a brief moment to do so now before turning to his guests.

"You certainly do have a way with her," he whispered to Connie.

It seemed to him that she had a way with children in general. What a pity that her record kept her from formally working in child care. He'd broached the subject with Miss Dabney early on and had been saddened to learn that Connie's situation effectively prevented her from being licensed to work with kids in most states, including Texas. He firmly believed that Connie had gotten a raw deal, but what was done was done.

Marcus glanced at the curly-haired toddler who sat with her cheek against Connie's chest. Larissa was asleep. Obviously, she had exhausted herself with her tantrum. Marcus hoped she wouldn't become too warm, as she was wearing her coat. Evidently, the nurse had expected Kendal to be there when she arrived with the child.

"She certainly seems fascinated by you," Miss Dabney said softly.

"I wonder if you look anything like her mother," Marcus mused.

Connie looked to those blond curls again, murmuring, "I hadn't thought of that."

"You don't," said a voice flatly, just before Kendal Oakes walked through the open doorway.

"Well, maybe a little around the eyes," he said a few minutes later, leaning forward from the edge of the pastor's desk. "And I suppose you're about the same size."

When he'd first heard the question and realized who it was being asked of, he felt a spurt of denial so fierce that it had momentarily rattled him, but then he took a look at his daughter, sleeping against Connie Wheeler's chest, and the feeling had fizzled into gratitude.

Larissa seemed at peace for the first time in memory. It had occurred to him that, sitting there together, the pair really could have been mother and child, and for the first time, he let himself really study Connie Wheeler.

She was beautiful.

Laura had been pretty in her own way. When they were dating, he'd thought her facial features were neat and symmetrical; later, they had seemed sharp and cold to him.

He couldn't imagine Connie Wheeler that way.

He shouldn't be imagining her any way, especially not with the good parson sitting right behind him.

Kendal realized that he really liked Marcus Wheeler. Moreover, Marcus and Connie made the perfect couple. Even their coloring was complementary. Both were golden, despite the minister's slightly darker hair.

Kendal rubbed his hands over his face, appalled at himself, and fixed his mind on his daughter.

"What happened?"

Miss Dabney explained, keeping her voice low, and despair swept through Kendal, followed swiftly by anger.

"I thought parents were supposed to remain outside of the classroom."

"Yes, they are," Miss Dabney admitted, "but it's a rule, not a law, and easily dealt with all in all. Larissa, on the other hand…"

The day care director darted her eyes at the minister.

Kendal closed his eyes, knowing what was coming even before the minister had cleared his throat. Larissa had already been dismissed from one day care center since they'd arrived in the Fort Worth area.

"We may not be best equipped to deal with her," Marcus said gently.

Kendal swallowed and rose from the corner of the desk, putting his back to the bookcase to face the others.

"I'm aware of Larissa's…special needs. I told you when we came that she's in treatment."

"Private care might be best," Miss Dabney said bluntly.

"I've tried that!" he said, struggling not to raise his voice.

The last thing he wanted was to wake his daughter and have her prove how difficult she could be, but the painful truth was that, in the months since her mother's death, they'd been through four private sitters, only one of whom had seemed able to control Larissa. Then he'd found out that she'd been giving his daughter sleeping pills! That was the closest he'd ever come to becoming violent.

"I'd stay home with her myself if I thought it would do any good," he admitted bitterly.

"Is there no one who could help you?" Connie asked softly. "No one you could trust?"

Kendal shook his head. He couldn't ask his step-mother to take over raising his daughter, and he wouldn't ask his late wife's mother. That would be the worst possible thing he could do.

All right, not the worst possible. The doctor suggested that residential care might be a solution, but Kendal couldn't even think of it. His daughter didn't need to be locked away, for pity's sake. She must already feel abandoned by her mother. How would she feel if he sent her away?

The idea that she might actually feel relief was almost more than he could bear.

If only he could somehow reach her, make her understand that he loved her and wanted to help.

"I simply don't know what to do," he admitted softly.

From the corner of his eye, he caught a look that passed from Connie to Marcus.

"Let's pray about it diligently for a few days," Marcus suggested after a moment, "and see what accommodations we can make."

Kendal nodded, aware of a lump in his throat. It was only a reprieve, of course, and Miss Dabney wasn't looking too pleased about it, but at this point he'd take anything he could get.

He straightened away from the bookcase and looked to Connie, trying his best to remain impassive.

"Thank you. I'll take her home now."

"Let me help you get her into the car," Connie whispered, sliding to the edge of her seat and starting to rise.

He stepped forward automatically, helping her to her feet with his hands cupped beneath her upper arms. Only when she fully stood up, his daughter cradled against her chest, did he realize that they were standing much too close. Abruptly, he released the woman and stepped back.

Larissa shifted, then seemed to settle once more as Connie carried her smoothly from the room. A glance in the pastor's direction showed no obvious signs of any connotation other than simple courtesy being applied to his actions. Nevertheless, Kendal felt guilt shadow him as he followed Connie.

The day care director returned to the day care center, leaving the pastor to bring up the rear.

Larissa grumbled when the bright sunlight and cold air hit her, but at least she was wearing her coat. Next time, she might not be. He made a mental note to put a blanket in the car for such occasions.

Opening up the car door, he stood aside as Connie went through the arduous task of getting a toddler into a car seat. Not surprisingly, Larissa awoke in the process. It was too much to hope that she wouldn't, of course, but once again it meant driving away with his daughter screaming for the woman.

A part of him felt the same way that Larissa did. When he looked into his rearview mirror before turning onto the street and saw Marcus and Connie Wheeler standing there arm in arm, watching his progress, his very soul seemed to plunge to the deepest level of despair.

Marcus placed the bowl of mashed potatoes on the table and took up his fork.

"Looks good," he said, surveying his full plate. "I always thank God that they taught you how to cook at that group home."

Connie smiled. "You always find something to be thankful for in every situation."

"I try," he admitted, cutting into his pan-grilled chicken breast. "I'm having a little trouble with the Oakes situation, though."

Connie steepled her hands over her plate, elbows braced against the tabletop.

"Marcus, you can't just put her out."

"I know. Unfortunately, I have to do something. I spent the afternoon talking to every other day care provider in the area and all of them said that it isn't fair to subject the other children to Larissa's problems, but how do we, as Christians, turn her away?"

"It is such a tragic situation," Connie commented, looking to her son with deep gratitude. Perhaps her own life had not been easy, but Russell was wonderful.

Thank God for Jolie!

Connie leaned forward and caught a dollop of mashed potato in her hand before it hit the floor. Russell grinned and shook his spoon again, sprinkling mashed potato on the tray of his high chair before tossing the spoon overboard and going after his dinner with his fingers. Connie patiently picked up the spoon, cleaned it and lay it aside. They would practice with it later once he'd knocked the edge off his hunger.

"You've no idea *how* tragic, really," Marcus said.

It wasn't the first time he'd made such a comment.

"Can you tell me?" Connie asked, aware that he was bound by ethical considerations.

Marcus thought it over and said, "I can tell you this much. Mrs. Oakes died from an allergic reaction while Kendal was out of town on business and Larissa spent nearly two whole days by herself before he returned."

Connie gasped. "Two days?"

"She was just over a year old at the time," Marcus went on. "I think it traumatized both father and child, and I don't think either one of them was prepared to deal with it. In the nine months since, I think it must have gone from bad to worse, but he's desperately trying. He moved here from Oklahoma because a certain doctor here was recommended to him. He opened a new branch office of his company and everything. My understanding is that the child has been diagnosed with some sort of detachment disorder."

"Oh my," Connie said, remembering that Kendal had mentioned a doctor earlier. "Isn't there anything that we can do?"

Marcus sighed. "There has to be a solution, but frankly, I haven't found one yet. We'll just have to keep praying about it."

"Yes, I will," she vowed, feeling a little guilty because lately her prayers seemed to have been all about her.

At least, she'd found a solution to her situation. She hoped she had anyway.

Broaching the topic with her brother at last, she waited anxiously for his reaction.

"What do you think?"

He wiped his mouth with a napkin and studied his plate for a long time.

"I'm all for education, Connie, you know that. But are you sure that dental hygiene is the right field for you?"

"Why wouldn't it be? It pays well and the hours are flexible."

"Those are good points," he agreed, "but I can't help thinking that you should pursue something that you're really passionate about."

She spread her hands. "Such as what?"

Marcus shrugged. "I don't know. You tell me. What do you feel most passionate about in your life?"

That was easy to answer, but it clearly offered no solution to her dilemma.

"I'm most passionate about being a mother," she said, "but that means that I have to do something to properly support my son."

"But there's no hurry," Marcus argued. "We're not hurting for money."

"It's *your* money, Marcus. I have to start earning my own way sometime."

"You already do. Just look at this fine meal you've cooked for me," he pointed out. Spreading his arms, he went on. "This was just a house before, Connie, somewhere to sleep and change my clothes. You've made it a real home for me."

"And what happens when you marry?" she asked pointedly.

He snorted and went back to his meal, muttering "That's not likely to happen anytime soon—if ever."

"You don't know that! Just look at Jolie and Vince. Six months ago, they didn't even know each other existed."

"Is that what this is about?" he asked with some exasperation. "Jolie's wedding has you thinking that I might be next? Connie, I haven't even been out on a date in... ages."

"And aren't likely to as long as I'm underfoot," she retorted.

He rolled his eyes. "That's not true."

"Then why aren't you dating?"

"I could ask the same thing of you," he pointed out.

"Me?" She thumped herself in the chest with her knuckles. "And who would date *me?*"

"Any man with eyes in his head."

"Any decent man would run fast in the opposite direction as soon as he found out about my past."

Marcus frowned. "You can't believe that."

"Okay, let me put it this way. I don't want anyone who *wouldn't* be upset by my past."

"Connie!" He dropped his fork. "Think about what you're saying. You're limiting God with that attitude. You realize that, don't you?"

"I'm not limiting God. I'm just being realistic," she argued.

"Connie, listen to me. You can't just shut yourself off from possibilities. I mean, we just don't know what God has in store for us. Think about it. Jolie would never have even met Vince if he had forwarded his mail before she moved into his old apartment! If God can use something that simple, surely He can use anything to bring whatever or whomever it is we need into our lives."

"I understand your point," Connie conceded, "and believe me, if God sends me a man who can overlook my past and be the father—"

"And husband," Marcus interrupted pointedly.

"And husband," she amended, "that Russell and I need, I'll be forever grateful."

"Excellent," he said, picking up his fork, "except I think it's *when* not *if,* and in the meantime, I hope you'll reconsider that school thing. I'd really like to see you find something you can be more passionate about than dental hygiene."

"Unfortunately," she pointed out with a sigh, "being a mom is not something about which the world is very passionate."

"Tell that to Larissa Oakes," he muttered.

Connie caught her breath. What if she could…but no. She shook her head.

Child care was not a viable option. Not even the day care center at her brother's church could hire her because of her record. She'd do better to go on to school. There were worse things than dental hygiene—much worse—and who knew, once she got into it, she might discover a passion for it. And so what if she didn't? She had Russell. He was all she needed.

For the moment, she dropped the subject of school, but she wasn't yet willing to let go of it entirely. Marcus meant well. Marcus always meant well because that's the kind of person her big brother had always been.

She, on the other hand, had made grave mistakes that she would have to pay for the rest of her life. Expecting anything else would be not only unrealistic but also presumptuous. After all, how much could a woman in her position expect? God had already blessed her much more richly than she deserved.

Chapter Four

"Baby, don't," Kendal pleaded, trying to pry Larissa's arms from around the day care teacher's neck.

His daughter hadn't been happy for a single moment in his company since she'd awakened after Connie Wheeler had belted her into her car seat the day before. Other times, he'd been able to distract her with music or books or food, but since yesterday, she'd howled every moment that she was awake and in his presence. He tried not to take it personally—he really did—but it was hard not to when his own daughter gave every sign of hating him.

Maybe I should give her up to her grandparents, he thought again, but everything in him rebelled against the idea. She was *his* daughter. He loved her and wanted her with him.

Besides, Laura's parents were cold, stiff people who, in his opinion, had scarred his late wife emotionally. He didn't want them doing the same thing to *his* daughter.

He supposed that his father and stepmother would

take Larissa if he asked, but since his father's retirement, they had become passionate about traveling. He
had never been comfortable asking Louise for anything
anyway.

He had been fourteen when his father married Louise. She had two daughters older than him and neither
had ever paid him much attention. Louise had always
been pleasant, and Kendal had long ago accepted that
she made his father happy, but he could never think of
her as his mother.

Exasperated by the whole situation, he momentarily stopped trying to take his daughter into his arms.
Larissa hung on to Miss Annette like a leech, but she
stopped howling when he stopped trying to take her
from the teacher.

He shoved a hand through his unruly hair. The
woman was a substitute, for pity's sake. She wasn't even
her regular teacher. Larissa couldn't have formed a real
attachment to her in such a short time. He could understand Connie Wheeler, but not her.

Swallowing his pride, he surrendered to the inevitable.

"Is Mrs. Wheeler around?"

Annette gave him a blank look.

"Connie Wheeler," he clarified. "Is she working
today?"

"Oh, Miss Connie doesn't work here," Annette stated
flatly.

He was surprised. She always seemed to be around.
Perhaps she worked elsewhere on the church grounds,
as a secretary or something.

"Where does she work?"

"I don't think she works anywhere," the day care teacher replied, screwing up her face as if thinking required much effort. "I heard she was looking for something, though."

Kendal glanced at his watch, filing that information away. Ministers didn't usually make very much money, and he assumed that the Wheelers could use a little extra income. That, however, was not his problem.

Looked like he was on his own.

Mentally fortifying himself, he reached for his daughter again. She bucked, arched her back and screamed. Resigned to another difficult evening, he physically pulled the child into his embrace. She thrashed for several seconds.

She stopped fighting him by the time he got her to the car and he prayed all the way home that this would be an end to it, at least for the evening.

Connie lifted her chin, pasted on a smile and did her best to set aside her troubling thoughts.

Her afternoon interview at the school had not gone as well as she'd hoped. The counselor had warned her point-blank that many prospective employers would not consider hiring her because of her record. He suggested that she consider a field that did not touch on medicine or the administration of drugs in any form, and he hadn't altered his advice one whit when she explained her situation.

Heartsick, Connie surveyed the school's course offerings again, but nothing that the counselor suggested had seemed workable.

She indulged in a bout of tears as she drove herself back to the church to pick up her son.

She wasn't even inside the building when she heard the commotion, and to her shock, Millie was not at her post. The frail woman came running the instant she heard the chime that signaled the door had been opened, and the look on her face said that the uproar had been going on for some time.

"Miss Connie!" she gasped. "Your brother is even back there."

"Larissa Oakes?" Connie guessed and Millie nodded, her mouth set in a distraught line.

"She didn't want to eat her lunch—not one bite—and when Miss Susan tried to feed her, she started to cry. Then Miss Dabney scolded her and she's been carrying on ever since."

"Is her father here?" Connie asked, already turning toward the hall.

"Yes, and if you ask me," Millie said, "that has only made matters worse."

Connie sent her a disapproving frown as she hurried away.

Anyone could see that the man was doing the best he could. She, for one, was tired of the implication that he was causing this.

Rounding the corner at a near run, she came to a sudden halt, taking in the chaos.

Larissa stood against the wall next to the infirmary door with both arms around the nurse's leg. She was trembling from head to toe, red in the face and wailing, nose and eyes running like faucets while Kendal Oakes and Miss Dabney glared at each other and Marcus and the nurse looked on helplessly.

"Just because she doesn't like corned beef is no reason to label her mentally deficient!" Kendal declared hotly.

"I'm only saying that we can't have her disrupting everything constantly!" Miss Dabney countered. "We have other children here—well children."

"What is *that* supposed to mean?" Kendal demanded. "Are you implying that my daughter is mentally ill?"

"This isn't helping!" Marcus insisted with steady authority. "Everyone just please calm down."

Miss Dabney swallowed whatever she was about to say, folding her arms mulishly. Kendal clamped his jaw, his hands at his waist. Even Larissa shut up, but Connie saw the child's eyes bulge.

She instantly knew what was happening and lunged forward, grabbing Larissa and turning her back on the doorway. A round trash can stood to one side of the door, and Connie pushed Larissa's head over it just as the child spewed the contents of her stomach. When she was finished, she screamed and reached for Connie, who plopped down on the floor beside her and pulled the child into her lap, Larissa's back to Connie's chest.

Kendal dropped to one knee beside them.

He cupped his daughter's cheek with one hand, and said to Connie, "Thank God you came."

Connie nodded. Larissa shuddered and rolled her

head against Connie's chest, but her wails had diminished to hiccupping sobs.

"We could use a damp towel," Connie pointed out softly.

The nurse slipped past them to fulfill that request as Kendal lay his big hand across his daughter's forehead. For once, Larissa did not object.

"Do you think she has a temperature?" he asked worriedly. "Maybe I should call a doctor."

"That's a good idea," Miss Dabney interjected from the doorway, "and she shouldn't return to day care until the doctor has given her a completely clean bill of health."

Kendal bowed his head, a muscle working in the hollow of his jaw.

Connie felt embarrassed for him. Miss Dabney couldn't have been more blatant about wanting Larissa out.

Marcus murmured something to the day care director, who left without another word to anyone.

Suddenly, Kendal lifted his head, looking directly into Connie's eyes.

"Help me," he whispered. "Please. You may be the only one who can."

The nurse handed a damp paper towel to Connie before she could reply to that astonishing plea. Her mind reeling, she mopped the girl's swollen face as Larissa lay gasping against her.

"I'll pay you whatever you ask," Kendal went on, "if you'll come to the house and take care of her."

Connie blew out a breath. For a moment, she couldn't

think, but then what came to mind was the idea that maybe she wasn't ready to go to school yet. She could always go later on. Maybe this was God's will. Maybe it was time that she gave something back for once instead of merely taking His many gifts.

She felt a movement beside her and looked up. Marcus stood in the doorway looking down at her.

"It might be the best solution for everyone," he said softly.

Somehow, Connie felt certain that it was. She looked at Kendal.

"I'd have to bring Russell with me."

"Of course. Whatever you think is best."

Wondering what really was best, Connie tried to take stock. First things first, she supposed.

She placed her hand on Larissa's forehead, which felt cool to the touch now that the child had calmed down.

"Should I call her pediatrician?" Kendal asked, concern etching grooves between his eyebrows.

Connie made a quick decision. A trip to the doctor might be more trouble that it was worth at the moment.

"I don't think so. Wait and see if she throws up again."

He nodded and let out a breath of relief. "All right. If she doesn't, do you think you could start tomorrow?"

Connie looked to Marcus, who shrugged slightly as if to say he didn't see why not. Connie nodded.

"What time would you like us there?"

"About eight. I usually need to be at my desk by half

past eight, but the office isn't even fifteen minutes from the house."

"I don't have your address," she pointed out.

He pulled a business card and an ink pen out of the pocket of his suit coat and quickly jotted down the address, speaking as he did so.

"It's not far. You turn right when you leave here. Go four blocks and make a left at the light. Then it's about three miles to the gates of the subdivision. I'll tell the guard to be expecting you and he'll guide you to the house."

Connie took the card, musing that it must be some house if it was in a gated community. She tucked the card into her pocket and shifted Larissa into a reclining position, her head tucked into the crook of Connie's elbow.

"Did you hear that?" Connie said to the child, wiping her nose again. "Tomorrow, Russell and I will come to see you at your house."

Larissa shuddered with an indrawn breath, her gaze lifting to Marcus before sliding to her father.

"Won't it be fun to have Miss Connie and her little boy come to our house?" Kendal said.

Larissa switched her gaze to Connie's face and Connie sensed that she understood. She sat the child up to face her.

"You be a good girl for Daddy tonight and eat a good dinner and Russell and I will come to your house to play in the morning. Okay?"

Larissa blinked but said nothing. Connie wondered if she ever spoke. She was certainly old enough, but then

Russell was, too, and he seldom spoke. Marcus teased that he was too lazy to talk, and he certainly was laid-back. Connie sensed that, in Larissa's case, the child was trapped behind a wall of confusion and doubt. She wondered, for a moment, if she could really help this child. Her experience was severely limited, after all. She concluded that she could hardly do worse than anyone else had done.

"If you'll take her, I'll walk out to the car with you," Connie said to Kendal.

She could see him steeling himself before reaching for his child. "It's time to go home now, Larissa, and Miss Connie and Russell will come to see you at our house tomorrow," said Kendal.

Larissa grunted, but she didn't fight or cry, at least not until Kendal was carrying her down the hallway and she realized that Connie was not keeping up. Connie saw it the moment that panic registered in Larissa's eyes, but it wasn't fear of her father that seized the child.

Connie knew that look. She'd seen it on the faces of her brother and sister; she'd seen it in the mirror.

It was the fear of being without someone.

No doubt, Larissa equated Connie—and perhaps any young woman—with her mother. She was obviously seeking comfort in the only way that she knew how. Connie knew exactly what she was feeling for she had felt it herself, the panic of abandonment, the desperation for attachment.

Feeling a tightness in her own chest, Connie ran to catch up, reaching out a hand to Larissa.

"It's okay," she said around the lump in her throat.

"You go with Daddy now and I'll come tomorrow with Russell. Promise."

But the panic had already set in. Larissa fought as Kendal belted her into her car seat, crying for Connie, who continually assured the child that she would see her again in the morning.

Once Larissa was securely belted in, Kendal turned to Connie.

"I don't know how to thank you. I *know* this is the best thing for her. I just know it."

Connie nodded, afraid she might cry if she tried to speak. He turned away and, in a moment, the car was turning right onto the street.

Connie felt Marcus at her elbow.

"Did you see that look on her face?" she whispered.

Marcus shifted his feet before answering. "Yes. And the awful truth is, her mama will never come back, either."

"But she has her father," Connie reminded them both, "and eventually, he'll find a way to make everything right for her. That's more than we had."

"I don't know about that," Marcus replied. Sliding his arm around her shoulders, he smiled at her. "We've always had one another."

Connie lay her head on his shoulder, confessing, "I thought we'd lost that, too."

"We may have lost Jo for a time," he said, "but I knew it couldn't be permanent. God always has a plan, Sis. He always has a plan."

She believed that. Maybe she'd stumbled onto His plan for her, unless…

"Kendal Oakes doesn't know about me, does he?" she said, worried.

Marcus shrugged. "I don't see what difference that makes. Tell him when you're ready. Meanwhile, remember that you may be his only chance right now."

"His only chance for what?"

"His only chance to have a normal life with his daughter."

Connie had her doubts about that, but Marcus had been her only chance to have a normal life with her son, and he'd risked much to be there for her. It seemed that the least she could do was return the favor now that the opportunity had presented itself.

All right, God, she prayed silently, *if this is what You want, I'll give it my best shot.*

If nothing else, she thought, she could perhaps give everyone some respite from the daily struggle. She would hope for more, but just that would be enough for now.

Larissa bowed her back and wailed. Connie calmly but firmly lifted the child off her lap and deposited her on the floor. Larissa promptly threw herself facedown, screeching like a banshee. But Connie had learned a thing or two over the past few days.

"If you want to sit on my lap while I feed Russell, you'll have to behave," Connie told her gently but firmly.

To Connie's immense relief and delight, Larissa

stopped wailing. She sat up, poking out her bottom lip and gasping pathetically. That was good enough for Connie. She reached out with both hands and Larissa climbed to her feet and walked into Connie's arms.

"That's my good girl," Connie cooed, as she lifted the girl onto her lap.

She began once more to oversee Russell's lunch.

Her son had shown no desire whatsoever to learn how to properly feed himself, but unlike Larissa, he didn't intentionally make a mess. Connie quickly learned that Larissa would throw her food around in a bid for attention or a fit of pique. Once appeased, she would demonstrate quick facility with a spoon, though.

Russell, on the other hand, preferred to sit there with his mouth open like a baby bird while she shoveled in the food. In a pinch, he'd use his hands, but he'd really rather be fed and he didn't care whether or not she fed him with Larissa on her lap.

Connie shook her head because, while she'd been dealing with Larissa, Russell had again abandoned his spoon and gobbled down as many green peas with his hands as he could. She suspected that more were mashed on his face than had actually gotten into his mouth. He grinned unrepentantly, proving her right. At least, he was unfailingly good-natured about the whole thing.

Chuckling, Connie took up the spoon and filled it with peas. Russell's mouth fell open and she poked the peas into it. While he chewed, she closed his fist around the handle of the spoon and helped him fill the bowl.

He made a swipe at his face with the thing and only half the peas rolled off the tip of the spoon this time before it got to his mouth. His second try was less successful because he couldn't load as many peas onto the spoon by himself as she could. After the third attempt, he once again abandoned the spoon and went after the peas with his hands.

Connie let him. Soon, at Jolie's suggestion, she would switch to foods that he could not eat easily with his hands, so he'd have no choice but to learn how to use the spoon.

From the beginning, Larissa had displayed a certain amount of jealousy toward Russell. Thankfully, he seemed completely unconcerned about her, which made things easier. Meanwhile, Connie had learned to use that dynamic in her favor, coercing and directing Larissa's behavior with praise for Russell's and reinforcing it with praise for Larissa's whenever she copied him. As a result, Larissa had begun to learn what behaviors got her what she wanted.

All in all, Connie felt that she'd had a certain amount of success with the girl. It was a pity that her father couldn't see it because Larissa consistently had a meltdown when it came time for Connie to leave.

She still didn't know what to do about that.

Before she could further ponder the problem, Larissa reached out and grabbed Russell's abandoned spoon. She scooped up a few peas on the end of it, but instead of eating them herself, as Connie expected, Larissa leaned forward and offered the peas to Russell.

He seemed bemused at first, but then he leaned down and opened his mouth. Connie held her breath as Larissa managed to deposit a couple of the tiny, green spheres into Russell's gaping maw. Afterward, she smacked down the spoon as if to challenge.

Connie laughed as Russell picked up the spoon and began to eat the remaining peas one at a time. As if coaching him, Larissa smacked her hands on the high chair tray. Russell seemed to ignore her, but he very studiously ate his peas.

"Well, aren't you the clever one," Connie praised, hugging Larissa.

Apparently, Larissa had decided that it was time to turn the tables. Instead of learning from Russell, she now seemed prepared to teach him a thing or two. That felt like real progress to Connie. She dropped a kiss on top of Russell's head, thinking that she'd have to report this development to Jolie as soon as the kids went down for their naps.

She'd started out putting them down in different rooms, but as their one-sided rivalry developed, she'd rethought that. Jolie had consulted her mother- and sisters-in-law and all had agreed that putting them down in the same room, perhaps even the same bed, was the right tack to take.

Since the house contained only one crib—and, of course, one high chair—Connie had gone the extra step and began to put them down in the same bed. As a result, the children now seemed to share a growing camaraderie and attachment.

Connie took great pleasure in having her judgment confirmed. Now if only she could convince Larissa that she would routinely return in the morning, all would be well.

Or would it?

Larissa still didn't appear to be bonding with her father. And what about the coming weekend?

Keeping Larissa calm on weekdays was one thing; the rest of her life was another.

Of course, Connie realized that she was not responsible for Larissa's total well-being, but she couldn't help feeling sorry for both father and daughter. She knew Kendal would sell himself short if his daughter could find some peace, and she feared that that was what he was doing.

They had spoken little since the inception of this arrangement. At first, he called several times a day to check on the situation, but by the third day, the routine had evolved into a quick goodbye in the morning, which Larissa routinely ignored, and a daily report by Connie in the evening. He always seemed pleased by the day's account, but afterward, when Connie took her leave, he seemed to accept Larissa's rejection and histrionics with tired resignation.

Connie couldn't help feeling that he should expect more—more from his daughter, more from himself, more from everyone, perhaps even the doctor to whom he dragged Larissa twice weekly.

But it wasn't her place to say what he should or should not do. After all, she was certainly not an expert on child-rearing. In actuality, she'd only been a mother for a few months. Besides, she reminded herself, Kendal and Larissa had professional help, high-powered professional help, at that, and yet, Connie couldn't help wondering how much progress Larissa had made under the doctor's care. It wasn't her business, of course, so she wouldn't ask. She was the sitter—nothing more—a well-paid sitter at the end of the week but still just the sitter nevertheless.

Oddly enough, she found the role of being Larissa's sitter almost as fulfilling as being Russell's mom, so much so that she had to remind herself, quite forcefully, that it was a temporary situation at best.

Children grow up, after all.

Needs—like circumstances—change.

When that happened, she could always go on to school, if that was part of God's plan for her. If not, then He would have something else in store.

In the meantime, she prayed that she could somehow make a real difference in the lives of Larissa and Kendal Oakes. It broke her heart to see sadness in their eyes.

Pain had become a tangible entity in the Oakes household, and Connie had begun to feel an overwhelming desire to banish it. With that in mind, she patiently put up with Larissa's possessiveness and repeated tantrums without slighting Russell or rewarding Larissa's unacceptable behavior. With repeated praise and reinforcement for good behavior, the tantrums were beginning to wane, thankfully.

"Let's go play," she suggested, setting Larissa on her feet and reaching for the tray of the high chair.

Larissa grabbed hold of her pant leg and tugged, but Connie just smiled down at her.

"One minute, baby. Let me get Russell cleaned up so we can go play. Okay?"

Larissa said nothing, but she watched with large, solemn eyes as Connie mopped Russell's hands and face before lifting him out of the chair.

Taking each child by the hand, Connie walked them into the large, comfortable den, where an array of toys had been scattered. Connie folded her legs beneath her and sat down. Larissa immediately crawled onto her lap.

"What shall we play?" Connie asked.

Russell grabbed a musical toy with which Larissa had earlier shown great fascination and, as expected, Larissa grunted and reached for it. Connie took it instead and coaxed Russell onto her lap beside Larissa. Holding the toy out of their reach, she pressed a button and waited a couple of seconds for the music to play. Then she began to rock from side to side and clap her hands in time with the tune.

Soon, Russell was clapping along, too, and finally Larissa began to join in.

A sense of satisfaction overwhelmed Connie. She laughed impulsively, and Russell put back his head, laughing with her, though he couldn't have known what he was laughing about. At once, Larissa copied his behavior, though her laughter contained no actual mirth. Connie hugged them both.

One day, she promised herself, *Larissa would know joy.* God willing, one day soon.

Chapter Five

Kendal stared at the two high chairs in his kitchen and marveled at the changes that had come to this household.

Connie had brought along a used high chair that very first morning, asking sheepishly if he minded and promising to make room for the extra chair in his kitchen. She had done that by moving a small potted tree to the corner near the bay window behind the breakfast table. It was something she could have moved to the garage, for all he cared. The decorator had placed it there and the housekeeper kept it watered during her twice-weekly visits.

He could have kicked himself for not realizing that she would need two high chairs. She had two children to feed, after all. Unfortunately, he hadn't thought of that because his world—he realized with a jolt—had pretty much narrowed to his concern for his daughter.

He'd learned to use work to hold his concern at bay during the day—otherwise, his business would have floundered by now—but it had never been about business. He'd used work to numb the pain of rejection long before Laura had died.

In the months since her death, thoughts of Larissa had never been far from the surface of his mind. Lately, those thoughts more often included some notion of Connie Wheeler, a development that he viewed with equal parts gratitude and dismay.

No one could deny that the woman was proving to be a godsend. At least for the hours that Connie was present, Larissa seemed happy. And though she routinely screamed and wailed when Connie left each evening, she seemed more content and more responsive—so much so that he'd taken to shamelessly bribing his little girl with promises of Connie's return.

"Eat your dinner, Larissa, and Connie will come again in the morning."

"Let Daddy soap your hair now, so you'll smell sweet for Connie tomorrow."

"Go to sleep and Connie will be here when you wake up."

Beyond the obvious benefit to his daughter, Kendal found that he liked having Connie and Russell around the house. Despite the fact that he did as much as he could to limit their interaction, having them there made the place feel more lived in—more like a real home.

It also somehow contributed to his loneliness.

He'd accepted the fact that Larissa might never come to care for him as a normal daughter ought to. That ugly pronouncement had come straight from the doctor's mouth, and he thought that he'd dealt with it. Yet, for some reason, walking around the house and seeing evidence of the Wheelers' presence made him feel as if he were on the outside looking in again.

That's how he'd felt with Laura after Larissa was born, on the outside looking in.

Maybe that's how he would always feel.

It wasn't a pleasant thought, but if Larissa could somehow grow up with some semblance of normalcy, he would strive to be content. Normalcy, however, was not yet achieved, for if the week had been somewhat less dramatic than most, the weekend was not.

Larissa was miserable when she realized that Connie wasn't coming on Saturday and had only consented to getting dressed for church on Sunday because he promised her that she would see Connie there. She searched the hallways for Connie once they arrived and then smiled with delight when she saw Russell in the nursery school. She actually called out for him.

"Russ!"

He looked up from the toy truck with which he was occupying himself, smiled and went back to playing, but when Larissa ran over and plopped down next to him, he included her in the game, pushing the truck at her and drawing it back, all the while providing the appropriate sound effects.

Kendal felt a spurt of delight. His daughter had a friend—a real friend. He tried not to think that she preferred her little friend to him, but he was not able to escape that reality when it came time to go home again.

He had promised Larissa that she would see Connie,

and he felt it was important that he keep his promises to his daughter. Connie, bless her, made time to sit down with Larissa for several minutes, but in the end, it was just as he'd feared. Larissa screamed and begged for Connie as he carried her to the car. Only promising her that she'd see Connie and Russell the next morning calmed her, but she was easily set off for the remainder of the day. Larissa's joy at seeing Connie again on Monday morning cut Kendal to the quick, but it was worth it to see his little girl actually happy for a time.

Letting himself into the house that afternoon, Kendal headed toward the back hallway, tired from a long day at work. When he heard giggles coming from the hallway, he stumbled to a halt. Was that Larissa?

Following the sound, he found himself standing at Larissa's bedroom door.

Connie sat on the floor, her legs folded. Larissa sat astride one jeaned thigh while Russell occupied the other. A book lay open on the floor in front of them and Connie was mimicking the goggle-eyed character on the page. Both children seemed to find this hilarious.

Kendal felt his heart sing at the sound of his daughter's laughter. She tossed her head back, curls bouncing, and let the sound trickle up out of her throat. He covered his mouth with his hand, momentarily overcome by emotion.

Connie suddenly realized he was there and jerked her head around, smiling lavishly over her shoulder.

"Hello."

Dropping his hand, he cleared his throat.

"Hi."

"We're reading a book," she said needlessly.

"I see that."

"I brought it from home. I hope you don't mind."

"Why should I?"

"Some parents would."

"I trust your judgment."

Connie dropped her gaze.

"Oh, thank you."

Kendal blinked. What had just happened? Had he made her uncomfortable with a simple statement of trust? Surely, she didn't think he would have her here in his home caring for his daughter if he didn't feel that he could trust her implicitly. Had he seemed too familiar, too personal?

He cleared his throat again.

"How is the good padre these days?"

Connie beamed a smile at him.

"Oh, Marcus is fine. Busy, but that's how he likes it."

"He's a good minister."

"Yes," she said proudly. "Yes, he is."

And a good husband and father, too, no doubt, Kendal thought.

Sighing inwardly, he clamped down on the envy stirring to life inside of him. It wasn't Marcus's fault that he'd succeeded where Kendal had so abysmally failed.

The hard fact of his life was that he had failed both Laura and Larissa. As a result, he would never be able to make it up to Laura now and his daughter preferred the company of almost anyone else to him.

A toxic brew of bitterness and guilt momentarily threatened to overwhelm him, but Connie's understanding smile kept him from wallowing in what would have been fruitless emotion. It would have been no more than he deserved, of course, and if punishing himself would give his daughter the peace and contentment that she deserved, he'd gladly endure a lifetime of self-recrimination. But such was not the case, at least, according to the doctors and the reverend.

Kendal couldn't help wondering how much the pastor had told his wife. How much of her understanding came from her knowledge of his culpability and how much from the goodness of her heart?

Those were questions, he quickly decided, that he didn't really want answered. It was best to keep his distance. He could do that. He'd had plenty of practice.

"How was your day?" Connie asked as she rose from the floor. It seemed the polite thing to do.

"Fine," he answered tersely. "Busy. And yours?"

"Pretty much the same," she replied, stooping slightly to scoop Russell up in her arms as he tried to climb her legs.

Larissa demanded the same treatment, yanking on Connie's jeans and lifting up onto her tiptoes with a whine. She cast wary glances at her father as Connie bent and wrapped an arm around her waist. Straightening, Connie parked a child on each hip. She noticed that Kendal stayed in the doorway and didn't interject himself into the scene physically.

"Do they do this to you often?" he asked.

"They sure do, but that's okay. The Cutlers say it'll get better soon."

"The Cutlers?" he echoed uncertainly.

"My sister's in-laws," Connie explained. "Her husband, Vince, comes from a large, gregarious family. They're a more-the-merrier group and they've kind of adopted Marcus and Russ and me."

"Ah."

She put her nose to Russell's and said, "You're wet, buddy boy. Better change you before we hit the road."

Carrying both kids to the change table, she sat Larissa on one end and lay Russell in the middle.

"Can you hold this for me?" she asked Larissa politely, handing her a diaper.

She'd learned that enlisting Larissa's help made her feel included and prevented her from demanding to be changed just because Russell was.

As she worked, Connie remained acutely aware of Kendal hovering in the doorway. Perhaps engaging him in conversation would dispel some of the awkwardness.

"So what about you? Do you have much family?"

"No."

"Neither do I." She took the diaper from Larissa, thanked her and lifted Russell to slide the diaper beneath him. "Just my brother and sister."

"I see."

"Do you have any brothers or sisters?"

"No, uh, just my father really."

"That's a blessing," Connie told him blandly. "I never knew my father."

Or maybe that was the blessing, she thought, smoothing down the tapes on the diaper. If her father was anything like Russell's, she was better off *not* knowing him.

She dreaded the day that she would have to explain his father's situation to her son and regretted that he would have to carry the name of a criminal for the rest of his days. It didn't seem fair. Russell certainly hadn't been given any choice in the matter.

Connie pulled up Russell's corduroys and lifted him into a sitting position. Larissa reached for her immediately and Connie smiled down at the girl before bending slightly to sweep an arm around each child and settle them once more on her hips.

Soon, they would be too big for this, she mused.

She turned to face Kendal knowing that he didn't try to take his daughter from her because he realized that Larissa preferred her. It would break her heart if the situation were reversed. She suspected that it was breaking his. His gaze lingered on Larissa for a moment, then lifted to meet Connie's.

He surprised her by asking, "How is it that you never knew your dad?"

"He just wasn't around," she said matter-of-factly. "I'm not sure my mother even knew who he was."

He blinked at her and she could tell that he was shocked, but maybe he needed to know that there were situations more dysfunctional than his own.

"I barely even knew my mom, actually," Connie went on. "She wasn't around much, and she left for good before I was seven."

"Left?" Kendal echoed, raising his eyebrows. "You mean, *left* as in passed away?"

"I mean *left* as in she took off with some guy and didn't come back."

There. If that didn't have him yanking his daughter out of her arms, maybe the rest of it wouldn't, either.

"Man, that sounds rough," he murmured, lifting a hand to the back of his neck.

"It was," Connie admitted. "We grew up in foster care, which, believe me, is not ideal."

"You seem to have turned out pretty well," he commented softly.

Connie felt her mouth flatten.

"I've made my share of mistakes, and then some." She should tell him now, she realized, all of it. But when she opened her mouth, something else entirely came out. "We later found out that our mother had died in an accident."

"That's tough," he said.

"She'd been gone a long time by then."

"It doesn't matter. I know what it's like to lose a parent. My own mother died when I was twelve. It was her heart."

"I'm sorry."

"I guess you just never know how life is going to turn out."

"You are certainly right about that."

"Maybe it's better that way," he mused.

"No doubt," she said, looking at Russell.

Would she have chosen the path she'd taken if she'd known what the consequences would be? Probably not. Not at the price of another person's life.

But then there would have been no Russell.

"Look, I don't mean to be abrupt," she said abruptly, "but it's my sister's birthday and we're expected for dinner, so I really have to run. Will you be all right?"

"Oh." He looked at Larissa, who had grasped fistfuls of Connie's shirt and was locking her legs around Connie's waist in anticipation of the inevitable parting. "We'll manage."

Warily, he reached for his daughter, who drew back and screeched.

"Now, now," Connie scolded gently, "where's my good girl?"

Larissa stopped screeching, but her eyes filled with tears and her bottom lip quivered mutinously.

"Tell you what," Connie said to Kendal. "You take Russell and let's go into the living room."

She held his gaze, telegraphing that they would make the switch there.

Kendal looked at the boy, who stared back at him expectantly. Connie twisted, placing Russell within his reach. Kendal swung the boy into his arms. Russell stared at him curiously for a moment, then reached up to pat his cheek as if assuring him that he wasn't going to bite.

"Hi, there," Kendal said, smiling warily.

Larissa instantly stiffened.

Well, well, thought Connie, *she wasn't as indifferent as she pretended.*

Connie moved forward, prompting Kendal to step back and clear the doorway. She turned into the hallway and walked down it, Larissa on her hip. Larissa looked back at her father as if she was trying to decide whether or not she liked this new arrangement.

Carrying Larissa, Connie led the way into the den. Along the way, Russell giggled at something Kendal did. Connie looked back over her shoulder in time to see Russell pulling up his shirt so Kendal could tickle him again. Kendal chuckled and complied.

"Tickling is one of his favorite games," Connie informed him, smiling indulgently as she came to a halt near the entry.

She had placed her things conveniently in hand earlier in anticipation of this moment. So far, Larissa seemed to be taking in everything with wary curiosity, but Connie knew that histrionics were soon to come.

It was a shame, Connie thought, *that she couldn't arrange a little more of this group interaction.* Larissa might come to look at her father a little differently. Russell certainly seemed taken with him.

"I, um, hope your sister enjoys her birthday," Kendal said, reminding her that it was time to go.

"Oh, she will," Connie assured him. "It's a surprise. Her husband has arranged it all."

"I see."

"Can you hold them both for a moment?" Connie asked.

"Uh, I'm not sure."

"I think you can," she told him meaningfully. "Let's try. All right?"

"I-if you think so."

Connie leaned in close to Larissa, who still didn't seem to know what to make of the situation. She stared hard at Russell as if trying to figure out what he could be thinking, and that's when Connie passed Larissa to Kendal. To his evident surprise, she went to him easily.

Kendal jostled both children awkwardly for a moment, then settled one on each hip as Connie had done earlier.

Russell leaned forward and touched Larissa's cheek with one hand, the other resting on Kendal's shoulder.

For an instant, Connie's heart stopped. Something about that scene literally stole her breath away, but then Kendal shifted and Connie reached for Russell.

Before his weight had even settled into her arms, Larissa was screeching and reaching for them.

Kendal quickly wrapped both arms around his daughter, who bucked and twisted in an attempt to free herself. Connie felt Kendal's disappointment as keenly as if it were her own.

"Larissa," she said loudly and sharply, but the child didn't even draw a breath. Connie tried again. "Larissa, I want you to be a good girl for Daddy. Russ and I will see you tomorrow."

Larissa howled and threw herself backward. Thankfully, Kendal kept her from falling.

Frustrated for him, Connie mouthed the words "I'm sorry."

He shook his head, clutching Larissa tightly. "No need. Go on now. We don't want you to be late for the surprise party."

Connie quickly turned away, stooped and snatched up her belongings: a large bag and their two coats. With one last look, she slipped into the entry hall, Russell riding her hip and hanging on with both hands. Larissa's outraged screams followed them through the door.

Pausing on the covered portico, Connie managed to get Russell's coat on him. It wasn't terribly cold, and her old car, which Jolie had given her after Vince had bought Jo a new one, was just steps away, so she wouldn't bother with her own coat.

Russell listened to the howls coming from inside the house, pointed to the door and commented solemnly, "Rissa."

"I know," Connie answered, "but she'll calm down soon. Her daddy will take care of her."

Russell pointed again. "Daddy," he said.

"Larissa's daddy," Connie clarified, her heart squeezing.

How soon, she wondered, before he asked that fateful question "Mommy, where's *my* daddy?"

What she wouldn't give for that day never to come.

Kendal plopped down in an armchair, his back to the foyer, with Larissa stiff as a board on his lap.

"They'll be back in the morning," he promised, jerking his head as Larissa's fist whizzed past his chin.

She hadn't really tried to hit him; she just wanted off

his lap. Easing his hold, he let her slip down onto the floor and then followed suit, trying to reason with her.

"Larissa, it's okay. I'm here and Connie will be back in the morning."

She threw herself backward, screaming at the top of her lungs.

He barely caught her in time to keep her from hitting her head on the floor.

"Larissa," Kendal said somewhat impatiently, "you know she's coming back in the morning. Don't do this to yourself."

Larissa wrenched out of his grasp and rolled onto her belly, wailing and kicking.

Suddenly, something inside Kendal snapped.

"Stop it!" he shouted.

She jerked her head up and froze, eyes and mouth wide.

He didn't know which one of them was more surprised.

Then she popped up on all fours and scuttled away from him. Before he even knew what was happening, she was under the coffee table, curled up into a ball and sobbing wildly.

Kendal sat stunned, so weary and appalled that he thought he might cry himself. She'd never really been afraid of him. At least, he didn't think she had.

Until now.

He closed his eyes, drew up his legs, propped his hands on his knees and dropped his head into them.

For one fleeting instant, he had felt what it was like to have a normal child—one who didn't screech and wail at the prospect of going into his arms. He hoped that Connie and Marcus knew how blessed they were.

What a delight it had been to hold little Russell!

Unlike Larissa, who always seemed stiff and tense, Russell had felt like a soft, heavy plush toy in his arms. He hadn't seemed frightened at all. In fact, he'd just wanted to play.

What Kendal wouldn't give just to play with his daughter!

Instead, she cowered under the coffee table, sobbing for Connie.

It wasn't fair to blame her, and he didn't. He really didn't, but it still hurt to be so thoroughly rejected.

He looked up at her, resigned to waiting out another fit.

How had this happened? he wondered. He'd had a fairy-tale childhood until his mother had taken ill, and even then, his parents had done everything in their power to keep her disease from negatively impacting his life.

Her loss had been devastating, but he'd never doubted her love for him for a moment, never wanted any other mom but her. Maybe that was why he had never quite been able to warm up to his stepmother. Louise was a nice lady, and Kendal didn't begrudge his father the companionship, but Katherine Barrett Oakes had left such an indelible mark on his life that he couldn't imagine anyone else actually taking her place—not that Louise had tried. She'd seemed to sense from the beginning that she couldn't hold a candle to his beloved mom.

If anyone should have turned out to be the expert

parent, it should have been him, not Connie Wheeler, who had never even known her father and lost her poor excuse for a mother much younger than he had lost his own excellent one. Yet, Connie was the happily married one, raising a perfectly well-adjusted child, while he…he was a failure, as a father, as a husband, even as a man.

Just look what had happened to his marriage.

Listen to his daughter begging for the babysitter instead of her only parent.

And the worst part of it was, he had no idea what to do about any of it.

Larissa did not eat her supper—not a single bite. No matter how much Kendal cajoled and pleaded, Larissa did nothing but sit in her high chair, scream and pull at her hair. He felt like pulling out his own hair before long.

Hoping that a bath might calm her, he ran a tub, but she fought him and slipped on the tile, nearly cracking her head again. He wanted to scream, wanted to lock himself in a quiet room somewhere and never come out.

The thought that he might lose control rattled him so much that he immediately calmed down. He dressed her in pajamas and tried to interest her in one of her favorite books. She knocked it from his hands.

He turned on some lullaby music. She drowned it out.

After hours of ceaseless tears, he was at his wit's end.

"God, what do I do?" he asked, sitting her on the floor at his feet. "What do I do?"

When he opened his eyes, he found her looking up at him with such anguish that it felt as if his heart were being ripped from his chest. The last shred of anger evaporated.

"Daddy's here," he said, scooping her up into his lap.

She collapsed against his chest with a pitiful wail—as if seeking comfort.

A horrid thought seized him. Could she possibly understand that her mother had *died?* Did she fear that every time Connie walked away from her that she, too, would die and never return?

He felt her wet cheek against his chest and clutched her heaving little body with both arms.

How did he make her understand that Connie was coming back?

Maybe, he thought suddenly, *if she could just hear Connie's voice on the telephone, that would help.*

Holding Larissa close, he shot to his feet and headed across the hall to the phone beside his bed. He'd programmed the Wheelers' home phone number on his speed dial the first day Connie had come to the house. Hitting the appropriate keys, he sat on the edge of the bed. As the phone dialed and rang, he rocked Larissa against him, murmuring that they were going to talk to Connie, that she would come tomorrow as usual, that everything was okay.

After what seemed like an eternity, Marcus answered the phone.

"Hello."

"Pastor!" Kendal began.

"I'm unable to take your call right now," Marcus's voice droned on. "I'm sorry I missed you, but please leave a message at the sound of the tone and I'll get back to you as soon as possible. If this is an emergency, please dial…"

Gritting his teeth, Kendal tried to memorize the number that the minister's voice reeled off. Telling himself that this *was* an emergency, he hung up and quickly punched in the numbers, praying he'd gotten them right.

Larissa slid into the crook of his arm, sobbing somewhat more softly now, and he knew that she was at the point of exhaustion.

On the second ring, the real Marcus answered. Kendal could hear laughter in the background and remembered that they had gone to her sister's surprise birthday party.

"Marcus Wheeler. How can I help you?"

Kendal closed his eyes, partly with relief, partly with mortification.

"Pastor, I'm so sorry to bother you, but I really, really need to speak to your wife."

For an instant, he actually thought the man was going to refuse and Kendal couldn't have said that he would blame him, but then Marcus asked, "Kendal, is that you?"

"Yes. Didn't I say? I'm sorry. I know it's an imposition, but could I please speak to her for just a moment?"

Another pause followed, then, "Connie, you mean. You want to speak to Connie?"

"Yes!" Kendal practically shouted it at him. "Yes, of course, I want to speak to—"

"My sister," Marcus interrupted pointedly.

Stunned, Kendal felt his world shift, tilt and tumble.

When it righted itself again, it was not the same world that he had known a moment earlier.

Chapter Six

Kendal looked around the room in disbelief. This was his bedroom in his house and his daughter whose quivering form he held in his lap. Yet, everything was somehow different.

He must be dreaming. Surely he was dreaming.

Except that *was* the phone that he held pressed hard against his ear. Too hard. Too hard, surely, to have heard correctly.

"Uh, did you say—"

"Connie is my sister," the pastor's voice confirmed carefully. "Hold on, she's coming over. Do I hear Larissa crying?"

Kendal thought he replied in the affirmative, but he couldn't be sure as the pastor then answered his own question.

"Yes, of course, poor baby. Neither of us is married, by the way. Here she is."

Not married? *Neither* of them married?

Kendal's mouth was hanging open when Connie came on the line.

"Ken? What's wrong? Is she okay? What can I do?"

"Uh." He clamped his jaw closed, swallowed and tried again. "Ju-just talk to her. She, uh, needs to know you're—" *Not married!* "Alive. I—I think. That is, I think if she could just hear your voice, she'd know you're coming back."

"Put the phone up to her ear," Connie directed.

He did that and said, "Larissa, it's Connie. Can you hear her?"

"Hi, baby," he heard Connie say from a great distance before his mind whirled off onto the logical tangent.

They weren't married! They were brother and sister!

Just my brother and sister, she had said. How was he supposed to know that Marcus was her brother? She talked all the time about her sister Jolie, but not once had she mentioned her brother, Marcus. Not once! All this time, he'd been thinking that she was the pastor's wife and she was the man's *sister!* How dare she let him think that they were married!

He realized that Larissa had grown quiet, save for a few gasps, as her breathing evened. Looking down, he saw that her eyes were tracking back and forth as she listened intently to whatever Connie was saying. Then she nodded as if in reply. She didn't know enough to actually speak into the phone yet, but *he* certainly did.

"I need to speak to Connie now," he muttered firmly,

pausing a moment to let them say goodbye before lifting the receiver to his own ear.

"I can't believe this," he said rather sharply.

"It's okay. You were right to call, and I think you were right about her thinking something might happen to me," Connie said.

"Obviously," he snapped. "That's not the point. You misled me."

"I what?"

"You misled me! I don't know if you did it on purpose or not, but you had me believing you were married!"

Silence followed that pronouncement and then the sound of a deep breath.

"I see. It was a reasonable assumption, I guess. I have—"

"The same last name!" he all but shouted.

"A child," she said at the same time.

At the moment, he wasn't quite sure what Russell had to do with anything. Child or no child, he'd have assumed they were married unless specifically told otherwise, which was exactly the point.

"What was I supposed to think?"

"I know. I'm sorry."

"Was it on purpose?"

"On purpose?" she echoed. "Uh, I'm not sure…"

Suddenly, he didn't even want to know. If she'd misled him on purpose, then she clearly had her reasons— reasons he probably wouldn't like—and if she hadn't misled him on purpose, he was an idiot.

Good grief. He *was* an idiot.

Biting back a groan, he closed his eyes again.

She'd never said they were married. No one had ever said they were married. He remembered the odd look he'd gotten when he'd referred to her as Mrs. Wheeler. This was his fault. He'd assumed, naturally, and he'd gone on assuming…

"I'm sorry," he said quickly.

"It's all right" was her somewhat-stilted reply. "As long as Larissa is okay, that's all that matters."

Larissa. He looked down at his daughter. She lay quietly in his arms, watching him beneath drooping eyelids, breathing through her mouth. He had to try to get some food into her before she collapsed entirely.

"Thank you," he said tautly to Connie.

"No problem," she replied tersely.

"E-enjoy your party."

"Right. Goodbye then."

"Bye," he said, just as the phone clicked.

He dropped the receiver into its cradle and bowed his head, wincing.

What had he done? Could he be a bigger idiot, make more of a fool of himself? He wouldn't blame her if she didn't show up tomorrow.

That thought brought a spurt of panic. Sitting up straight, he glanced at Larissa. Surely, Connie would come. She wouldn't disappoint Larissa, would she?

He couldn't believe that she would, but just in case, he decided that he'd better arrange to take the day off. At the very least, he had some explaining to do—some apologizing, more like—and in the meantime, he had a daughter who needed care.

"Come on," he said miserably, rising to his feet, "let's

eat and get some sleep. I, for one, am going to need my strength tomorrow."

Not to mention a good deal of prayer and contrition.

Connie hitched Russell a little higher on her hip, took a deep breath and gave the bell a quick ring before opening the door and stepping inside. Early on, Kendal had said to just come on in, but she always liked to give him a little warning first, and that was especially true today. Once in the foyer, she let Russell slide down to the floor, catching the strap of her heavy bag in her hand.

"Hello," he called to anyone who might be listening.

Dreading what she knew must come, Connie caught his hand in hers and started forward.

It was all her fault, of course. Even if Kendal had made some erroneous assumptions on his own, they were logical assumptions. She, on the other hand, had withheld the truth—and a very unsavory truth at that. Nothing could excuse the fact that she hadn't told him everything about herself right up front.

Before they had even traversed the foyer, Kendal appeared in the open doorway to the living room. His expression appeared solemn, if somewhat relieved, and, oddly, he was dressed in comfortable jeans and a long-sleeved polo shirt.

"I wasn't sure you'd come."

Surprised, she stopped in her tracks, asking, "Why on earth would you think that?"

He just shook his head wryly.

"Take off your coats and come into the kitchen. I've just finished feeding Larissa."

Connie wasn't sure whether that was a good sign or not, but she did as he instructed, divesting first Russell and then herself of their outerwear, which she tucked into a small hall closet. Russell was halfway across the living room by the time she turned to follow him, dropping the bag into a corner.

She moved past the formal dining room and the den, musing about how much she liked this house with its spacious, open floor plan and wondering whether or not she would be spending time here after today. Most likely not, considering how upset he'd been about his own erroneous assumptions. Nevertheless, she'd prayed about the matter all through the night and she knew that she must confess all.

When she entered the kitchen, Kendal was just setting Larissa onto her feet. The girl smiled brightly at Connie, but she ran straight to Russell and threw her arms around his neck. Russell growled like a bear, and the embrace went from hug to wrestling match in a twinkling. Kendal chuckled, but Connie immediately stepped in to gently separate the children.

"Do you drink coffee?" Kendal asked, lifting the pot from its burner.

"Yes."

"How do you take it?"

"Black."

He nodded and filled a mug. "Sit down."

She pulled out a chair and sat.

He placed two mugs on the round table and joined

her, his chair angled sideways so he could cross his long legs comfortably.

"Shouldn't you be getting ready for work?" she asked.

"I took the morning off."

"Oh."

He looked her straight in the eye, admitting, "I have some apologizing to do, so here goes. I'm sorry about last night."

"No, you were right to call," she said quickly.

"That's not what I mean, although I hated having to bother you at your party. I appreciate you talking to her, by the way. It helped a great deal."

"I'm glad."

"She slept peacefully though the night and hasn't given me a bit of trouble this morning," he went on, reaching for his cup.

Connie nodded and picked up her own cup to sip from. The coffee was strong and bitter, but she kept her face impassive. They had important matters to discuss, and she was not one for putting off the disagreeable. She set down the mug again.

"Kendal, we need to talk."

"I know. I was wrong to blame you—even for a moment—for my own stupidity."

She shook her head. "It was an innocent misconception, completely understandable."

"It won't happen again, I promise."

"I'm sure it won't," she began, distracted as Larissa began climbing up onto her lap. Connie helped her up, then ducked her head to acknowledge the child, smiling and rubbing foreheads with her. Larissa turned so that she could wrap her arms around Connie's neck and lay her head on Connie's shoulder with a sigh.

"She loves you," Kendal said wistfully.

Connie closed her eyes and hugged her little body tight, whispering, "I love her, too."

"Thank you for that," he said.

An instant later, he chuckled and she heard him set down his coffee. She opened her eyes again to see Russell crawling up his leg.

"Well, at least somebody around here likes me," Kendal announced with a grin, lifting the boy up onto his knee. "Or is it that any lap will do in a pinch?"

Connie tilted her head. How awful to feel that your own daughter doesn't love you.

After pushing his coffee to the center of the table, Kendal playfully poked a finger into Russell's navel. Immediately, Russell bared his belly, eyes dancing.

Kendal covered that fat little tummy with one hand and shook it, teasing, "I bet that belly sees lots of daylight."

Russell fell back into the crook of Kendal's arm, laughing and eager to play. Kendal seemed just as eager to oblige him. Connie couldn't help smiling, especially as Larissa suddenly swung around to see what the fun was all about. She stared without expression at her father and Russell for several seconds before turning a clearly puzzled look on Connie.

"Silly boys," Connie said softly, hugging her close.

Larissa watched a bit longer, frowning, before she suddenly shouted, "Russ!"

Kendal looked up, but Russell ignored Larissa and reached out to tug Kendal's chin down and reclaim his attention. Once more, Kendal obliged, but the giggling had barely resumed before Larissa twisted and slid her way to the floor, shoving at Connie to get free. She ran to her father's side and tugged at Russell's shirt, as if wanting him to get down off her daddy's lap.

For a moment, Connie assumed that she wanted to take his place, but then Kendal set Russell on his feet and Larissa immediately squeezed in between them, her back to her father. She bumped up against Russell, clearly trying to engage him in play and just as obviously trying to shut out her father. Connie glimpsed the look of hurt on Kendal's face before he quickly shuttered his expression.

Connie knew exactly how Kendal must feel, remembering all too well the first time she saw Russell after getting out of prison. She'd been nothing to him. Even Marcus was more familiar and had garnered much more interest than she had. It had felt like a knife to her heart. All she'd been able to think of for months was cuddling him, kissing him, telling him how much she loved him and wanted him and he simply hadn't been interested. His attention had been centered on Jolie, who had been—for all intents and purposes—his mother.

Intellectually, Connie had understood that she was a stranger to her own child, mostly by choice. She hadn't wanted Russell inside the prison, hadn't wanted to risk the smallest chance that he might remember her in those surroundings, but the reality had been devastating all the same. She had felt hopeless, lost, useless, guilty and unlovable. If it wasn't for Marcus, she might have slunk away, found a dark hole and disappeared into it. Then, even after she realized that she couldn't let Russell go through life believing that his own mother hadn't wanted him, it was Marcus who'd shown her how to really be a mother to her son.

The transition had been easier than she had anticipated, really, but since Russell had come home to her, they had experienced moments when he'd wanted Jolie rather than Connie. That, too, had hurt, but patience had been all that was required to see the situation changed.

Such was not the case for Kendal.

For whatever reason, he obviously needed help teaching his daughter to accept him. In that, at least, Connie had actual experience. Surely, God intended her to use it. Even if this was to be her last day with them, she would try to fulfill God's purpose for bringing her into the lives of Kendal and Larissa Oakes.

If she could do that, it would be enough.

Connie slipped off her chair to sit cross-legged on the floor, pulling Russell down on one side and Larissa down on the other so that the children sat facing each other.

"Who wants to play patty-cake?" she asked brightly. Looking pointedly at Kendal, she said, "Daddy wants to play, don't you?"

He blinked at her, but he went along.

"Sure." He didn't sound very certain about it, but he got up, pushed back his chair and sat down on the kitchen floor.

"Let's show them how," she said to him, lifting her hands. She repeated the old nursery rhyme and went slowly through the motions. "Patty-cake, patty-cake, baker's man, bake me a cake as fast as you can, roll it up, roll it up, throw it in the pan!"

Kendal did his best to match his motions to hers, and on the second try, they were perfect. They went through it twice more, the children occasionally clapping their hands together, but while Russell looked between her and Kendal, Larissa looked only at Connie.

That, Connie sensed, was something she had been *taught*. Setting aside the questions that assumption raised, Connie concentrated instead on retraining Larissa. She started by involving Russell first.

"Want to play, Russell? Clap your hands and then clap Kendal's."

Kendal caught on fast, holding his hand down for Russell to slap. Familiar with the old "give-me-five" game, Russell slapped his palm against Kendal's.

"Good job!" Connie praised, keeping the motion going with Kendal. "Clap your hands again," she instructed the boy. He did so and she held out her own palm. "Now me." He slapped her hand with his and beamed when Kendal gave him praise this time.

"Good! You're getting it."

"Your turn, Larissa," Connie said brightly, renewing the pattern with Kendal. "Clap your hands."

The girl did so. It wasn't much of a clap because she already had her hands pressed together, but she got the idea.

"Now clap Daddy's hand," Connie instructed, but

Larissa never took her eyes off Connie. She ignored Kendal completely.

Connie glanced at Kendal. Holding her gaze, he kept up the pattern.

"Clap your hands," she instructed Larissa again, and this time, Larissa gave them a good clap. "Now mine." Connie held out her hand and Larissa gave it a tepid pat. "Good. Your turn again, Russ."

Clap, clap, clap. Kendal held down his hand. Russell slapped it and clapped. Connie and Kendal repeated the pattern. Russell hesitated a moment before realizing what was expected of him, but then he slapped her hand and clapped his.

"Good job!" Connie and Kendal proclaimed at the same time and Russell literally applauded himself.

Connie looked at Kendal and said, "Your turn again, Larissa."

They picked up the pattern. Kendal repeated the rhyme with her this time while Connie willed Larissa to cooperate. When the moment came, he held out his hand. Connie held her breath. She didn't look at Larissa; she merely stared at Kendal's hand expectantly. After a long time, Larissa touched her palm to her father's.

Elated, Connie calmly launched straight back into the game, reciting the rhyme and clapping hands with Ken. She no longer dared to look into his eyes for fear that one of them would tear up. Then the time came for her to offer her hand to Larissa. This time, she got a smart slap. Looking up, she caught the gleam of delight in Larissa's eye, but Connie bit back her praise until Kendal had offered his.

"Good job, honey!"

Larissa seemed startled. She looked sharply to her father and then back to Connie.

"Isn't this fun?" Connie said brightly. "I'm so proud of you both. You're learning this game. Let's do it again."

She held up her hands and looked to Kendal. His gaze touched hers and a poignant smile spread slowly across his face as he lifted his hands into position.

"Patty-cake, patty-cake," he began.

Connie joined him, covering his sudden hoarseness with her own bright tones. They played several more rounds, each lavishing praise and Larissa did not miss her father's hand a single time.

"Sweet dreams, baby," Kendal said softly, patting Larissa's pale-blond curls. "You, too, buddy." Smiling, he smoothed Russell's bright red hair, then followed Connie out of the room, closing the door softly behind them.

It had been a busy morning and one of the best mornings of his life. He and his daughter had played together—really played—with Connie's and Russell's help. He'd been walking around with his heart in his throat for hours now.

"Will they really sleep like that, do you think?" he whispered as he followed Connie down the hall. He was surprised to find that Connie put them down together in Larissa's crib. Connie looked back over her shoulder.

"Oh, yes. They're used to it." She had a neat, compact but curvy figure, even from the back. "Besides," she said, "Larissa was half-asleep over lunch. We wore them out this morning."

He drew her to a stop just as they entered the den, his hands clasped lightly around her upper arms.

"I can't thank you enough. That's the most fun I've ever had with my daughter. All the therapists and doctors to date haven't managed what you have in one short morning. Even lunch was a joy. I have to cajole and plead with her to get every bite into her when you're not here."

Connie seemed embarrassed, even troubled, by his words. She dropped her gaze, murmuring, "She'll learn."

He was entirely serious, though. In fact, he had never meant anything more, and he wanted her to know it.

"I thank God for bringing you and Russell to us," he told her flatly.

She looked up sharply at that.

"Even though I'm not married?"

It seemed an odd question to ask, but he had been wondering about it. How could any woman so sweet and lovely and gentle and caring *not* be married? And why did she expect it to bother him?

"Was it a divorce?" he asked.

That, at least, would explain some of her reticence.

Abruptly, she dropped her gaze again and turned away from him, breaking his hold on her.

"No."

He felt a jolt of surprise. That must mean she was widowed, like him. It seemed a lot to have in common—especially with children so close in age—

and highly significant. Then she suddenly turned back to him.

"It's not what you think."

He tilted his head, asking "How so?"

"Let's sit down," she said, moving toward the leather sectional sofa. "I have a lot to tell you."

He felt sure that he wanted to hear it, but the longer she talked, the more he wished that he didn't have to. From what she'd already said, it hadn't taken a genius to deduce that her childhood had not been picture-perfect, but he'd never dreamed how dysfunctional her family had been.

He tried to imagine never having known his father or having his mother leave him in the care of siblings only a year or two older than him for days at a time without adequate food or even, on occasion, utilities. Wrapping his mind around the idea of his wonderful mother bouncing from one man to another proved impossible.

The nightmarish stories that he'd heard about foster care were at least partially proven by Connie's account of her childhood experiences, although she bluntly admitted that her own attitude created many of the problems.

"I was angry, I suppose, especially after they split us up, and I never seemed to quite fit in. But it was more than that, too. Looking back, I realize that whenever I started to feel the least bit happy, guilt would fill me up. I mean, how could I be happy when my family had been destroyed? It didn't seem right."

He nodded at that, thinking of his own experiences. After his mom died, it seemed as if he would never feel happiness again. She had suffered so much with her illness. A virus had damaged her heart, which had failed bit by bit over time. Sadness had hung over their household for years, especially after she'd gone into the hospital for the last time. She died waiting for a transplant. It seemed disrespectful to her memory to be happy after that.

Was that why he hadn't been?

The thought shook him because he knew that if that was the case it was his own fault. His mother had loved him; she would have wanted him to be happy. At least, he had that assurance.

Connie, unfortunately, did not. Her mother had literally abandoned her. It was what came after foster care that truly chilled him, though.

"I met Jessup Kennard when I was nineteen years old," she said softly, her gaze targeted—as it had been throughout—on her hands. "Six months later, I finally gave in and we started going out. Within the year, everyone was telling me that he was no good, but I—I…he was so charming and I didn't want to be like my mother, going from relationship to relationship." She closed her eyes. "I kept thinking that if I was patient, he would change, and then he finally gave me a ring. He said we would get married as soon as we saved some money and then—" she gulped "—he convinced me that we could save much faster if we weren't both paying rent."

Kendal saw a tear drop onto her hand and impulsively covered it with his own. She flashed him a surprised look before carefully removing her hand from beneath his.

"I think I know what's coming next," he said gently, wanting her to understand that he wouldn't—couldn't—judge her. He had made his own mistakes, too many to pass judgment on anyone else.

She shook her head, sniffled and dried her eyes with the sleeve of her sweater.

"No," she said, and her certainty shook him to the bone. "No, you don't. It's worse. Much worse."

Chapter Seven

Connie tugged on her left earlobe, took a deep breath and began her narrative, folding her hands in her lap. She had prayed for hours about this and now she had to trust God with the outcome. Whatever it would be, she was prepared—or so she told herself.

"I, um, I finally gave Jessup an ultimatum," she began, "and I guess he believed me. Or maybe it was just an excuse. I don't know. He announced that we would drive to Las Vegas and get married right away. He said we just had to stop by the bank first."

Suddenly, she could see it all again in her mind's eye: the gleam in his vivid, blue gaze, the little half smile that he'd worn. How happy she had been! She related the story haltingly: how he'd asked her to drive and how she'd stayed in the car, which was parked just to the side of the front door, while he went into the bank.

"I remember that he was wearing a lightweight, black nylon jacket with a hood." That hadn't seemed important at the time—completely unremarkable. If only she had known! "He was in there five or six minutes when I—I heard a screech of some sort and then clanging and finally loud, popping noises."

She put her hands over her ears, hearing the sounds again, feeling them shiver up and down her spine.

Kendal angled his body a little more toward her and asked "What happened? Was he killed?"

Once, she'd wished that were so! Now, she tried hard not to. Shaking her head, she gulped and went on.

"He came running out and jumped in the car. He said the bank had been robbed, and to get out of there quick before they came for us. I—I thought he had escaped, that the robbers would be coming after us with guns!" Tears sprang into her eyes and rolled down her face as she admitted, "I didn't know until much later that *he* was the robber."

"Oh, no." Kendal straightened sharply.

"He was carrying a gun and a mask in his jacket," she went on, forcing her voice from its near whisper. "He'd killed the guard—an off-duty police officer."

"What happened next?" Kendal asked.

She wrung her hands, knowing how it must've sounded.

"I wanted to call the police. Surely, I thought he'd be needed to give testimony, but he said he didn't want to put off marrying me for a moment longer than necessary, that we'd call them once we arrived in Vegas."

"And you believed him," Kendal surmised.

How she'd wanted to believe him! But she hadn't. Deep down inside, she hadn't.

"He was very insistent, but I just wasn't comfortable.

He made me pull over and he got behind the wheel." She sighed and added, "We didn't even make it to New Mexico before I heard a description of our car on the radio. I only turned it on because he'd gone in a convenience store in El Paso and I was bored waiting outside."

How many times, she wondered, *had she mentally kicked herself for not turning on the radio right away?* She hadn't even thought of it! She just sat there, wringing her hands much as she was now, while Jessup slid a disc into the CD player. Her stomach roiled the entire time, but she hadn't been able to let herself think about the truth.

"What did you do?" Kendal asked, interrupting her thoughts.

"I—I didn't know *what* to do. I guess I was in shock, but I knew. At *that* point, I knew. I jumped out of the car and ran. All I could think about was getting away, and I was so afraid that he would catch me."

"Did he?"

She shook her head, shamefaced.

"No. He didn't even try. He had to get out of Texas, you see, but I didn't think of that until later—until after I'd caught a ride with a trucker headed to Dallas. And that was my big mistake."

"I don't understand."

She put a hand to her head in agitation. "No one else did, either, but at first, all I could think about was getting away from him. Then once I calmed down, I realized that I *had* to go to the police. By that time, we were in the middle of nowhere, so I asked the trucker to drop me off in Midland and then found a policeman."

"You turned him in."

"That was my intention." She closed her eyes and admitted, "Oh, I handled it badly. The first words that fell out of my mouth were 'We robbed a bank.' That thought had been going around and around inside my head for hours, you see. I couldn't get over the fact that he robbed a bank and I just sat there and let it happen! I just blurted it out." She bowed her head. "I never convinced the district attorney that I didn't know what Jessup intended, so naturally I was a suspect."

Kendal covered his lower face with his hand. "They charged you?"

"Yes," she whispered in a pained voice. "A police officer had died. They don't take that lightly, whatever the circumstances."

"But you came forward!" Ken argued desperately.

"Only after Jessup had had time to get out of the state," she pointed out.

Kendal's eyes widened. "Surely, you weren't convicted?"

She lowered her gaze again. "It didn't go to trial. I pled guilty to a reduced charge."

"What?"

"A man had died—a police officer. I gave Jessup time to get away. The legal aid attorney said it was the best I could hope for."

Kendal looked stunned, horrified.

"They—they must have given you probation or—"

"I served eighteen months, two weeks and four days of a four-year sentence," she told him softly, "over a year of it before they caught Jessup in Arizona."

Kendal bowed his head, lifting his palms to his face. Connie made herself go on as dispassionately as possible.

"I didn't know I was pregnant when I went in or I might have had the courage to fight the charges. By the time I found out, it was too late, so I did the time as best I could and, eventually, I was released early for good behavior."

"Thank God for that, at least," Kendal exclaimed, leaning forward to brace his elbows on his knees and uncover his face.

"We were never married," she went on miserably, "but Russell has his father's last name, and that's a burden he'll have to carry for the rest of his life. It's bad enough that he was born in prison, but once they convict Jessup, Russell will also have to carry the name of a murderer."

"That's why your sister had him," Kendal surmised correctly, "because he was born while you were—"

She spared him the distasteful act of actually finishing that thought. "Yes. My sister took him and loved him like her own. I never even expected to have the chance to be a mother to him, frankly." She balled her hand into a fist. "I didn't think I'd survive prison. But I did, and I realized that I couldn't let my son grow up believing that I didn't love him enough to fight for him. Trust me when I tell you that knowing your mother doesn't want you is a constant, abiding pain. You always wonder if you're good enough. I *had* to take him back."

"You had no choice," Kendal agreed firmly, and fresh tears brimmed in Connie's eyes.

"I know, but it hurt Jolie so badly. She wouldn't speak to me for several weeks. If it hadn't been for Marcus…"

She rushed on, relieved to have something positive to say for a change.

"I owe everything to my brother. I found the Lord because of him. He's the reason I have my son—and my sister. He has supported us and given us a place to live, a new start, a real chance at a good life." Her enthusiasm waned at this point, but she forged on. "I can't live with my brother forever, though. I have to find a way to take care of my son on my own. It won't be easy, but in five years, my record will be expunged. Until then, I have a felony conviction and that limits the kind of work I can do, so I've been thinking about school and preparing myself for a career."

She sat back, feeling both relieved and horribly burdened. He hadn't leapt to his feet and tossed her out on her ear yet, but she knew that the possibility remained. Frankly, in his position, she wasn't sure what she would do.

"I—I'll understand if you think I'm not fit to care for Larissa."

To her immense gratification, Kendal captured her hands in his, exclaiming, "No! I meant what I said. You've made a huge difference. Larissa *needs* you. *I* need you. And believe me, Connie, I've had too many failures in my own life to judge you for yours."

Her expression must have clearly shown her skepticism for he told her then just how disastrous his marriage had been, how the woman who had reminded him so much of his late mother in looks had turned out to be her polar opposite. According to him, virtually overnight Larissa's mother had gone from an almost-too-adoring wife to a cool, unreceptive one.

"Nothing existed for her but the baby," he finished hollowly. "It was as if she couldn't love us both at one time, as if she just turned off her feelings for me."

"I wish I'd known how to do that," Connie admitted ruefully. "Had I been able to turn off my feelings for Jessup, I wouldn't have made such terrible mistakes with him."

"But then you wouldn't have Russell," Kendal pointed out, sweeping his thumbs across her knuckles. Only then did she realize that he was still holding her hands.

As casually as she could manage, she slipped free and folded her arms.

"True," she said. "Still, I wish I'd been more sensible, more disciplined." Grimacing, she added, "Someday, I'll have to tell him. Russell will never know his father, but he'll never know a moment's pride in the man, either. What will he think of me when he knows the truth?"

"Russell will love you then as he loves you now," Kendal assured her confidently. "You must know what a gift that is."

Suddenly, Connie understood what he was thinking and it broke her heart. She leaned toward him.

"She loves you, Kendal. Larissa loves you. Don't ever think that she doesn't."

"What if she's like her mother?" he worried aloud.

"What if it's some crazy quirk of DNA and she *can't* love?"

"But you told me that Laura *adored* Larissa," Connie reminded him. "You said that Laura smothered Larissa with attention—so much so that she had none left over for you. I don't think it was that Laura *couldn't* love but rather that she punished you for every little disappointment by *withholding* her love. That is learned behavior."

He propped his forearms on his knees, considering that argument. After a moment, he nodded.

"You're right. It was what Laura had been taught, to freeze out anyone who displeased her. It's what her parents, especially her mother, had done to *her* in many ways. Agnes—Mrs. Conklin—wouldn't speak to Laura for weeks and Laura would agonize over what she might have said or done to displease her."

"And eventually Laura repeated that very behavior with you," Connie pointed out.

He sat up straight and crossed his legs, not quite meeting Connie's gaze any longer.

"When I first met Laura," he said carefully, "I felt that she was desperate for someone to love her, and I believed *that* someone was supposed to be me. After we were married, I had to work a lot and that sometimes upset her, but she always came around—until she became pregnant with Larissa."

"She closed you out and focused all her love on her child," Connie said softly, "and then she taught Larissa to do the same."

"That's exactly what happened, and I knew it at

the time. I just didn't know what to do about it. I still don't."

"We simply have to retrain Larissa," Connie stated confidently. "She's bright and she's loving, but she's confused. And who can blame her after what she's been through?"

"You really don't think there's anything fundamentally wrong with her?" he asked hopefully.

"Not at all. Yes, she's very emotional and easily over-stimulated, but she's almost two, for pity's sake. That's how two-year-olds are. That's why they call them the terrible twos."

He smiled. "I'm glad we talked. You don't know what a blessing—"

A screech from the direction of Larissa's room interrupted him. Connie glanced at her wrist, checking the time.

"Oh, my word!" She popped up and hurried away, saying over her shoulder, "I can't believe we've been talking for more than two hours!" She flapped her arms, exclaiming, "It's a good thing you aren't home every day. I'd never get anything done!"

She swept down the hall and into Larissa's room. True to form, Larissa was standing up, eager to get out of the crib and on with something else while Russell continued to loll, in no hurry to exert himself. He smiled when he saw Connie and sat up. Connie laughed, feeling light and hopeful.

Thank you, Lord, she thought.

Everyone could go forward now. The air had been cleared. Kendal was not showing her the door. Larissa was learning to relate to her daddy. Connie was finally earning some money and removing some of the financial burden from Marcus. Yes, that was more than enough to make her truly grateful.

Kendal blinked. Two hours! He'd been sitting here on this couch talking to Connie for *two hours?* When had *that* ever happened?

Then again, when had he ever known a woman with so much to talk about?

When he thought about everything that Connie had been through, well, it humbled him. It certainly put *his* problems in perspective. Not that he was denigrating the death of his mother or his wife or underestimating the problem with his daughter. Nevertheless, his own childhood—at least, his early childhood—had been idyllic, and he realized now that he'd rather have experienced his mother's illness and the strength of her love throughout that time than to have lived the kind of life that Connie had known. He had never for a moment doubted the love of his parents; Connie had never known anything but such doubt.

That probably explained why she had fallen for a character like Jessup Kennard.

When Kendal thought about her actually serving time behind bars because of that man, his blood ran cold— and then hot. He'd known a moment of overwhelming rage at Jessup when Connie told him that she'd been charged with abetting his crime. He hoped that the man would spend the rest of his life locked away, but Kendal couldn't help feeling that Russell had gotten the short end of the stick in this deal.

He wished there was some way to make life better for both Connie and Russell. God had used them to improve his life enormously so far. He still couldn't believe that he'd actually played with his daughter this morning! Or that he'd spent two whole hours in conversation with Connie.

She was right. It was a good thing that he wasn't home every day.

Or was it? Hmm. What strides might they make if he could spend his days with Connie, Larissa and Russell? Just quitting work was not an option, of course, but it was certainly worth thinking about taking some time off.

Kendal followed Connie to Larissa's room. Connie was lifting Russell onto one hip; Larissa already occupied the other. Moving to the change table, she tried to get dry diapers on both children, who were chattering cheerfully.

"Here," Kendal decided aloud, "let me help."

It was time, he told himself, *that he stopped living on the sidelines of his daughter's life and got into the game*. He immediately went about changing her. It was something he'd done many times these past months, but he'd never actually *enjoyed* it before.

He enjoyed it now partly because Russell kept trying to engage his attention. Russell lay next to Larissa on the change table and allowed his mom to put on a dry diaper, but all the while, the child smiled up at Kendal, waggling his eyebrows and babbling incoherent words.

Kendal couldn't help laughing. Before he knew what he was doing, he found himself making silly sounds just to get a giggle out of the boy.

After a moment, Connie nudged him. Kendal glanced at her and then followed her gaze downward. Larissa was watching him with intense concentration, a slight frown on her face. Her attention slid momentarily to Russell, then back to her dad. The look in her narrowed little eyes seemed to say, "Back off, buddy. He's *my* dad."

Was it possible? Could she be just a tiny bit jealous?

Cautiously, Kendal poked a finger into her belly, twisted it and made a creaking sound. She didn't laugh, but she brightened visibly and turned such a smug look on Russell that Kendal felt his eyes fill with tears.

There was hope for them yet. For the first time, he had real hope that he and his daughter would one day enjoy a normal, healthy, loving relationship.

Thank You, Lord, for sending us Connie and Russell, he thought.

The afternoon passed much as the morning had. Kendal felt as if he were living someone else's life, right up until the moment when Connie and Russell left for the day. Larissa had her usual meltdown—reaching and crying for Connie—but one thing had changed. Instead of struggling to get away from her father, she actually allowed him to comfort her. She sat in his lap, her damp little cheek pressed to his shirt front, and huffed and snuffled until he began to suspect that much of it was for show or out of sheer habit. Nevertheless, he held her, crooning sympathetic nonsense.

"There, there, baby. It'll be all right. You know it'll be all right. We're here together now, Larissa and Daddy. It'll be okay."

Eventually, she allowed him to carry her into the kitchen and deposit her in the high chair while he prepared another less than stellar but hopefully edible dinner. At least she didn't complain, and she made less of a mess than usual, too. Even though she didn't always look at him when he talked to her or fed her, it seemed that Connie was right that flinging her food around was Larissa's way of asking for attention.

Bath time was not without its rough patches, but they'd had worse—much worse—and when he lay Larissa in her crib for the night, she only tried to get up twice. Both times he gently but firmly laid her back down and covered her with a soft blanket.

"Night-night, Larissa. Sleep well. See you in the morning."

Maybe they would play again tomorrow, or would it be unreasonable to try for two good days in a row? He was still undecided on the matter when he turned in for the night, but he awoke in the morning knowing that God had given him an incredible opportunity.

He made arrangements before Connie showed up the next morning. It had meant calling his secretary at home—something he didn't like to do—but the moment it was done, he knew that it had been the right thing. Nevertheless, an inexplicable nervousness seized him as soon as Connie smiled at him.

"Not going in again today?" she asked, her gaze skimming over his casual attire.

Suddenly wondering what had made him think that she would welcome having him around, he tried not to gulp.

"I thought I'd stay home the rest of the week. U-unless you object?"

Her eyebrows went up in tandem. "Why would I object? I'm sure it's none of my business."

"I don't want to be underfoot."

"In your own home?"

"It's my home, but it's your place of employment."

"My point exactly."

He scuffed a toe against the carpet. "I just don't want to be in the way."

She laughed lightly. "I'm glad for the help. Any coffee?"

A weight seemed to lift from his shoulders. He headed for the kitchen.

"I'll pour you a cup."

"Could I have a little milk this time?"

He stopped and looked back over his shoulder. "Milk?"

She wrinkled her nose and admitted, "I'd prefer a lot of milk, actually. We drink a weak brew in the Wheeler household."

She hadn't really liked his coffee but had been too polite to say so.

"How about I brew a compromise pot, as my stepmother would say, and you go with just a little milk?"

"Sounds good."

It did sound good, and it was. The whole day was, and the next day as well, and the day after that.

Larissa had had her moments. At one point, she pitched an absolute fit over a stuffed doll that she'd never paid the least attention to before Russell developed an interest in it. Another time, she actually told her father. *"No"* when he was trying to give her a drink, but Connie just smiled wryly and said, "Get used to it. You'll be hearing a lot of that over the next few months. It's what a normal almost-two-year-old does, you know."

A normal almost-two-year-old she wasn't, of course. Larissa still preferred Connie much more. She never came to him of her own impulse, but she did tolerate his presence and he began to notice something significant: She looked at him. She *really* looked at him, made actual eye contact.

It never lasted very long, and she often made a point of snubbing him afterward, but eye contact with him began to seem more and more casual. Perhaps he would never be the center of his daughter's life, but, at least, he was an acknowledged part of it now. That was something, at least. It was almost enough.

Then came the weekend.

Larissa continued to make Connie's evening departures difficult. At one point, Kendal even suggested that it might be easier if Connie merely slipped away as unobtrusively as possible, but that proved impossible. Larissa never went anywhere alone with him willingly, and it was as if she kept one eye on Connie at all times. Besides, as Connie pointed out, Larissa had to learn to deal with the reality of the situation, so they continued to struggle at the end of each day.

On Saturday, Larissa awoke in a good mood, but breakfast wasn't over before she began asking for Connie. He never told her that Connie wasn't coming; instead, he started saying that they would see Connie at church the next day. By evening, Larissa was in old form again, demanding Connie and throwing her food. She refused to let him get her ready for bed, and his promise that they would see Connie tomorrow only seemed to enrage her.

He considered calling Connie on the phone again, but something told him that this was more about Larissa getting what she wanted than her fears of anything happening to her mother figure. He toughed it out and finally got her down for the night.

She was sullen and groggy on Sunday morning and hadn't rested very well. When she saw Connie at church, she didn't perk up as usual. Instead, she grabbed on, just as she had in the beginning, as if Connie were her only lifeline in a vast, turbulent sea. The parting was especially histrionic afterward and Kendal couldn't help feeling that he'd taken one step forward and two steps back, especially since Larissa seemed to blame him for the situation. She actually took a swipe at him after they got home and he was so shocked that he didn't quite know what to do about it.

In the end, he did nothing—just stepped back and let her howl. Even after the storm waned, Larissa wouldn't let him hold or comfort her in any way. By Sunday evening, he was pretty much in the same shape that Larissa was, wishing fervently that Connie and Russell were there to facilitate the situation.

Connie knew how to help him deal with his daughter's emotional outbursts, and Russell provided a much-needed distraction for him and Larissa. Somehow, that little boy helped Kendal believe that he could be an effective father, while Connie, who knew instinctively how to handle Larissa, showed him just how to manage it.

Unfortunately, it was as if he forgot what to do when she wasn't around and reverted to old habits and old resentments. How he wanted to be finished with those!

Kendal feared that he was losing all the hard-won ground that he'd so recently gained. He stared bleakly at the week ahead, telling himself that he had to go back to work. The idyll was over and real life hovered oppressively near, threatening failure after so much hope.

What will happen, he wondered, *when Connie leaves them to go to school?* The very idea of it made panic clutch at his chest, and that was when he knew that he had to find a way to keep Connie and Russell in his and Larissa's life.

Permanently.

Chapter Eight

Kendal tugged on the cuff of his shirt sleeve and self-consciously straightened his tie.

Ridiculous, of course. Appearances had nothing to do with anything. This was all about reason—sound, solid, carefully constructed reason.

However, it was also about desperation and it was the desperation that drove him now, pricking his self-confidence with spurs of sharp doubt.

He glanced at the children on the den floor. Larissa was greedily hoarding blocks, gathering as many as she could manage while keeping a possessive eye on Connie. Meanwhile, Russell was scattering the blocks with languid sweeps of his arms and legs and lazy little kicks, which was precisely why Larissa worked so hard to gather them up.

Connie smiled indulgently from her seat in the armchair, one leg folded beneath her. Her sweater, he noticed, did not quite match her pants, and her shoes were very worn. Well, she could afford to buy matching outfits and new shoes soon enough, provided his arguments were as sound as he thought them to be.

He leaned forward, balanced his forearms on his knees and clasped his hands, presenting as earnest a picture as he could.

"I've thought this through very carefully," he began. "I wouldn't want you to think I haven't, considering the seriousness of it. I hardly slept last night, praying about it."

Connie tilted her head and gave him her attention, visibly tensing. The smile faded from her jade-green eyes.

"What is it, Ken? Are you having second thoughts about my suitability?"

"No, no. It's not that at all," he hastened to assure her.

She relaxed again. "Well, then, what could be so serious? Has something come up?"

He still wasn't quite sure how to put it. All his well-rehearsed statements seemed ineffectual or, worse, inappropriate. The words that he finally found were not exactly what he'd intended.

"I want you and Russ to live here with us."

For a moment, it was as if time stood still. Connie stared at him, unmoving, unblinking. She didn't even seem to breathe. Then she abruptly straightened her leg and sat up tall, shoulders squared.

"I can't do that."

He'd put it badly. He knew he'd put it badly.

"Hear me out. Please. It's not what you think."

She wasn't listening; she was shaking her head.

"We simply can't move in here. You're a single man. I'm a single woman. Days are one thing, nights another. We can't live here. It just can't be done." She slid to the very edge of the chair, her lips compressed.

"We could get married," he said simply.

Suddenly, she was on her feet, her mouth ajar, one hand in her hair.

"We'd have to get married," he reiterated quickly, adamantly. "I mean, of course we'd get married."

"You're asking me to *marry* you?" she demanded incredulously.

Since that was obvious, he didn't think it warranted a reply. She threw up her arms, spun on one heel and then back again.

"I don't believe this!"

He got to his feet, quelling the urge to reach out for her, to hold her in place and make her listen.

"Think of it as a partnership," he argued. "Legally, it would be marriage, but in reality, it would be a partnership."

She stopped twisting around long enough to stare at him.

"Not a real marriage then?"

"Yes, of course, a real marriage but with limitations."

She folded her arms and he actually did reach out this time, but he quickly forced his hands back to his sides.

"Such as?" she demanded.

He tried to think of how to phrase it so he wouldn't embarrass her.

"We, uh, we already have children, so *that* wouldn't be an issue."

She tilted her head slowly as she processed that, and when she finally came to the right conclusion, her cheeks pinked.

"You mean, a marriage in name only?"

"Yes."

She seemed to catch her breath, and fearing that was a bad sign, he plunged on, arguing, "It would work. We'd sign a prenup. You can set the ground rules. Plus, you'll be financially independent. You could even go to school! We'd have to work it out, but I know it's one of your goals and I'd help you achieve it. This would be a means to that end."

She stared at him for a long time, as if he were a stranger, as if only just now seeing him.

Finally, she demanded, "And what do *you* get out of this? A convenient babysitter?"

"No! Not a babysitter. You've never been *just a babysitter*. But you aren't her mother, either, and that's what I want. It's what Larissa *needs*."

He glanced at his daughter, sitting at attention now, her pointed gaze moving back and forth between him and Connie. He wondered how much she understood, what she thought. Did she even sense how hard he was fighting for her right now? He felt as if he were wound tight as a spring, and it seemed impossible that everyone else in the room couldn't feel it, too.

"Listen," he said urgently, stepping closer to Connie, "we've both been hurt. Maybe on our own, we'd never seek to marry again, but we each have a child who needs two parents. And we're a good team. We proved that last week. Despite our different backgrounds, we have similar values. We…" He struggled for the right phrase. "We *balance* each other somehow. I don't know any other way to explain it."

Connie heaved out an agitated breath and abruptly sat down again, this time on the end of the sofa. Kendal dropped down next to her.

"I can't believe this."

"I know it's come out of the blue," he said, "but if you'll just think about it, it makes sense. You want to be independent of your brother. This accomplishes that."

"And makes me dependent on you," she asserted.

"Not at all," he refuted calmly. "Connie, you bring so much to this relationship that I could never adequately compensate you for it. Frankly, I wouldn't even try. But I can give you a measure of independence financially. We'll create a portfolio for you. I'll teach you how to manage it. Whatever happens, if it doesn't work out between us, that will be yours."

Connie shook her hands at him. "'This relationship,' you said. *What* relationship? I *work* for you."

"Now you'll be my partner."

"And your *wife!*"

He knew that he was tiptoeing through a minefield here, that now more than ever he must choose his words carefully. *Lord, give me the words*, he thought. *If this is really Your will, give me the words.*

Before those words arrived, Russell did. Kendal felt a small hand on his thigh and looked down to find that bright red head tilting back to look up at him. His first impulse was to reach down and scoop the child onto his lap, but he couldn't afford to be distracted at the moment.

He patted the boy's shoulder instead, and said, "Russ, Daddy needs to talk to Mommy right now. We'll play later, okay?"

He didn't even realize what he'd said until he'd done it, and then it struck him that those were exactly the right words.

"That's it," he said, looking up at Connie. "Don't you see? It's not about husband and wife. I'm Daddy. You're Mommy. And that's how it's supposed to be. That's what our kids need. That's what we have to find a way to give them. Can you think of a better way to do it?"

Connie stared at him for so long that he began to think she wouldn't reply at all. Then she bit her lip and shook her head.

"No," she whispered, "No, I can't."

The deal wasn't closed, he knew that, but she was listening, swaying.

He picked up Russell and placed the boy astride his lap. From the corner of his eye, he saw Larissa drop her blocks and move toward them. Yes, this was right. This was exactly what had to happen.

"It's as important to me that I get to be Russ's daddy as it is that you be Larissa's mommy," he said. "In fact, I'd like to formally adopt Russell."

Connie's gaze sharpened. Gradually, as she took in that idea, her whole face lit up. Her shoulders rose as if a great burden had been lifted from them.

"You'd do that?"

She had no idea how happily he'd adopt her son as his own. To have just one child to whom he could truly be a father would be a joy. He would never discount Larissa, but what a relief—and a joy—it would be to have a real relationship with Russell.

"In a heartbeat," he said flatly.

She put one hand over her mouth and her eyes filled with tears that made them sparkle like polished gems.

After a moment, she dropped her hand and asked in a small voice, "Could I adopt Larissa, do you think?"

He almost collapsed, his fears sucked away with a great sigh of relief. He had to gulp before he could reply.

"Absolutely."

A real mother. He could give his daughter a real mother—not a stepmother—but a *real* mother. And he would get to be a real dad, to both of these kids.

It was almost too much to hope for.

Larissa toddled over to Connie and leaned against her leg, but she was looking at Kendal and Russell as if she was trying to decide whether or not to protest the seating arrangement. He wanted to gather all three of them close and hold on for dear life. He settled for looping an arm around Russell and pulling him back against his chest.

A son. Kendal had put away dreams of a son soon after Larissa was born when Laura announced that there would be no more children.

"It wouldn't be fair," she'd said, and indeed it would not have been, considering her inability to love more than one person at a time.

Now he could have a family.

They might make an unconventional family, but that didn't matter because it was so much more than he'd hoped for, so much more than he alone could give his daughter. Even if it didn't work out—even if he and Connie eventually decided that they couldn't live together happily—Larissa would still have Connie in her life and Russell would still have him.

It was important, though, to be as fair to Connie as he possibly could.

"I'm thinking that a civil ceremony might be preferable," he said, "and a platonic relationship makes dissolution simple. If, for some unforeseen reason, it doesn't work out as we planned, an annulment would take care of it."

"I wouldn't want to be divorced," she agreed.

"But adoption is set in stone," he insisted.

"We want to give our children stability. That commitment has to be unshakable."

"Exactly."

"I'm not saying 'yes' yet," she warned him. "I have to talk to my brother first. I just couldn't do something like this without his blessing."

Kendal had expected that and was ready for it.

"Let's talk to him together. I imagine he'll have some questions for me, as I would in his shoes."

Biting her lip, she considered it for a moment.

"Yes, that might be best. We should do it here, I think." She glanced around her, and Larissa took advantage of the moment to snag her attention and ask to be lifted up.

Connie tugged Larissa onto her lap and hugged her.

"That's my girl," she cooed. "Oh, I still can't believe this!"

"Believe it," Kendal said, smoothing a hand over the top of Russell's bright red head.

Maybe his daughter would never come to him like this, but his son would and, at least, he could give her what she—they—so obviously needed. Nothing should get in the way of that.

"Will you pray with me?" he asked, aware of the thickness and depth of his voice.

Connie bowed her head. "Yes."

Kendal closed his eyes, feeling Russell's warm, heavy little body against him.

"Lord, I've prayed for this for so long and here it is. Here *they* are. It all seems so simple now, so right. I, for one, can't thank You enough. I just can't believe that this would not be Your will, but if it's not, please show us because it is really about what's best for everyone. And we know that even if we have this figured out right, there are still hurdles to be overcome and we can't get over them without Your help. Forgive me for doubting for so long, Lord, and help me be the father and partner You would have me be. In the name of Your Son, Amen."

"Amen," Connie whispered.

She looked up and smiled, and suddenly it hit Kendal that this was his chance to make up for all his failures, as a father and as a husband. *It hadn't all been Laura's fault,* he admitted to himself. He'd let his pain at her rejection overshadow his responsibilities to both her and Larissa, but that would never happen again, he vowed.

If God gave him this second chance, he would let nothing get in the way. He would be the best family man ever made. He was sure of it.

Connie sat down with a plop, the damp rag with which she'd been cleaning the kitchen table forgotten in her hand.

Every time she thought about marrying Kendal, his proposal stunned her all over again. Even more shocking than his proposal was the fact that she was considering accepting it!

Considering, my eye, she thought ruefully. *I'm planning on it!* Unless, of course, her brother shot down the whole idea, which he just might.

She couldn't really blame him. The notion of a platonic marriage was pretty outlandish. Yet, in this case, it made an elegant kind of sense—for a lot of reasons.

For one thing, this might be her only opportunity to give Russell the kind of father that he deserved. After all, what other decent man would want her? That brought up a second point: Kendal needed her. Larissa needed her. What a joy it was to be able to fulfill those needs!

She'd be able to go to school now—not that she'd really *have* to since Kendal promised to solve her financial problems. Still, to be able to attend school without any worries was a gift beyond her dreams.

The last reason was in many ways the most important, though—at least personally.

Marriage to Kendal would prevent her from repeating the mistakes of her past. She would be forever safe from the wrong sort of attraction to the wrong sort of men. She knew one thing for sure about herself: She would never be able to betray a marriage vow, however unconventional the marriage.

No one else would ever know how much she wanted that insurance—that protection—even if she was only protecting herself from herself! Experience had taught her the necessity of such, and surely God would not have put her in this situation if it was not His will for her.

Would He?

She shook her head, unable and unwilling now to believe that marrying Kendal was not the best—the right—thing to do.

Still, she could understand why Marcus might need some convincing, which meant that they'd better go about presenting the idea very carefully.

She wondered what Kendal would think about her organizing a small dinner party here for the five of them. Marcus should definitely see this house. She'd told him about it, of course, but if he actually saw the place, he'd have a better understanding of what her life would be like here. Some good food wouldn't hurt, either.

Yes, she'd definitely propose a dinner. In fact, she'd do more than that. She'd actually plan the thing and present it to Kendal when he came home that evening. Better yet, she'd call him at work.

Smiling, she looked around the well-appointed kitchen, with its brick walls and sleek modern appliances. She especially liked the arches over the cooktop and sink window and the pot rack over the work island.

This would be *her* kitchen, if all went as planned.

Now *that* was something she wouldn't have believed even that morning!

They'd eat in here, she decided, rather than the formal dining room. It was cozier, more family oriented.

She went to check out the pantry to determine what Kendal had that she could use. There wasn't much, actually—lots of macaroni and cheese and canned vegetables—not particularly imaginative or nutritious alternatives, but workable. There were tins of fruit and one enormous can of boneless chicken. He also had staples such as flour, sugar, salt and even a biscuit mix. The cocktail wieners and lettuce that she found in the refrigerator helped, too, as did a bag of frozen broccoli and a few spices in the cabinet above the stove.

She made a mental note to move those, as the steam from cooking below them could affect their potency.

After jotting down a menu, she went to the phone and called Kendal. He gave the plan his hearty approval. Then she had a final request.

"Could you bring home a couple of apples, paprika and some butter? Real butter, not margarine. Salted."

"That's *P-A-P-P*—"

"Only two *P's*, *P-A-P-R-I-K-A*. It's in the spice section."

"Got it," he said. "If you need anything else, just give me a shout."

"I think that'll do."

"I'll see you when I get home then. And Connie?"

"Yeah?"

"This is right."

"I think so, too."

The surprising thing was, she really did.

Marcus was not particularly surprised, frankly, when Connie called to say that Kendal wanted to invite him to join them for dinner that evening. He'd heard the shock and interest in Kendal's voice when he'd disabused the man of the mistaken notion that he and Connie were anything other than brother and sister. Given that Connie and Kendal—whom she often referred to as Ken—had essentially spent all of last week together, a dinner invitation was not surprising, especially when he considered how drawn Connie had been to Kendal and his daughter from the beginning.

Marcus just hoped that they'd take their time and not let themselves be carried away by infatuation. Neither could afford another romantic blunder, and more was involved here than just their feelings.

Their children had a large stake in any relationship developing between them. Moreover, each brought a certain amount of baggage and some issues that still needed to be resolved. Nevertheless, Marcus couldn't say that he was necessarily displeased, especially with the advances Larissa seemed to have been making—at least, according to Connie.

As he drove toward the Oakes home, Marcus thought about Kendal's assumption that he and Connie were married. He had to smile. In retrospect, Marcus supposed that he should've realized someone would get the wrong idea. He and Connie did have the same last name, after all. But Connie and Russell had been with him for months now; he'd stopped feeling as if it was necessary to make explanations a while ago.

He shook his head. God certainly did work in mysterious ways sometimes. First, Jolie met Vince because he forgot to have his mail forwarded, and then Connie met Kendal because his daughter developed a fixation with her. It's a pity that God didn't seem to have any tricks like that up His proverbial sleeve for Marcus, but maybe someday...

It would be nice to find a simple, easygoing woman who wouldn't mind living in the fishbowl that is a minister's life—a real helpmate, someone diplomatic and organized, maybe with a little musical talent. That always came in handy. She wouldn't have to be gorgeous or even particularly stylish—just modest and unassuming and selfless. The demands on a minister's wife were many, as many as the demands on the minister.

Marcus allowed his attention to be distracted by the neighborhood in which Kendal Oakes lived. He'd suspected that Oakes was well off; he hadn't suspected that he was *this* well off. Connie could do worse. But then, money wasn't everything. Sometimes, in fact, it was nothing but trouble. That didn't seem to be the case here, but Marcus couldn't be sure, so he'd reserve judgment until later.

He found the house and turned off onto the drive. It made a large loop at the end. Parking his vehicle at the crest of the loop, he got out and walked up the broad, brick-lined path to the front door, which sat far back behind several brick columns beneath the overhang of a slate roof.

Connie answered the door with her customary smile and a kiss for his cheek. Her gaze did not quite meet his long enough for him to feel that she was perfectly calm, though. Very telling.

Smiling to himself, he followed her into the spacious, well-dressed house—well dressed but not particularly homey—until they reached the den, which was scattered with toys and warmed by the muted noise of a large-screen television. Kendal quickly popped up off the leather sectional and clicked off the television with the remote. He was holding Russell.

"Marca!" Russell greeted him enthusiastically.

Marcus reached out and took his nephew's weight into his arms.

"Hey, pal. How are you?"

"Rissa," he said, pointing toward Larissa as if he was making introductions.

She sat on the couch with her legs stretched out in front of her. It was the first time Marcus had ever actually seen her quiet and composed.

"Hello, Larissa," Marcus said.

She just looked at him, then at Connie.

"Give me a minute," Connie said to no one in particular. "We'll eat very soon."

"No problem," Kendal said. "Have a seat, Marcus."

They sat. Russell slid down off Marcus's lap and went to play with a plastic dump truck. Larissa flopped over onto her tummy before hitting the floor with her feet. She looked at Marcus again, strangely solemn, a little wary, and then sat down and took Russell's truck away from him. He grabbed it right back. Kendal bent, picked up a toy car and handed it to Larissa. She took it without a sound and rolled it up Russell's leg. He dropped the dump truck in her lap and took the car for himself.

Marcus chuckled. "They seem to get along well enough."

"Oh, yes," Kendal said. "They're real buddies. He's been great for her. He's been great for me, too." He reached out and rubbed the top of Russell's head fondly.

Larissa jerked her head around sharply and glared at her father.

"Someone is jealous," Marcus noted.

"Sure enough, but of whom?" Kendal wondered aloud.

Moving slowly and deliberately, he brushed a hand across Larissa's curls. She looked down at the dump truck in her lap, snubbing her father but apparently content.

"She seems like a different child," Marcus murmured.

"Very nearly," Kendal agreed.

"Dinner is on the table," Connie announced just then.

"Great! Let's eat." Kendal rose and bent to lift the children to their feet, each by one arm.

Marcus rose, too.

"Go to your chairs," Connie instructed the children, coming into the room.

Russell didn't have to be told twice. As usual, he was more than ready to eat. He ran into the kitchen. Larissa went with Connie, staying close to her side, but once they reached the kitchen, it was her father who lifted her without resistance into her high chair.

As Kendal secured the trays, Connie pointed Marcus to a seat. He moved behind the chair, but he didn't sit down. Instead, he just stood there and watched, his heart climbing into his throat.

He didn't know how they had become a family so quickly and so seamlessly, especially given what had brought them together, but even if they didn't know it yet, that's what they were. He watched Connie and Kendal portioning out food and screwing the tops on spillproof cups, anticipating each other's needs and moving in concert, with hardly a word spoken between them. Finally, they turned to the table and their own chairs. Kendal automatically pulled out Connie's chair for her, and it was then that he seemed to realize that Marcus hadn't seated himself. He paused and Connie looked up.

"What?"

Marcus aimed his smile at the floor.

"So," he said, sliding a hand into the pocket of his slacks, "when is the wedding?"

Connie jerked in surprise. Kendal placed a steadying hand at the small of her back and they traded looks. Kendal cleared his throat.

"Soon."

"Provided you agree," Connie added hastily.

Marcus quelled a sudden urge to laugh. How long had it been—five weeks, six—since he'd performed the rites for his other sister? He clearly remembered saying to Connie at the wedding reception that she could be next, but she'd dismissed the idea. What decent man, she'd asked, would have her?

Well, he was looking at him.

He was looking at a matched set, in fact.

He looked at Connie standing next to Kendal and saw a pair, a team.

He looked at their two kids sitting there side by side, calmly stuffing their precious little faces, and just marveled because it was so very obvious.

Russell had a sister. And a father. Connie had a daughter. Larissa had a mother. Apart they were fractured, shards of what should have been. Together they were whole, a unit.

Even now, Marcus thought, *the wisdom of God never ceases to amaze me.*

Chapter Nine

Marcus pushed away his plate and smiled at his sister. He was going to miss her cooking. The woman could work wonders with packaged macaroni, canned chicken, frozen broccoli and a few spices, and he dearly loved those little sausages wrapped in biscuits. This wedding discussion had been hanging over them for nearly an hour now.

"That was great, Sis. Thanks."

"My pleasure."

Kendal had already praised the meal, remarking that he could never make macaroni taste this good and that every casserole dish he'd ever attempted had looked like it had been through the garbage disposal. Connie had beamed.

Nevertheless, despite their natural affinity, Marcus sensed that all was not just as it should be. Oh, they were a couple, all right, and yet something didn't quite meld.

Glancing at the children, who were still working

on their dinners but with less gusto than earlier on, he edged back from the table, crossed his legs and folded his hands.

"All right, let's hear it."

Connie and Kendal traded looks. It was something they seemed to do quite often, silently telegraphing messages to each other. Then Kendal lay his hand lightly over hers and began to speak.

"First off, I want you to know that Connie will be well taken care of. I've instructed my attorney to draw up a prenuptial agreement that—"

"Whoa." Marcus lifted a hand. "A prenup? Is that really necessary?"

"Under the circumstances, yes, I think it is."

"Well, to my mind, if you aren't sure that she isn't marrying you for your money, then you don't have any business getting married at all," Marcus said bluntly.

"It isn't like that!" Connie objected, and Marcus saw Kendal's hand tighten fractionally around hers.

She subsided instantly, obviously prepared to let Kendal handle this. That said to Marcus that his sister trusted this man, which was no mean accomplishment on Kendal's part, considering what she'd been through.

"The object here is to make absolutely certain that Connie is financially independent no matter what happens," Kendal informed him.

Marcus frowned.

"In the event of a divorce, you mean," he clarified. "Otherwise, a simple will would take care of the situation."

"There will be no divorce," Ken stated flatly. Then he looked Marcus squarely in the eye. "If this union is ever dissolved, it will be by annulment."

Momentarily taken aback, Marcus rubbed his ear, a stalling tactic to allow him time to start his thought processes again. Once his brain kicked into gear again, he came up with the only obvious conclusion.

"I'm no legal scholar and I'm not in the habit of making ecclesiastical pronouncements, but this sounds suspiciously to me like a marriage in name only."

"More or less," Kendal conceded.

"We've each tried romance, Marcus," Connie put in, "and you know how that turned out."

"I think of it as an arranged marriage," Kendal said. "We just arranged this one ourselves."

"And what about love?" Marcus asked lightly, his mind reeling.

They looked so *right* together, so perfectly paired, so aware of each other. But perhaps they weren't as *aware* as they thought they were.

Kendal picked up Connie's hand and covered it with both of his hands.

"There are many kinds of love, I'm sure you know, and I promise you that mine is genuine where both Connie and Russell are concerned. I can't begin to tell you what a difference they've made to me and my daughter or how far I would go to keep them a part of our lives. I intend to adopt Russell, and Connie wants to do the same for Larissa. We've thought it through very carefully and we're both convinced that this is for the best."

"I see."

Marcus saw that they believed everything they were saying. He saw, too, that this platonic arrangement had about as much chance of succeeding as a ski competition in Sundance Square in downtown Fort Worth. He wondered what it was going to take for them to see that.

Maybe it was going to take a wedding.

"I have to pray about this," he finally said, and they both nodded.

"We all should pray about it," Kendal added, "and keep praying about it until everyone's mind is at ease."

Marcus couldn't argue with that.

"Let's begin now," he suggested, leaning forward and reaching out to cover their joined hands with his. It was very much like what he'd do if he were marrying them.

They bowed their heads and went to God. He asked for wisdom and an understanding of God's will, as well as for a deep and intimate understanding between the two of them. When he was done, he had the feeling that it was already settled, but he wasn't quite ready to put his stamp of approval on the thing.

"I just don't like to see anyone go into marriage by planning for its demise," he said, "but if you're determined to do this, I suppose I'd better clear my calendar."

"That's not necessary," Connie told him softly, a hint of apology in her voice.

"Under the circumstances, we thought a civil ceremony might be best," Kendal explained.

Marcus shook his head. On this issue, he would not budge.

"If you don't want to do it in church, that's one thing, but when any sister of mine gets married, I expect to do the honors. That's one privilege I absolutely reserve for myself."

He could tell that Connie was relieved by that.

"Does that mean that we have your blessing?" Kendal asked.

"Not necessarily," Marcus replied honestly. "This is not a business arrangement, no matter what your attorney says."

"Believe me, it's not my intention to treat it like one," Kendal insisted. "I intend to be the best father and husband that a man can be."

"In that case," Marcus said, somewhat mollified, "I expect you'll be wanting this marriage properly blessed in church one day, and when that happens, then you'll have *my* full blessing. Until that point, I can live with doing it your way."

There was that look again, the one that only two people in love—even if they didn't know it yet—could share.

Marcus sighed inwardly. He half envied, half pitied them. Perhaps in their positions, he'd be looking at this the same way they were, which probably meant he wouldn't have been able to see that rocky road just ahead, either.

Well, sometimes that was best. Perhaps it wasn't as important to see the boulders in the pathway as it was to trust God to get you past them. And should they fail to navigate this pathway together, better that they should fail under these conditions than most others.

Meanwhile, he'd be praying that no one would come away with a broken heart.

"I now pronounce you husband and wife."

Connie heard a sniffle behind her and knew that Jolie was crying. No doubt, she was remembering her own recent nuptials, though this quiet, private little ceremony before the fireplace in Kendal's living room—*their* living room, rather—was a far cry from Jolie's elegant Valentine's Day event.

With only themselves, Marcus, Jolie and Vince in attendance, it hardly seemed like a wedding at all to Connie, except that her brother had just pronounced them husband and wife.

Connie wondered if it felt as surreal to Kendal as it did to her, but his steady gaze gave away nothing. She wondered again if they should have had the children attend rather than schedule the short service during their nap, but then Marcus said the words that she'd been dreading and she remembered why this was best.

"You may kiss the bride."

Connie locked her trembling knees and tried to keep everything else relaxed.

Really, what was there to fear from a simple kiss?

She felt a moment's panic when Kendal bent his head toward hers.

Then his lips brushed across hers and a light flashed on the camera wielded by Vince. Connie winced inwardly. She didn't want to look at that photo in the years to come, knowing that it was all fake.

Kendal wrapped his arms around her and folded her close in an affectionate hug and she realized that her heart was hammering like a drum. *She didn't know how to do this,* she told herself wildly.

They were supposed to be friends—platonic friends— and though Marcus had warned her that marriage could not be a business arrangement, that was essentially how she'd envisioned theirs. Panic swept through her, right behind the realization that Marcus was, unfortunately, right. Affection had to play some part in a spousal relationship, after all.

Affection, not love, she reminded herself, *not romantic love.*

She did her best to relax, allowing Kendal to turn her to face her sister and brother-in-law. They stood side by side, beaming, but then they didn't know the facts.

Connie wanted it that way, and Marcus had agreed with her. Jolie was so in love with her husband that she wouldn't be able to take an objective view of Connie's situation with Kendal. And once again, Connie admitted privately, Jolie would know that she had done better than her baby sister.

Connie felt her stomach sink, hating the feeling of inadequacy.

Why, she wondered for the millionth time, *couldn't she be more like Jolie?*

Vince tucked away the camera and offered his hand to Kendal. Connie marveled at the width of Kendal's—her husband's—grin as he allowed Vince to pump his arm while she found herself perilously close to weeping.

Jolie noticed. She threw her arms around Connie and asked, "What is it about weddings that turns on the tears?"

Connie could only shake her head. *It should have been joy,* she thought. It should have been, but it wasn't. Instead, it was fear, the stark, ravening terror of doubt.

She'd made a mistake. Surely, she'd made a mistake. This wasn't going to work. It couldn't possibly, not when she felt butterflies every time Kendal came near. It felt as if they were beating her to death with their delicate little wings. The effort of smiling strained her resolve, especially when Kendal's arm slid around her.

"I guess we should cut the cake," he said, adding jovially "before the kids wake up."

The children. Yes, of course. That's what this was about.

Connie felt a little better. She allowed Kendal to lead her across the living room and into the formal dining area.

It was a large, airy space, open to the foyer on one end and a sheltered patio on the other through double-wide French doors. A swinging door in a third wall opened onto a small butler's pantry, which opened onto the kitchen. It was the perfect space for entertaining. Kendal said that it was fitting that the first event to be held there would be their wedding celebration, but it felt like a travesty to Connie.

She couldn't help thinking what an utter fraud she

was, posing there with her hand clutching the pearl handle of a beribboned cake knife, Kendal's larger one wrapped around hers. Vince snapped more photos as they pushed the blade down through the small, two-layer confection. White on the outside, pink on the inside, it featured a pile of sugar roses in its midst and could have easily marked someone's birthday instead of a wedding.

"Strawberry," Jolie said, "your favorite."

Connie forced a smile. "Ken ordered it special."

They didn't bother with the pretense of feeding each other. Instead, Connie quickly cut and served enough pieces for everyone.

"Um, good," Vince commented after forking a bite into his mouth.

Everyone else nodded in agreement.

It was the most pathetic attempt at celebration that Connie could recall. She'd marked holidays in prison with more enthusiasm.

Lord, what's wrong with me? she thought. *I know this is best. I know what blessings this marriage will bring. Help me.*

It was with great relief that she heard Larissa cry out.

"Guess that means nap time is over," Kendal quipped, setting aside his plate.

"I'll go, if you like," Jolie offered, but Connie waved that away.

"Oh, thank you, but we'll manage."

"Larissa can be difficult," Kendal admitted. "Help

yourselves to some punch and take a seat in the living room. We won't be long."

Connie would have preferred to get the children up and dress them herself, but she would not say so, fearing that Kendal would take it wrongly. Or, rather, that he would take it correctly.

"It's going to be all right," he told her softly as they moved through the house. "Relax. The worst is over."

She shot him a smile for that, wondering how obvious her distress was.

"It's just that Jolie has always been the one to do everything right," she whispered. "You should have seen her wedding last month."

Kendal drew her to a stop in the hallway.

"It's not a competition, Connie. What works for them won't necessarily work for us and vice versa. Don't judge yourself—or us—by someone else's standards, all right?"

Connie nodded, feeling better. "Thank you."

"Don't mention it, Mrs. Oakes," he said, reaching up to brush a strand of hair from her cheek.

Just like that, the butterflies were back.

There must be something wrong with me, Connie thought as they headed once more for Larissa's room.

But, of course, there was. She was the one who'd thrown her future away on a man who thought stealing and murder were justifiable. She was the one who'd served time in prison, the one who had a child out of wedlock. *If she was ever foolish enough to feel cheated in this marriage,* she told herself, *she had only to remember those facts.*

The truth was, only God's good grace had brought Kendal into her life. She wouldn't grieve the fact that he didn't love her as she'd always imagined her husband would. Together they were a whole family, and that counted most.

So why did this feel so suspiciously like self-pity?

Kendal couldn't account for the level of his emotions. He felt like laughing, like singing. It was ridiculous. His marriage to Laura hadn't made him giddy like this and he believed that he was marrying for love that day.

Their wedding had been a dignified, subdued, very traditional affair—not this rushed, sparse, almost furtive ceremony—and yet, he was quite sure that he hadn't been this...happy.

How long had it been since he had even thought that word in relation to himself? Too long, he decided, walking down the hallway beside...his wife.

Funny, but he felt more married at this moment than ever before. He suspected, though, that Connie did not share his sense of connection. He feared that she was having second thoughts, and all of a sudden, their relationship seemed tenuous at best.

This marriage was right for everyone involved. He would simply make certain that Connie's doubts were put to rest. To that end, Kendal forced himself to relax, allowing himself the small pleasure of placing a proprietary hand at the small of her back just as they reached the door to Larissa's bedroom.

Russell had been given a room on the same side of the hallway as Larissa, the two bedrooms separated by an adjoining bathroom. Connie's room was across from Russell's, next to Kendal's. Their rooms were also separated by a bathroom, but this opened only onto Connie's room, which afforded the adults personal privacy while allowing them both to remain in close proximity to the children.

They decided that Russell would continue to sleep in Larissa's room for the time being. In a day or two, they would move his crib into the room with Larissa's and he would sleep in his own bed. Then in a week or so they would move Russell's crib into his room but leave the adjoining bathroom doors open. In this way, they hoped to accustom the children to living together without having them become too dependent on each other.

Kendal pushed open the door, following it into the room. True to form, Larissa stood at one end of her pale, frilly crib, anxious to get on with this business of getting out and about, while Russell patiently lolled on his back, wide-awake but in no apparent hurry to exert himself. He climbed to his chubby feet as soon as the adults entered the room. Kendal moved quickly to the crib and swept both children into an exuberant hug, lifting them over the side rail.

"Here, Mommy," he said, turning to Connie.

A smile lit up her face. Larissa leaned toward her and Connie obliged by taking her weight from Kendal. He tossed Russell lightly, making him giggle before starting to change his clothing. Connie had laid out wedding finery for both children before their naps.

"Uncle Vince is going to take your picture," she said to Larissa.

"Oh, that's right," Kendal said, suddenly struck by the fact that his daughter would now have aunts and uncles. "We sure got the better end of this deal. All you and Russ got was us, but we got Jolie, Vince and Marcus in the bargain."

"There are your parents," Connie pointed out, "and your stepsisters."

He hadn't even thought of them, actually, but now that he had, it didn't make much difference.

"Well, my father, anyway," he said, "and I guess Louise to an extent, but Janelle and Lisa have their own lives."

Connie lifted an eyebrow at that, but before she could make a comment or ask a question, Russell decided that he was as dressed as he wanted to be. He attempted to flop over onto his belly, as if he might be able to just slide down off the change table as easily as he normally slid off the couch or a chair.

"Whoa, there, pardner. You can't go to a wedding reception without your britches," Kendal said.

"Russ," Larissa ordered sternly. "Stop it."

Kendal looked at his daughter in surprise. She spoke often enough, but mostly it was unintelligible garble. This time, however, she had enunciated as plainly as any adult. Kendal glanced at Connie and saw that she was as surprised as he was. He rolled Russell onto his back once more and held him there with a hand splayed across his chest, then addressed his daughter, a lump in his throat.

"Thank you, Larissa, but Daddy has it under control."

"Takin picher," she said with a nod, as if that settled it.

"That's right," Connie told her, thrusting the toe of her white tights onto one little foot. "Uncle Vince is going to take Russ's picture, too. He's going to take a picture of all of us."

"Larissa, Russell, Mommy and Daddy," Kendal said softly, looking at Connie. "Our first family photo."

Connie smiled and Kendal felt his heart swell inside his chest.

This family was going to be all right. Everything was going to be just fine.

It had to be.

He could not endure another failure.

"Good night, sweetie."

"Good night, Russ."

"Sweet dreams."

Connie closed the door and breathed a sigh of relief. Such a day. She felt tied up in knots. Even after she'd changed out of her hastily purchased, pale-tan wedding suit into comfortable slacks and a turtleneck, she hadn't been able to shake the nerve-racking knowledge that this was her wedding day. Correction. This was now her wedding night.

As if to illustrate that fact, Kendal yawned.

"Mmm, sorry. Long day."

"Tell me about it," Connie sighed, moving down the hallway. "My feet are killing me."

"My mom used to soak her aching feet in an herbal tea concoction," Kendal said, following her.

"Frankly, I'd rather drink it by the cup," Connie quipped.

He tsk-tsked. "Would you settle for a cup of cocoa?"

Now that sounded like an excellent idea, but she hadn't seen any mix in the pantry.

"Are you sure you have any?"

"I have cocoa powder," he said.

She grimaced. "Not the same thing."

They reached the den, where he came to a stop, causing her to turn to face him.

"Don't tell me that you've never had cocoa made from scratch."

Connie tugged her earlobe, folding one arm across her middle. She hoped that he didn't expect her to whip up a batch, good as it sounded.

"Sorry," she told him, "outside of my field of expertise."

"Not outside of mine," he drawled, strolling toward her with a pointed look.

Connie dropped her jaw, laughing. "This I've gotta see."

He wagged a finger at her. "Uh-uh. A man—even a married man—is allowed his little secrets."

"Oh, I see how it is," Connie teased.

Kendal stopped—close by, *too* close—and chucked her under the chin, seizing the tip of it between the pad of his thumb and the curl of his forefinger. A subtle smile curved his lips.

"Prepare to be impressed," he warned.

Suddenly, Connie couldn't breathe. If they were *really* married, she knew, he would kiss her now. Horrified to realize that she wanted him to, she spun away, pretending a great interest in the view beyond the ceiling-to-floor window.

In truth, as the moon had not yet risen, there was nothing to see beyond the large, covered patio except the subtle glow of the pool lights and the black stripes of the tall, wrought-iron fence around the pool. On the street in front of the house, there were lights tastefully tucked into the trees and landscaping, but the common green had been left in a more natural state—if manicured lawns and artfully winding graveled pathways could be deemed natural. At the moment, it was nothing more than black contours against a black backdrop, but it suddenly seemed more comfortable than the warm, opulent house in which she was standing.

Please, she prayed silently, *don't let me mess this up.*

Connie poured herself coffee and lifted the cup, leaning back against the kitchen counter. She had passed another restless night, and she was vexed with herself because of it. What was wrong with her anyway? After nearly a week as Mrs. Kendal Oakes, she ought to have settled in by now, but her room still felt, well, like the guest room, despite the familiarity of her own things around her.

She was missing Marcus. That must be it.

She could talk to Marcus, confide in him.

Once she'd been able to, anyway. Now she hardly knew what she would say to him if he were here—certainly not what was really on her mind. She kept thinking about her husband, wondering if he felt as restless and unsettled as she did.

As if summoned by the mere thought of him, Kendal walked into the kitchen, knotting his tie.

"Morning," he said cheerfully and began dropping smiles on everyone.

He started with Russell, tweaking a chin smeared with oatmeal. A blob of the same plopped onto the high chair tray, dripping from the spoon that Russell hadn't quite kept steady. He immediately concentrated on the blob, smearing it with the tip of one finger.

Larissa did not lift her face at her father's greeting, but the ghost of a smile curved her Cupid's bow mouth, even as she slid her spoon into her bowl for another bite. That was enough to make Kendal beam as he turned to Connie.

She suppressed a stab of longing as she presented him a cool smile, keeping her gaze averted.

"Good morning."

He reached behind her for the mug she'd set out, and said, "You're looking lovely, as usual, but a little tired. Didn't you sleep well?"

She stepped aside so he could pour his coffee. "I was reading until late."

It wasn't exactly a lie. She had read her Bible until late into the night. He didn't have to know that she hadn't picked it up until she'd tossed and turned past her endurance.

"Good book?" he asked lightly.

"The best."

"Ah. Well, why don't you take a nap when the kids

do? That way, you'll be rested for our session with Dr. Stenhope this afternoon."

"We'll see," she hedged, turning toward the stove. "I have some ham to go with the oatmeal, if you like."

"No oatmeal. I'll slap the ham between a couple pieces of toast and eat it on the way. I ought to get in early since I'm going to leave early."

"I'll wrap it in a napkin for you," she said, dropping two pieces of bread into the toaster.

"You're spoiling me," he noted cheerfully.

"By making breakfast?"

"Just by being here."

She didn't know what to say to that. At any rate, her heart was beating too wildly to allow her to reply.

He moved to the table and sat down to drink his coffee while the toaster took forever to brown the bread.

Connie made the sandwich and wrapped it in a napkin, then picked up a banana and carried everything over to him.

"What time should Larissa and I be ready to leave?"

"Three-thirty."

"I'll have Jolie here by three-fifteen then."

"Are you sure she doesn't mind coming over?"

"Trust me, she'll love sitting Russ."

Nodding, he rose. "I'm really glad you're coming with us today."

"Me, too."

He took the sandwich and banana from her. "Have a good day."

"We will."

"And get some rest."

"Don't worry."

"I won't if you promise me that you'll get some rest."

"I promise."

Smiling, he leaned forward and kissed her cheek, just as any normal husband might. Then he left the room, leaving her standing frozen in the center of the floor.

The moment he disappeared from sight, Russell threw down his spoon and yelled "Da-a-a!" so loud that Connie jumped.

A heartbeat later, Kendal stepped back into the doorway that led to the back hall and the garage. He looked at Connie and his eyes said it all.

He cleared his throat twice and glanced at Connie again before saying, "I'll see you later, Son. You, too, Larissa. Be good for Mom. I love you both." With that, he turned and left again, his eyes glinting suspiciously.

Connie turned away so that the children wouldn't see her tears, but the awful truth was that, unlike Kendal's, hers were not tears of joy. They were not tears of sadness, either. Hers were more like tears of shame.

She felt ashamed because something seemed to be fundamentally wrong with her. Otherwise, she wouldn't be wallowing in self-pity half the night because she'd gotten exactly what she'd bargained for in this marriage. Her heart wouldn't have clenched because he'd told the children that he loved them and hadn't told her the same.

She wouldn't be so miserably ungrateful when her every prayer had been answered.

She wouldn't be falling in love with her husband.

Chapter Ten

Kendal resisted the urge to drape his arm loosely around Connie's shoulders or even take her hand in a show of support. Such physical gestures—however innocent—were not welcome.

Oh, she never said anything. One thing he had learned about his lovely wife over the past few weeks was that she did not complain, not about anything. It was if she thought she'd lost the right to complain when she'd sat ignorantly outside that bank while Jessup Kennard had shot a man.

No, she didn't complain when Kendal touched her. She stiffened, though, and subtly moved away, never realizing that it was the same to him as being stabbed. As a consequence, much of the time Kendal felt as though he were bleeding from dozens of small cuts. It was, he'd realized bleakly, even worse than Laura's cold, blunt rejection in the past. He didn't know why, but it was.

Still, he wouldn't change anything. If only for his

daughter's sake, he'd make the same bargain all over again—and somehow find a way to live with it.

"I'm sorry, Dr. Stenhope," Connie said softly, "but I can't agree with you."

Robust and middle-aged, with straight gray hair chopped bluntly just below the nape, Dr. Stenhope had an air of superiority that was, admittedly, supported by her reputation and credentials. On rare occasions, though, such as this one, her clinical detachment slipped.

"So you're not just her stepmother. Now you are a clinician, as well?"

"Connie is not and will never be *just* Larissa's step-mother," Kendal said somewhat tartly. "She is going to formally adopt Larissa."

Curling her lip slightly, Dr. Stenhope waved that away as inconsequential.

"My experience with detachment disorders has shown that adoption makes little or no difference."

"But that's just it," Connie pointed out. "I don't believe that Larissa has a detachment disorder, not in the clinical sense."

The doctor made a show of rearranging papers on her desk.

"Oh? And you think your diagnosis is superior to mine?"

Kendal frowned at Dr. Stenhope's flippant tone, but Connie kept her voice serene and polite.

"Larissa was traumatized by her mother's death. There can be no doubt about that. But I believe that her attitude toward her father is a combination of her own strong will and conditioning."

"Learned behavior, yes, I think you mentioned that," the doctor said, sounding amused. "However, I must warn you, Mrs. Oakes, that a child's personality and temperament are set by the time she is Larissa's age."

"I understand that, and I have no problem with Larissa's personality or her temperament," Connie went on doggedly, "but I do believe that Larissa can be taught to love and respect her father."

"Retraining is not impossible," the doctor demurred, pursing her lips. "It is most certainly one of our goals."

Connie tugged on her left earlobe. Kendal had come to realize that it was a nervous habit—a stalling tactic—and he slipped his hand around her wrist in a gesture of support.

"I suppose the problem is that I don't understand how your methods will achieve that goal," Connie said to the doctor, "more specifically, I don't understand the need for medication."

The doctor seemed exasperated. She folded her hands over her desk blotter and adopted a somewhat patronizing tone.

"I am not surprised by that, ma'am, but you must appreciate the fact that psychiatry is not an exact science. Granted, some of our methods are experimental, and perhaps they will not help Larissa. We need to monitor her under medication closely to determine if she improves."

"Meanwhile, Larissa is not learning one whit about

getting along in this world," Connie said rather forcefully.

"Our methods are accepted in the field," the doctor argued acerbically. "Her treatment plan is cutting-edge medicine."

"That may be," Connie said, rising to her feet, "but it doesn't change the fact that Larissa has learned more about being a normal, happy child in the past six weeks than in all the months before that. Maybe we don't know anything about regressive play therapy, psychoanalysis or the newest drugs, but I do know that our daughter is calmer, more satisfied and more interactive than she was before I met her."

"No one is disputing that fact," Dr. Stenhope said quickly, but Connie was on a roll, and she wasn't going to be derailed.

"I know that she loves her father and she's learning to show it," Connie went on doggedly. "She's taking on a big-sister role with Russell, though there are only a few months between them. Now I call that progress!"

She turned to Kendal her pretty mouth set mulishly.

"I'm sorry, Ken, but I can't stand idly by while they put our daughter on drugs for no good reason."

Kendal stood up and realized he could have kissed her. He *wanted* to kiss her. That was part of the problem, frankly—one he spent a lot of time trying not to think about lately. He hadn't bargained on that. Not that he hadn't always found her attractive. It just hadn't become an issue until she was living in the house with him, until he had married her.

Somehow, he wasn't prepared for the kind of interaction they shared, which was absurd because he, at least, had been married before. But not like this.

With Laura, the marriage had grown colder, not warmer from the moment she said, "I do." Certainly, he'd expected this marriage to be different, but it wasn't supposed to be like this. Affection, yes. Trust, absolutely. Admiration, of course. He had expected a partnership, and they certainly had that, but this tenderness was blossoming into profound love.

One thing gave him great comfort, though. He adored how ardently Connie loved and fought for their daughter.

He drew in a deep, calming breath and switched his attention to Dr. Stenhope.

"I agree one hundred percent with my wife, doctor. Larissa is not going to take your medication."

Dr. Stenhope's face grew stern.

"Kendal, I must remind you that I am the foremost expert in my field—"

He lifted one hand, interrupting her. "Your credentials are unassailable, doctor, but nothing you can say is going to change my mind at this point. God brought Connie to us for a reason, and Larissa is blooming in the safe, structured, consistent environment that we are able to provide for her now. My faith insists that this is the right path for us."

Dr. Stenhope placed her hands flat on her desk and pushed up to her full height.

"In that case," she decreed, "perhaps you would be better satisfied with a *less progressive* therapist."

Kendal glanced at Connie, who bowed her head without comment.

"I'm sorry you feel that way, doctor," he said. "I know you've done your best for Larissa, but I believe that God has other plans for her now."

Dr. Stenhope inclined her head, polite in defeat if not exactly gracious.

They took their leave quickly, collected Larissa from the windowed therapy chamber where she waited under the watchful eye of an assistant and walked out to the car.

It was a glorious spring afternoon, the kind of day that saw problems seem to melt away. As the couple headed to the car, each holding one of their daughter's small hands, Larissa seemed at peace.

"What Russ doing?" she asked.

"I don't know what Russ is doing at the moment, sweetie," Connie answered. "Maybe Daddy will take you both outside for a swing for a little while before supper, though."

"Would you like Daddy to take you out for a swing when we get home?" Kendal asked, unlocking the car with the remote.

Larissa made no reply.

Connie opened the back door and Kendal lifted Larissa into her seat.

"I bet a hug would convince Daddy to take you out for a swing," Connie suggested.

Larissa kept her gaze averted, but she dutifully wrapped her arms around Kendal's neck as he bent over her in the car.

He closed his eyes, basking in the moment. It still took Connie's prompting, but his daughter was now at least willing to interact with him for whatever she wanted. Connie insisted that Larissa's feelings for him were genuine and deep. He was not so sure, but he was willing to take whatever he could get, frankly. If only Connie would...

No, he wouldn't think like that. What he had now with Connie, Russell and Larissa was so much more than he'd had before that he wouldn't second-guess it. Perhaps it was not *all* that he wanted, but it was exactly what he'd bargained for, and he was grateful for it.

After he got Larissa safely harnessed into her seat, he walked Connie around to the passenger's side and opened the door for her. Oddly enough, he enjoyed these small, husbandly gestures as much as he enjoyed his daughter's hugs and his son's laughter. He told himself that he couldn't ask for more.

Throughout the remainder of the afternoon and into the evening, Kendal felt as if he existed in a bubble of golden light. Great pleasure was found in the simple things—swinging with his children on the bench swing beneath the arbor in the side yard, their fumbling attempts to wash up for dinner, another excellent meal, an hour or so of television with his family in the den, the ritual of bedtime. He could only marvel at how radically his life had changed and knew that he was blessed.

Then the children were in bed and the day wound down to that awkward hour when it was just him and Connie. That was when the pain resurfaced and when he wondered how much longer he could endure her politeness and distance.

Out of sheer habit, he looked for a distraction. Sometimes it was work, sometimes television or a book. This time, Connie provided the distraction as they returned to the den together.

"So what do you think we should do about Larissa's therapy?"

His thoughts had touched on the subject off and on throughout the evening, but he hadn't wanted to rush to any judgment.

"I think we need to pray about it."

"I agree," she said simply, sinking into the couch.

He took a seat next to her but not too close. They bowed their heads and he began to ask God for guidance. Connie, too, prayed for understanding and wisdom, surprising him by saying aloud that she didn't want her dislike of the doctor to influence their decision. Afterward, Kendal couldn't help expressing his amused surprise.

"So you don't like the doctor?"

Connie wrinkled her nose. "She reminds me of a warden."

Suddenly, her confession didn't seem quite so amusing.

"I keep forgetting about that. Prison must have been a horrible experience."

She shrugged. "Yes and no. I tried to take away as much good from it as I could. I think I came out a better person than I went in."

He shook his head in awe.

"I don't know how you can have that attitude when you weren't even guilty of anything."

"We're all guilty of something, Ken," she said. "I was at least guilty of not listening when God tried to get my attention, and like Marcus says, 'If you don't go to your knees willingly, then you leave God no choice but to drive you to them.'"

"My mother used to say something like that. The way she put it was that we should humble ourselves before God or He would do it for us."

"She must have been very wise."

"She was. She had that same spiritual wisdom that I sense in Marcus but also an unusual maturity and a patience borne of much suffering."

"I wish I had known her."

Kendal nodded. "You don't know how often I've wished I could seek her advice, especially since Laura died."

Connie nodded. "I'm very thankful that I have Marcus."

"Do you think he could recommend a competent therapist?"

"I don't know, but I'm sure he'd be willing to listen if you want to discuss the matter with him."

"I think I might." Kendal furrowed his brow. "You know, I came to Fort Worth expressly to get Larissa into therapy with Dr. Stenhope. Now I wonder if the therapist was the real reason God brought me here."

"Whatever the reason," Connie said, "I'm glad you made the move."

He had her hand in his before he realized what he was doing.

"I think you're the reason," he told her softly. "You and Russ."

Her hand lay still and stiff in his.

"I doubt God would put you and Larissa through all that turmoil and pain just for my benefit."

"I was looking at it the other way around," he confessed. "You are a godsend, Connie. The difference you've made in our lives is simply amazing."

She squeezed his hand, and said, "I think I've gotten more than I've given."

"Never," he whispered, lifting his arm around her.

To his delight, she smiled and lay her head on his shoulder. He folded her close, overwhelmed with hope. *Might this be the moment that their real marriage begins?* he wondered. His heart pounding, he curled a finger beneath her chin and turned her face up. His gaze slid to her mouth and her pretty lips parted slightly, but as he lowered his head, she suddenly straightened and turned her face away.

His fledgling hope crashed and shattered. Loss and pain howled through him. His muscles tightened as he fought to keep his expression impassive, undisturbed.

"Well," he said, feeling strangled and wounded, "I think I'll turn in early."

She smiled and nodded, but her gaze did not quite meet his.

He rose quickly and went to his room—his lonely, solitary room—where he fell on his face, spread-eagle on his bed.

He had no right to feel this disappointment, no right to the expectations that had led to it, no right to wish that it might be different.

Help me to not love her, he prayed. But that couldn't be right. He amended his prayer. *Show me how to love her as I should. I want to be the husband that You want me to be, the husband and father that I wasn't before.*

The father. Yes, that was it. To be the husband that Connie deserved and God ordained, he had to first be the father.

"What's this?" Connie asked, eyeing the envelope that Kendal placed on the counter with obvious suspicion.

"Open it and see."

He folded his arms, smiling complacently while she picked up the large manila envelope, lifted the flap and reached inside. Grasping a sheaf of papers, she pulled them free of the envelope and began to read. Her heart swelled and tears stung her eyes.

"Oh, Ken."

"It's not done yet," he warned. "We have to petition the court to sever Jessup's ties first, and he could fight us on it, but our attorney assures me that it would only delay matters, nothing more."

"Russell Wheeler Oakes," she read aloud, brushing her fingertips over the name printed on the page.

"It has a nice sound to it, don't you think?"

She nodded. "I can't tell you what this means to me, what it will mean to him."

He smiled at that.

"You'll have to sign in front of a notary. Then the attorney can file."

"I'll do it first thing tomorrow. Miss Dabney is a notary."

He made a face and she laughed, knowing that he was thinking of how Miss Dabney had essentially forced Larissa out of day care.

"I'll take the children and rub her nose in it," she promised, tongue in cheek.

"No, you won't," he refuted, tapping her on the end of her nose. "You're too much a lady."

She made the face this time.

"You're right. It wouldn't be nice."

"Besides, when you think about it, she did us a favor."

"It has worked out, hasn't it?" Connie said, keeping her smile in place as she turned away and opened a cabinet.

She stowed the papers safely out of sight so she could finish dinner preparations without worrying about getting something on the important forms. She wondered if she should broach the subject of adopting Larissa or let it go for now. On one hand, she worried that her record would complicate matters; on the other, it would be one more tie binding them together.

Perhaps they were already bound too tightly.

She wasn't as good at this marriage-in-name-only business as Kendal. Too often, she found herself yearning for something more. She had begun to fear that she might be the sort who could never be satisfied, always wanting more and more. Her mother had been like that: always seeking something more.

Connie had begun to think about what might happen if Kendal were to actually fall in love with her. Would that be enough? Or would she find herself wondering what else, who else, might be waiting for her out there? She couldn't quite believe that she would ever want any other man, but was that because her love for her husband remained unrequited? She'd once thought the same about Jessup, after all.

The fact that Jessup Kennard was nothing at all like Kendal Oakes meant little because she had known, deep down, that Jessup was not all he should have been and still she had loved him, wanted him.

It was better, she decided, if she never found out what being loved by Kendal would mean, not that it was likely to happen. Why would he love her? And why should she want him to?

What they had was too precious to risk on the mere thrill of romance and the chance that she was as fickle at heart as her mother.

She would be satisfied with what she had.

How could she ask for more, really, when she'd already been given so very much?

"You don't mind?" Kendal asked, not for the first time.

"No, of course not," Connie insisted yet again. "I understand perfectly why you'd want your father and stepmother to think that ours is a marriage like any other."

"It's not that I want to lie to them," he said, not for the first time. "It's just that explanations could be awkward and—"

"Ken, it's not as if they're spending the night," Connie interrupted, keeping her voice low in deference to the children. "Just visiting for a few hours. Besides, they're here now. It's too late to change our minds."

Nodding, he took a deep breath and expelled it as the white luxury sedan rolled to a stop at the top of the drive. The driver's door opened and Russell immediately started forward, but Kendal reached down and snatched the boy up into the safety of his arms. Larissa, meanwhile, wrapped herself around Connie's legs and turned her face away from the newcomers. Connie patted her back encouragingly.

Gordon Oakes climbed out of the car and turned to wave as he moved around to the passenger's side. He didn't look much like Kendal, actually, being shorter, heavier and bald. Of course, at sixty-six, he had thirty-six years on his son, but his features were too soft, his face too round, his jawline not quite as chiseled as Ken's, who obviously took after his late mother.

Kendal's stepmother emerged from the sedan.

Louise Oakes was tall and rawboned, with improbably red hair caught in a large black bow at the nape of her neck. She beamed a toothy smile at them and hurried forward, a black handbag dangling from her elbow. Wearing black pants and a brightly colored blouse with white shoes, she was not exactly a fashion plate. Then again, in his pale-blue seersucker pants and white pull-over with brown socks and shoes, Gordon was not nearly as well turned out as his son, either.

For some reason, Connie relaxed a little.

Kendal stepped forward, reaching out to his father.

"Dad. Louise. It's so good to see you."

Gordon pounded Kendal's back enthusiastically.

"Hello, Son. How are you? Don't even need to ask, do I? Just look at this pretty thing standing beside you. Whoa, look at this little one, Lu, another redhead in the mix!"

Kendal slid an arm around Connie's waist, smiling at the boy in his arms.

"Honey, this is my dad."

"It's Gordon, young lady," he said, shaking her hand and clapping her on the shoulder.

"Connie," she got in before he disappeared.

Squatting, he took himself down to eye level with Larissa.

"Hello, Larissa! Can you hug your old grandpa's neck?"

Connie urged Larissa forward a step. Tentatively, Larissa lifted one arm and hung it stiffly around Gordon's neck before zipping back to Connie. Obviously surprised, Gordon shot a look up at Kendal.

"Well," he said, pushing himself back up to full height.

Kendal nodded, smiling. Suddenly, Gordon engulfed Connie in a bear hug.

"Little lady, Ken pegged you right when he said you were an answered prayer."

It was Connie's turn to send a surprised look at her

husband, but then her attention was distracted by Louise, who held her arms out to Russell.

"Who is this little darlin'?"

Russell didn't know the woman, but that didn't prevent him from sliding into her arms.

"This is Russell," Kendal said, rubbing the boy's little head proudly.

Louise hugged the boy as if hungry for the experience, her gaze dropping to Larissa.

"Russ," Larissa said seriously, pointing, just in case Louise hadn't gotten the message.

Louise bent down, Russell clinging to her, and kissed the top of Larissa's head.

"You have grown so much! Look how pretty you are."

Larissa ducked her chin, smiling slightly. Louise straightened.

"It's so good to see you all!" she exclaimed and abruptly burst into tears.

Chapter Eleven

"I'm not some silly old woman, you know," Louise said, slicing into the lemon that Connie had removed from the refrigerator.

"No, of course you aren't," Connie told her lightly, pouring hot water over the tea bags in the pitcher. "Think nothing of it."

"It's just that we've been so worried," Louise confided, wielding the knife swiftly. "We've tried not to interfere, really we have."

"I'm sure Ken realizes and appreciates that," Connie murmured, wondering if he did.

She set the timer and reached up into the cabinet for glass tumblers.

"It's just that we didn't know what to expect, you see," Louise went on, picking seeds out of the lemon slices. "Larissa was so troubled and Ken was so stoic and bleak all the time." She shook her head and slapped the knife down on the countertop. "It was that woman's fault. God forgive me, but I never liked her. She was so cold, so—" Louise crossed her arms and shivered "—unbalanced."

Connie said nothing. She didn't want to criticize, and God knew that she had no room or right to judge anyone. Besides, this was Larissa's birth mother they were talking about.

"When Ken called and said he got married again, we were shocked," Louise stated bluntly. "We didn't know what to think."

"It was sudden," Connie admitted.

"What a relief to walk in here and find you!" Louise exclaimed, and Connie flushed.

She felt like a fraud. These people didn't know about her prison record or the circumstances of Russell's birth—not that she blamed Kendal for keeping them in the dark. Still, it made things awkward.

"And to see the change in that child," Louise went on, clutching her hands together and lifting them toward the ceiling in a gesture of thanks. Then she sighed. "You're so lucky. Larissa will never remember a time when you weren't her mother."

"I feel very blessed," Connie agreed, trying not to think that she'd missed the infancy of both children.

It struck her quite forcefully that she would never know those first precious days of life and discovery—not so long as her marriage remained chaste.

"What's this new treatment Ken mentioned?" Louise asked.

Connie shook herself out of her reverie. "We're, uh, moving into a different type of therapy now, more of a family-therapy situation. It's all about building and blending relationships."

Louise waved a hand as if to dismiss that and said, "You're already a family. She even calls you Mommy. It's so wonderful!"

Connie laughed. Her heart skipped a beat and the world seemed a brighter, sunnier place whenever one of the children called her Mommy.

"That's Kendal's doing, frankly. I guess it just seemed natural to him. He certainly had Russell calling him Daddy in no time."

She would always be so grateful for that.

Louise reached out a hand to Connie. Smiling, Connie clasped hands with her and understanding flashed between them. It was the last thing Connie had expected: to have such a rapport with her mother-in-law. She didn't know if Kendal would approve of her calling Louise that, but she couldn't think of the woman any other way now. No doubt, she'd have loved Kendal's birth mother, but she couldn't imagine that she'd have found any more acceptance. Certainly, they wouldn't have had this much in common.

It was amazing, Connie thought, *how it had all worked out.* She just hoped that her past wouldn't rise up to somehow mar the present.

Kendal glanced back over his shoulder as he moved toward the kitchen to check on how the iced tea was coming along. He had a fierce thirst, but more than that, he wanted to give his dad a few moments alone with the kids.

It wasn't an entirely normal situation. Larissa tended to ignore her grandfather in much the same manner that she tried to ignore Kendal, but she could be engaged through Russell, who stood at the center of her attention whenever Connie wasn't around. His dad was eating that up.

Gordon sat on the couch, Larissa on one knee, Russell on the other.

"Can you say *Grandpa?*" he urged. "Who can say *Grandpa?* Come on, which one of you is going to say it first? *Grandpa.* I'm Grandpa." He pointed to each of them in turn. "Larissa, Russell, Grandpa."

Ken chuckled. One of them had better learn to say it before the day was through. The old man was determined.

Kendal reached for the louvered swinging door and paused, hearing his stepmother's voice and Connie's laughter.

He began to push the door inward, only to halt again as Louise exclaimed, "I envy you so much!"

Drawing back his hand, Kendal cocked his head.

"I'd be thrilled if Larissa would call me *Grandma,*" Louise said. "I so wanted Ken to call me *Mom.* Of course, he was older when I married Gordon, and he was so close to Katherine. I never wanted to get in the way of that. She deserved to be remembered, to keep that place in his heart, but I'd have been so happy if he could've thought of me as his mother."

Kendal reeled backward a step.

He hadn't realized that it mattered to Louise one way

or the other. Louise was so…demonstrative, so *blatant,* that he always just assumed she'd speak up if she wasn't happy about something. It hadn't occurred to him that she was even capable of holding back.

"I'm sure Ken is fond of you," Connie said. "I know he's grateful that his dad has you."

"I always wanted a son," Louise said wistfully, and Kendal recognized all too well the note of yearning in her voice. "My girls have never understood that. They've been a little jealous of Kendal. They say I stick my nose into their business at the drop of a hat but that I've always shown him much more restraint." Louise chuckled. "I guess they're right, but my mother always said that men—boys—are different. You'd understand that. You have a son."

"It's so true," Connie said with a laugh. "Even now, if you give Larissa a doll, she holds and pats it, but to Russ, a doll is a car with legs. He'll literally drive it, pushing it around on the floor. He even adds sound effects."

The conversation went on in that vein for some time, but Kendal couldn't concentrate on what was being said. He was too caught up in the idea that he'd misjudged his stepmother. It hadn't seemed to him that she'd cared one way or another about a relationship with him, but he wondered now if he just hadn't given her a chance.

He knew what that was like. Oh, did he know what that was like!

His lungs felt as if he'd taken a blow to the chest. *What else had he missed?* He wondered.

The answer was painfully obvious.

He turned to look at his daughter with new eyes. *Learned behavior.* Connie kept using that phrase. In her mind, Larissa's behavior reflected exactly what she'd been taught—and he had been as responsible for what she'd been taught as her mother, maybe more so.

A warmth spread through his chest. Gasping, he only then understood how cold he had been, how closed off. He'd cheated himself and Louise of a relationship. Had he also cheated his wife and his daughter?

He had.

He knew he had.

Ever since the death of his mother, he'd been that poor boy who'd been hurt by the loss of someone dear. When had he withdrawn from those who cared most about him? Why hadn't he realized what he was doing?

Yes, Louise was exuberant and demonstrative—too much so, he'd always thought—but now he remembered the warmth and exuberance of his mother's hug and the hearty laughter that she had shared with his father and he knew that the problem wasn't Louise. She hadn't been too blatant. He had been too reserved.

A sudden urge seized him.

He strode across the room, swept his daughter up into his arms and carried her to the wall of glass that overlooked the gentle slope of the backyard. She didn't resist. She didn't even stiffen. She looked at him—not with surprise or shock or fear but with a solemn, soul-deep sadness that nearly reduced him to tears.

"Oh, baby," he said, trying to be quiet, trying to be gentle as he hugged her close. "I love you so much. Daddy loves you so much."

He held her and rocked her gently, swaying from side to side, until her arms and legs slowly crept around him. He put his head back, overwhelmed with emotion. This was what he needed, what she needed, and this was the way it was going to be from now on.

This is the new me, he thought, *the real me. This is who I will be, and this is how I'm going to help my daughter be who she should be.*

He would not, he vowed, mope around waiting to be loved. From now on, he would do the loving and count whatever came from it as gain, even if what should come was heartbreak.

"Can we talk?"

Side by side on the couch, his father and stepmother looked up at Kendal.

"Sure," Gordon said, flapping a hand lightly against the back of the sofa. "What's up?"

"Actually, I was speaking specifically to Louise," Kendal divulged, dropping down next to Connie.

His stepmother glanced around as if to find the other Louise in the room before she again looked at him. She leaned forward slightly, a certain apprehension in her eyes. He had never before realized what a soft, clear gray they were, with just a hint of purple about them.

"I know you have to be going soon, but I wanted to wait until the kids were down for their naps," he began.

Louise traded a look with his father before she asked, "Is something wrong?"

Kendal shook his head. "No. Well, yes." The apprehension in her eyes sparked to alarm, so he hastened to add "I heard what you said to Connie in the kitchen earlier."

Louise looked confused. She might not understand yet, but Kendal realized that Connie knew exactly what he was talking about. He groped for his wife's hand, found it and kept it as he leaned forward, bracing his elbows on his knees.

"Louise, I'm sorry," he said, and Connie squeezed his hand encouragingly.

"Sorry?" Louise echoed, furrowing her brow.

He licked his lips, suddenly realizing that he hadn't rehearsed what he would say but plunging ahead anyway. "I never realized how much my…coldness hurt you."

Her jaw literally dropped.

"What are you talking about?" Gordon demanded, his face screwed up in confusion.

Kendal felt his lips twitch in a smile. It wasn't the least bit funny, especially when he felt on the verge of tears, so he couldn't imagine why that smile wanted out. Alternately, he felt as if he wanted to hide his face and as if sunlight might burst from his chest at any moment. He composed himself and explained.

"I heard Louise tell Connie that she'd always wanted me to call her *Mom,* and I didn't, and I'm apologizing for that."

Louise cupped one hand over her mouth. The muscles of Gordon's lower face began to quiver.

"You—" He cleared his throat. "The way your mother suffered—"

"No," Kendal said. "That's no excuse. God gave me a second mother—not a replacement, but a second one—and I didn't know how to be thankful for that." He tightened his hold on Connie's hand. "Now God has given my daughter a second mother, and I will be forever grateful for that, but I'm realizing now how little I appreciated what I had."

"Oh, no, Ken," Louise managed in a shaky voice. "You've had such hard times, we realize that."

"We all have hard times," he said. "That's part of life. Mine didn't have to be quite as difficult as I've made them, I think, but I can't do anything about the past. All we can do now is go forward. I suppose it's a little late for me to begin calling you *Mom,* but I want you to know that my children will always think of you as their grandmother, just as Larissa will always know Connie as her mother and Russ will think of me, I hope, as his father."

"It's n-n-never too late!" Louise wailed, throwing out her arms and coming up off the couch.

Kendal rose to meet her, bending to accept her hug. "Thank you," he whispered. "Thank you for being my mom even when I wasn't smart enough or loving enough to be your son."

She sobbed with all the enthusiasm with which she did everything else. He patted her, not quite sure what else to do. Then he saw the tears in his father's eyes and he knew that he didn't have to do anything. He just had to accept what had for so long been offered.

Connie stood at the door, watching as Kendal said goodbye to his parents. They all seemed so happy. Louise couldn't stop talking about how she wished they could stay longer.

"Next time," she said, "we'll stay the night."

Ken never batted an eye, but Connie couldn't help thinking that her room was the guest room. Of course, she could always bunk with one of the kids, but that would mean explaining their situation to her in-laws or outright lying to them with some made-up excuse. Neither idea appealed to Connie in the least.

She was thrilled that Kendal had come to fully accept his stepmother at last, but this new chapter in their relationship presented certain problems. Connie felt a little guilty about not telling Gordon and Louise the truth concerning their marriage, but she couldn't deny that she preferred not to do so, either. The guilt intensified when Gordon broke away from his wife and son and bore down on her with arms and smile wide.

"Here's the gal we have to thank for making this such a great visit," he boomed heartily, engulfing her in a hug. "You found the right one this time, Ken."

"Yes," Kendal agreed warmly, "I sure did."

Connie felt the sting of heat in her cheeks. Thankfully they didn't know what a fraud she was! What would they think of their daughter-in-law if they knew she was an ex-con and an unwed mother who'd been raised in the child-welfare system?

No, she reminded herself, not unwed, not any longer. But for how long? A marriage in name only was easily broken if—and when—the time came, and the time would surely come when Larissa and Kendal no longer needed her.

Louise garnered everyone's attention by loudly blowing her nose.

"I wish we didn't have to go!" she wailed.

"If we hadn't bought those nonrefundable cruise tickets..." Gordon opined, shaking his head.

"It'll be at least two months before we can come back," Louise observed mournfully. She planted a kiss on Kendal's cheek and said, "We travel too much anyway, and you know what? It's just not as much fun as it used to be."

Gordon concurred with a thoughtful nod. "We'll have to cut back. A growing family needs more time."

"Speaking of growing families," Louise said, pulling Kendal forward so she could wrap an arm around Connie's waist as well as his, "you kids won't want to wait too long before you add another grandbaby to the mix. Wouldn't that be lovely, Gordon?"

"Fan-n-n-tastic!" Gordon exclaimed.

Connie felt the color drain from her face. Her gaze zipped up to meet Kendal's.

He didn't bat an eyelash, didn't seem the least uncomfortable by the topic, didn't voice a single cautionary word.

Longing stabbed Connie out of the blue. She had a sudden vision of a tiny bundle with warm-brown hair and big eyes the color of cinnamon. *Plus,* she thought, *a baby would bind her to Kendal in a way that their sham marriage never could.* Appalled at herself, she quickly turned away, groping blindly for the doorknob.

Gordon and Louise left soon after that—Louise beseeching them to kiss the grandbabies for her, Gordon proclaiming loudly that he expected someone to be saying "Grandpa" by the time he returned. Kendal came to stand beside Connie in the doorway, one arm slanted casually over her shoulder and across her back as he waved his parents away with the other. Only when the sedan turned down the drive did they step back inside.

"That went well," he announced happily.

"I'm glad," Connie told him, moving into the foyer. "I like them."

He caught her hand before she slipped out of reach, drawing her to a halt and saying, "They love you. Dad told me over and over again how good you've been for us. But he wasn't telling me anything I didn't already know."

"You were the one who made this visit special for them, Ken," she told him with a shake of her head. "What you did for Louise was very kind."

He snorted at that. "I should have done it long ago. If I hadn't been such a self-absorbed twit, I'd have realized—"

She cut him off, impulsively placing her fingertips over his mouth.

"You said it yourself, the past is the past. We go on from here."

Sighing, he pulled her close, wrapping his arms loosely around her.

"I love you, you know," he said softly.

For one wild moment, her heart soared, but then she quickly reeled it in. He didn't mean it *that* way.

Or did he? she wondered when he curled his fingers beneath her chin and tilted her head back. Then his face descended and his lips pressed gently on the center of her forehead.

No, he didn't mean it in any romantic sense. Her heart plummeted, even as she told herself that what she felt was relief.

It was better this way, she insisted silently as they turned toward the living room arm in arm. In many ways, Kendal had become her best friend. They made good partners. She only had to look at the children to know.

Larissa and Russell seemed to be rubbing the sharp edges off each other, imparting something of themselves to the other. Russell beamed all the time now. He seemed a bit more aggressive in a secure, confident way, while Larissa was softening, and becoming gentler. At times, she appeared very uncertain, but she was much more willing to interact now, especially with her father.

Yes, this marriage had been good for the children. For their sake, Connie would never regret her bargain with Kendal.

For herself, Connie sometimes secretly wished that she had never laid eyes on Kendal Oakes. What he made her feel on a daily basis terrified her. Sometimes she yearned for a closeness and intimacy that she knew could be a disaster waiting to happen, and yet she somehow couldn't put it aside. That seemed like the very worst confirmation of her greatest fear: that she was like her mother, neediness bred into the bone. How could she saddle Ken with that?

He deserved better, which meant that she could not tie him to her permanently. She had no choice but to pull back emotionally, but that had become more and more difficult to do. Maintaining physical contact at the same time was a virtual impossibility, so Connie quickly and casually disengaged from Kendal the instant they emerged from the foyer.

He stood silently watching her as she busily moved around the house, straightening and tidying. She even picked up the kids' toys, which they would pull out again as soon as they awoke from their naps. That shouldn't be long now, thankfully. Then she could start dinner, keeping herself busy almost until bedtime, which reminded her…

What would she do when Kendal's parents returned for that overnight visit?

Would she even still be here?

"Eat your peas, sweetie," Kendal instructed patiently. Larissa gave him a bland look but then daintily picked up a single pea between the thumb and forefinger of her right hand and popped it into her mouth. "Good girl," Kendal praised.

Abruptly, Russell grabbed a handful of peas from his own plate, smashed them in his fist and crammed them into his mouth. Mostly. Kendal chortled even as Connie reprimanded the boy.

"Russell, no! Use your spoon."

"Don't scold him," Kendal said offhandedly. "He's just trying to be a good boy and do what Daddy says. Aren't you, son?"

"At this rate, he's going to be smashing food all over his face when he's in kindergarten," Connie complained, rising from the table to wipe Russell's hands and face.

Kendal looked down at his plate and tried not to take offense.

Lately, he found himself regularly plummeting from the mountain peak of elation to the valley of despair. On one hand, the children were responding beautifully. When he remembered the stiff, depressed and depressing father that he used to be, he could have wept. On the other hand, Connie was another matter altogether.

No matter what he tried, she just seemed to pull further and further away. In the four days since his parents had visited, everything had shifted. He'd had a sort of epiphany that day. Or, at least, he thought he had. In one blinding moment of insight, he realized that he'd never really allowed himself to love again after the death of his mother, and he vowed to be different. He *was* different, and yet his relationship with his wife had only become more strained and confusing.

It was almost Laura all over again. The more he wanted to love Connie, the more she hardened against him.

What am I doing wrong, Lord?

He'd asked that same question a dozen times already,

and so far, he had no answers. He was no closer to understanding how to make his farce of a marriage real than he had been the first time he'd fashioned that prayer. Yet, what could he do other than keep trying? Determined, he picked up his fork once more.

They ate in near silence, discounting the screeches and grunts of toddler talk and the accompanying background music of banging feet and eating utensils. Then Russell shoved his plate off his high chair tray, a sure sign that the meal had ended. Fortunately, Kendal caught it before it flipped over and decorated the floor with half-eaten veggies and shredded beef. But Connie was incensed, or as incensed as Connie ever got.

"Russell Wheeler Oakes!" she snapped, leaping to her feet. "You are going to learn some table manners, young man, or you're going to eat alone!"

"No harm done," Kendal pointed out in a low voice.

Connie didn't appear to hear him as she yanked the tray off the high chair and unclipped the safety belt with quick, agitated movements.

She lifted Russell from his high chair and deposited him on his feet, ordering, "Time-out!"

Instead of going to the time-out chair in the corner, Russell sat down with a plop and began to cry. Kendal reached down and picked up Russell, setting the boy in his lap, his little head tucked beneath Kendal's chin. Connie turned her back and began busily wiping down the kitchen counters.

"You have to learn to eat with a spoon and fork like

Daddy," Kendal said to the sniffling Russell. "I know it seems like a lot of bother, but that's what big boys do. You'll keep trying and you'll learn. Okay?"

Russell, of course, made no reply. A wide-eyed Larissa did, though. She pointed a finger at Russell and instructed, "Kiss him."

Kendal smiled, delighted.

"Okay, I'll kiss him." He began smacking kisses all over Russell's head. Soon, Russell was laughing. "But if I kiss Russ, I have to kiss you, too!" he told Larissa, scooting to the edge of the chair to reach her.

She grinned as wide as her face, belying her nonchalant pose.

Kendal had never been happier than in that moment when his daughter had eagerly turned up her face to him. He trapped Russell against him with one arm, crouched beside Larissa's chair and tickled her with baby kisses until they were all laughing.

He lifted himself and slid back onto the seat of his chair, glancing up at Connie. She stood with her back to the counter, her hands braced against its edge, a soft, almost-yearning smile on her face. He smiled back, seeking her gaze with his, and she abruptly turned around again, reaching for something in the sink.

Kendal felt the sting of a figurative slap.

This roller coaster had never been any fun, he told himself. He had to get off. But how?

He kept asking himself that question during the evening ritual of family time in front of the television and getting the children ready for bed. He was still asking himself the question as he closed the door to Larissa's bedroom. Lately, Connie had taken to avoiding any time alone with him, so he was surprised when she did not immediately go to her room but instead moved back into the den.

Confused, he asked if she wanted to talk and she said that she did. They sat down, both of them tense, while he waited for her to begin. She seemed to have trouble getting to the point.

Finally, she blurted, "I should think about enrolling in school soon."

The statement caught him off guard. His first thought was that she was looking for an escape, but on reflection, he reminded himself that he'd promised her an education when he proposed. Still, the timing seemed... odd.

"Do you think Larissa is ready for that kind of separation?"

Connie bit her lip.

"Possibly."

He didn't argue with her. She was probably right, and he always trusted that she had the best interests of the children at heart.

"Jolie has said that she'd like to watch the kids for us. I-it wouldn't be every day. We could work up to it, get Larissa used to spending time with her aunt."

He nodded, not quite trusting himself to speak yet, and cleared his throat.

"Whenever you think she's ready then."

"I haven't even decided what to study yet," Connie backpedaled quickly. "I just thought it was time to, you know, start investigating."

"Whenever you're ready," he reiterated. "I promised I'd pay for tuition and I will. No need to worry about that."

Connie looked down at her hands and, for a moment, he thought she would say something more, but then she murmured "Thank you," rose and left him sitting there, feeling more alone than he'd ever felt in his life.

Chapter Twelve

"I have to warn you," Kendal said, sitting across the breakfast table from her, "this won't be like last time."

"I understand," Connie murmured.

What she understood was that it would be much more difficult to present a "normal" marriage now than in the past. They were both miserable and Connie feared that it would be obvious to anyone who spent more than ten minutes in their company. For that reason, she'd pretty much held off her own family with lightning-fast visits and brief phone conversations full of happy chatter.

"The Conklins were upset when they heard I'd remarried," Kendal said. "I didn't tell you at the time because I didn't want to worry you. Besides, in the overall scheme of things, it really doesn't matter."

"But they're Larissa's grandparents," Connie pointed out.

"Which is why I can't tell them not to come for her second birthday," Kendal stated apologetically.

At least it was only one day, Connie thought. Thankfully, they wouldn't have to worry about overnight guests. Yet.

"We'll get through it," she said stoically.

He covered her hands with his, squeezing gently.

"Thank you."

Connie looked away, not wanting him to read the love in her eyes, and changed the subject. "I'm thinking that we should keep the celebration small."

He released her.

"Oh, uh, right."

"I'll plan a simple menu," she went on, tucking her hands safely beneath the tabletop. "You can buy Larissa that family play set that the therapist mentioned."

The therapist had also mentioned that he'd like to speak to the two of them alone on occasion, but she wasn't about to let that happen. She could just imagine what he would say about their so-called marriage if he ever truly understood the limitations of the relationship. Besides, this was about Larissa's interaction with her father, not his interaction—or lack of it—with Connie.

Through the monitor on the kitchen counter, she heard Larissa waking up and used that as her excuse to end the discussion.

Kendal checked his watch as she hurried from the kitchen, and Connie took that to mean that he was about to leave for work. She was surprised then when he walked into the room just as she'd finished changing Larissa.

Instantly, the little girl brightened. Kendal swept her

into his arms, kissing her chubby cheeks enthusiastically.

"That's my sweet girl. Be good for Mommy today, okay? And kiss Russ for me. Tell him Daddy loves you both."

"Lus you bof!" Larissa echoed.

"That's right. Daddy loves you both. Bye-bye now."

He passed her back to Connie, dropped a quick kiss on her cheek, too, and strode from the room, Larissa calling behind him, "Bye-bye."

Such a simple thing, a father and daughter saying a temporary goodbye, but only a few months ago, it would have been an anomaly in this household.

No longer. Praise God, no longer.

Larissa lay her head on Connie's shoulder in a hug and softly repeated, "Lus you bof."

The tears caught Connie off guard. One moment, she was hugging her daughter close, the next she was sobbing.

Obviously startled and troubled, Larissa patted her clumsily, saying over and over again "Mommy cry? Mommy cry?" until finally Connie got herself together again.

"It's all right, baby," she sniffed.

But it wasn't.

It wasn't all right, and she didn't know how to make it better.

"Would you like some more coffee, Mrs. Conklin?" Connie asked, picking up the glass carafe from the coffeemaker.

Agnes Conklin turned up her long, sharp nose disdainfully. "No, thank you."

"I'll have another," her husband, Whitney, said, pushing his cup forward.

The rusty tenor of his voice gave the impression that it was rarely used. As round as Agnes was angular, he looked like a jolly sort, but Connie had found him as dour and unapproachable as his wife. They looked to be opposites, with Agnes all shades of gray, including her chilly eyes and short, crimped hair, and Whitney a study in pink flesh with a white, fluffy fringe around his balding head. Yet, as far as manner and tone were concerned, they had much in common.

"Takes two cups of this to equal one real cup, I expect," Whitney groused, staring morosely into his cup.

Connie blanched, mumbling, "I'm sorry. Is it too weak?"

"The coffee's fine," Kendal said tersely. "The Conklins are known to take a strong cup. Laura used to say that her parents' coffee could stand up and walk by itself."

Mrs. Conklin dropped her jaw as if shocked that Kendal would so casually mention his late wife by name. Connie had the feeling that, no matter what she or Kendal did, the Conklins would be shocked and hostile, but she so wished that it could be different.

These were Larissa's grandparents, yet they had shown no apparent interest in the child, despite having come, ostensibly, for her birthday. It seemed more likely that they were on a fact-finding mission, or, rather, a fault-finding mission. Unfortunately, plenty could be found at fault with Connie, or so she believed.

She refilled Whitney's cup and quietly resumed her place at the kitchen table. The formal dining table in the other room had been decked out with a cake, balloons and other decorations to celebrate Larissa's second birthday. Mrs. Conklin had grimaced as if she found the whole thing tacky and then turned away. They were waiting now for Jolie, Vince and Marcus to arrive so they could cut the cake.

Several more minutes of desultory small talk had to be endured, with Kendal doing most of the talking, before the doorbell finally rang. Connie jumped to her feet in relief.

"If you'll excuse me," she murmured and almost ran from the room.

Behind her, she heard Kendal say, "Looks like our company has arrived. Let's get the kids to the dining room."

Connie rushed to the front door and yanked it open. Her brother smiled at her, his hands in his pockets.

"Hey, Sis." His smile turned upside down as he took in her worried expression. "What's wrong?"

She flapped a hand at him, trying to make light of it.

"Oh, I'm a little nervous, that's all. I want Larissa to enjoy today."

"She will," he assured her, crossing the threshold.

Connie shut the door and stepped close, whispering, "I don't think her grandparents like me."

"Nonsense," Marcus whispered back, slipping an arm

around her. "What's not to like? You're adorable and always have been. Why, when you were a kid, everyone who saw you exclaimed, "Isn't she adorable!'"

"You're making that up."

He grinned unrepentantly. "Yeah, I am. Most of them said, "Look at those enormous eyes."' He tweaked her nose. "At least, you finally grew into them. They used to cover ninety percent of your face."

"Oh, please."

The doorbell rang again. Feeling better, Connie opened up to let in Jolie and Vince. They exchanged kisses and hugs. Connie remarked that Jolie looked prettier and happier every time she saw her.

"It's marriage," Jolie said. "It agrees with me."

"Who'd have thought?" Vince teased.

Everyone laughed, but Connie felt a twinge of the old jealousy. Her sister's marriage, according to evidence, was perfect, while hers…well, she was hardly married at all. Sighing inwardly, Connie shepherded her family into the dining room.

Kendal had put the children in their high chairs, which had been moved into the room for that purpose. They sat side by side at one end of the long, rectangular table. The Conklins had taken seats at the table, as if to say that one should sit at a dining table, not merely gather around it. Following their lead, Connie directed everyone else to their chairs. Jolie and Vince looked at her a little oddly, but they sat. Just as they sat, though, Agnes got to her feet.

"I believe introductions are in order," she announced imperiously.

Connie blushed, stammering, "Oh, o-of c-course. How silly of me. Mr. and Mrs. Conklin, this is my sister, Jolie, her husband, Vince, and my brother, Marcus."

During this, Marcus and Vince were climbing to their feet once more. Marcus immediately held out his hand, bowing slightly from the waist. Agnes looked horrified and dropped into her seat without so much as an acknowledgment. She glared at Kendal.

"What are these people doing here?"

For a moment, Kendal seemed at a loss for words, but then he stated the obvious. "They've come for the party."

"Why?" Agnes demanded. "These people are no relation to Larissa."

Kendal's jaw tightened and he muttered, "No blood relation, perhaps."

Terribly embarrassed, Connie stepped in to try to smooth things over.

"They're very fond of Larissa," she began.

"Young woman, when I want your opinion, I'll ask for it," Agnes snapped.

Connie jerked back. Jolie leaned forward as if about to defend Connie, but Marcus laid a quelling hand on her arm, giving Kendal time to say, "My wife will speak when she pleases in her own house."

Agnes lifted her chin, her cold eyes narrowing into slits. The expression reminded Connie of a snake, and she shivered involuntarily.

"I think it's time to light the candles," she squeaked, whirling away to find the lighter that she'd tucked into a drawer of the buffet.

Striking the propane to flame, she lit the first candle. Both children instantly stared at the golden flicker, but it was Russell who pointed a moist finger and commanded excitedly, "Dadda, look!"

"I see it," Kendal told him, a smile in his voice.

Suddenly, Agnes was on her feet again, a horrified expression tightening her face as she gasped, "He called you Daddy!"

Kendal glanced in her direction, frowning. "Yes, of course. Why wouldn't he?"

"You're not his father!"

"Oh, but I am."

Mr. Conklin rose. "I'd bet his real father would have something to say about that."

"Trust me," Jolie muttered, "his real father couldn't care less."

"I find that difficult to believe," Agnes argued.

"Believe it," Kendal said flatly. "As a matter of fact, I'm in the process of adopting Russell."

Agnes clutched her chest as if she'd been stabbed. "You expect to raise my granddaughter with that—that *stranger?*"

Kendal rose, his hands going to his waist.

"I hardly think that her brother can be classified as a stranger."

"Brother!" Agnes pointed accusingly at Connie. "Next you'll tell me that my granddaughter will be allowed to call that woman *Mother!*"

"Privileged is more like it," Marcus said calmly, also rising.

"As a matter of fact," Kendal stated, "she already

does, because in every way that counts, Connie is her mother."

Agnes reeled as if she'd taken a blow.

"How dare you?"

Unnerved by the strife, Larissa reached for Connie then, beginning to make nervous, huffing sounds. Connie tried to reassure her.

"It's okay, honey."

Kendal, meanwhile, was on the verge of losing his temper.

"How dare I what?" he demanded. "How dare I give my daughter a wonderful, loving mother?"

"My daughter has barely been dead a year!" Agnes bawled.

Marcus attempted to reason with her. "Mrs. Conklin, surely you see how good this marriage has been for Larissa."

"I see no such thing!"

"That's right," Kendal derided. "How could you when you never had any care for Larissa, anyway? You were never around longer than it took to make Laura feel small and unloved!"

"If she had listened to me, she never would have married you!" Agnes shrieked.

That's when Russell began to cry. Connie sent a beseeching look at Jolie, who was already on her feet and moving toward him. Vince rose and tried to take Larissa, but Larissa wailed and hung on to Connie. Within moments, Jolie had swept Russell out of the room.

"It's not right!" Agnes shouted, looking at Larissa.

"She should miss her mother the rest of her life, not forget her!"

"No one wants her to forget her mother," Marcus said at the same time that Kendal vowed, "I pray to God that she forgets her!"

Connie moaned, jiggling Larissa, who was working up quite a paroxysm of tears.

"Ken, no," she pleaded, but he didn't seem to hear her.

"I can't believe Laura wouldn't want that, too!" he went on. "She loved our daughter, and she would want her to be happy and whole."

"Not if it meant being forgotten!" Agnes shouted.

Kendal shook his head in consternation. Connie turned and hurried from the room with a weeping, wailing Larissa in her arms, but she heard Kendal speaking behind her.

"Laura won't be forgotten. Larissa will be told about Laura when she's old enough to understand, but Connie is her mother now."

"Never!" Agnes shouted. "I'll take you to court first. I'll sue you for custody if that's what it takes to preserve her connection to her mother!"

"You can try!" Vince exclaimed.

"But you won't get it done," Kendal said flatly.

Connie all but ran into Larissa's room. As she passed through the den, Jolie fell in behind her with Russell, now calm but wide-eyed. Even as they moved down the hallway, though, they could hear the argument being waged loudly in the dining room. Connie was on the verge of tears herself, but she desperately needed to calm

Larissa. She dropped into the rocking chair and began to rock, murmuring comforting words.

A stricken Jolie plopped down on the floor at her feet, Russell in her lap.

"Connie, I'm so sorry."

"Not your fault," she managed.

"It's not yours, either," Jolie said warmly.

Connie felt her facial muscles begin to quiver.

"Oh, Jo," she whispered raggedly, "what if they find out about me? They'll use it against Ken, I know they will."

"Now, now," Jolie soothed, smoothing a calming hand over Russell's head, "let's not borrow trouble."

Connie squeezed her eyes shut. "I'll never forgive myself if—"

"Stop," Jolie said. "Stop right now." Then she began to pray. "God, protect this family. You know that they belong together. You know that Connie is the best mother little Larissa could hope to have. Please comfort Mrs. Conklin and bring her to her senses. Help her— help them—to understand that what's best for Larissa is a family that loves and understands her. Thank You so much for bringing Kendal into my sister's life. She deserves to be happy and loved."

But did she? Connie wondered. *Did she deserve to be happy?* She did not think she truly deserved to be loved. Otherwise, God would have brought her the same kind of marriage that he had brought Jolie.

She added her silent prayer to Jolie's. *God, forgive me for wanting more than what You've given me. Please*

*don't let Larissa and Ken suffer because of my mistakes
and my past. Please. I'll do anything. Anything. I'll even
give them up.*

The party—when it finally took place, minus the
Conklins—was a dismal thing at best, rather reminiscent of their wedding reception, Kendal mused. Nevertheless, they all put on their best faces and tried to make
it fun for Larissa, who could not be coaxed to blow out
the candles, even from Connie's lap.

Russell performed the honors instead. He also ate the
cake, which Larissa refused. Then he zipped around the
room on a sugar high while Connie and Kendal opened
Larissa's gifts for her and tried to pretend that she was
doing it herself.

The books that Marcus brought elicited no interest
whatsoever, but Larissa did pay scant attention to the
musical toy that Jolie and Vince had purchased for her,
though she refused to leave Connie's lap to play with
it by herself. When Kendal opened the small, plastic
house that served as the carrying case for the hand-high
figurines inside, she perked up a bit.

"Look at these," he said soothingly. "Here's the daddy
and the mommy and the brother and the sister. They're
just like us."

Larissa reached out her hand and snatched one of the
tiny dolls, clutching it against her. It happened to be the
daddy doll; whether by design or accident, no one could
say, but his heart gave a kick anyway.

"Here's one more," Jolie said, handing over a soft
package.

Kendal showed it to Larissa, who flicked her eyes back and forth between the gift and him expectantly but did not move so much as another muscle. Bitter anger suffused Kendal. Part of it was directed at himself. He should have known that the Conklins would pull something like this, and he should have held his temper, but it infuriated him that Agnes would put Larissa's welfare behind what she deemed proper and right.

Couldn't she see how much Larissa had improved under Connie's care? Didn't she want her granddaughter to be well and happy?

He really suspected that she did not, and the injustice—the insanity—of that just floored him. Nevertheless, he had no intention of allowing the Conklins to dictate to him—not when it came to the welfare of his daughter or indeed his whole family.

He looked at Connie and wanted desperately to offer her comfort and reassurance, but he sensed that she was hanging on to her aplomb by a thread now. A kind word from him could well push her over the edge, so he bided his time.

The package from Connie contained a pretty sweater with a girl and a boy appliquéd on the front. Larissa touched the appliqué with a slow finger, but then she tucked her hand under her chin and closed her eyes.

"Someone's sleepy," Kendal said, caressing her cheek.

"Nap time," Connie announced softly, straightening away from the back of the dining room chair.

Russell screeched and ran at the table, dropping onto his knees just in time to slide beneath it.

"Good luck," Vince drawled wryly.

Marcus chuckled and got down on all fours to fish his nephew out from under the table.

"Come on, sport, before you knock your head off."

He passed Russell up to Kendal and got to his feet.

"Thanks," Kendal said, offering his hand. "And thanks for coming, too. Sorry it turned into such a mess."

"Hey, can't say it wasn't interesting."

"A little too interesting," Kendal sighed.

Marcus slapped him on the shoulder. "Don't concern yourself. We'll lay this at God's feet and let Him deal with it."

Kendal nodded and Marcus moved away, to be replaced by Vince. Connie rose to her feet, Larissa cradled against her, and called goodbye to her brother. Meanwhile, Russell reached out and tried to take Larissa's doll, but Larissa held on tight until Kendal could move Russell out of grabbing range.

Vince laughed and gave Russell's back a rub. "Your day's coming, buddy."

"That's right. Just you wait until August," Jolie said, going on tiptoe to give Russell a kiss on the cheek.

Russell immediately turned and smacked a kiss on Kendal's cheek. Everyone laughed.

"Guess he didn't want Dad to get left out," Jolie said, ruffling his hair.

"That's right. Everyone knows Dad has to have his fair share of kisses around here," Kendal teased.

Connie, of course, was the exception to that rule, but he pushed that ache aside.

"Thanks for coming, guys."

"Our pleasure," Vince said, patting Larissa on the back. She scrunched up her shoulders but otherwise did not respond.

"She's tired," Connie said, and Vince nodded his understanding before ushering Jolie out.

Kendal looked at his wife. She had never seemed quite so fragile before, and he was truly sorry for his part in that. Could he make it up to her?

"Let's get these guys down."

She nodded and led the way to the back of the house.

They went through the familiar routine of putting the kids down for their naps, but instead of doing both together, Connie put Larissa down and Kendal took care of Russell. It required considerable patience to get Russell down that day, but finally he was on his way to dreamland. Kendal slipped out of the room and ambled into the den, thankful for a few minutes of peace and quiet.

Connie sat on the leather sectional, her feet drawn up beneath her.

"I don't know about you," he said, reaching up to massage a tight muscle in his neck, "but I could use a nap myself this afternoon."

"A nap won't fix this," she said with a sigh. "Maybe it's time we called a halt."

"A halt?" he echoed. "What are you talking about?"

She straightened, slipping her feet down to the floor and folding her hands in her lap.

"Ken, we knew the time might come when it would

be wise to end our arrangement. That's why we agreed on a marriage in name only."

He felt poleaxed.

"You want out of the marriage?"

"I'm becoming a liability to you," she said, looking down at her hands.

"That's absurd!"

"Ken, please think."

"*You* think!" he shot back desperately. "Think about Larissa! She's the reason we did this. Larissa *and* Russell!"

"You'll be Russell's legal father soon," Connie argued, "and you know I won't abandon Larissa."

"But that's what you're doing now!"

"No! No, it isn't."

"She needs you. Larissa's well-being depends on you, Connie!"

"What Larissa needs—what she's always needed—is a fully engaged father, and she has that now."

"What Larissa needs is a normal, happy family!" he pointed out.

Connie came to her feet, slashing the air with her arms.

"Well, we certainly aren't that!"

"We could be," Kendal insisted.

She turned away, shaking her head.

He wanted to tear out his hair. Didn't she understand how he felt about her yet? How could she not know? He had tried to tell her, show her. Perhaps it was time that he took the next step and demonstrated his feelings in the only way he could think of.

Reaching out at the same moment that he stepped forward, he turned her into his arms and found her lips with his. For a long moment, the world was again sane, right. She softened against him, her hands splayed against his chest, joining him with her kiss.

Such love flowed out of him that he swayed with the force of it. He hadn't known that he could love this much, and for that moment, that one instant, she seemed to accept the love he so desperately wanted to give her.

Then it was over.

She jerked away, a look of horror on her face.

"What do you think you're doing?" she demanded.

Suddenly the clock seemed to turn back. It was Laura all over again.

Once more, his wife was rejecting him.

He felt gutted, hollow, except for the pain that whistled through him like wind through a tunnel.

Connie reeled and ran from the room. Dimly, through the strange roaring in his ears, he heard her footfalls and then the click of her bedroom door. Then finally, he heard his own voice.

Fool! he said to himself. *Did you really believe she wanted a true marriage to you?*

Stiffly, Ken dropped onto the edge of the sofa and put his dazed head in his hands.

Whatever was wrong with him, whatever tainted him, he knew that he had no one to blame but himself. He'd known what he was getting into with this marriage. He'd engineered the agreement! Why had he thought Connie would or should change her mind just because he had changed his?

His thoughts skipped to Larissa and he tried to imagine what it would be like for her without Connie there day in and day out.

"Dear God, what have I done?" he whispered. And could he possibly undo it?

Chapter Thirteen

"I didn't think you'd be awake."

At the sound of her husband's voice, Connie sat up, peering over the high back of the leather sectional at the shadowy form in the doorway. The flickering light from the television did not extend to the kitchen, despite the massive size of the screen.

For two weeks now, he'd worked almost nonstop, coming home late at night and leaving again very early in the morning. She knew perfectly well that he was avoiding her. In the process, he was also avoiding the children, and she'd had enough of that.

"Did you get it done?" she asked, referring to the contract that had supposedly been keeping him away from home.

Kendal sighed and moved farther into the room, his steps dragging. He carried his suit coat draped over his back from the expedient hook of one finger, his briefcase clutched in the other hand.

The dark shadow of his beard struck Connie as

strangely intimate since she rarely saw him unshaven. Yes, he always wore a bit of a five o'clock shadow at the end of the day, but he emerged from his bedroom cleanly shaved the next morning, even on weekends. She'd never seen him looking quite so unkempt, but then he wasn't getting much sleep lately.

"Yes, but that's the problem with my business," he was saying. "There's always another proposal, always another report, always another prospectus, always another form to fill out or file."

In other words, Connie mused silently, this was going to happen again. She wondered if he even realized that he had reverted to old habits.

"You haven't eaten dinner with the children since last weekend," she pointed out needlessly.

He cleared his throat.

"I'm aware of that, Connie. Has there been a problem?"

"Only that they keep asking for you."

"They?"

She heard the hope that underlay the doubt in his tone.

"Yes, Ken, both of them. Just tonight when we were sitting at the dinner table, Larissa pointed at your chair and said, 'Daddy?' as if to ask where you were. Later, she followed Russell down the hall to the door of your study. He knocked on the door, and she called out to you."

"She actually *called* for me?"

"She actually called for you," Connie confirmed.

He bowed his head and she watched his throat work as he swallowed.

Guilt swamped her. She knew that she was responsible for the distance that had grown between them. It was up to her to do something about it if she could, at least as far as the children were concerned.

"They need you, Ken."

He waved that away with a negligent gesture of his hand. "You're the one they really need. I'm sure they're fine."

"They're fine so far," she argued, "but they need us both, Kendal. Don't think for a moment that they don't."

"I'll look in on them before I go to bed," he said softly, "and we'll do something special tomorrow—the three of us—if you think that'll work."

She noticed that she was not included in those plans and gulped. All right, so be it. That way was probably safer.

"I take it that you have the weekend off, then?"

"Yeah, of course."

"Good," she said briskly, pivoting to put her feet on the floor and stand. "I want to do some shopping tomorrow, and it will be best for everyone if you keep the kids here with you while I do it."

"Okay, sure."

"I'll say good-night then." She reached across the back of the couch and handed him the remote control, since the television was the only light source in the room, before moving toward the hallway. "You should get some sleep, too," she added gently. "You look tired."

"I *am* tired," he muttered, "more tired than you can possibly know."

"Sleep in tomorrow morning, then," she suggested, pausing.

"No, I want to have breakfast with the kids."

She wasn't about to argue that point. "They'll like that."

"I *have* missed them," he said softly.

For a moment, she thought he would say more, but then he pointed the remote at the television and pushed the power button, shutting off the set.

Connie stood for several seconds, letting her eyes adjust to the dark, then turned and started down the hallway.

"Good night, Ken."

"Good night, Connie."

A faint, blue night-light guided her to her bedroom door. She slipped inside and reached for the light switch. The lamp beside her bed flicked on. Though familiar, the green-and-apricot room felt empty and cold tonight, just as the house had come to feel the longer Kendal had been absent.

Connie sat down on the edge of her comfortable bed and removed her shoes and socks, a deep sadness filling her.

How had it come to this that she had to invent reasons to leave him alone with the children?

Perhaps she should just take herself out of the way

entirely, but how could she do that and be fair to the children?

Once before, she'd brought up the prospect of ending the marriage, but she didn't really want to do that. Russell needed Kendal; Larissa needed her. They all needed one another. So her only real option seemed to be to work out some livable arrangement that fulfilled the children's needs and kept her out of Kendal's way.

She saw again—as she had so often—the look on his face after she'd broken away from his kiss. She felt again the agonizing longing and the paralyzing fear that his kiss had evoked.

If only she could trust herself to be a true wife to Kendal, they might have a chance at being a normal family, but how could she do that when Kendal didn't love her as a true husband should?

Sighing, she resigned herself to a Saturday spent shopping alone. She wasn't much of a shopper, really.

For one thing, she'd never really had the opportunity or the funds to buy more than the necessities, and why tantalize herself with things that she couldn't afford? For another, errands were difficult enough with one child, let alone two, especially when that second child had what Larissa's new therapist called a "low threshold for overstimulation."

At least, she'd get that new steam iron and the stain remover that she needed.

Might as well look for shoes, too, she decided. The soles of her loafers had holes in them.

It occurred to her that she could also buy a pair of

capri pants, something new for spring and summer. She'd wanted a pair ever since they'd become popular.

Meanwhile, the children would enjoy a full day of their father's attention. Everybody won.

So why did she feel as if she'd lost something very important?

She had lunch in a nice little café and later coffee in a popular specialty shop. In between, she browsed through an Arlington mall. In the end, though, she made her purchases at a familiar discount department store.

She suspected that Kendal would not approve, but she just wasn't comfortable spending more than she had to for what she needed.

A glance at the clock on the dashboard informed her that she hadn't spent as much time away from the house as it had seemed, but she told herself that Kendal would surely welcome her help getting the kids down for their afternoon naps.

When she walked into the house from the cavernous garage, though, she wondered if he had put them down early, for the place was as quiet as a chapel.

Strolling into the den, she saw that the French doors overlooking the patio and back lawn were open and realized at once that Kendal and the children were outdoors. That was good. With the warmer weather, the children wanted to be outside every day, but over the past week, several days of rain had trapped them inside.

After leaving her purchases and her handbag in her room, Connie wandered outside. The measured cadence of Kendal's voice reached out to her. Recognizing the rhyming words of one of the children's most beloved books, she headed toward the leafy arbor just beyond the corner of the covered patio. The landscaper had placed a large bench swing beneath the ivy-covered, wrought iron pergola, and since the weather had warmed, it had become a favorite place for the kids.

Connie rounded the corner and stopped.

Kendal sat in the center of the swing, Larissa snuggled up on one side, Russell on the other, the book open on his lap. The children alternately looked down at the book and up at Kendal as he read. They were such a beautiful sight, the three of them, that her heart turned over in her chest.

Before she could make herself known, Kendal reached the part that Larissa always liked best.

Laughing, Larissa poked the book with her finger, exclaiming, "Bunny!"

The look of joy on Kendal's face nearly undid Connie. He hugged his daughter.

"That's right. That's the bunny. What a smart girl you are."

Larissa turned her face up, pursing her mouth for a kiss, and Connie clapped a hand over her own trembling lips. Kendal left the book in his lap and tenderly cupped her tiny face, kissing her gently.

Russell tugged on his arm, smacking his lips demandingly. It was the same sound he made when he wanted something to eat.

Kendal laughed and dropped an arm around each of the children, exclaiming "Oh, I love you both so much!"

"Lus you bof!" Larissa echoed.

To Connie's surprise, Kendal suddenly dropped his head.

"Oh, Lord, help me," he said, crying out from his heart. "Lord, show me what I should do."

Quickly, Connie stepped back out of sight.

She didn't know what had spurred Kendal to petition the Almighty with such obvious desperation, but she knew that whatever it was had ripped him apart. Was he that unhappy? Had she done that to him?

For a moment, she pondered turning around and walking out of the house, just disappearing, but how could she do that to Russell and Larissa? What she and Kendal shared with those children was far too precious to risk.

All right, perhaps they weren't a normal family, but whatever they were, it was working on too many levels to think of ending it. What she had just seen proved that.

Connie put her back to the rough stone wall and bowed her head, echoing Kendal's prayer.

Realization came quickly. Somehow, she had to find a way to mend her relationship with Kendal. If they couldn't regain the friendship with which they'd started their marriage, then they had to find some other comfortable ground.

Unfortunately, she didn't have the slightest idea what that might be.

"Hey! I'm home!"

At the sound of Connie's voice, both kids looked up

expectantly. Kendal heard the excited pitch in Larissa's breath and smiled sadly.

She made only a minor fuss when Connie left the house earlier, but no one could deny that she adored her mommy. In the meantime, she seemed happy with him and Russell, but Connie would probably always take center stage in her life. At least, until she grew up and married.

Funny, but he had never really considered that before. Now that she was becoming a normal little girl, though, he was beginning to realize that he must do so.

He hoped that she would marry well. Russell, too. Kendal promised himself that he was going to start praying now that his children would not make the same mistakes he had.

As Connie rounded the corner and strode toward them, her beauty struck Kendal squarely in the heart. He thought of how she had changed his life, and he knew that he was wrong to think of her as a mistake.

Perhaps the marriage had been a mistake, but he couldn't quite believe that, either. No, his mistake had been in framing the marriage as he had. He'd thought he was being so smart; he should have realized that he couldn't fix everything himself. Only God could manage that.

Father, help me. Show me what to do.

It was the same prayer he'd been praying for days now.

Connie waved, smiling, as she approached and he closed the book. They'd been through it once already anyway.

"Hi. How was the shopping?"

She wrinkled her nose.

"I got everything I went for anyway. How are you guys?"

Larissa reached for her and Connie bent at the waist to pick her up. At the same time, she ruffled Russell's hair and kissed his cheek.

"Daddy weeds bunny," Larissa announced.

"Daddy read you the bunny book?" Connie said. "What a good daddy." She looked down at him. "Any problems?"

He shook his head. "Nope."

Only that my wife doesn't love me.

Grimacing inwardly, he told himself to get a grip and stop feeling sorry for himself.

Russell yawned and leaned over until his head was in Kendal's lap. Kendal glanced at his wristwatch.

"I see it's that time."

Gathering Russell up into his arms, he stood up, feeling the swing bump against the backs of his legs. Together, they carried the children into the house.

Larissa said that she was "firsty," so they gave drinks to both children before taking them off to their beds. Kendal got Russell down for his nap, while Connie did the same for Larissa, but they each looked in on the other child before leaving them alone.

Afterward, the awkwardness that had come to characterize their personal relationship descended once more. Kendal didn't know what else to do, so he took himself off to his study, saying that he needed to check some papers.

The papers were right where he'd left them, of course. Having checked them, he sat behind his desk for almost two hours, playing solitaire on the computer and wondering what Connie was doing.

When he heard the children stirring, he emerged from his self-imposed exile to find that Connie was preparing dinner. He called out that he would take care of the kids and then did so.

The evening passed pleasantly enough.

The kids seemed delighted that they were all sitting down to dinner together, but once Larissa and Russell went to their beds again, Connie announced that she was going to read and left him on his own. By the time he sought his own bed, he knew that something had to give.

The next morning was too busy to really think about it. Sunday mornings were always busy, but the busy times were the easiest.

Those moments when he found himself alone with Connie—or without her—were the worst.

It was during the sermon that Kendal decided he had to speak to Connie about the situation. When Marcus began reading the Scripture reference, Kendal knew that he had made mistakes that needed to be admitted, beginning with God and ending with his wife. He bowed his head, right there in the middle of the service, and began to pray silently.

Lord, I was arrogant and ignorant to think that a marriage in name only was Your will. I should have realized that it was all about my expedience and desperation and nothing more. Why couldn't I see that I would fall in love with her? What am I talking about? You know perfectly well that I was half in love with Connie from the beginning. I've made so many mistakes, Lord, and yet You've blessed me. Thank You for making Larissa better and for giving me Russell. Hebrews says that You sympathize with our weaknesses and that we can draw near Your throne confident in Your mercy and grace, so that's what I'm doing now, Lord. Please help me fix what I've messed up.

He felt better after that, but he knew that the most difficult part was yet to come. It was so difficult, in fact, that he put it off, managing to avoid the discussion that evening and the next.

By Tuesday, though, he couldn't bear it anymore. When he glanced at the clock on his desk at the office and saw that it was time for the kids to go down for their naps, he knew that the moment had arrived.

Rising, he told his secretary that he was going home for the day and didn't know whether he would be back that afternoon. Then he got in the car and drove home.

When he let himself into the house, Connie was sitting at the kitchen table thumbing through a magazine. He noticed that she wore a pair of short pants and a slender, sleeveless top that made her look neat and feminine without being fussy.

She glanced up in surprise when he walked into the kitchen.

"Ken, what's wrong?"

He pulled out a chair and sat down, folding his forearms against the tabletop.

Without a preamble, he said, "Connie, this isn't working."

She closed the magazine and slumped back in her chair.

"What do you want to do?"

It was telling that she neither expressed shock nor argued with him. Obviously, he had blundered badly with that kiss. He shoved his hands through his hair, trying to think.

"First of all, I want to apologize for losing sight of the reality of our…arrangement. I know I've made you uncomfortable, and I regret that, but—" He broke off, swallowing. "I think we made a mistake, Connie, and maybe it would be best if I left the house."

She folded her arms and asked in a small, whispery voice, "Is that what you want?"

What he wanted was a real marriage, a wife who loved him and wanted a real marriage with him, but that was not what she'd signed on for.

"I could rent a small apartment nearby," he said evasively. "I'd spend as much time with the children as you thought wise."

"Is that what you want?" she repeated, tears in her eyes.

He bowed his head.

"I just can't go on as we are."

She was silent for a long while. Then he heard her shift and lifted his head. Sitting forward, she dried her cheeks with her hands.

"What if the Conklins found out you weren't living here?" she said. "They could use that against you, couldn't they?"

He sighed, weary, so weary.

"I don't know. Maybe. But if you adopt Larissa first, it won't matter."

"You think they won't fight that? I think they will, and I can't imagine that a judge wouldn't agree with them."

He shook his head, arguing, "They gave Russell back to you."

"That's different, Ken, and you know it."

All he really knew was that he was tired of living like this.

"We have to do something."

"I know." She reached across the table and squeezed his hand. "I've missed you. Can't we be friends again?"

Friends. That was so much less than he wanted but also more than he had now. He turned his palm into hers and gave her back the same question she'd asked him twice now.

"Is that what you want?"

She nodded, smiling gently.

"Yes."

His heart contracted. Tracing the line of her jaw with the tip of one finger, he allowed his longing free rein for a moment, but then he dropped his hand and took a deep breath. He'd made this bed; it looked like he was going to have to lie in it.

"All right. We'll try to go on as we are, then."

"Not as we've been, though," she said quickly.

"I'll try to do better," he promised.

"It's not just you," she told him. "I have to do my part, too."

"You've always done your part."

"I haven't," she argued, "but I've realized something recently."

"What's that?"

"You became my best friend for a while, and I've missed that."

He squeezed her hand. Well, that was something, wasn't it? Maybe they could build on that.

"But we need to be partners again, Kendal," she went on, "for the children's sake."

She was right, of course.

Would he ever learn to put others first? he wondered.

"You'll have to help me," he said.

Connie smiled.

"That's what partners do. They share the load."

Partners. Friends. Even best friends. It would have to do, unless…

Dear God, his soul whispered, *I need a miracle.*

Connie watched her hands as she peeled a potato, preparing dinner, but her mind was on Kendal, as it had been since she'd looked up and found him standing in the kitchen in the middle of the workday earlier that week. On one hand, she was glad that they'd come to a new understanding. On the other hand, she couldn't help thinking that their new understanding was basically their old understanding, and that hadn't seemed to work too well in the first place.

She put down the knife, scolding herself for her negativity.

The fact was that their "arrangement," as Kendal called it, had worked very well indeed—for the children. And that had always been the point. She could not afford to lose sight of that fact.

Besides, what did she have to complain about?

Not so long ago, she was in prison. Her life now was a paradise by comparison. She would not, she vowed, feel sorry for herself or regret that her life had not turned out as she'd always dreamed.

Kendal was a good man. They made a good team. They had a good life. Best of all, the children were well and happy. She wouldn't jeopardize that for some unrealistic dream of romance as her mother had done.

She was resolved on that issue, absolutely determined.

Why then did she feel this vague, uneasy yearning?

Why wasn't this enough for her?

And why couldn't she seem to put it aside?

She heard the sound of the garage door opening up and quickly picked up the knife and potato again. Her heartbeat sped up as she anticipated the moment when her husband would walk into the room.

"Hi," he said, doing just that.

She turned her smile toward him.

"How was your day?"

"Okay. Yours?"

"Busy."

"Where are the kids?"

"In front of the TV. Their program's been switched from morning to afternoon."

"That's convenient."

She nodded.

"Until they switch it again."

"I'll go in and say hello, then I'll help you get dinner ready," Kendal said.

"Don't be surprised if they ignore you," she warned. "That single half hour of television has become a big deal lately. I'm glad we decided to restrict it, though."

He leaned one hip against the counter as she placed the peeled potato in the sink and reached for another.

"They're growing up so fast," he said.

"Yes, they are."

"How long do you suppose we can hold them to a half hour of television a day?"

"You're not counting the couple of hours in the evening when we're watching our programs while they're in the room," she reminded him.

He looked toward the den.

"Maybe we should turn it off completely, do something else."

"We could play patty-cake," she said with a smile.

He chuckled.

"I'm warning you, I've been practicing."

She laughed and he dropped a hand onto her shoulder in an affectionate pat, her only warning before he dipped his head and kissed her cheek.

He took off after that to greet the children, leaving Connie with her heart pounding.

She quickly turned her attention to the potato in her hand, but she didn't put the knife to it. The tears in her eyes, a product of bone-deep regret, prevented her from seeing well enough to wield a blade.

Chapter Fourteen

She read. She prayed. She worried. She prayed some more. She tossed and turned. Finally, she just couldn't bear another minute.

Throwing back the covers, Connie hit the floor in her bare feet and reached for the cotton duster draped across the end of her bed. *What,* she wondered, *would help her sleep?*

She fondly remembered the cup of cocoa that Kendal had made her on their wedding night. Sweet and rich, it had filled her mouth and throat with soothing chocolate. It was too warm for hot drinks, though, too cool for a cold soda or iced tea. Besides, Kendal wouldn't be there to share it.

Oh, well, she told herself, *she sure didn't need the caffeine*.

What she needed was to calm her restless soul. Then perhaps, she could relax. But how to achieve the peace that she sought?

A lifelong fan of old movies made in the 1930s and

1940s, she briefly contemplated checking the TV listings but rejected the idea for fear of waking the family. She decided instead on a glass of water from the tap and a quiet swing watching the stars through the ivy-covered pergola.

Relishing the thought of the cool grass beneath her bare feet, Connie slipped out of her room.

The hour was late. She knew this even though she hadn't bothered to check the time because, even in a busy world of twenty-four-hour grocery stores and fast food, the night possessed a stillness at its depth. Beyond that, the weary restlessness of her own body testified to the long hours of struggling to go to bed.

One benefit of spending hours in the dark was that one's eyes adjusted, so she didn't bother flipping on lights that might wake up the rest of the household. Instead, she walked steadily down the darkened hallway with only a single faint, blue light at knee level to guide her, one hand trailing along the paneled wall.

Turning into the den, she felt the silence in which the house steeped and knew that her children slept peacefully in their beds. She would not think of Kendal at all.

Making her way to the kitchen, she opened a cabinet door, gleaming in the moonlight that fell through the window behind the breakfast table, and took down a tumbler, which she filled with cool water from the tap. She stood for a moment, her back to the sink, letting the water slide down her throat, quenching her thirst before refilling the glass.

Back into the den she went, drawn by the night-backed windows that showed her a scene washed in the pale rays of the moon. Beyond the corner of the pool, the lawn fell away in a gentle roll that led down to the common green. In the distance, she could make out the fold in the contours of the land where a small stream ran, and beyond that, the silver mirror of the duck pond. The dark, mushroom shapes of trees dotted the lustrous grass.

This was a world at peace, she mused, and yet she had such turmoil.

She opened the French doors and stepped outside, never thinking that they should have been locked.

The patio was dark beneath its sturdy cover, its surface chilling her feet as she wove swiftly through the wrought-iron furniture there to the grass beyond. The fragrance of spring wafted up to tickle her nostrils, even as the silvered blades of grass tickled the sides of her feet. Then she turned the corner of the house and slammed into a hard, warm barrier.

The glass fell from her hand, bouncing harmlessly on the sod and spraying her legs with water. At the same time, long, strong arms came around her. Her heart slamming inside her chest, her beleaguered mind instantly registered the masculine form against which she was trapped.

"Kendal!"

"Connie? What are you doing out here?"

The words just fell out of her mouth. "I couldn't sleep."

He released her from his embrace but not his hands, which closed around her upper arms.

"Are you all right? What was that you dropped?"

"Just a glass of water," she said, grimacing.

He moved a foot experimentally, and she heard a faint clink.

"It didn't break," he concluded, turning her away from it anyway. "Sit down. Let me get it out of the way. I don't want you stepping on it."

She let him lead her to the arbor, although she didn't need the assistance. It wasn't as if she could miss the thing even in the dark. He waited until she slid onto the seat of the swing before moving away again.

At a distance, she could see that he wore jeans and a simple T-shirt. Like hers, his feet were bare and his hair tousled. He found the glass, bent and picked it up, then set it carefully on the ground next to the house.

Turning his head, he stared into the gloom of the arbor for several long moments, but Connie knew that he could not possibly see her. Finally, he started toward her. She bit her lip. This was not helping her relax! Nevertheless, she made no attempt to stop or evade him; she merely waited until he turned and sat on the swing next to her.

"So you couldn't sleep either, huh?"

"Must be something in the air tonight," she murmured.

He drew up one knee, lifting one foot onto the seat of the swing and pushing off with the other. The bench glided backward in a slight arc before swinging forward again.

"Beautiful weather," he said.

Connie filled her lungs with air, and said, "It smells like spring."

"Yep."

They drifted back and forth in the shadows for some time, the arc gradually diminishing.

"So why couldn't you sleep?" she asked inanely, expecting to hear that a business deal was troubling him or some such nonsense.

Instead, he brought the swing to a halt by simply placing his feet on the ground and said, "I was thinking about us."

Connie's heart slunk inside her chest. She closed her eyes, whispering, "Me, too."

He sighed and draped an arm around her shoulders, pulling her close. Her head found a natural resting place in the hollow of his chest. His free hand journeyed up to skim her face, brushing at the tendrils of hair that wisped about her head. Tears seeped into the seams of her eyelids.

If only he could love her...

If only she could believe that would be enough...

She thought of her mother, always chasing after a new man, flush with the promise of true love, always slamming back into the house, sobbing or bitterly raging.

Velma Wheeler had chased that happy high, that hope of endless ecstasy. It was responsible for her death, every bit as responsible as the drunk who'd driven his car into the side of a building with Velma in the passenger's seat, leaving her three children to the impersonal mercy of the state.

Jolie and Marcus had turned out strong, determined.

Connie had latched on to the first man who'd come along and followed him right into prison.

She was her mother's daughter.

Or was she?

Connie could say this much in her favor: She was a better mother than her own had ever been. She would never allow her children to suffer abandonment and doubt. She would do what she needed to protect them and provide for them. No, her children would never face the scalding pity or numbing disdain of strangers charged with their care.

It was Kendal for whom she feared, Kendal who had married her in name only and come to regret even that. Perhaps she should find a way to free him. He might yet discover someone to love.

But what of the children? Oh, she knew that he would never abandon them, but how would they adjust to seeing their father with another woman?

How would *she* adjust?

Chilled, she rubbed at her forearms.

"Connie," Kendal suddenly said, sitting forward and twisting slightly to face her. "I promised myself I wouldn't do this, but I just have to." He groped for her hand, found it and lifted it in his. "Connie, is there any way to make this a *true* marriage?"

Her breath ceased. A *true* marriage? A true marriage meant two people who loved each other, a lifetime commitment, a soul-deep joining. They had none of that. None!

But what they did have was surely worth saving, if only for the sake of their children.

She tamped down her panic and heard herself ask, "Are you so unhappy then?" The raspy quality of her voice surprised her.

He took her by the shoulders as if he might shake her.

"Don't you see? We made a mistake. I was wrong to think we could make it work this way. I need more than this. I never expected to, but I do!"

Connie gulped. "I—I don't know what to s-say."

His hands flexed, a warm, precious weight on her shoulders.

"What if we were married in church? Marcus said—"

"*True* marriage is about more than vows or buildings!" she exclaimed.

He stared at her for a moment, then he snatched his hands away and rose, walking off a short distance.

"It's hopeless," he said, as much to himself as her. "God, forgive me. What have I done?"

"Kendal," Connie began.

Tears clogged her throat.

She should release him. She knew that. But how could she?

He turned, holding out his arms and shaking his head, his expression indiscernible in the dark of night.

"I'll just have to try harder, won't I? Find some way to keep my distance without impacting our—"

He broke off, but that word didn't need vocalization. They had married for the sake of their children. They would stay married for the sake of their children.

At least, until one or both of them simply couldn't

bear it anymore. Connie sensed that Kendal was very nearly to that point, and his pain wounded her in a way she had never realized it could.

She rose, but he stepped back, and the next instant he had turned and was striding away, his head down, shoulders slumped. She watched him go, her heart breaking open inside her chest.

Sobs welled up. She plopped back down onto the seat of the swing, bending over with the weight of her sorrow. After a few minutes, she found herself beseeching God.

"What should I do? What can I do?"

Kendal was so unhappy that he was obviously in pain and she didn't know how to help him. She didn't know how to help herself, either. Straightening, she brought a hand to her head, trying to think. She thought of her brother and sister.

Marcus had been her rock for a long time now, and she trusted his judgment implicitly, but Marcus was single, not the person to give her advice at this point. Even had he been, she wasn't sure that she could go to him with this for fear of disappointing him.

Jolie, on the other hand, not only was a married woman but also knew Connie's faults. If anyone in this world understood what a failure Connie had been, it was her sister, Jolie. *In that case,* Connie thought, wiping her constantly leaking eyes, *what did she have to lose?*

Rising from the swing, she left the arbor and went into the house. She walked straight to her room and exchanged her nightgown and duster for a pair of sweats and tennis shoes. Grabbing her purse, she headed out the door again, seeing and speaking to no one.

As she aimed her little car down the driveway, her chest heaved. Swiping at her eyes again, she shifted gears and kept going.

Twenty minutes later, she fell into her sister's arms, weeping like that frightened little girl she had once been. Connie wouldn't have blamed Jolie if she'd given her a good scolding and sent her home. It was the wee hours of the morning! But she didn't expect that, and she wasn't disappointed. Even Vince, who had opened the door, his hair standing up on end and a rough black beard shadowing his lower face, showed nothing but support.

"Is there something I can do?" he asked sleepily.

It was Jolie who answered him. "Just give us a few minutes."

He patted Connie awkwardly and trudged out of the room, struggling with a yawn. Jolie guided Connie to the couch in her large, Texas-chic den and dropped onto it with her. Connie sniffed and tried to dry her eyes while Jolie shoved back her hair and sucked in a deep breath.

"Okay. What's going on?"

"I-it's K-Kendal."

"I figured. What did he do?"

"He wants a real marriage!" Connie exclaimed, surprised by the anger in her own voice.

Jolie blinked and swept her bangs up, then down again.

"My brain's foggy, so you're going to have to explain that."

Connie started from the beginning, revealing, for the first time, the conditions under which she had married Kendal Oakes.

"Okay," Jolie said, sounding exasperated after several minutes of explanation, "let me see if I've got this straight. You married Kendal in name only for the sake of his daughter and your son?"

Sniffling, Connie nodded and waited for the explosion, the condemnation. Instead, Jolie merely sounded confused.

"So you don't love him then?"

"Well, of course I do!" Connie snapped.

For pity's sake, what did *that* have to do with anything?

Jolie stared at her for a full minute before tilting her head to one side speculatively.

"I don't get it."

Connie rolled her eyes, saying, "Goodness gracious, Jolie, you've met the man! What's not to love? Oh, he's not macho like Vince. Or Jessup, for that matter. Not that Vince has anything else in common with Jessup, mind you."

"Absolutely not," Jolie agreed indignantly.

Connie, frankly, wasn't paying much attention as her thoughts centered on her husband.

"Kendal is a smart, sensitive, emotional man who—"

"Wants a real wife," Jolie interrupted flatly.

Connie glanced at her sister, her chin beginning to tremble.

"Exactly!" she wailed.

Jolie growled, literally, the sound rumbling up from the bottom of her throat.

"And the problem is?" she demanded.

Tears began to roll down Connie's cheeks again.

"Isn't it obvious?"

"Uh, no-o-o."

"Well, it's obvious to me!" Connie sobbed.

Jolie scooted closer and wrapped an arm around Connie's heaving shoulders.

"Is it that you aren't sure *he* loves you?" she asked gently.

Connie made a face, wondering why she had to spell it all out. What other logical conclusions were there, after all?

"Partly," she grumbled. "Oh, he says he does, you know, but of course he would, wouldn't he?"

Jolie drew back, eyeing her like she'd taken leave of her senses.

"Uh, no."

Her brow wrinkling, Connie swiped at her cheeks.

"What do you mean?"

"Think about it. Lots of guys who love their wives never bother to say so because, well, why should they? They're already married, and they seem to figure they've said it enough to get to that point. Then, on the other hand, there are those guys who say it without any intention of getting married. Maybe they're in it for a few nights or until the woman they're saying it to stops providing whatever satisfaction they're after."

"That would be Jessup," Connie muttered.

"Yeah, well, the question is, which of those guys is Kendal?"

Frowning, Connie replied, "Neither."

"So what's he got to gain by saying that he loves you?" Jolie asked.

"A physical relationship, for one thing."

"Which means that the marriage becomes tighter, even more difficult to get out of, the relationship richer, deeper. That's a bad thing?"

Connie jumped to her feet.

"You don't understand. He doesn't mean it like that. He says he loves me the same way he says he loves the kids!"

"But you don't doubt that he loves the kids."

"Of course not."

"And he's said that he wants a 'real' marriage?" Jolie crooked her fingers to indicate quotation marks around the word *real*.

"That's why I'm here!"

Jolie sat back, folding her arms.

"I don't get it. You love your husband, he loves you and your kids, but when he says he wants a *real* marriage, you freak out."

"True," Connie muttered, trying to figure out why this sounded so different now than before she'd mentioned it to Jolie. Seeing Jolie's smirk, she expounded. "He said he wanted a 'true' marriage."

"And you don't?" Jolie asked skeptically.

"It's not what we agreed to," Connie said, looking away.

"That's a yes or no question, Connie."

But she didn't have a yes or no answer. She sat down again, leaning forward and running her hands through her hair.

Jolie sat forward, too.

"Connie, why don't you tell me what's really going on?"

Connie shook her head, whining. "I don't know. It all seemed so perfect in the beginning. Larissa needed me. Kendal needed me. Russ needed a daddy. I needed to let Marcus off the hook, to find some way to provide for us." She looked up, wanting no mistake about this. "Kendal's been more than generous."

"Looks like it's worked out pretty well," Jolie commented.

Sniffling, Connie nodded.

"I've been good for Larissa. I'm not being conceited when I say that."

"No one doubts that you've been a good mother to her, Connie. Why, Marcus says she's a different child now."

"And Ken's been good for Russell, too. You should see them together."

"I've seen them," Jolie said softly, "and I agree with you. Now tell me why you're afraid to take this marriage beyond name only."

Connie looked up, the tracks of her tears stiffening on her face.

"We always said we wouldn't be like Mama," she reminded her sister.

"Yes, we did," Jolie confirmed. "What does that have to do with anything?"

Connie sighed, feeling tired, drained, weak. Fresh tears welled in her eyes. She was sick to death of feeling ashamed for her mistakes.

Marcus said that she shouldn't feel guilt or shame any longer because God had not only forgiven her but also forgotten about all her transgressions. Now, according to Marcus, all she had to do was let herself forgive and forget, but how could she do that without the risk of repeating her mistakes?

"Are you ever afraid," she asked Jolie, "that Vince won't be enough for you?"

"Never," Jolie said firmly. "Vince completes me in a way I didn't even know I was incomplete. Now if you'd asked me that before last Christmas…"

"What changed?" Connie wanted to know.

"I did. I stopped being angry about everything and started realizing how God had always met my needs, how He had blessed me—first with you and Marcus, then with Russell and now with Vince."

"You just stopped?"

"I just turned it all over to God, Connie. I just let go of it, and once I did that, Vince's love flowed right in and took its place."

Connie bit her lip, whispering, "But you haven't made the mistakes I have, Jo."

Jolie smiled with understanding.

"We all make our own mistakes, Connie. Maybe the mistakes are different, but the solution is the same."

"But what if I turn out to be like Mama? What if, once I have him, I don't want him anymore?"

Jolie laughed.

"Sis, you're not like Mom. Why would you think you are?"

Connie looked down. "You know how she was always falling in and out of love."

"So?"

"I loved Jessup. Now…"

"You *thought* you loved him," Jolie scoffed. "I doubt you thought that for very long, but you were so afraid of being like Mama, so determined to make it work, that you hung in long after any other woman would have walked away. Now you're holding back with Kendal for the same reason, aren't you?"

Connie closed her eyes.

"I—I don't know."

"Okay." Jolie spread her hands. "Let's say that's not the case. Then what is it?"

"Maybe what he feels for me isn't what it should be," Connie said.

Her brother-in-law strode into the room just then.

"Sorry, kiddo. Won't wash." He shrugged. "Hey, I don't usually hang around doorways eavesdropping, but in this case, I'm glad I did."

Connie sat back abruptly, even as Jolie chuckled and lifted a hand to her husband. Vince perched on the back of the sofa, one foot braced against the floor, and folded his wife's hand in both of his.

"I take it you're going to put in your two cents' worth," she remarked.

"Absolutely." He looked to Connie and said, "Listen, I know all about you Wheeler girls and your fear of turning out like your mom and, from where I'm sitting, that looks like so much bologna, frankly, but I understand why it's a factor. That said, you better rethink Kendal's end of the equation."

Connie frowned, a tad miffed, truth be told, that Vince had interjected into a private conversation like this. Nevertheless, he had done so—with Jolie's tacit approval—and, short of outright rudeness, she could find no way to oust him again. In fact, considering that he hadn't closed the door in her face when she'd shown up sobbing on his doorstep earlier, she would have to add ungrateful to rude if she asked him to stay out of it. All of which meant that a reply of some sort was in order.

"I, uh, what does that mean, 'rethink Kendal's end of the equation'?"

"You say he doesn't love you like he should. I say, open your eyes, woman. Kendal looks—and sounds— like a man totally in love to me. And you know what they say." He winked at Jolie. "Takes one to know one."

Jolie grinned and, with some obvious effort, switched her attention back to Connie.

"Look, Sis, you can't have it both ways. You can't be afraid on one hand that you'll suddenly morph into our mother and fall out of love with Kendal the instant that you're sure he loves you and, on the other hand, worry that he doesn't really love you at all."

"I'm not doing that," Connie argued. "Why would I do that?"

Jolie glanced at Vince before saying gently, "Because

the truth is, you just don't really believe you're worth someone like Kendal."

Connie opened her mouth to argue that point. Then she realized that the words on the tip of her tongue were "I'm not."

She closed her mouth again, admitting silently that Jolie was right.

"Is that how *you* felt?" she asked after a long moment of thought.

"Yes," Jolie admitted forthrightly. "Now I know better."

Connie felt the rise of hope.

"Really?"

"Sure," Jolie said offhandedly. "I finally realized that Vince just isn't that great."

"Hey!"

Laughing, Jolie twisted and pushed up onto her knees, wrapping her arms around her indignant husband.

"Just kidding. He's the best." She tilted her head back, looking up at him. "He's absolutely the best thing that has ever happened to me."

"Yeah, and don't you forget it," he quipped, planting a kiss right in the middle of her forehead.

Jolie turned her head, smiling at Connie.

"Now you tell me, is that how you feel about Kendal? Aren't he and Larissa the best thing that's ever happened to you and Russ?"

A lump rose in Connie's throat. She pushed a single word out around it. "Yes."

"Then it seems to me," Vince said, "that the next

question is, are you going to let the past rob you of it?"

Connie blinked. Was that really what she was doing? By refusing to put the past to rest, was she risking the future that God had designed for her? If Kendal really did love her, what was there to fear? Only herself. The self God had forgiven and blessed.

Let us therefore draw near with confidence to the throne of grace, that we may receive mercy and may find grace to help in time of need.

The verse from Hebrews ran through her mind, warming and electrifying her. Suddenly, she found herself on her feet again. In some ways, she was more confused than ever, but she suddenly knew one thing.

"I have to go home."

Jolie followed her to the door, fretting. "You sure? It's awful late. Maybe you ought to sack out for a little while."

Connie shook her head, feeling great urgency.

"I have to go home."

"Just be careful, okay?" Jolie lectured.

Connie turned back long enough to hug her sister and say, "Thank you."

"Aw, what are sisters for?"

Smiling, Connie looked past Jolie to Vince, hovering in the distance.

"And thank you."

He shrugged and said, "Just give him a chance, kiddo. I figure he's worth it, don't you?"

Nodding, she hurried away, uncertain what she had accomplished but sure now that the ultimate answers were waiting for her right where she'd left them: At home.

Chapter Fifteen

Kendal shoved a hand through his hair, frantic with worry. Intellectually, he knew that Marcus wouldn't lie to him, but desperation goaded his response.

"How can you *not* have seen her?" he barked into the wireless telephone receiver. "Where else would she go?"

It seemed like forever since he'd heard her car driving away. A glance at the digital display on the front of the microwave told him that it had been, in fact, almost ninety minutes. Ninety minutes was long enough to imagine all sorts of ridiculous scenarios.

She'd left him. That seemed the most obvious reason for a middle-of-the-night departure. She felt responsible for his unhappiness so she'd packed up and disappeared in the dead of night. What a selfish slug he was to lay that on her!

Oh, God, what will I do if she's left me? How will I cope?

His children would hate him, and he couldn't blame them in the least.

The calm, rational, sleepy voice of his brother-in-law droned in his ear, but Kendal was too upset to take comfort in what he heard.

"Granted it's not like her, but I'm sure there's a reasonable explanation."

How upset had she been, Kendal wondered, *too upset to drive? Was her car now a mangled heap on the side of the road somewhere?*

A rumbling sound penetrated the fog of distress that surrounded him. At about the same instant that he identified that rumble as the garage door being lifted or lowered, another door opened in the back hallway and footsteps moved toward him. He held his breath until she appeared in the kitchen doorway.

"Connie!"

She had been crying. Even in the shadows cast by the half light of the small bulb that he'd switched on over the stove, he could see her tear-ravaged face clearly. Without another thought for his beleaguered brother-in-law, Kendal put the phone down on the breakfast table and hurried toward her.

"Honey, what's wrong? Are you all right?"

She nodded, but the listlessness of her actions did not reassure him. Quickly, he ran his hands over her arms, shoulders, neck and face.

"Were you in an accident?"

She shook her head, her chin wobbling alarmingly.

"Thank God!"

He pulled her to him, wanting nothing more than reassurance, and closed his eyes with poignant delight when she tucked her face into the hollow of his throat, her arms circling his waist.

She was all right. She was fine. She hadn't left him.

So where had she taken off to, and didn't she know that she'd scared him half out of his wits?

Frowning, he pushed her away, holding her at arm's length.

"Where on earth have you been? It's 4:00 a.m.!"

"I know," she answered in a quavering voice. "I went to see my sister."

"Your sister?" he echoed in disbelief, remembering to moderate his voice only at the end. "At this time of night, or should I say morning?"

She nodded miserably and all the panic and fear that had filled him earlier evaporated in a burst of pure outrage.

"Are you nuts?" he demanded.

Tears trickled from her eyes and she fixed him with such a woebegone expression that his heart instantly melted into a glob of jelly.

"M-may-b-be!" she warbled, and then she began to sob in noisy gasps that shook him down to the tips of his toes.

"Oh, no, honey, don't," he pleaded, holding her close again. "Sweetheart, please. I can't bear it when you cry like this."

"I'm so-r-r-ry!" she blubbered, and he felt like the biggest heel in creation.

"It's not your fault," he crooned. "*I* should be apologizing to you. I upset you earlier, I know, and I'm so sorry. I don't know what's wrong with me."

"I do," she gasped, clasping the fabric of his T-shirt in both hands. She lifted her head, her eyes sparkling with tears. Her breathing hitched and slowed. Finally, in a tiny voice, she said, "I haven't been a good wife to you."

"That's not true." He shook his head, then pressed his forehead to hers. "You've been the perfect partner, a wonderful mother. You've far surpassed the terms of our agreement."

"But I haven't been a *wife* to you," she insisted softly.

He lifted his head, confused, hopeful and wary all at the same time.

"You've given me a family, Connie. You've made this house into a real home. In my book, those are the most important parts of being a wife."

"I'm just so tired of it all," she said and panic ripped through him again.

"What are you saying?"

Sighing, she pulled away, went to a chair and plopped down at the table. Propping one elbow on the tabletop, she rubbed her hand across her face. Kendal pulled out a chair and joined her, his heart thudding painfully in his chest.

"I've been so afraid," she began. "My whole life I've been afraid. First was the fear of being alone in the house at night with just my brother and sister. Anything could've happened, and young as I was, even I knew it.

Then I was afraid that my mother would leave one day and not come back."

"Which is exactly what she did," Kendal commented, cupping her cheek in his palm.

"Exactly," she echoed. "I was afraid of losing that shabby little apartment we called home, and that fear, too, came true." She waved a hand helplessly. "After that, I was afraid of losing everyone else I loved, and when they separated me from my brother and sister…"

"Another fear fulfilled," he concluded gently, brushing back a tendril of her pale hair.

"I was always afraid of losing the next placement, the next family, and I always did."

He closed his eyes, hurting for her.

"I'm so sorry."

"When I met Jessup," she went on doggedly, "I was very afraid that he was a mistake, and that's why I tried so hard to make it work out with him."

"He wasn't worth the heartache he caused you," Kendal stated firmly, "but that's not your fault!"

Only the blink of her eyelids indicated that she'd even heard him.

"I can't tell you what prison was like," she whispered, trembling. "Every moment was a nightmare, every day, every night, awake, asleep, one long nightmare of fear."

Alarmed by the suddenly vacant look in her eyes, Kendal seized her shoulders and shook her.

"That's enough! It's over. You're safe here with me, and I'll never let anything bad touch you again, I promise."

She smiled, a slow curving of her lips that seemed to take great effort. Her gaze held his, telegraphing warmth and gratitude.

"You can't protect me from myself, Kendal."

Sadness tinged her smile and she tilted her head as if it had suddenly become too heavy to hold upright.

"I can try," he gritted out, knowing in that moment that he would do, say, be anything that she needed. Her rock. Her soft place to fall. Her champion. Her scapegoat. Her friend. Her husband. Anything that she would let him be. He started to tell her so, but as if sensing that he was about to say more than she wanted to hear, she held up her hand, barring his words with her fingertips.

"Let me finish," she insisted softly. "The thing I've been most afraid of," she went on, taking away her hand "is being like my mother."

He shook his head adamantly.

"Not possible."

"How can you say that? You didn't even know her."

"I know that she left her children," he said, "and that's something you could never do, although—" he looked down, admitting,"—I did think that perhaps you'd left me."

She made a pained sound and he looked up to find her crying again. His heart stopped. Was she going to do it? Was that the point to all this?

"Not so long ago," she reminded him, "*you* were the one talking about leaving."

"I wouldn't," he vowed. "I couldn't! And it was never

what I wanted, Connie. Believe me, it was never what I wanted."

She gulped and he watched her square her shoulders, her chin rising an inch as she pulled in a deep, steadying breath.

She asked forthrightly, "What is it that you do want, Kendal?"

Such a simple question, one that deserved and demanded an answer. Whether his answer would be the beginning or the end of their life together, he couldn't even guess, but he knew that the time had come to speak his heart. Matching her resolve with his own, he drew himself up tall, whispered a silent prayer and prepared to tell her what she needed to know.

Connie hadn't realized that silence could have weight and substance, that the air could actually grow heavy and cold with it. Yet, she felt it as she watched Kendal gather himself in preparation for answering her question.

She saw the way his chest expanded and his shoulders leveled, how his jaw, shadowed by the dark growth of his beard, firmed. His hands flexed before coming to rest on his knees.

They were strong hands, less used to doing hard labor than wielding a pen but wide with long, tapered fingers. Gentle hands, capable hands. Just like Kendal himself.

She thought about what he did for a living, juggling numbers and people, deals and personalities. It was a complex business with many pieces and possibilities, but he handled it all with an easy poise. Even while struggling with his personal life, a life largely devoid of support and human comfort, a life that had at times reduced him to shreds inside, he had made the business work, grow, thrive.

He had lived on faith and sheer determination, accepting rejection and resentment while constantly striving to do what was right and best.

Such a man this was!

How he had fought to build this life they shared, to give his daughter the mother that she needed, to make them all into a family. To think that God had dropped him right into her lap—and she hadn't had the courage to claim him!

What a fool she had been, paddling against him, determined to head upstream instead of following the easier path designed by God. It would serve her right if Kendal said that what he truly wanted was his freedom. She wouldn't believe it. She wouldn't believe it because she couldn't bear to.

After all she'd been through in her life—all the loss and the pain, the mistakes and the doubt—she had finally come to a possibility that she could not endure. It was worse—far worse—than any foolish fears that her mother's weaknesses might lurk within her. It was akin to that horror of every loving parent: the chance, the theory, of losing a child. Every parent knew that such gambles existed, but none could willingly face it. She could no more bear to lose Kendal, she realized, than she could have borne losing one of her children. And so it could not happen.

I mean it, Lord, she thought. *It can't happen. I've been foolish and cowardly, but I've suffered enough loss. I can't lose Kendal. You gave him to me, and I'm trusting You to keep this family, this marriage, together.*

Kendal ratcheted his gaze up to meet hers. Such a lovely, warm brown his eyes were, surely the most beautiful color in a universe of wonders.

"What do I want?" he asked rhetorically. "Simply put, Connie, what I want more than anything else in this world is to spend the rest of my life with you, to be your husband in every sense of the word, to —"

She came off her chair, her arms flying around his neck.

"I love you!" she gasped.

Time stopped. The room did a lazy spin on its axis and then his long, strong arms banded about her.

"I want to love you as you deserve to be loved," he finished in a whisper. "Thank God. Oh, thank You, God!"

"I don't deserve you," she told him brokenly.

Turning her slightly, he sat her on his knee, keeping his arms looped lightly about her waist.

"Listen to me," he said. "No one deserves what we've been blessed with. I sure don't." He lifted a hand to push her hair back out of her face, as if he didn't want her to miss a word of what he had to say next. "I haven't loved God as I should," he confessed. "I've carried around a lot of anger and self-pity because of my mom's death, and I've blamed God for my own shortcomings and mistakes. Yet He's given me everything I've needed, more than enough to build a happy, rewarding life for myself, including a loving, patient stepmother whom I ignored for years, not one but two beautiful children and the most wonderful woman to love."

She shook her head.

"That's the thing you have to understand. I'm not wonderful. I've made such horrible mistakes."

He chuckled about that, actually chuckled!

"Honey, you've made no more or worse mistakes than I have. We've both suffered for the choices we've made, but that's how we became who we are now. That's why I am this man who loves you so much, who treasures his family more than his own life. That's how you got to be the woman I can't live without, the sweetest, dearest mother and—"

She kissed him, seized his head in both her hands and kissed him for all she was worth.

Somewhere in the distance, she began to hear an odd sound, something between a whistle and a bellow. Odder still, it seemed somehow familiar. Not a chorus of angels, then, and not a siren of any sort, either. Reluctantly, she broke the kiss and poised to listen.

"What is that?"

"Hmm?" was the dreamy reply.

"A part of her smiled even as she asked, "That sound? Don't you hear it?"

For an instant, she wondered if she was imagining it. Then Kendal bolted upright in his chair, nearly dumping her on the floor.

"Oh, no!"

"What? What is it?"

"Marcus!" he exclaimed, making a grab for something behind her. He came up with the telephone receiver, which he slapped to his ear, already speaking. "Oh, man, I'm sorry! I forgot all about you! Connie came in and—"

He cleared his throat and turned an interesting shade of red, nodding his head sheepishly. After a minute, he rolled his eyes, but he settled back in his chair again, pulling her into the curve of his arm.

"Uh-huh, right," he replied dryly to whatever Marcus had said, "like you were snoozing there on the other end of the line, Reverend I-Told-You-So."

Connie gasped and slapped her hands to her warming cheeks. Marcus had been listening this whole time?

Kendal laughed.

"You just try it, preacher man, and you'll look a whole less pretty the next time you step onto the pulpit," he quipped.

Connie gasped. Again.

"Kendal!"

He just tightened the arm looped about her waist.

"She's staying right here where she belongs," he said into the phone, winking up at her, "but since I know she values your blessing and we've already interrupted your beauty sleep, we might as well get this ball rolling. Hold on."

He lay the phone down. Bodily sliding her off his lap, he rose, walked her to the opposite chair and pushed her into it before getting on one knee.

"Connie," he said loudly, glancing at the telephone receiver, "I love you! Will you marry me?"

She started to laugh.

He held up a stalling finger and added, "In church. Soon!"

She slipped an arm around his neck, leaned close to the telephone receiver and shouted, "Yes! I love you, too!"

Grinning, he grabbed the receiver again.

"Go back to sleep, Marcus."

"But first, call Jo!" Connie instructed loudly, just before Kendal disconnected.

She looked at Kendal, love radiating from every pore. "Do you think we woke the kids?"

"Better go check," he said, getting up off the floor, her hand in his.

They strolled unhurriedly through the darkened house, relishing the closeness, the unspoken promises that they'd made to each other. Together, they slipped into Larissa's room.

She slept soundly, her hands tucked beneath her sweet face. Tears of happiness gathered in Connie's eyes. Maybe she would never formally adopt Larissa, but this little girl was still her daughter, and she need never fear that she would be separated from her until Larissa herself decided that it was time to make her own life. What a gift that was! She hugged Kendal, trying to tell him without words how grateful she was.

Kendal led her out of Larissa's room and into Russell's. He lay there half-awake. Whether he had been woken by their voices earlier or their entry into his room didn't matter.

"Go back to sleep, Son," Kendal whispered, smoothing Russell's rumpled hair with one hand. "Mommy and Daddy are here to watch over you."

"And we always will be," Connie added, "both of us."

Russell sighed and rolled over. Kendal pressed a kiss to her temple as she patted Russell's back rhythmically. Several seconds later, they tiptoed out into the hall and stood there, between their bedroom doors, an unspoken question in the air.

"I know we're already legally married," she said softly, "but do you mind if we wait for the real wedding?"

"No," he said, then "yes," and finally "no."

Connie smiled. "Me, too."

He locked his hands at the small of her back and bent slightly to touch his nose to hers.

"Do you mind if I buy you an engagement ring?"

"No," she said flatly, thrilled, "and, um, no."

He chuckled.

"Want to pick it out or can I surprise you?"

She thought about it. "Surprise me."

"Good choice. We'll both be a lot happier with the result that way. I might even finally get to spoil you a little."

She poked his chest with a finger, warning, "Just don't get too extravagant."

He arched an eyebrow, grinned and drawled, "Yes, dear."

"Oh, that was very good," she teased.

Grinning, he hugged her.

"I haven't had a wink of sleep," he said, "and it's sure not happening now."

"Mmm, I know what you mean. So what shall we do?"

"Make a pot of coffee?" he suggested. "Plan our *last* wedding?"

Connie chortled. "Now that's a plan."

She grabbed his hand and started back down the hallway, so happy that her feet hardly seemed to touch the floor, but in the den, he tugged her to a stop.

"What?"

"Maybe we didn't get the marriage part right the first time," he said, "but we started this thing by taking it to God, and that's how we should go on."

"Who says we didn't get it right?" Connie asked. "I think we're exactly where He meant for us to be."

"I know we are," Kendal said, "which just goes to prove that you can't go wrong on your knees."

Smiling, Connie nodded.

They knelt together in front of the windows overlooking the back lawn, hands clasped, heads bowed.

"Dear Lord," Kendal began.

"Thank You so much," Connie added.

As Kendal took up the prayer again, she felt peace and joy filling her to the brim. Every fear fell away.

A sadness welled up in her then for her mother.

Velma Wheeler had never known anything like this. Perhaps she had been unable to feel it. Perhaps she simply hadn't known what real love was. Connie certainly hadn't. Otherwise, she never would have doubted that this could be enough.

More than enough.

* * * * *

Dear Reader,

Many of my books are inspired by personal experience, often providing the barest germ of an idea with which my fertile imagination can work, as in this case, where I've been privileged to watch the creation of a family from very diverse ingredients.

God has blessed me with a friend at church, a single woman by the name of Stacy. A lovely person, inside and out, and a successful businesswoman, Stacy has always held a deep conviction that God means for her to be a mother. Eventually Stacy came to feel that God was steering her toward adopting a child from Russia. Then Stacy announced that she was adopting not one child but two, virtual twins, unrelated children very close in age, adopted into the same family at the same time. What a challenge!

After many months, a great deal of expense, major remodeling of her home and several arduous trips abroad, Stacy brought home dark, exotic Julia from Siberia and blond, cuddly Dimitri from near Moscow. These two content, supremely normal toddlers could not have been blessed with a better mom, formed a more cohesive family unit or provided greater inspiration. From such diverse seeds a beautiful, healthy family has grown, proof that real families are born of God's will and our willingness to love.

What a joy it's been to watch! Stacy, Julia and Dimitri, thank you.

God bless,

Arlene James

Enjoy these four heartwarming stories
from your favorite Love Inspired authors!

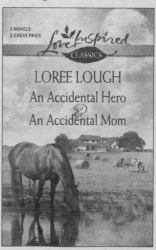

Lois Richer
THIS CHILD OF MINE
and
HIS ANSWERED PRAYER

Loree Lough
AN ACCIDENTAL HERO
and
AN ACCIDENTAL MOM

Steeple
Hill®

*Available in May 2011
wherever books are sold.*

www.SteepleHill.com

LIC0511

REQUEST YOUR FREE BOOKS!

2 FREE INSPIRATIONAL NOVELS
PLUS 2
FREE
MYSTERY GIFTS

Love Inspired®

YES! Please send me 2 FREE Love Inspired® novels and my 2 FREE mystery gifts (gifts are worth about $10). After receiving them, if I don't wish to receive any more books, I can return the shipping statement marked "cancel." If I don't cancel, I will receive 6 brand-new novels every month and be billed just $4.24 per book in the U.S. or $4.74 per book in Canada. That's a saving of at least 23% off the cover price. It's quite a bargain! Shipping and handling is just 50¢ per book in the U.S. and 75¢ per book in Canada.* I understand that accepting the 2 free books and gifts places me under no obligation to buy anything. I can always return a shipment and cancel at any time. Even if I never buy another book, the two free books and gifts are mine to keep forever.

105/305 IDN FDA5

Name _____ (PLEASE PRINT)

Address _____ Apt. #

City _____ State/Prov. _____ Zip/Postal Code

Signature (if under 18, a parent or guardian must sign)

Mail to the **Reader Service:**
IN U.S.A.: P.O. Box 1867, Buffalo, NY 14240-1867
IN CANADA: P.O. Box 609, Fort Erie, Ontario L2A 5X3

Not valid for current subscribers to Love Inspired books.

**Are you a subscriber to Love Inspired books
and want to receive the larger-print edition?
Call 1-800-873-8635 or visit www.ReaderService.com.**

* Terms and prices subject to change without notice. Prices do not include applicable taxes. Sales tax applicable in N.Y. Canadian residents will be charged applicable taxes. Offer not valid in Quebec. This offer is limited to one order per household. All orders subject to credit approval. Credit or debit balances in a customer's account(s) may be offset by any other outstanding balance owed by or to the customer. Please allow 4 to 6 weeks for delivery. Offer available while quantities last.

Your Privacy—The Reader Service is committed to protecting your privacy. Our Privacy Policy is available online at www.ReaderService.com or upon request from the Reader Service.

We make a portion of our mailing list available to reputable third parties that offer products we believe may interest you. If you prefer that we not exchange your name with third parties, or if you wish to clarify or modify your communication preferences, please visit us at www.ReaderService.com/consumerschoice or write to us at Reader Service Preference Service, P.O. Box 9062, Buffalo, NY 14269. Include your complete name and address.

LIREG11

*When David Foster comes across an unconscious woman
on his friends' doorstep, she evokes his natural born
instinct to take care of her.*

*Read on for a sneak peek of A BABY BY EASTER
by Lois Richer, available April, only from Love Inspired.*

"You could marry Davy, Susannah. He would look after
you. He looks after me." Darla's bright voice dropped. "He
had a girlfriend. They were going to get married, but she
didn't want me. She wanted Davy to send me away."

David almost groaned. How had his sister found out?
He'd been so careful—

"I'm sure your brother is very nice, Darla. And I'm glad
he's taking care of you. But I don't want to marry him. I
don't want to marry anyone," Susannah said. "I only came
to Connie's to see if I could stay here for a while."

"But Davy needs someone to love him. Somebody else
but me." Darla's face crumpled, the way it always did before she lost her temper. David was about to step forward
when Susannah reached out and hugged his sister.

"Thank you for offering, Darla. You're very generous. I
think your brother is lucky to have you love him." Susannah
brushed the bangs from Darla's sad face. "If I end up staying with Connie, I promise I'll see you lots. We could go to
that playground you talked about."

Susannah's foster sister Connie breezed into the room.
"I'm so glad to see you, Suze. But you're ill." She leaned
back to study the circles of red now dotting Susannah's
cheeks. "You're very pale. I think you need to see a doctor."

"I'm pregnant." The words burst out of Susannah in a
rush. Then she lifted her head and looked David straight in
the eye, as if awaiting his condemnation.

SHLIEXP0411R

But it wasn't condemnation David felt. It was hurt. He'd prayed so long, so hard, for a family, a wife, a child. And he'd lost all chance of that—not once, but twice.

How could God deny him the longing of his heart, yet give this ill woman a child she was in no way prepared to care for?

Although David has given up on his dream of having a family, will he offer to help Susannah in her time of need? Find out in A BABY BY EASTER, available April, only from Love Inspired.